AF555921

RSS

Praise for the Book

Over the past 50 years there has been an exponential rise in the growth and national importance of the RSS. Unfortunately, this development hasn't coincided with a more rounded understanding of the factors that have contributed to this phenomenon. There still exists a gap between how the RSS perceives its public role and how a big section of the English language media and commentators understand the organization. Through his media interventions, veteran swayamsevak Ratan Sharda has attempted to bridge the gap. Now, in this much overdue book, he has analysed the RSS through the contributions of its six Sarsanghchaalaks and the context of their leadership. This book is a very valuable addition to the study of public life in India and will contribute immeasurably to a better understanding of today's India.

Swapan Dasgupta
MP (Rajya Sabha), Senior journalist, Writer

Rarely has an organization as consequential as the RSS, been so-little understood. A key reason for this may be that most books on the RSS have been written in non-English, Indian languages. Almost none in English. Ratan Shardaji sets right this lacuna in his book, *RSS: Evolution from an Organization to a Movement.* It is not easy to encapsulate an organization with over 85 million members. In addition, it is the ideological fountainhead of 28 all-India organizations with their own mass bases. It has been in existence for 95 years. If you wish to understand the RSS, through an English language book, you can do no better than reading this masterpiece from Ratanji. It is a must-read!

Amish Tripathi
Bestselling author

Understanding the origins and history of the RSS is essential for understanding India today, and how its influence continues to shape the country. Ratan Sharda provides an excellent and detailed examination of the development of the largest service organization in India and perhaps the entire world.

David Frawley (Acharya Vamdev Shastri)
Author, Vedic scholar, Public intellectual

I always wondered what RSS is. Ratan Sharda met me a couple of years back. I asked him, 'How can I help you?' 'No, I need nothing. Just came to visit you and understand what you think of the RSS,' he responded. I told him, 'You need to tell people about yourself. Even I have no clue.' And we had a polite discussion. I was intrigued. Now he is out with his new book to tell us about the RSS. It covers almost a century of RSS journey, told in an engaging manner.

Anupam Kher
Actor, Writer

Ratan Sharda deserves accolades for taking up a subject which has only drawn opinions in extremes. Love RSS or hate RSS. But do you understand what the RSS is all about? Get on this journey with Ratan. From Hedgawar to Bhagwat, this is a seminal work of scholarship on a subject which is an extremely difficult one to delve into.

Bhupendra Chaubey
Editor in Chief: India Ahead and Andhra Prabha Group

It is rather easy to demonize or deify the RSS. After all, painting an entity as villain or hero requires no analysis, merely a preconceived notion. But Ratan Sharda does neither. He manages to compress a near-century of material into a crisp narrative that describes the evolution of the RSS, in size, structure, systems, priorities, ideology and objectives. In doing so, he plugs the gaps between perception and reality. For anyone seeking a better understanding of the RSS, this book is a great reference.

Ashwin Sanghi
Bestselling author

Shri Ratan Sharda through his scholarship has demystified the RSS for the layperson, being an insider as well as a scholar, he presents a unique and well researched perspective on the organisation, graced with sublime familiarity and objectivity. A must read for scholars as well as those curious about the RSS.

Advaita Kala
Author, Award-winning film writer, Social activist

The RSS as an organization has played, and continues to play, an important role in the Indian public and socio-cultural life. Whether or not one agrees with its activities, it certainly cannot be ignored. Unfortunately, almost all English language writing about the RSS has come from its critics that present it as a secretive organization. Ratan Sharda's book provides a necessary counterbalance—an insider's view of the organization, its objectives and its evolution.

Sanjeev Sanyal
Economist, Bestselling author

His new book on the RSS is not just the history of the RSS but an in-depth and insightful study of independent India's evolution and how one organization kept it together with hard groundwork, focus, commitment and sacrifice. This book will also inspire the younger generation for service and patriotism. Ratanji's simplicity of thoughts and rational approach reflects beautifully in this book. This book will become the reference point for future generations to understand why the RSS is integral to India's unity. And why the language of service is silence. Ratan Shardaji has done a great service by telling the untold story of the RSS. A must-read.

Vivek Agnihotri
Award-winning film maker, Writer

The RSS is a movement, less understood and seen through a million oblique and obtuse prisms by one and all. Attempts to skirt its surface has led to myriad descriptions, that depict the 'projection' of the author's thought process far and wide rather than the true layered flesh and bones of the organization. Ratan Sharda, an insider in the anthropological sense attempts at viewing the last of the revolution. He honestly attempts to simplify the struggle without oversimplifying it to the lay man. A book that chronicles men and milestones is a must read for all!

Dr Harish Shetty
Renowned psychiatrist, Social activist for mental health

One cannot understand the RSS without a proper understanding of India and its hoary past. Ratan Sharda is eminently suited to write on the subject with his background and decades of association with the organization. The book gives a good account of the thought processes and evolution of the RSS.

Chamarthy Umamaheswara Rao
President, Vidya Bharati, South Region;
ex-Principal Secretary, Government of AP

RSS

EVOLUTION FROM AN ORGANIZATION TO A MOVEMENT

Ratan Sharda

RUPA

Published by
Rupa Publications India Pvt. Ltd 2020
161-B/4, Gulmohar House,
Yusuf Sarai Community Centre,
New Delhi 110049

Sales centres:
Bengaluru Chennai
Hyderabad Kolkata Mumbai

ISBN: 978-93-90356-31-7

Tenth impression 2026

15 14 13 12 11 10

Printed in India

Contents

Foreword
by Makarand R. Paranjape

I
95 Years of Tapascharya

Founded on 27 September 1925 by Dr Keshav Baliram Hedgewar, the Rashtriya Swayamsevak Sangh (RSS), will soon be ninety-five years old. Ninety-five years of *tapasya*, rigorous penance and austerity, for the sake of the Hindu nation is how its eventful journey may be described.[1]

It is impossible to determine the exact number of the members of the RSS. But with estimates upward of 8 million, it is probably the largest voluntary organization in the world. Daily, over 60,000 *shakhas* or meetings of the RSS take place in all parts of India and in several places outside the country.

The RSS has also germinated, nurtured and established some thirty all-India organizations. The prominent ones include Vidya Bharati, which runs 14,000 schools, Saraswati Shishu Mandir, also under Vidya Bharati umbrella, which runs 25,000 schools and the one lakh single-teacher schools called Ekal Vidyalayas. Besides India's largest workers and students unions, Bharatiya Mazdoor Sangh (BMS) and Akhil Bharatiya Vidyarthi Parishad (ABVP), the RSS is also credited with founding and supporting the Vishwa Hindu Parishad (VHP). In addition, there are over a lakh *sewa* or service bodies founded and supported by the RSS.

---

[1]Portions of this Foreword have appeared in earlier versions in some of my earlier writings, including columns in *Daily News and Analysis* (DNA), *Mail Today* and *The Print*. I thank these publications for carrying my views in their pages and websites.

The unique and distinguishing feature of the RSS is its almost infinite creativity and fecundity. It is manifest in the Sangh's capacity to create any number of near-autonomous organizations touching almost every sphere of life. As one insider puts it, 'There is no limit on the number of organizations that can be seeded to support the multiple issues in society that necessitate intervention.'[2] *Sangh Srishti,* or the creative and innovative resourcefulness of the RSS, is the prominent, largely non-political but socially crucial and culturally transformative aspect of the Sangh.

The other side is its political intervention through the RSS inspired and created current ruling party, the Bharatiya Janata Party (BJP) and its predecessor, the Bharatiya Jan Sangh. The BJP was formed on 6 April 1980. Today, with a vaunted membership of 100 million people, it is the world's largest political organization. What is more, from a dismal tally of just two seats in 1984, the first general elections after it was founded, it notched up in 2014 an impressive 282 seats in the 543-seat Lok Sabha. In the 2019 general elections, it fared even better, with 303 out of 543 on its own accord. What an incredible success story, even its harshest critics would admit.

In its earlier avatar, it was known as the Akhil Bharatiya Jan Sangh or Jan Sangh, for short. The Jan Sangh was started on 21 October 1951. Unfortunately, its founder and first president, Shyama Prasad Mukherjee, died in Srinagar less than two years later, on 23 June 1953. Mukherjee entered Kashmir on 21 May 1953 to protest against Article 370 granting special status to the state. His slogan, '*Ek desh me do nishan, do pradhan, nahin chalenge, nahin chalenge*,' had become popular all over India at that time.

Mukherjee was arrested at Lakhanpur soon after he had crossed the 'border,' then transferred to Srinagar Central Jail. He died in circumstances which many regard as 'suspicious.' No post-

[2]Sunil Ambekar, *The RSS: Roadmaps for the 21st Century* (New Delhi: Rupa, 2019), p. 145.

mortem was conducted, nor did Prime Minister Jawaharlal Nehru agree to an inquiry.[3]

If Mukherjee was its founder, Deendayal Upadhyay, a towering personality from the RSS, was Jan Sangh's most influential ideologue.[4] His 'Integral Humanism' remains the guiding philosophy of the BJP. Upadhyay became President of Jan Sangh in December 1967. Just a couple of months afterwards, he was murdered on 11 February 1968. Around 2:00 a.m., he was pushed out of a moving train nearing Mughalsarai Junction.

In August 2018, Mughalsarai was renamed Pt. Deendayal Upadhyay Junction.

During the anti- and post-Emergency period of 1977-1980, the Jan Sangh merged into the Janata Party. This conglomeration of ideologically diverse pollical forces, which had come together to oust Indira Gandhi from power, fell apart, giving rise to most of the non-Congress political formations that are present till today in our complex electoral arrangements. The issue flagged by the opponents of the Jan Sangh faction within the Janata Party was the former's 'dual membership' or link with the other 'Sangh,' their parent organization, the RSS. Indeed, it is this umbilical cord that actually defines the BJP's distinctive identity in our political spectrum.

That is why the two 'real' progenitors of the BJP must not be overlooked. 'Guruji' Madhav Sadashiv Golwalkar became the Sarsanghchaalak or head of the RSS in 1940. He inspired Mukherjee, giving him several RSS workers to start a political party. Before him, 'Doctorji' Keshav Baliram Hedgewar, the founder and first Sarsanghchaalak of the RSS, had already recognized the need for a political party to safeguard the interests of the Hindus. He

---

[3]The best book on this great patriot remains *Dr Syama Prasad Mookerjee: A Biography* (New Delhi: Deep Prakashan, 1954) by senior Jan Sangh leader, Balraj Madhok.

[4]A 15-volume edition of his collected works, edited by Dr. Mahesh Sharma, was published by Prabhat Prakashan in 2019. It is now available in an English translation too.

and the party's supremo, current Prime Minister of India, Narendra Modi, both are RSS creations. Earlier, Atal Bihari Vajpayee served as India's prime minister for two consecutive terms from 1998 to 2004.[5] He, too, like Narendra Modi, was not only an RSS swayamsevak (volunteer), but *prachaarak* (dedicated worker) for several years. Presidents, Vice-Presidents, former Vice-Presidents, senior Cabinet ministers, chief ministers, and prominent political leaders at all levels of Indian democracy have been proudly shaped by their RSS background. The RSS remains steadfast in its commitment to the Indian nation, to what Sri Aurobindo called 'Bharat Shakti' in *Foundations of Indian Culture.*

Perhaps more than any other organization, it is the RSS which has worked for Hindu and Indian national unity. It is this emphasis that is best summed up in the RSS slogan, *Sanghe Shakti Kaliyuge,* or unity is the source of strength in Kaliyuga. It would therefore not be an exaggeration to say that with its hundreds of main and ancillary associations, millions of volunteers, and thousands of prominent leaders, the RSS is India's most power and influential organization.

Truly, *Sangh samaj ban gaya hai*—the Sangh has permeated into every part of Indian society.

II
RSS: Travails, Trials, Triumphs

RSS founder, Hedgewar, or Doctorji, as a student at the Calcutta Medical College, was associated with the secret, revolutionary society, Anushilan Samiti, which believed in an armed overthrow of colonial rule. Later, like many young patriots and nationalists,

[5]Himself a prolific poet, writer, and renowned orator, Vajpayee's many works, including collections of his speeches, are easily available. Recent biographies by N.P. Ullekh included *The Untold Vajpayee: Politician and Paradox* (New Delhi: Penguin, 2018). Of the hundreds of books by and on Narendra Modi, *Centrestage* (New Delhi: Penguin, 2014) and *Marching with a Billion* (New Delhi: Penguin, 2018) by Uday Mahurkar try to come to grips with his phenomenal popular appeal as well as impressive governance record.

Doctorji too joined the Congress, which was spearheading India's freedom struggle.

In fact, on 27 September 1925, when the Sangh was founded, Doctorji was still a Congressman. He had already spent a year in jail in support of Gandhiji's Non-cooperation *andolan* (agitation) in 1921–1922 that ran parallel to the Khilafat agitation. Leaving the RSS in charge of acting Sarsanghchaalak, Dr L. V. Paranjpe, he would spend another stint in British prisons during the Non-cooperation Movement in 1930–1931, this time sentenced to hard labour.

Doctorji came in contact with all shades of nationalists, but his inclination was towards the 'garam dal,' the extremist wing of the Congress, led by leaders such as Lala Lajpat Rai, Lokmanya Tilak, and Bipin Chandra Pal. He was also close to Pandit Madan Mohan Malaviya and Dr B.S. Moonje.

Though he respected Gandhiji, Doctorji believed that fetishizing non-violence as the sole method to throw out the British would be counterproductive in the long run. He was also alarmed at what he saw as the incessant appeasement and submission to the increasingly dangerous Muslim demands, all in the interest of the much-desired but somewhat unrealistic goal of Hindu-Muslim unity.[6]

After the partition of Bengal (*Banga Bhanga*) in 1905, the setting up of the Muslim League in 1906, and the Morley-Minto reforms of 1909, which allowed separate electorates to Muslims, the Punjab Hindu Mahasabha was formed. Its key movers were Rai Bahadur Lala Lal Chand and Col. U.N. Mukherji. It was the latter who first propounded the idea of the demographic decline and political impotency of the Hindus.[7]

The failed Khilafat *andolan* (1919-1924) and the gruesome anti-Hindu Moplah Rebellion (1921) made Doctorji realise that the Congress, although a political organization made up

---

[6]See *Dr Keshav Baliram Hedgewar* (New Delhi: Publications Division, 2017) by Dr Rakesh Sinha.

[7]U.N. Mukherji, *Hindus—A Dying Race* (Calcutta; M. Bannerjee, 1909).

overwhelmingly of Hindus, could not be relied upon to protect them or fight for their demands. He felt, instead, that the best safeguard for the future of India was the unity and empowerment of Hindu society. A new, largely non-political organization, based on Hindu ideological, cultural, and spiritual principles was needed. Hence the RSS.

In March 1940 the Muslim League passed the 'Pakistan Resolution' committing itself to an independent Islamic country. Later that year, Gandhiji declared in anguish, 'vivisect me before you vivisect India.' What was the way out? That year, Doctorji also passed away.

In 1942, Mahatma Gandhi announced the 'Quit India' movement. All the prominent leaders, including Gandhi, were sent to prison. In response to Gandhiji's call, 'Do or die,' Guruji reportedly responded, the 'part about 'dying' is clear in the slogan 'Do or Die.' But what is to be 'Done'? Has the Congress working committee given any directions about it?'[8]

India hurtled towards a bloody and calamitous independence, which culminated in the creation of two states, India and Pakistan on 15 August 1947. The partition of Bharat on religion lines had proved Doctorji's prescient premonition to be true. The Mahatma did not fast against the partition of India. The Congress did not have an answer. It conceded Pakistan. Instead, Gandhiji was assassinated by Nathuram Godse and a small band of accomplices on 30 January 1948, less than six months after the independence of a truncated and divided India.

On the following day, the Sarsanghchaalak (head) of the RSS, 'Guruji' Madhav Sadashiv Golwalkar, wrote to Jawaharlal Nehru, India's prime minister:

> Yesterday at Madras I heard the shocking news that some thoughtless perverted soul has committed the heinous act

---

[8]This was part of the seven questions that Guruji sent Balasaheb Deoras to ask Jayaprakash Narayan, then an underground leader. —Ratan Sharda, *RSS 360°: Demystifying Rashtriya Swayamsevak Sangh*. E-book.

> of putting a sudden and ghastly end to the life of Poojya Mahatmaji by the bullet. This vile act is a blot on our Society in the eyes of the world. Even if it had been at the hands of one from an enemy country, this act would have been unpardonable, for the life of Mahatmaji was dedicated to the good of the entire humanity crossing the borders of particular groups of people. No wonder that every one of our countrymen will be filled with unbearable agony to see that one of our own countrymen has perpetrated his most inconceivable, abominable act. Since the moment I heard the news a void has pervaded my heart. My heart is laden with anxiety at the terrible prospects of the near future due to the absence of that great unifier. The attack on such a deft helmsmen who held so many diverse natures in a single string bringing them to the right path, is indeed an act treacherous not merely to an individual but to the whole country. No doubt you, that is the Government authorities of the day, will deal suitably with that traitorous individual. However severe that dealing be, it is bound to be too mild when compared to the loss sustained.... On behalf of the Organization which has been moulded on these very lines, and intensely sharing the bereavement of the Nation at this crucial hour and invoking the sacred memories of that departed soul, I pray at the Feet of the All-Merciful Almighty that He bless us with the necessary inspiration and wisdom to establish a real everlasting oneness of our people.

On the same day, he sent another letter to 'Sardar' Vallabhbhai Patel, India's deputy prime minister and home minster:

> Yesterday at Madras I heard the news of the ghastly incident, which has shaken all humanity. Such a heinous and abominable incident has probably never been witnessed before. My heart is wrung with extreme agony. It is difficult to find words to condemn the person who has committed this crime. Even the idea of such an unprovoked wickedness passes comprehension. What can be said about the man who has thus

> plunged the whole world into indescribable grief? ... On behalf of the Organization which is built on this faith and on this basis of oneness I pray at the Feet of the All-Merciful Lord to guide all the children of this Nation on the right path and inspire them for the building up of a pure and powerful national life.

Both letters were signed with the same parting salutation, 'Yours in the Service of the Mother.'[9]

However, on 4 February 1948, the RSS was banned. Guruji himself was arrested. Before the ban was lifted, over 70,000 RSS workers had offered arrest and been into jail in post-independence India. As a part of the agreement between Guruji and the government to lift the ban on the RSS, a written constitution was framed for the first time. Guruji was released from prison on 6 August 1949.[10]

Since few have read this important document, it is important to quote from it. It gives us an idea of what the RSS officially stands for. According to the Preamble, the RSS was founded to unite the country and to stop its disintegration. Its main objectives include:

(a) to eradicate the fissiparous tendencies arising from diversities of sect, faith, caste and creed and from political, economic, linguistic and provincial differences, amongst Hindus;
(b) to make them realise the greatness of their past;
(c) to inculcate in them a spirit of service, sacrifice and selfless devotion to the Society;
(d) to build up an organized and well-disciplined corporate life; and
(e) to bring about an all-round regeneration of the Hindu Samaj on the basis of its Dharma and its Sanskriti.

It is important also to quote from Article 4 of the RSS constitution:

---

[9]http://www.hvk.org/specialarticles/justice/justice.html.

[10]The RSS Constitution is not easily available. Some excerpts have been posted on https://www.sabhlokcity.com/2015/04/the-constitution-of-the-rashtriya-swayamsevak-sangh/

'In consonance with the cultural heritage of the Hindu Samaj, the Sangh has abiding faith in the fundamental principle of tolerance towards all faiths. The Sangh as such, has no politics and is devoted to purely cultural work. The individual Swayamsevaks, however, may join any political party, except such parties as believe in or resort to violent and secret methods to achieve their ends; persons owing allegiance to such parties or believing in such methods shall have no place in the Sangh.'

During the 1975 Emergency imposed by another Congress Prime Minister, Nehru's daughter, Indira Gandhi, thousands of RSS workers again went to jail fighting for our civil rights and liberties. This alone should have put paid to accusations that the RSS is fascist or anti-democratic. Thrice a victim of state intolerance, the RSS is against any curtailing of civil liberties or democratic freedoms.

In *Bunch of Thoughts*[11], first published in 1966, Guruji had already forecast how the Congress would behave after Independence, when it will come to power. There were the 'two types of movements against the British rule in our country,' Guruji wrote, 'One was the armed revolution resorted to by the revolutionaries and the other, passive resistance led by the Indian National Congress.' The latter had 'more disastrous and degrading effects on the country. Most of the tragedies and evils that have overtaken our country during the last few decades and are even today corroding our national life are its direct outcome.' The ills of the Congress culture continue to this day, in a legacy of scams and dynastic politics.

When Doctorji started out, the Congress was the mother of almost all Indian political, social, and cultural formations. Today, as the RSS enters its 95th year, the scales of history seem to have reversed. Almost every major political, social, and cultural organization in India today bears the stamp or influence of the RSS.

---

[11]The reprint of the 3rd edition was published in 2000 by Sahitya Sindhu Prakashana, Bengaluru. An e-version is available at http://www.golwalkarguruji.org/Encyc/2017/10/18/BunchofThoughtsBook.html.

III
Hindutva and Hind Swaraj

Mahatma Gandhi gave his life for Hindu-Muslim unity. But, as I have shown, by the time he had witnessed the horrors of the Partition, he had reconciled to the fact that unity was an impossible dream.[12] Even amity would do. Or if not amity, at the very least, peaceful coexistence. But what would be the terms on which this might be ensured, at least within India?

The communalization of Indian politics had commenced long before the Partition. Among the many communal riots that had erupted, a particularly gruesome one in September 1924 resulted in the ethnic cleansing of Hindus from Kohat. Gandhiji embarked upon a severe, penitential, twenty-one day fast at the residence of Muhammad Ali in Delhi. He wanted, more than anything, to restore Hindu-Muslim unity.

On 17 September, the very first day of the fast, his secretary, Mahadev Desai, asked what error of his had forced him to resort to such hard penance. Gandhiji replied:

> My error? Why, I may be charged with having committed a breach of faith with the Hindus. I asked them to befriend Muslims, I asked them to lay their lives and their property at the disposal of the Mussalmans for the protection of their holy places. Even today I am asking them to practice Ahimsa, to settle quarrels by dying but not by killing. And what do I find to be the result? How many temples have been desecrated? How many sisters come to me with complaints ... Hindu woman are in mortal terror of the Mussalman goondas. .... How can I bear the way in which his (a letter writer's) little children were molested?' [13]

The deeper causes of Muslim separatism in India have been

[12]*The Death and Afterlife of Mahatma Gandhi* (New Delhi: Penguin, 2015).

[13]Mahadev H. Desai, *Day to Day with Gandhi: Secretary's Diary*, Vol. IV (Varanasi: Sarva Seva Sangh Prakashan, 1969), p. 195.

identified by Sita Ram Goel in his eponymous book.[14]

Leader after leader, including Bhai Parmanand, Lala Lajpat Rai, Swami Shraddhanand, V.D. Savarkar, Sri Aurobindo, M.S. Aney and Subhas Chandra Bose, disagreed with Gandhi's idea of pacifist absolutism. Although for Gandhi, ahimsa did not mean cowardice, few Hindu victims of violence could practice the non-violence of the brave. It was too tall an order, apparently contrary to human nature. Self-defence has been permitted in all religious traditions, but Gandhi wanted to reform human nature itself. It was a noble ideal, but quite impractical for most.

Doctorji had himself witnessed communal riots in Nagpur in 1923 and 1924. It was largely because of organised Hindu resistance, rather than non-violence, that peace had been restored in Nagpur. Doctorji trained Hindu youth, armed only with lathis, to patrol neighbourhoods. The *shakhas* of the RSS were modelled on *akhadas* or gymnasiums. Their primary purpose was to instil patriotism, unity, and fearlessness. The organization was named Rashtriya, rather than Hindu, Swayamsevak Sangh because it was devoted to the national cause of swaraj or political independence from British rule. As Devendra Swarup puts it,

> In a way, RSS was born out of the deep concern felt by all the national leaders including Gandhiji, Malaviyaji, Lala Lajpat Rai and Swami Shraddhanand. It was to free the Hindu society of its cowardice, social disharmony and inequality and to infuse with a spirit of selfless patriotism and nationalism.[15]

Ratan Sharda's book, *The Sangh & Swaraj: Role of RSS in Freedom Struggle* (New Delhi: Prabhat Prakashan, 2020), is a detailed refutation of the propaganda of the Left-Liberals that the RSS did not participate in the freedom struggle or that the Congress was

---

[14]*Muslim Separatism: Causes and Consequences* (New Delhi: Voice of Dharma, 1995).

[15]See Devendra Swarup, "Gandhiji, Hedgewar and the R.S.S.," *Dialogue* 22.2 (October-December 2010) for a detailed account (https://www.asthabharati.org/Dia_Oct%20010/dev.htm.)

the only party that fought for India's freedom.

What is increasingly clear is that the dichotomy between Gandhi's idea of Hind Swaraj and Hindutva as propagated by the RSS is not as sharply defined as it may seem at first. Hindutva and Hind Swaraj are not binaries. They encompass many shades of views and positions, all of which go to making us a great nation. This is exactly what the Supreme Court ruled on 25 October 2016, when it confirmed that Hindutva is a way of life, not a religion.

IV
Mainstreaming Hindutva

In 2019, the Vijayadashami speech by RSS Sarsanghchaalak Dr Mohan Rao Bhagwat was delivered on Thursday, 18 October at the Reshimbagh Maidan, Nagpur. Bhagwat began by recalling how we would soon celebrate the 550th Prakash Parv or anniversary of Guru Nanak. Bhagwat stressed how Guru Nanak opened a 'new path of self-enlightenment' by a 'spiritual practice commensurate with the times.' The Guru created a new sense of oneness in a society beaten and brutalised by 'cruel, intolerant, savage foreign invaders.'

When Babar conquered Punjab, it is recorded that Guru Nanak was himself taken captive. Bhagwat also acknowledged the Sikh Guru parampara: 'It is his [Guru Nanak's] legacy that gave the country a magnificent and majestic tradition of 10 Gurus who removed our state of penury and inferiority.'

Next Bhagwat remembered Mahatma Gandhi, whose 150th anniversary we are celebrating. Gandhi, according to Bhagwat, provided 'the political foundation of truth and nonviolence to the independence movement of the country.' He was one in a long line of 'several great personalities of this country' who inspired 'continuous enlightenment' and strengthened our 'inclusive culture, based on love and truth.'

Gandhi 'inspired the common man of the country to come out of his home and stand firmly with a moral force against the British oppression.' Mohanji paid homage to martyrs of the Jallianwala

Bagh massacre, which took place 100 years back on Vaisakhi 1919, when soldiers of the British Indian army killed nearly 1,000 unarmed men and women.

Seventy-one years after our independence, our struggle to regain our self, our '*swa*,' is still far from over. Indian social and cultural life is yet to be fully decolonized. To preserve our swaraj or independence, Bhagwat noted, both defence and economic security are absolutely essential.

Bhagwat was also unsparing in his self-criticism of Indian society, identifying 'ignorance, dearth of development and amenities, unemployment, injustice, exploitation, discrimination and absence of sensitivity and sanity' as root causes of our sorry state. On the other hand, 'urban Maoists' are taking advantage of social tensions and divisions. Their 'cohorts' are 'already established in social and other media, intellectual circles and other institutions.' Bhagwat called this sort of ideological warfare 'Mantrayuddh.'

Why is it that in independent Bharat, our rulers are yet 'to make the administration people-centric'? Obviously, 'political freedom' without all dimensions of our national life 'reorganized on the basis of "swa" (self)' is not complete. That is why the rebuilding of the Ram temple was so important. Its main aim was to restore the self-esteem of the people. But all elements of society needed to come together to accomplish this task. Similarly, on Sabarimala, the sentiments of the people had to be considered; just judicial intervention would not be sufficient. To adapt and adopt our '*swa*' to the times was how to make Bharat great once again, he said.

Mohanji may be described as a modest, even self-effacing man. But since 2009, when he took over the reins of what is arguably the world's largest cultural organization, he has shown both admirers and detractors of the RSS that he means business. Today, no one can doubt his visionary ambition, not just for his organization, but for India that is Bharat.

Few will forget the coup he pulled off in getting India's former President and senior Congressman, Pranab Mukherjee, to share the dais with him. On 7 June 2018, Mukherjee not only addressed the nation from the Sangh platform at the RSS headquarters in Nagpur, but traversed the narrow and congested lanes in the heart of the city to pay homage to founder Dr Keshav Baliram Hedgewar at the latter's erstwhile home, now a memorial. Mukherjee said, 'Today, I came here to pay my respectful homage to a great son of Mother India.'

To anyone who cared, Mohanji was sending an unmistakeable message: the RSS, despite nearly hundred years of negative propaganda and relentless battering, was not only alive and well, but in great spirits and fighting fit. What is more, the Sangh was no longer 'untouchable.' Instead, it had become one of India's central and most significant organizations, playing a vital role in shaping the nation's destiny. Indeed, mainstreaming the RSS and internationalising Hindutva may be summed up as Bhagwat's greatest achievements.

The Deoras doctrine expanded the Sangh's horizons from what some perceived as Golwalkar's hardliner stance: 'We do believe in the one-culture and one-nation Hindu rashtra. But our definition of Hindu is not limited to any particular kind of faith. Our definition of Hindu includes those who believe in the one-culture and one-nation theory of this country. ... So by Hindu we do not mean any particular type of faith. We use the word Hindu in a broader sense.'

If Deoras broadened the idea of Hindutva, Bhagwat has tried to abolish the dichotomy between Hinduism and Hindutva. While Hindu Dharma is indeed a way of life, Hindus cannot afford not to assert their religious and political identities by harnessing or consolidating the essential principles of Hinduism. These essential 'tatvas' or codes of conduct, ideas, values, opinions, and doctrines all constitute the bedrock of Hindutva. Though these core ideas may be age-old, their application or presentation must be context-specific and contemporary.

Hindutva, in order to be relevant and meaningful, must be as flexible, plural, and responsive to the times as Hinduism itself. Bhagwat has thus endeavoured to rescue Hindutva from the narrow straitjacket into which it has been confined for over seventy years. Dubbed and slandered as a supposedly fascist and chauvinist ideology, Hindutva has had consistently bad press. Bhagwat has rehabilitated it as the proud identity badge of new age Indians and globalised Hindus.

To end the civil war between different factions of Hindus has been his dream: 'Why should we try to bring everyone under one flag or one banner?' he asks. 'It is enough that we all work for India. All patriotic Indians should strive to work together for the welfare of Bharat.'

At the Bharatiya Vihar Manch Valedictory address on 3 February 2019 in Ahmedabad, Bhagwat gave the slogan of 'working together differently' as the key to the success of Hindu *samaj* or society. This was the '*vyuha rachana*,' the strategic formation, needed to identify and network all those who are active in the larger mission of working for the welfare of India. '*Mil jul ke raho; satya khojo; yehi Hindutva hai*,' (Mingle and live together peaceably; find the truth; that is Hindutva) he stressed. Who could object to that?

Like other key members of the RSS and other Hindu organizations, Bhagwat also believes in India's special mission as the 'Jagatguru,' the world's teacher. Call it our own version of Indian exceptionalism. The underlying idea is that India's wisdom traditions have the knowledge to save humanity from predatory and irresponsible consumption, which is the fallout of self-destructive and nature-exploiting modernity. We are all today the slaves of this inhumane globalised machine, which is eating into the very vitals of our personal, social, and economic relations. This critique of modernity is not very different from Mahatma Gandhi's in *Hind Swaraj* (1909). Gandhi considered modernity a veritable Kali Yuga, the Godless age of greed and immorality, destructive of civilization. He wanted Indians to cleave to India's ancient way of life as they would to 'mother's milk.'

Bhagwat's Hindutva has the added component of respect for

modern science as a parallel quest for truth, quite in keeping with the spiritual imperative of the ancient Vedic Rishi Dharma, propounded and practised by Rishis. A revitalized and contemporized version of this wisdom tradition is the best antidote to the ills that plague the modern world, according to him. India was, is, and will remain a spiritual and spiritualising civilisation; that, to Bhagwat, is our strength and the true implication of Hindutva.

The Hindu nation and the state of India both have to be strong because they are custodians and protectors of this Dharma. As Sri Aurobindo famously said in his Uttarpara speech, 'When it is said that India shall expand and extend herself, it is the Sanatan Dharma that shall expand and extend itself over the world. It is for the dharma and by the dharma that India exists.'

V
Ratan Sharda's *Evolution of RSS*

As I have tried to demonstrate so far, the saga of the birth, growth, and development of the RSS is also the story of new India. It is this phenomenal chronicle that Dr Ratan Sharda's present book gives voice to.

Even if not part of the Congress-dominated political order, the RSS has been far more mainstream than the elitist voices of Lutyens Delhi have maintained. Even in their lean decades, Eknath Ranade (1914-1982) pulled off the incredible feat of building the Vivekananda Rock Memorial and the Vivekananda Kendra over a period of nine years from 1963-1972. This stupendous achievement was the result of a nationwide campaign and consensus building across political and ideological boundaries.[16] If RSS ideology is currently centre-stage, this is neither accidental nor unforeseen. They have worked and struggled tirelessly for over 95 years to this end.

There is scarcely an area of India's extended social, cultural,

[16]Senior BJP leader L.K, Advani has himself recorded this in his autobiography, *My Country My Life* (New Delhi: Rupa, 2008).

of political sphere, including the diaspora, where the RSS is not active or influential.

But this was not always the case.

In fact, far from being powerful and influential, the RSS was India's least understood and most reviled organization. Banned once in British India and thrice after Independence, it was systematically slandered and ridiculed by the ruling dispensation. A systematic disinformation campaign was conducted against it over decades. Its members were branded as Hindutva fanatics and fascists. Even those associated with it were excluded from positions of importance, whether in the government or civil society. Even in Indian academia, the 'taint' of the RSS was enough to ensure one's boycott or marginalisation.

If so, then how has the RSS come to occupy centre-stage in Indian life? How has this massive and decisive transformation occurred?

Ratanji's book is an attempt to answer precisely this question. In documenting the evolution and ascendency of the RSS, Ratanji adopts the unique and useful method of taking us through the life, work, and achievement of its five Sarsanghchaalaks or head coordinators, Keshav Baliram Hedgewar (1925–1930), Madhav Sadashiv Golwalkar (1940–1973), Madhukar Dattatraya Deoras (1973–1993), Rajendra Singh (1993–2000), K.S. Sudarshan (2000–2009), and the current incumbent, Mohan Rao Bhagwat (March 2009 onwards). In addition, he gives us a wealth of factual information combined with useful analysis and explanation to help us understand the growth and inner workings of the RSS.

He is in a good position to do so because he has been, since his childhood, an RSS member. He has served in various RSS organizations in a variety of capacities. He was an ABVP activist and student leader, the general secretary of his college's student union during the Emergency and was jailed. He went on to do his M.A. and, much later, wrote a PhD on 'Understanding RSS through Its Resolutions, with Focus on North East, Jammu and Kashmir and Punjab' at the Hindu University of America.

To my mind, Ratanji's book is of crucial importance because it appears when the public perception of the RSS is at an inflection point. No longer is it necessary to take either a pro- or anti-RSS position. To the curious and unbiased, who also wish to be well-informed, there is now a plethora of material on the RSS. Not just by its sworn critics or neutral commentators, but members, insiders, and sympathisers have written a spate of books in recent years highlighting various aspects of the RSS.

After Koenraad Elst's pioneering volume, *Decolonizing The Hindu Mind: Ideological Development Of Hindu Revivalism* (New Delhi: Rupa, 2001), which appeared nearly twenty years ago, notable contributions include *RSS's Tryst With Politics: From Hedgewar to Sudarshan* (New Delhi: Manohar, 2002) by Pralay Kanungo, *Lost Years of the RSS* (New Delhi: Sage Publications, 2011) by Sanjeev Kelker, *The RSS: A View* (New Delhi: Penguin, 2017), *The Incomparable Guru Golwalkar* (New Delhi: Prabhat Prakashan, 2018) by Ranga Hari, *RSS: A View to the Inside* (New Delhi: Penguin, 2018) and *The Brotherhood in Saffron: The Rashtriya Swayamsevak Sangh and Hindu Revivalism* (New Delhi: Penguin, 2019) by Walter Andersen and Shridhar Damle, *Know About RSS* (New Delhi: Prabhat Books, 2019) and *The Saffron Surge Untold Story of RSS Leadership* (New Delhi: Prabhat Prakashan, 2019) by Arun Anand *The RSS: Roadmaps for the 21st Century* (New Delhi: Rupa, 2019) by Sunil Ambekar, *Disaster Relief and the RSS: Resurrecting 'Religion' through Humanitarianism* by Malini Bhattacharjee (New Delhi: Sage, 2019), and *Hindutva for the Changing Times* (Ghaziabad, UP: Indus Scroll Pres, 2020) by J Nandakumar. Ratanji's earlier book *RSS 360: Demystifying Rashtriya Swayamsevak Sangh* (New Delhi: Bloomsbury, 2018) is itself an important part of this list.

In addition, the RSS has opened itself not just to interaction but even to inquiry by serious scholars and important members of the public. Its present Sarsanghchaalak, Dr Bhagwat, has embarked upon an unprecedented outreach programme involving wide-ranging talks, discussions, and meetings with all sections of

Indian society.[17] We do not, in other words, have an excuse to remain ignorant about the RSS. We cannot hide behind prejudice or bigotry, but must take the trouble to engage sincerely with its intriguing if not amazing history. What is more, we are free and able to form an informed and independent view which is neither identical with that of the official RSS position nor brainwashed by the anti-RSS lobby or its malicious propaganda.

It is this inflection point in the discourse on the RSS that Ratanji's book marks and underscores. Hence its historic importance. Given the phenomenal, almost miraculous success of the RSS, it continues to attract many disparagers and nay-sayers. Sharda's book is a welcome and salutary corrective to such misconstructions.

Neither an academic study nor an exercise in apologetics, Sharda's account is unpretentious, even anecdotal, which is what adds to its readability and authenticity. But it is thoroughly documented, with every source clearly cited. Though a staunch supporter, Sharda is also critical of some aspects of the RSS, which goes to show his independence of opinion. As a sincere attempt to explain, clarify, and correct several misunderstandings, Sharda's book is a welcome addition to the gradually growing literature on the RSS.

The RSS-led Hindu resurgence appears irreversible. But will it be merely a powerful reassertion or a genuine and wide-ranging renaissance? This is the key question. The next decade or two will give us the answer. I am sure Ratanji will be around to write about the role of the RSS in the exciting times yet to unfold.

Makarand R. Paranjape
Director, Indian Institute of Advanced Study, Shimla

[17]The latest of these was a wide-ranging *vichar* (discussion) with journalists, writers and opinion makers held on 18 February 2020 at Terapanth Bhawan, Adhyaatm Sadhna Kendra, Chhatarpur, New Delhi.

Introduction

The first thing that would strike anyone about the Rashtriya Swayamsevak Sangh (RSS) is that it is a unique organization not just in India but globally. Its objectives and its philosophy have been inspected with a magnifying glass and bookish analyses of its methodology have also been done. However, one problem with these analyses is that there is not enough available literature on the RSS, especially in English. This is especially noteworthy because most of its critics come from English-speaking backgrounds. Their harsh critique is mainly dependant on two books from the RSS. First, the book *We Our Nationhood Defined* that was disowned by writer M.S. Golwalkar, that is, Guruji himself, in the immediate years following his appointment as the Sarsanghchaalak. The second book is titled *Bunch of Thoughts*, which is a collection of Guruji's speeches till 1964. Guruji spearheaded the RSS through its most crucial phase, up to 1973. Being lectures, they reflect his views during those periods, including the worst period of Partition and its aftermath.

The complete works of Guruji were published in the following years. A newly compiled version with 12 volumes titled *Guruji Samagra Darshan*, was published in 2006. However, none of the critics or analysts seem to be inclined to read them. They present his views that are perennial in nature. Thus, most of the books and essays on the RSS are based on poor study and written by Left-oriented intellectuals and academicians, essentially biased against the RSS, and coloured with a priori conclusions.

One of the reasons for this gap in perception and reality is also a lack of enough material from the RSS in English, and many researchers have admitted this to me personally. However, there is good amount of material in Hindi and other regional languages, but efforts to procure them seem to be too much for researchers. The blame, thus, also can be put at the door of the RSS, for not making its literature easily available. Therefore, the viewpoints we read are a standpoint built on a Western ideological and political framework. These exercises map 200–300-year-old Western idioms of religion, nation state and secularism on to at least 8,000 years of documented Hindu way of life, which has a different conceptualization of the civilizational narrative that speaks of *Dharma, Samskriti, Rashtra* and *Nirvana*—realization of the Ultimate Truth that can be discovered through various paths.

It was this vacuum and huge gap in perception and reality of the RSS that made me write about it. The positive response I have received for my efforts so far has convinced me that people are eager to understand the RSS better, and that the bias against it can be corrected with objective dissemination of information covering its various aspects. My earlier books have not been written to counter critics, but to provide the right information in an easy way to both the seekers and the critics.

This book is written in the same vein, but goes a step ahead from my earlier works. It is an ambitious project that tries to encompass ninety-five years of RSS history and also look at its evolution through its inner organizational dynamics. It attempts to explain, with enough documentary evidence, how the RSS has reached where it is now. I have tried to connect various turns in its history to bring out how a tightly knit cadre-based organization has morphed into a massive people's movement.

The Sarsanghchaalak is the public face of the RSS. He becomes synonymous with the organization. The Sarsanghchaalak of the RSS personifies the RSS. His views are taken as the most authoritative. His word is considered as the final word for and of the organization. The elected top executive of the RSS is Sarkaryavaah, who runs the day-to-day operations and coordinates its activities within and outside the RSS. However, by virtue of the ultimate authority he has, the Sarsanghchaalak is the one who more or less shapes the organization. Therefore, I have chosen to observe this evolution through the lives of the six Sarsanghchaalaks.

For this purpose, I have studied the lives of all the Sarsanghchaalaks, reviewed the organization's work and referred to some rare books about the RSS written by insiders. As expected, most of the resources I referred to are in regional languages (Hindi and Marathi). I also had some invigorating discussions with many of my colleagues and seniors in the RSS. I am fortunate that I have met all the Sarsanghchaalaks except the founder. I was quite young when Guruji was the guiding light of the RSS, though I saw him in my shakha and heard him in the RSS camps. I got to really understand and appreciate him only when I translated two of his books written by Shri Ranga Hari. However, with all others, I was fortunate enough to observe them from close quarters during my work as an the RSS karyakarta (worker).

I recall many inspiring and humbling moments that I experienced with the RSS veterans—many of whom, people outside the RSS, hardly know but who were the foundation stones of this huge citadel of a Bharat-centric movement. Their selfless sacrifice at the altar of the motherland remains mostly unknown and will be lost to future generations unless more literature is created to document their work. Watching them from close quarters and conversing with them helped me understand the conduct of the Sarsanghchaalaks, and the secret of the RSS growth.

The RSS is a finely structured organization established on the basic building blocks of strong interpersonal relationships and team spirit. If one considers the RSS as a living organic entity, then the 'shakha' is the very basic cell of its body that communicates with the top Akhil Bharatiya Pratinidhi Sabha (ABPS), which is the highest decision-making body through finely designed operational units at various levels. Information and feedback flow from bottom to top; decisions based on these inputs are taken by elected and nominated ex-officio members of ABPS that again flow down to the shakha level. Execution of these decisions is mostly left to local state and district levels and finally to individual shakhas. Thus, it is a highly federal yet unified structure with enough room for autonomous actions. Many programmes are conducted at local shakha and district levels, which are undertaken independently by these units without any need for permission from higher office-bearers. Only some national-level campaigns might have a more structured approach.

Elections to the ABPS are done through an electoral college. This is not the place to go into details of this process. This ABPS elects the Sarkaryavaah (general secretary), who is the executive head of the RSS. The Sarkaryavaah then nominates his central working committee known as Kendriya Karyakarini. It is on such a vast finely honed organizational structure that the Sarsanghchaalak presides.

Consensus-building is an art that is imbibed in swayamsevaks (volunteers) from their early days. This has led to a model democratic organization that has never seen any split—a rarity in the Indian socio-political scene. Even the name of the organization 'Rashtriya Swayamsevak Sangh' was finalized after consultation and voting by all members of the founding committee. However, like any other organization, there can be serious differences too but the consensus-building exercise and close brotherly relations between workers within the organization have helped overcome this natural human tendency. We can catch a glimpse of such inner conflicts and resolutions in this book.

A Sarsanghchaalak is always nominated by the previous Sarsanghchaalak. But, this nomination too goes through a process of long discussions with senior karyakartas. He chooses within the shortlisted names, so it is not a purely personal choice. The post of the Sarsanghchaalak has no fixed tenure. The first two Sarsanghchaalaks were in office till their demise. Apart from these two, all the others handed over the rein to their respective successors voluntarily when they felt that they couldn't carry on the responsibility due to failing health.

Organizations affiliated with the RSS also look up to the Sarsanghchaalak to advise them and provide necessary moral support. At this time, there are over 60,000 daily shakha meetings and 25,000 weekly and monthly shakha meetings. There are about

85 million swayamsevaks directly involved in RSS work, considering that each shakha has a list of approximately 100 members in the locality. Add to this, twenty-eight all-India organizations, excluding the BJP, many of them with their own mass base. For example, an organization such as Vidya Bharati has around 14,000 schools and Ekal Vidyalaya has around 80,000 single teacher schools. There are also 130,000 social service or sewa organizations. Then, there are mass organizations such as the ABVP, Bharatiya Mazdoor Sangh (BMS) and Vishwa Hindu Parishad (VHP), and hundreds of smaller organizations. The reader can thus imagine the influence that the Sarsanghchaalak carries and the responsibility that comes with this post.

No karyakarta or worker can rise in the ranks on the whims of an individual in the RSS. A person in the RSS rises only through systemic processes and filters through numerous ranks before he reaches a high-enough stage where he can be a possible candidate for the post of the Sarsanghchaalak.

A Sarsanghchaalak can start the process of forming new policies by giving certain guidelines. This is where his role becomes critical in the way the organization moves ahead in a specific direction. In this sense, the Sangh, at a particular time, becomes a reflection of the then Sarsanghchaalak's views and thinking. According to the present Sarkaryavaah, Bhaiyyaji Joshi, 'Sarsanghchaalak plays an important role when it comes to structure, scope and direction of the organisation.' (Anand 2019, 201).

The Sarsanghchaalak is not just the face of the organization, but takes on the mantle of its guide and philosopher. His unassailable position and respect can change the direction of the organization, help stabilize it and smoothen relations with other sister organizations. This is an important reason for the reticence of the Sarsanghchaalaks in public life.

The objective of this study is to examine how within all these constraints and historic flow of events, various RSS chiefs seeded new ideas, moulded its working and took the organization forward. The book will try to see how their personalities impacted the socio-political scene of Bharat, i.e., India. This is not a compilation of biographies of various Sarsanghchaalaks. Since the personality and ideas of a person mould his social behaviour, I have created light sketches of their biographies to capture the essence of their personalities and analysed their actions to study the evolution of the RSS.

While it was not easy to compress ninety-five years of the life of an organization of this size and scale within the constraints of a single book, I have tried my best to keep it brief and engaging, with interesting anecdotes and by recounting critical historical turns in the life of the RSS. It is a veritable walk through the history of the RSS. Through this analysis, the reader will be able to understand how the RSS evolved slowly from a tightly knit cadre-based organization to a mass movement.

Sarsanghchaalak as an Institution

As we go through the lives of successive Sarsanghchaalaks sketchily drawn in this book, we will find some common traits in all of them, despite having very different personalities. This is a result of the training methodology institutionalized by the RSS, whereby it nurtures certain qualities in its cadres. These qualities are refined as they grow within the ranks. In fact, these traits can be seen not just in Sarsanghchaalaks but in all the top leaders of the Sangh who have undergone this training over the years and worked their way up the ranks. Many senior swayamsevaks, who are not in senior hierarchy, too imbibe these qualities because they too, have gone through a similar process.

Bhagwan Krishna tells Arjun:

Yad yad ācharati śhreṣhṭhas tat tad evetaro janaḥ
sa yat pramāṇaṁ kurute lokas tad anuvartate

— Bhagavad Gita, Chapter 3, Shloka 21

Meaning, 'Whatever actions great persons perform, the common people follow. Whatever standards they set, all the world pursues.'

There are some tangible and some intangible organizational processes that hone the personalities of the swayamsevaks that tune them as karyakartas. Expectations from their conduct grow higher as they rise higher in the ranks. It is not just processes, but also their interactions with other team members during baithaks and collective programmes that sharpen the personality of karyakartas and take them to the next level. These interactions at each level are organizational filters that are personal yet impersonal.

Irrespective of whether a person comes from South or North, East or West, his community or the language that he may speak, the approach of looking at issues and responding to them in a balanced manner evolves from within. It is very common to hear people say, 'I instinctively felt he is a swayamsevak.' If you ask people why they feel so, the answer is usually, 'By his language, his conduct.' Having said this, each swayamsevak is a unique personality, and therefore it is only after thorough discussions and thousands of man-hours that conclusions are arrived at and a final consensus is reached. This is a skill an individual acquires with patience.

The Sarsanghchaalak is looked upon as the head of the organization to whom every person within and outside looks up to, because he is the person whose conduct mirrors the RSS itself. This puts an enormous burden on him as he is supposed to personify the best traditions of the RSS. The message that the nation is larger than the organization and that no individual is more important than the organization and the nation is strongly ingrained in all swayamsevaks.

Hindu society's readiness, rather, its eagerness to convert a great leader into a god was discouraged by Dr K.B. Hedgewar. Nana Palkar, in his biography of Dr Hedgewar, writes about Dr Hedgewar's visit to the princely state, Aundh in Sangli. At the time of his visit, Dr Hedgewar was taken to the family temple of the royal household and shown a grand painting depicting Bhagwan Shiv being incarnated as Shivaji through the revered Jijabai. On seeing the painting, he is said to have turned to his host, and said, 'Sir, this idea of avatar has damaged our society. Why do you wish to deify a great person who awakened the society with unequalled efforts and unparalleled courage?' The king thought for a while and finally said, 'Doctor, what you say is correct.' (Palkar 2000, 323)

The reader will find in this book some of the prominent common traits of Sarsanghchaalaks. Most of these are inherent in their personality, and probably that is what helps them stand out amongst thousands of RSS workers.

All the Sarsanghchaalaks have a very high intelligence quotient (IQ). They are academically brilliant. They are at the top in their field; yet, they forsake the fruits of their success for service to the society. They are insatiable readers and don't drop their reading habits despite their hectic schedules. Their hunger for knowledge is never satiated. Beginning from Dr Hedgewar to all Sarsanghchaalaks down the line, the reader will note this common trait.

They also have a high emotional quotient (EQ). A compassionate and sensitive nature is one of the most important qualities of an RSS karyakarta. One can see it in every Sarsanghchaalak. Most would have stayed awake at nights to care for a sick junior, or taken care of someone's personal problems, career, family emergency and so on. Most would have gone out of their way to provide succour to a citizen in every possible way. They maintain good relations with the families they stay with during tours, and keep in touch with most people—not just RSS workers—they come in contact with.

Lastly, they also have a high social quotient (SQ). There is a sense of responsibility towards the society that keeps them mindful of any problem to the society and the nation. They mingle with any team, group or community very easily. There are countless instances of a pure vegetarian prachaarak eating non-vegetarian food in order to be one with their hosts, as in the North East where non-vegetarianism is the norm. Every prachaarak also puts in an effort to learn the local language of the place where they are working so that they can write and converse like the locals. Some even become an authority on their adopted language. They avoid confrontation or negative discussions with ideological adversaries as they treat all—even critics—as their future ally. Many adversaries have, indeed, become allies at a later time. Their behaviour clearly shows that they treat all persons as well as every region and faith as their own and speak of people and religions with great respect.

All of them have a brilliant memory. While some maybe are naturally gifted, others may have trained themselves to remember people, names and places. This quality is very important in order to connect with people. Everyone likes to be addressed by their name and be recognized. It is amazing that despite so much of travelling and being stationed in different places during their stint as prachaaraks, they can remember thousands of faces, their families and their qualities.

All senior leaders, especially Sarsanghchaalaks have punishing travelling schedules. As one climbs higher in the ranks of the RSS, one must travel to places further off and more frequently. The top leaders may be assigned different RSS centres as their place of stay during their responsibility, but the address is only for reference, getting documents or other materials. They stay there only for a couple of days before they go out on tour again. Most of the travel is by modest means. Only in case of urgent matters do they travel by air. Earlier prachaaraks had a very hard life.

All Sarsanghchaalaks and other top leaders lead simple, frugal lifestyles with very few belongings. They live with swayamsevaks' families or at RSS offices. These families become their extended family. They are their mothers, sisters, brothers, nephews, uncles and aunts, while they leave behind their own families when they become prachaaraks. Though some lifestyles have changed today, the idea of frugality remains deeply ingrained. For example, today they may possess mobiles and electronic tablets as they are necessities of a technology-driven society or give up jholas (cloth bags) for better quality bags, yet their daily expenses are so low they would shock anyone. Also, their expenses do not increase as they rise up in the hierarchy. A Sarsanghchaalak may be spending more or less similar to what a district prachaarak spends.

Their humility and transparency in their behaviour with people—irrespective of the person they are talking to—is another quality that would strike anyone. They are always balanced in their behaviour, radiate happiness and show no ego, despite being a part of one of the biggest voluntary organizations in the world. They are not provoked easily. In short, they fit into the description of a *sthitpragya* as described in the Gita—meaning one who is not easily moved by what is happening around them.

Even in their deaths, Sarsanghchaalaks have left a message.

A veteran prachaarak, Ranga Hariji, points out that all Sarsanghchaalaks must leave instructions on how they should be cremated. The founding Sarsanghchaalak had said that he did not want a military-style cremation; rather he wanted it to be like the cremation of an ordinary family person. It was necessary to give this instruction as most people assumed the Sangh to be a paramilitary organization. Some members of the RSS would have also thought on these lines. Doctorji, as he was known, wished to convey the message that it is actually a family organization.

The second Sarsanghchaalak, Guruji, had instructed that there should be no memorial except that of the founder. Dr Hedgewar Smarak Samiti was formed in 1962 under his chairmanship. He understood the emotions of the swayamsevaks. It was necessary to avoid any confusion within the organization and so he left this message. He understood that it could mean another memorial in the same campus.

The third Sarsanghchaalak was practical. He had told his personal assistant, Shri Shrikant Joshi, that his cremation should be in a public crematorium. He remembered that Guruji's cremation was done at the RSS office campus because it was a decision taken by some top RSS leaders of the time. He did not wish to leave behind a tradition whereby Reshimbagh would become a place where multiple *chhatris* or small memorials of succeeding Sarsanghchaalaks would come up.

The fourth, Rajju Bhaiyya, had said, 'Wherever I die, my last rites should be done there. Entire Bharat is my home. There is no reason to shift my dead body anywhere.' He died in Pune and he was cremated there, though his native place was Prayag. Sudarshanji followed the same tradition.

What the brilliant veteran writer-prachaarak Shivrai Telang said at the time of the demise of Shri Balasahab Deoras, can actually be said about the entire successive top leadership of RSS.

> All the three Sarsanghchaalaks had the same vision of the nation and they presented it to the society as per situation of

> those times. For this purpose, all three worked as per demand of the times in tune with their respective personalities. Sangh has never encouraged production of clones. No one is like another, still all of them are same.

Each Sarsanghchaalak gave new dimensions to the mission of RSS, which was and still is, in consonance with what the first Sarsanghchaalak had envisioned. Ultimately, they too underline the doctrine that the mission is more important than the personality. Their lives are an inspiration for millions of swayamsevaks. This is the reason why the post of the Sarsanghchaalak has become an institution in itself.

While taking over as Sarsanghchaalak, Guruji said that the seat of Sarsanghchaalak is like the throne of Vikramaditya, sitting on which even a shepherd would dispense justice well. On assuming the responsibility of Sarsanghchaalak, Balasaheb Deoras had said that though he was nowhere near Doctorji or Guruji in qualities, he was confident that he would do justice to the post of the Sarsanghchaalak because he was blessed with a wonderful team of workers that even god would not find easily. Succeeding Sarsanghchaalaks have made this post an institution, and this institution has in turn influenced the succeeding Sarsanghchaalaks.

Dr Hedgewar: The Founder of a Unique Organizational Model (1925–1940)

Dr Keshav Baliram Hedgewar, or Doctorji as he is generally known, was a quintessential product of the Indian Independence struggle. Born on 1 April 1889 as per the Gregorian calendar and on Hindu New Year's Day as per the Hindu calendar, Keshav was the son of Baliram Hedgewar who was a scholar of the Vedas and Agnihotra. Baliram had three sons and three daughters.

The Hedgewar family belonged to Kundkurti village on the banks of the confluence of three rivers—Godavari, Vanjara and Haridra. It was a traditional scholarly family that had even hosted Jagadguru Shankaracharya at one time. The people of this village were of strong built, with wrestling as their main hobby. The people of this area spoke three languages: Telugu, Kannada and Marathi. They left their hearth and homes about 150–200 years back in search of a better life in Nagpur, which could be reached in three or four days on foot. Mughal persecution, hence poor life and rise of the Bhonsale kings in Madhya Prant, persuaded them to migrate (Palkar 2000, 2–3).

Keshav was the youngest of three brothers. The family, though not rich, lived a happy and satisfied life. The eldest son was very fond of body-building and built a gymkhana at their home, thus motivating his two brothers to start body-building as well. Keshav was admitted to a *Vedshala* (school for Vedic studies). After noticing his son's hunger for knowledge and reading, his father admitted him to an English-medium school called Neil City High.

He was eight years old when his school celebrated the sixtieth birthday of the Queen of England. The school celebrated it in a big way. Young Keshav too received sweets. He brought the packet home and threw it into the dustbin. When the other children asked him about his missing packet, he said that he had received it but questioned, 'Why should he celebrate the birthday of a queen who defeated the Bhonsales?' After four years, in 1901, when it was time to celebrate the coronation of the English king, Keshav refused to participate in the celebrations (Palkar 2000, 8).

Unfortunately, at that time, there was a plague epidemic in Nagpur and surrounding areas. In the fourteen years of the disease in India, around ten million people lost their lives. It is said that people would tell that in Nagpur, in a locality of one hundred thousand, around 300 people would die each day. Keshav lost both his parents on the same day despite taking all precautions for cleanliness and hygiene, as well as Ayurvedic medication from Baliram's brothers. Nothing worked.

His eldest brother fell into bad habits. So, the two younger brothers were left to fend for themselves. They would get food sometimes, sometimes they would sleep hungry. But Keshav kept up his spirits, making friends, playing and wandering around in Nagpur. He began to enjoy speaking in public on various subjects. It was here that Dr Munje, who was a prominent Hindu Mahasabha leader, discovered him and decided to take on the responsibility of the young boy's education. Keshav had a revolutionary bent of mind. The year 1905 became a landmark year due to 'Bang Bhang' efforts of the government and rise of *Vande Mataram* as the battle cry. The year 1906 witnessed the Swadeshi Movement. This atmosphere influenced him deeply (Palkar 2000, 20–21).

This was the mood in 1908 when a visit of the education inspector to his school was scheduled. His agitation at that time—he was in Matric (present-day SSC)—is noteworthy. As a protest against the infamous 'Risley Circular' that had banned the slogan of *Vande Mataram* in 1906, he organized students in senior classes to raise this slogan when the inspector came on his visit. When the inspector threatened action, the agitation intensified with boycotting of class. This went on for nearly a month. No student would divulge his name despite threats of dismissal. Ultimately, Keshav himself came into the open as he didn't want his friends to suffer. He was expelled from school (Palkar 2000, 21–22).

He was staying with Dr Munje at that time but he would manage his food in different places, sometimes even staying hungry. Through an introduction from Dr Munje, he got into Rashtriya Shala with a hostel in Yavatmal. After completing school, he returned to Nagpur and went back to public life. Anushilan Samiti, a revolutionary group, had a team in Nagpur too. This group managed to collect some funds and send Keshav to National Medical College, Calcutta, where he could receive more information and knowledge about revolutionary activities. According to his revolutionary friend Ramlal Vajpayee, Keshav was sent with financial support from Dajisaheb Buti to work under Shri Pulin Bihari Das to learn more about revolution than medicine (Palkar 2000, 30). In Calcutta too, Keshav made friends with people who had come to study there from all over the country. His heart and soul were fired up with the desire to free India from British rule.

His colleague in Anushilan Samiti, Shri Trailokyanath Chakravarty, mentions him and his work in his autobiography, *Jail Mein Tees Baras*. He also included Keshav's photograph as a team member in this book (Palkar 2000, 37). Keshav's code name in the police files was 'cocain' (Sinha 2004, 19). His colleagues used to recount his absence from the guesthouse at odd hours in the night (Palkar 2000, 39). There is a mention of his learning bomb-making in Palkar's book.

Early Experiences in Public Life

A strange rule had been passed by the British that students passing out of National Medical College (from where he graduated) had a right to practice medicine but they had no right to give any sickness certificate to the patients. It was passed by Sir Parde Lucis through Cabinet. It was meant to insult Indians. News began to appear in various newspapers about this patently unjust law and a demand to rescind it began to rise. The law began to be known as 'Bogus Medical Degrees Bill'.

Dr Hedgewar had met Dr Ashutosh Mukherjee before beginning this agitation. He also met editors of many newspapers such as Motilal Ghosh from *Amrit Bazar Patrika*. They all supported Dr Hedgewar. There was a lot of noise made about many meetings, even though ninety per cent of the public meetings never actually took place. When police went for enquiry, the owners of the hall and the named chairman would confirm that the meeting took place, creating enough buzz for the cause.

Once the propaganda created a wave, a huge meeting was held under the chairmanship of Shri Surendranath Banerjee. When a resolution was passed at this meeting, opposing the bill, the government of the day had to listen to it and the law was amended to allow the medical graduates to give certificates. The agitation was concluded successfully. This episode tells us that Dr Hedgewar understood how to exploit the power of the media to create the right environment. However, as we will see later, he consciously refused to use it for the expansion of RSS work. We will also come to understand the reason for such an approach. After completing his one-year internship, Dr Hedgewar returned to Nagpur in 1916 (Palkar 2000, 51).

From 1916 to 1918, he participated in serious revolutionary activities with his close friend Bhauji Kavre in Madhya Prant. The spread was from Punjab to Goa. Arms were purchased and serious conspiracies were worked out. Meanwhile, Britain won World War I (WWI) and began heavy action against revolutionaries. Many young people retreated into a shell; plans were abandoned. During this time, Dr Hedgewar used to give highly provocative lectures at Ganesh festivals (Palkar 2000, 58–64). Having seen and experienced revolutionary activities from close quarters, he realized that sporadic isolated acts couldn't bring the desired impact and independence.

He was clear in his mind that he would not marry and would

dedicate his life to the freedom of the nation. He told his paternal uncle about his priorities in life. He saw family responsibilities as a hurdle to his life's mission, which involved a deep commitment, hectic work schedule and risks. He could sense from others that obligations of family duties could weaken one's focus. He decided to join the Indian National Congress and formally joined it in 1918.

During this period, some more events took place. 13 April 1919 witnessed the ghastly firing by General Dyer in Jallianwala Bagh in Amritsar, where people had collected to protest against the infamous Rowlatt Act. Hundreds had perished and it had shaken the conscience of the nation.

This period saw the demise of one of the tallest leaders of the freedom struggle, Lokmanya Tilak, who had made a clarion call 'Swaraj is my birthright and I shall have it.'

Dr Hedgewar's Innings in Congress

Dr Hedgewar had previously worked in Tilak's Home Rule League for some time. He also helped gain readership for a Hindi weekly that was brought out by an organization, Rashtriya Mandal. Since his views were more aggressive than those of the Congress, he formed an organization, Nagpur National Union, with his other friends and gave fiery lectures to students and young. He used Hindu festivals to inculcate national spirit among the masses (Karandikar 1999, 68). Rashtriya Mandal used to publish a periodical *Sankalp*, and Dr Hedgewar was given the responsibility of increasing its circulation. He toured the entire Madhya Prant by various means and worked hard to raise both funds and circulation.

An episode illustrates his burning passion for the nation. As he was going home after hearing of Tilak's death, he saw some boys playing cricket. He couldn't control himself and he shouted at them, 'Such a great leader has expired and you are playing cricket?' The boys stopped the game. Interestingly, one boy, Dadarao Paramarth, was so moved by the pain expressed by Dr Hedgewar that he went on to become a swayamsevak of the first RSS shakha and was one of the most respected prachaaraks of the RSS (Karandikar 1999, 67). It was a period of high ferment.

His urge for social reforms in society was very strong. During this time he visited Arvi, a town in Maharashtra, where his friend Gangadhar Deshpande told him about his niece being married off to an old man. Dr Hedgewar was quite upset on hearing this. He asked his friend whether he was fine with the match, Deshpande admitted that he was not. So, Dr Hedgewar hatched a detailed plan of taking the young girl to Nagpur. The plan was successfully executed, even though it led to some legal cases against the two friends. The girl was later married off to a suitable young man (Karandikar 1999, 71). Dr Hedgewar's ever-present sense of social duty made him do many such spontaneous acts in his life.

Dr Hedgewar also would get together people with different viewpoints; he would engage in discussions and exchange ideas with them. Among them was also a Communist leader, Comrade Rambhau Ruikar. He was such a good friend that he would be invited to the milk-drinking session on *Kojagiri Poornima* (full moon night before Diwali). The number of friends coming together for such sessions would sometime reach seventy-five or eighty! Such groups also included eminent personalities like Dr Munje and Raje Laxmanrao Bhonsale. This *Kojagiri* get-together lasted till Dr Hedgewar founded RSS in 1925–26.

After he joined the Congress, preparatory meetings and public lectures had begun for the preparation of the Congress plenary session in Nagpur in December 1920. Dr Munje and Dr Hedgewar mostly led these meetings. One would be a speaker while the other would be the chairman alternately in these programmes. Nagpur Congress members were keen that Lokmanya Tilak should be the president of the session. Unfortunately, Tilak died on 1 August of the same year.

Under the circumstances, Dr Munje wished to ask Aurobindo Ghosh to take over the political leadership. Both Dr Munje and Dr Hedgewar went to Pondicherry in September 1920 with this request. But, he had taken a spiritual turn and he refused (Palkar 2000, 75).

Dr Hedgewar was the joint secretary of Nagpur branch of the

Congress at a time when the national session of the Congress was being planned in Nagpur in 1920. Dr L.V. Paranjape formed Bharat Swayamsevak Dal in January 1920 itself to take care of the arrangements. Dr Hedgewar was fully involved in this exercise. This was done to involve young volunteers in organizing the session. However, more attention was paid from September onwards. When the idea for uniforms for the volunteers was being discussed, many felt that it would be unwise to spend money just for one meeting. A circular was released by the two assuring all that the volunteers would be involved in different nation-building activities including processions and lectures during various festivals. Around 1,000 volunteers were recruited for this session. It is said that this session was the biggest and grandest until then. The next big session took place in 1928 in Calcutta (Karandikar 1999, 72-73).

Dr Hedgewar did such a good job that his stature in the party and his following rose sharply. The Congress till that time was only demanding 'Self Rule' as a dominion under British rule. The line of thought was followed in this session too. However, Dr Hedgewar had also presented a resolution to the Resolution Committee, of which he was a member that demanded 'Complete Freedom.' It was, however, rejected by the committee.

The proposed resolution read:

> Goal of [the] Congress is to achieve complete freedom and establish Indian republic; and to liberate the other nations of the world from exploitation and atrocities of capitalist imperialism. (Palkar 2000, 97)

The periodical *Modern Review* in its March 1921 issue reflected its disappointment.

> But, the proposed resolution which excited laughter among serious-minded people deserved a better fate than what it met with the subject committee. (Palkar 2000, 80)

This session would also be long remembered for the untimely death of Tilak just before the session he was to preside over. This session also saw the beginning of the rise of Mahatma Gandhi as the unrivalled Congress leader.

It is noteworthy that the Congress declared its resolve for complete independence after nine years at the 1929 Lahore conference. This shows that Dr Hedgewar was much ahead of the leaders of his times about his vision for India. Not only did he want India to become an independent nation, but also help other colonized countries to gain independence from what he called 'Capitalist Imperialism'. It is notable that he welcomed the 1929 resolution unconditionally and celebrated it as per Congress' direction.

Gandhiji presided over the 1920 session. He had begun his innings by supporting the Khilafat agitation that was launched by the Muslim leadership to reinstate the Caliph of Turkey who had been overthrown by Kemal Atatürk. Till then, the King or Caliph of Turkey was supposed to be the lord of the entire global community of Muslims. Neither did Dr Hedgewar like the idea of going overboard in this support to Muslims in the name of Hindu–Muslim unity, nor did he get a satisfactory reply from Gandhiji (Karandikar 1999, 71).

The Non-cooperation Movement launched by Gandhiji and the Khilafat agitation ran parallel during that time. The former led to the formation of the All-India Khadi Gramodyog Sangh to promote swadeshi goods (Karandikar 1999, 74–75). The call for 'Independence in one year' found great resonance among the people of the country and led to the establishment of Rashtriya Schools and the owning of charkhas (spinning wheels) in every household. Dr Hedgewar and Dr Munje wholeheartedly joined the Non-cooperation Movement and gave immensely provocative lectures in Madhya Prant and Maharashtra (Karandikar 1999, 79).

This movement took place around the same time that the Khilafat Movement gathered momentum with active support from Gandhiji and the Congress. There was disquiet in the Congress about support to the Khilafat agitation, especially in Nagpur, which was a major centre for Tilak's followers. They felt that linking the Khilafat Movement to the freedom movement was not a good idea. Though Dr Hedgewar was also against the Khilafat Movement, he did not want Gandhiji's Non-cooperation Movement to be weakened. So he jumped right into the movement with full energy so that the larger fight for freedom from colonial rule did not suffer.

To give the Non-cooperation Movement a push, Dr Chaulkar, Samimullah Khan and Dr Hedgewar became very active. The fact that Doctorji worked with Samimullah Khan, who was an avid supporter of the Khilafat Movement, shows his sagacity and commitment to the freedom struggle. He did this simply for the sake of providing momentum to the Non-cooperation Movement. He was sent repeated notices by the government to refrain from making inflammatory speeches, but he did not stop. On 23 February 1921, he was sent a notice to refrain from making any speeches for a whole month, but he flouted this too. Finally, he was charged with making objectionable speeches and the judge told him that his speeches were seditious. This case was a result of his refusal to toe the government line. He was also told by the court to not give such speeches for one year, as well as submit two bail amounts of ₹1,000 each and a personal surety of ₹1,000. However, he refused saying, whatever the decision, he considered himself innocent. As a result, he was imprisoned for one year with hard labour (Karandikar 1999, 80).

Though he willingly went to jail refusing to plead guilty, he was clear that going to jail was not the only thing one could do for the freedom struggle. Before entering jail, he said in his speech,

> Just as it is true that one should always be ready to be imprisoned, or be sent to Kala Pani, or get hanged; it is also true that one should not at all be in confusion that going to prison is like reaching heavens, as if this imprisonment itself means achieving freedom. One should definitely not understand that filling prisons will get us freedom or swarajya. The truth

> is that one can serve the nation in many ways by being out of prison. (Palkar 2000, 91)

While in jail, he observed the behaviour of Khilafat volunteers, who would openly say, 'For [us], Islam is first and the nation second' (Palkar 2000, 95). Savarkar had a similar experience of Muslim inmates' blind hatred for Hindus during his Kala Pani imprisonment in the Andaman Islands (Karandikar 1999, 101).

Doctorji was further disturbed by Gandhiji's reaction to Moplah violence against Hindus during Khilafat. 'Brave, God-fearing Moplahs who were fighting for what they consider religion and in a manner they consider religious.' When the bloodshed went out of control, the British used brute power to suppress the violence. The imprisoned Moplahs were transferred in a railway bogey and sixty-six of the prisoners died of suffocation. It was very disturbing news. However, Jawaharlal Nehru, who didn't speak up against the wanton violence against Hindus, said, 'The Moplah rising and its extraordinary cruel suppression—what a horrible thing was the baking to death of the Moplah prisoners in the closed railway vans!' (Palkar 2000, 103)

Later, Gandhiji did introspect and probably realized his mistake. In his biography, Mahadevbhai Desai wrote about his admission.

> I made a mistake. I may be blamed for being a traitor to Hindus. I have seen the result of me [sic] keep saying that Hindus should follow non-violence in the face of Muslims' violence; die instead of killing to stop the fight. I have seen what the result of my views is. Large numbers of temples have been destroyed. Many sisters have come to me with their complaints. How can I tell Hindus to bear with it with patience? (Karandikar 1999, 93)

The Non-cooperation Movement fizzled out by 1923, and people returned to their professions and schools by the time Nehru was released from jail. Politics became an unwelcome word. A similar rise and fall of enthusiasm and consciousness was also seen when

Tilak was sentenced to imprisonment in Mandalay and when he was released after six years. It was around that time when Aurobindo too was released from Alipore Jail. When he went to jail, there was huge rise in fiery agitation of 'Bang Bhang'. By the time he returned, the fire had cooled down (Karandikar 1999, 85).

All these episodes in the freedom struggle agitated Dr Hedgewar. He realized that it was necessary to have a regular programme that would inculcate a spirit of patriotism and nurture *sanskaras* to keep it burning.

Though he had many differences with Gandhiji on Khilafat and absolute non-violence, he respected him unconditionally. When Gandhiji was awarded a six years' jail term on 18 March 1922, every eighteenth day of the month was celebrated as Gandhi Din. Dr Hedgewar gave a lecture in October 1922, paying his respect to Gandhiji and remembering him for his sterling qualities.

> Today is a sacred day. It is the day to remember the great qualities of the great soul like Mahatma Gandhi and ponder over them. Sacrifice of every kind of selfishness is the biggest quality of Gandhiji. If we wish to be called the followers of Gandhi, we should give up our family life and give our life for the national cause. (Palkar 2000, 109)

In 1923, he also promoted a newspaper *Swaatyantra* and worked hard, without any remuneration, to keep it running. Many prominent names were brought in. It used to be full of inspiring stories about Independence. Many articles in support of Savarkar were also published. The 238th volume, dated 6 November 1923, was the last edition of this newspaper (Palkar 2000, 123).

Many severe communal riots broke out in 1924 all over India, as noted by Pattabhi Sitharamaiyya in his book, *History of the Indian National Congress*. These could be a sequel to the Moplah violence unleashed in the aftermath of the failure of the Khilafat agitation. Some were plain massacres of Hindus by Muslims. Kohat, now in Pakistan, is one of the places where genocide of Hindus took place in 1924, after the Moplah violence of 1921.

Dr Munje made a tour of all the riot-affected areas from Malabar in Kerala, which was the Moplah home ground, as well as Uttar Pradesh and the Central Province. The situation was really bad. Dr Munje exclaimed, 'This is the most widespread and biggest attack on Hindus after the end of Muslim rule' (Karandikar 1999, 94).

Mahatma Gandhi went on a hunger strike that resulted in the formation of peace committees. Writing about these attempts, Dr B.R. Ambedkar noted, 'The unity conferences produced nothing but pious resolutions, which were broken as soon as they were announced' (Palkar 2000, 128). While Gandhiji could not see the long-term effect of appeasement of extremist elements in Muslim society, other observers could. Dr Ambedkar asked, 'Can any sane man go so far for the sake of Hindu–Muslim unity?' (Karandikar 1999, 100)

Overall, the period from 1920 to 1924 was a highly turbulent time for the nation when Indian society went through great turmoil. It was during this time that Gandhiji admitted, 'There is no doubt in my mind that in the majority of quarrels the Hindus come out second best. But my own experience confirms the opinion that the Mussalman as a rule is a bully, and the Hindu as a rule is a coward' (Gandhi 1924, 35–36). Nehru in his biography noted that Hindus were busy working as clerks and were asleep (Palkar 2000, 129).

During this time, Dr N.S. Hardikar began his work on the Hindustani Seva Dal and established it in time for the Kakinada session in 1923. Nehru also liked the idea, but he was in for a surprise when he realized later that many leaders strongly objected to any such organization as that could create a spirit of militarism if they were brought together in a disciplined manner. This would be contrary to the objective of ahimsa, or non-violence. Nehru was surprised at this strong reaction because the Seva Dal itself had many luminous Congress leaders. He wrote,

> We were surprised to find later how much opposition there was to the Seva Dal among leading Congressmen. Some said that this was a dangerous departure, as it meant introducing military element in the Congress and the military arm might overpower the civil authority! (Palkar 2000, 105)

Decision to Reform Hindu Society and Birth of RSS

While being active in the freedom movement, one question that always bothered Dr Hedgewar was how a handful of Britishers coming from 7,000 km across the seas, could rule such a huge nation. He realized that there was something wrong with Indians. In all his years in public life, he realized that Indian society had forgotten its own history and was fragmented on the lines of caste, language and region. He saw that it was disorganized and stifled by oppressive customs that could be exploited by British. If the country did not change even after gaining Independence, history would repeat itself. One oppressor would replace another—that is all. Therefore, the most important work was to raise the nation above caste and creed, reform it, organize it, help it get rid of its oppressive customs and ultimately raise national consciousness. He could see that it was possible only by keeping away from politics, propaganda and working silently in a sustained manner.

He discussed the issue of a Hindu organization, its reform and unity, with many of his friends. He met Bhauji Kavre, Appaji Joshi, Vishwanath Kelkar and many others. He was clear that the proposed Hindu unity was not to be against Muslims and was not meant to beat them up. He would speak about Hindus having their only land Bharat, a society that had the heritage of great dharma, and the *sanskriti* or cultural values needed to unite and be organized in a disciplined way. This exercise needed to be above politics, allowing leaders to keep working within their own political space. However, Appaji Joshi noted, 'Various leaders whom Doctor Hedgewar met were mostly aligned to different political parties who carried influence of Gandhiji's movement—

some were influenced by Swarajya Party, thus nothing came of it' (Palkar 2000, 130–131). Thus, Doctorji gave up on all such attempts and decided to work for Hindu renaissance on his own.

Dr Hedgewar first began with a wrestling school for which he called back an ex-revolutionary Ganga Prasad to train youth in wrestling. The idea was to get youth involved in a long-term effort for which they needed to be physically strong (Palkar 2000, 88). Thus, it can be seen that experiments towards organizing the youth had already begun.

Finally, he founded the Rashtriya Swayamsevak Sangh in 1925 on Vijayadashami day at a meeting in his home with twenty-two of his friends. However, the name of the new organization was decided through voting later in April 1926. The three names that were suggested are Rashtriya Swayamsevak Sangh, Jaripatka Mandal and Bharatoddharak Mandal. Rashtriya Swayamsevak Sangh received 20 out of 26 votes, Jaripatka Mandal received 5, and Bharatoddharak, 1 (Palkar 2000, 136).

The day of Vijayadashami too was significant as it is a day that celebrates valour and victory of 'dharmic' forces over 'adharmic' forces—victory of good over evil. In Maharashtra, it is also celebrated as *Seemolanghan,* meaning the crossing of boundaries, in which villagers from one village crossed over to another and staged mock fights. In short, it signified getting over one's own limitations.

Some questions came to the fore: If one wished to organize Hindu society, then why not name it Hindu Swayamsevak Sangh? If a Hindu organization is called Rashtriya, then Hindu and Rashtriya become synonymous. If that is so, does it mean non-Hindus are not Rashtriya? But, Doctorji had no such negative ideas. For him, all those who reside in Hindustan, have love for the nation and have the full right to serve it. He was clear that this nation has a culture and history that is thousands of years old. It was a country that had great personalities, which preceded the history of Western nations. Indeed, there was much to be proud of (Karandikar 1999, 15). It is interesting to note that when Dr Hardikar had named the

Seva Dal as Hindustani Seva Dal, there was no objection to it at the time. However, the word 'Hindustani' was dropped later. We don't know whether it was done because it had the word 'Hindu' in it (Karandikar 1999, 21).

In the foundation of the RSS, we see the unorthodox approach of Dr Hedgewar. He formed an organization with a clear objective but did not give it a name. He named the organization only after due consultation with his team many months later.

Doctorji moulded his own personality to suit the ideals of the new organization he had in mind. For the sake of organizing society on the strength of positivity, he let go of his aggressive approach and hot-tempered avatar. It is noted in his biography that in his early avatar, when he spoke, he used to spit fire and brimstone. His eyes would burn with anger while speaking about the British. This aggressive and angry persona was in his genes. His family was known for its hot temper. However, from the day he founded the RSS, he changed his entire persona to suit the need of an organization that he wished to build on the strength of brotherly affection and bonding. It was the new persona of an organizer, not of a revolutionary or an agitator. No one ever heard him raise his voice again. If people wished to try something different in a shakha programme, he would allow them to do it and learn from their mistakes; he did not stop or scold anyone. He became patient and did not lose his humorous vein till the very end.

Even after establishing the RSS, he had warm relations with political and social leaders from all walks of life, even those who held opinions different from his own. Once, there was a hot debate in a meeting on whether Gandhi was better or Savarkar. Asked about his views, Dr Hedgewar's responded by saying, 'This debate is like debating whether the rose is better or mogra (*Jasminum sambac*). It is a matter of inclination and choice. At such a time, you should not crush one flower, but enjoy the beauty of the flower you like' (Palkar 2000, 223). Therefore, one can see in Doctorji a clear knack for harmonizing different points of view. He used to stress that the RSS was not against anybody. Rather, it was to unite and strengthen Hindu society.

After officially declaring the formation of his organization, Dr Hedgewar would go to various *vyayamshalas* (gymnasiums) to find talented and enthusiastic youth with a burning desire for freedom. He would then get them trained in whatever sport they were good at. To bring such youth together, his friends established two new gyms but it only led to negative competition. That is when he decided to begin his own shakha. After this, he began bringing his swayamsevaks together once a week for political and intellectual training. Finally, he came up with the idea of a daily shakha and was organized in a rundown place called Mohite Wada in Nagpur. He cleaned up the place with his young wards and began a daily shakha. Mohite Wada was purchased by well-wishers many years later, and the first RSS *karyalaya* (office) came up there. It houses a small RSS museum today and a few residential quarters for senior prachaaraks.

In fact, the methodology adopted by Dr Hedgewar was taken from akhadas that were there in all villages at the time. As per records of the British India government, there were 230 akhadas in Nagpur division in 1921. By the 1931 census, these numbers had doubled to reach 575 (Karandikar 1999, 25). However, Dr Hedgewar found that a value system was missing from these akhadas—the focus was only on physical fitness. To remedy this, he added more programmes to this basic idea.

The revolutionary movement had an even bigger role to play in the working style of the Sangh. When he was a student of Calcutta Medical College from 1910 to 1916, he was a member of Anushilan Samiti, an organization with a similar outward structure. Anushilan Samiti was formed in March 1902. As per British intelligence report, drill and lathis were integral parts of its working. Every member had to arrange for his own lathi. He had a dagger, a small lathi and a bigger lathi. The smaller lathi was used for training in sword fighting. During a raid, the police found 158 books about training in sword, dagger, yoga and drill-related activities—all that would have seemed harmless to an outsider (Swaroop 2017, 26). Members of the samiti used to call themselves 'Hindu santaan,' meaning Hindu children. It seems the oath-taking ceremony in the RSS was also inspired by Anushilan Samiti. Thus, we note that the search for inspiration of the RSS working methodology was from within the Indian revolutionary movement (Swaroop 2017, 27). Bhagini Nivedita too was a member of the working committee of Anushilan Samiti.

Bhagini Nivedita had told Satishchandra Basu, one of the founders of Anushilan Samiti, 'You are aware of Swamiji's [Vivekananda] wish. Therefore, you should improve your health; and other exercises including lathi training should be done.' Swami Shraddhanand, a disciple of Swami Vivekananda, had told Satishchandra Basu earlier that he must work for freedom. He had quoted Swamiji as saying, 'Even a crow bound by rope flaps and struggles hard to get free. Why should you not sacrifice your lives for the freedom of our nation?' (Swaroop 2017, 31–32).

In conversation with his disciple and intellectual daughter, Christine Greenstidel, he noted, 'Nivedita is new to politics [...] I first wish to organize a team of volunteers who would take an oath of celibacy, educate people and inject the nation with a new energy' (Swaroop 2017, 33–34).

This is what Dr Hedgewarji had also realized with his many years of experience. Dr Hedgewar got his friend, Martandrao Jog, to give training in military discipline, marching, and so on. Jog was also the head of Congress Seva Dal. This was around December 1926 (Palkar 2000, 145). His other friend, Anna Sohoni, organized physical training and created a syllabus for physical drills, including lathi training. Lathi was called danda by Dr Hedgewar because Shivaji's guru, Swami Samarth, used to carry it and called it 'dand.' Some other martial physical programmes like spear and cane were also introduced to inculcate martial spirit and discipline (Karandikar 1999, 30).

Dr Hedgewar's intervention during the September 1927 Muslim–Hindu riots saw the end to riots in Nagpur that were routinely happening then. They were the last of the riots. Muslim goons had their way for all these years, but that year Dr Hedgewar decided to teach the goons a lesson. A determined band of 100–125 swayamsevaks with only lathis, but engaged in a planned manner, turned the tables with smart thinking. The riots went on for three days. Muslims had to take asylum in the Gond King's Fort. However, after this incident, Nagpur never saw riots. Muslim leaders realized that Hindus too can retaliate. And if they do, their false sense of being unbeatable will mean nothing (Palkar 2000, 164–65). This episode led to rising respect for Dr Hedgewar in many circles. He was invited to the Hindu Mahasabha plenary session in Ahmedabad. Since he could not go, he sent some swayamsevaks and Balaji Huddar.

This was the time when the intellectual leaders began to take Dr Hedgewar's RSS seriously. In a meeting they asked, 'OK, you want to organize Hindus? What will the RSS do when it is able to organize the society?' Doctorji's famous reply was, 'RSS will do nothing, but swayamsevaks will do everything.' This reply showed his clarity. The RSS's role was to create people with character and dedication to the nation. These people in turn will bring in the requisite change and work in different areas as per society's requirements.

Balaji Huddar was appointed the first Sarkaryavaah of the RSS. However, in 1931, while Dr Hedgewar was in jail due to his 'Jungle Satyagraha,' Balaji Huddar indulged in political dacoity as a revolutionary. Doctorji was highly disturbed. After he returned from jail, he asked Balaji to resign and the latter went his own way. Balaji went to England to study world politics, and with the rise of General Franco, he left for Spain to fight in the civil war. He returned to India later as a Communist (Karandikar 1999, 30).

Such was Dr Hedgewar's belief in human relations that he invited Balaji Huddar to address the swayamsevaks after his return from Spain. Balaji spoke at length. He spoke of the struggle between the capitalist and the labour. In his remarks later, Dr Hedgewar indicated that while Huddar could speak about progress and development of labour in the Sangh, he should not use the divisive language of 'labour' versus 'owner' (Palkar 2000, 334). This is the thought that Shri Madhav Sadashiv Golwalkar (better known as Guruji) later carried forward when he guided Dattopant Thengdi who organized the labour union, Bharatiya Mazdoor Sangh.

The idea of a uniform emerged when Dr Hedgewar wanted to take his swayamsevaks for a darshan to a temple during a festival. He felt that to create the right impact, they needed a uniform. The uniform adopted was based on the one that he and Dr Paranjape had created for young volunteers at the 1920 Congress plenary in Nagpur. It was a khaki-coloured half pant and shirt with a brown cap with two folds. A broad leather belt, calf-length socks and military-style shoes were also added to the uniform (Karandikar 1999, 31).

Somewhere around 1929, Anna Sohoni, who had designed the physical drills for the RSS, left the organization. He believed in a militant approach, preparing the youth with wrestling lessons, and drills to help members respond to violence against Hindus in any place. Dr Hedgewar's view was long term—his vision was to strengthen society itself so that such attacks simply did not take place. This difference in approach saw Sohoni leave the organization (Karandikar 1999, 134). Thus, from the initial group, his two most important friends had parted company with him. However, at a personal level, Dr Hedgewar continued his friendship with them till the end.

The Organization Takes Shape

From the beginning Dr Hedgewar created an atmosphere of family-like brotherhood in the shakha, where members would worry about each other's well-being like brothers. This was the cementing factor of the Sangh. This aspect was more important than the intellectual programmes, meetings, training workshops, discussions on national issues to inculcate patriotism and sanskaar. He exhibited this with his own conduct (Karandikar 1999, 35). For example, if somebody didn't turn up in a shakha, he would visit the person and ask about his well-being with affection. This habit was imbibed by his juniors, thereby strengthening the ties between the members. This approach is still basic to all RSS shakhas.

Dr Hedgewar himself gave a clear positive aspect of his objective of Hindu consolidation. He wrote in his diary:

> At the heart of Hindusthan, there is Hindu *sanskriti*, therefore defending Hindusthan means defending Hindu culture. That is our first duty. If Hindu culture is destroyed in Hindusthan, then just the piece of land is left without this soul, there would be no pride in calling this land as Hindusthan or Hindu nation. Because, a nation is not just a piece of land. Hindu society is the inheritor of this Hindu culture—to revive it is therefore a national duty, and so describing this organization as Rashtriya is correct. (Karandikar 1999, 17–19)

Annie Besant had noted on 15 January 1906 at the Grand Theatre, Calcutta:

> Make no mistake; without Hinduism, India has no future. Hinduism is the soil into which India's roots are struck, and torn of that she will inevitably wither, as a tree torn out from its place. Many are the religions and many are the races flourishing in India, but none of them stretches back into the far dawn of her past, nor are they necessary for her endurance as a nation. Everyone might pass away as they came and India would still remain. But let Hinduism vanish and what is she? A geographical expression of the past, a dim memory of a perished glory, her literature, her art, her monuments, all have Hindudom written across them. And if Hindus do not maintain Hinduism, who shall save it? If India's own children do not cling to her faith, who shall guard it? India alone can save India, and India and Hinduism are one.[1]

[1]Refer to http://www.stephen-knapp.com (lasted accessed on 6 June 2020).

Dr Hedgewar decided to leave the Congress and organize the RSS as he realized the limitations of the political approach of the Congress to India's problems. But, as was his wont, he kept supporting the Congress in the struggle for freedom. Dr Hedgewar's differences with the Congress on the issue of a national renaissance were spelt out by him in his diary.

> Congress has, unfortunately, not paid attention nor stopped violent attacks by non-Hindus on Hindu dharm and Hindu Sanskriti. RSS is needed to take care of this urgent work. Inspite of it, Sangh has no opposition to Congress. We have been cooperating with Congress in independence struggle so that national culture is not hurt. (Karandikar 1999, 191)

Dr Hedgewar was a person in a hurry. He had a clear understanding of his goal of achieving results in a time-bound manner. Explaining the stand of the RSS on its objective, Dr Hedgewar said,

> Sangh is not a gymnasium, nor a club or a military school. We have pledged to see completion of our work [freedom for Bharat] with our very eyes. Sangh doesn't wish that its work should continue for centuries like a club or a school. If you work like a student who begins running around hard just when examinations are on his head, you will be left rubbing your hands in disappointment. (Swaroop 2017, 144)

In Marathi, his words were '*yaachi deha yaachi dole*,' in our own lifetime. Satisfied with the work and approach of the RSS, many smaller Hindu organizations merged with the RSS during the initial period of its growth. One of them was Sant Pachlegaokar Maharaj who merged his Mukteshwar Dal in 1934. Tilak Vyayamshala in Umred also disbanded itself and merged into the RSS (Karandikar 1999, 203–04). He was invited to many other youth organizations working for the freedom of Bharat.

Dr Hedgewar had a modern outlook and he was unorthodox. There is an incident from his childhood. Once, a gentleman with rigorous religious habits came to his home as a guest. After his bath, he sat down to recite the Bhagavad Gita. After completing his recitation, he placed flowers very reverently on the sacred book and bowed to it. Doctorji asked him, 'You must be surely trying to walk the path shown by the Gita.' The honoured guest was highly incensed by the intemperate statement from the youngster and scolded him, saying, 'The Bhagavad Gita is something to be read. This, itself, leads to salvation of the human being.' The young boy shot back, 'But, it is not mentioned anywhere in our sacred Hindu religious scriptures nor is there any tradition which says that one can attain salvation just by worshipping without attaining high character and developing virtuous qualities in oneself' (Golwalkar 2008, 117).

On reforming Hindu society, he had more faith in evolution rather than revolution. He believed that centuries of distortions and deep-seated prejudices can't be removed by agitations, force or revolution. They can't change hearts. It needs persuasion and taking everybody along (Karandikar 1999, 108). Swami Vivekananda had expressed similar views on his return from the United States of America.

> I am more reformist than the reformists. They are doing a great job. But, I have serious differences with them on one point. Their path is of breaking and destruction. My path is of joining and bringing people together. They talk revolution. I don't believe in revolution, but in internal evolution. (Karandikar 1999, 108)

Dr Hedgewar received support from Veer Savarkar's younger brother Narayanrao Savarkar for Sangh work and travelled with him to spread Sangh work. He read Savarkar's book on Hindutva, gifted to him by Narayanrao and also went with him to meet Veer Savarkar in Ratnagiri. Again, though he did not entirely agree with Savarkar's definition of a 'Hindu,' he did not get into a debate with him; instead, he took inspiration from him to work (Karandikar 1999, 205).

The system of *pratigya* or oath-taking was introduced in the RSS in March 1928 (Karandikar 1999, 136). While other organizations would charge a subscription fee and fill up a form, Dr Hedgewar felt that by taking an oath to serve the motherland was a much more serious commitment.

The oath was in Marathi and read:

> *Sarva shaktiman Shri Parmeshvara's ani aaplyaa purvajaans smaroon, me ashi pratgiya karto kee, Hindu dharma, Hindu Sanskriti, va Hindu samaaj yanche sanrakshan karun, hindu rashtra la swatantra karnya sathi mee Rashtriya Swayamsevak Sangha cha ghatak jhalo aahe. Mee sanghaa che kaam praamaanikpane, niswarth buddhine, tan man dhan purvak kareen ani hey vrat aajanm paleen.* (Karandikar 1999, 138)
>
> Meaning,
>
> Remembering the all-powerful Supreme Being and my forefathers, I take this pledge that I have become a part of Rashtriya Swayamsevak Sangh to protect Hindu Dharma, Hindu Sanskriti and Hindu society and to free Hindu Rashtra. I will do my duty for Sangh with honesty, selflessly and with body, mind and wealth. I will follow this oath throughout my life.

After the independence of Bharat, the only words that were changed were 'to free Hindu Rashtra' and they were changed to 'for great prosperity of Hindu Rashtra'.

Dr Hedgewar attended the Calcutta session in 1928 as a member of the Congress working committee of Madhya Prant. He was introduced to Netaji Subhas Chandra Bose and also Rajguru, a colleague of Bhagwat Singh. He told Netaji about his new organization, the RSS. After Saunder's killing, Rajguru had come to Nagpur, where Dr Hedgewar requested his colleague Appaji Joshi to look after him while he was underground. He also cautioned Rajguru not to move out anywhere. However, Rajguru's urge to go to his village near Pune undid this effort and led to his arrest when he went there (Palkar 2000, 187).

Netaji seems to have kept a tab on the progress of the RSS. He even went to meet Dr Hedgewar at the RSS office on 18 June 1940 in Nagpur. But Doctorji was seriously ill and could hardly sleep. When Netaji came, he had just dozed off. Understanding about his frail health, Netaji refused to disturb him and returned. When Doctorji was told about it later, he was very upset and emotional that he had lost a chance to meet Netaji (Palkar 2000, 396).

As the Sangh grew, lack of resources began worrying Doctorji. He was somehow managing this by raising required funds through his well-wishers. But, he must have realized that it would not be possible to expand with such an unstructured approach. He hit upon another innovation that was totally voluntary and non-discriminatory. That was raising funds through guru dakshina (offerings to the guru). India has a long history of guru dakshina wherein a disciple repaid his debt to the guru through making an offering according to his/her capacity. Since gurukuls had no fee, they had both rich and poor students. This non-discriminatory submission of offering was a highly respectful way of contributing to the running of the gurukul.

The first Guru Pujan Utsav was organized on the day of Guru Purnima in July 1928, and Dr Hedgewar gave a day's prior notice to his young swayamsevaks. Guru Purnima is an ancient Hindu tradition, and is like Teacher's Day that was introduced in independent India on the birthday of the second Indian president, Dr S. Radhakrishnan, to honour him. However, Guru Purnima is not in honour of any one guru but for all gurus in the world. Disciples or students pay their respect and worship their guru or teacher on this day. Thus, it was an appropriate day chosen by Doctorji.

All he said was, 'Tomorrow, we will celebrate Guru Pujan festival. All of you should bring flowers and guru dakshina. There is no expectation, but each can bring dakshina as per his will.'

Nobody had any clue—whom would they worship on the day—Dr Hedgewar or someone else? The next day in his lecture about the importance of the guru, he finally said, '*Bhagwa Dhwaj* [saffron flag] is our guru.' Dr Hedgewar said,

> A person can be of very high stature, but he can never be complete, without any shortcomings. A person can slip up, witness weakening of qualities as he rises higher. However, ideas and principles are perennial and don't change. The history of this nation is ancient, there are very elevating thoughts in our sanskriti. Our nation has witnessed a long history and inspiration since long. *Bhagwa dhwaj* reflects all these qualities. (Karandikar 1999, 141)

The total collection of the first guru dakshina was ₹84 and a few paisa. This is the only day in the RSS where each swayamsevak salutes the *Bhagwa dhwaj* individually, not collectively. It represents a personal commitment and dedication to the cause. This practice of running the organization totally from voluntary contribution is still followed with care. This may be one of the critical reasons why no political power has been able to suppress RSS work. It is not dependent on any individual or party to run it.

Dr Hedgewar was against any kind of personality cult as he realized that even the best of people can have some flaws in their personality and work. They are prone to corruption whether physical or spiritual. Thus, he chose the flag that was greatly respected and has been in use since eons from the Vedic times to Ramayana to current times. It is a symbol that represents the history, culture, bravery, sacrifice and perennial history of Bharat. With this, he also underlined the fact that no person was greater than the nation and the society.

The importance of *Bhagwa* in national life is explained by the fact that the flag committee of the Congress in 1926–27 had recommended a *Bhagwa* flag with a blue charkha on the left top corner. Its committee report is available in Nehru Memorial Museum and Library (File 11/27/1927). Sardar Patel was the chairman of the committee. Other members were Jawaharlal Nehru, Maulana Azad, Dr N.S. Hardikar, Kaka Kalelkar and Master Tara Singh, among others. The decision was unanimous. This is mentioned in Pattabhi Sitaramaiyya's history of the Congress (Karandikar 1999, 144). Mahatma Gandhi objected to this recommendation, though the committee had representation of all sections of society. They didn't see *Bhagwa* or saffron as communal or Hindu. It was only later with the intervention of Gandhiji that the decision was reversed and the tricolour became the flag of the Congress and the nation.

After Guru Pujan, three more festivals were added that had social relevance and nurtured a sense of family. On Makar Sankranti, swayamsevaks go with *til-gud* sweets to meet people, fostering a sense of social bonding. Varsh Pratipada, known as Gudi Padwa in Maharashtra, is the first day of the Hindu New Year. It is celebrated all over the country though different names are used to refer to it. Shalivahan Shak is used by the Government of India as the Hindu calendar along with the British Gregorian calendar.

The third and last is Chhatrapati Shivaji Maharaj's ascension to the throne as a Hindu king, which marked the epoch-making day. A Hindu kingdom rose a century after the defeat of the Vijaynagara Empire. This was the renaissance of Hindu national life. This seed of a Hindu nation was laid that day by Shivaji and bore the fruits of the mighty Maratha Empire that reached its zenith with the Marathas reaching Delhi spearheaded by the Peshwas. Contrary to popular perception, the British snatched power from the Marathas on their way to creating the British Empire. This is the background for the celebration of Hindu Samrajya Din by the RSS.

Later on, Raksha Bandhan or Rakhi was revived as a festival of brotherhood. This was a recalling of the many ways through which fraternal love was celebrated, such as the relationship between a king and priest, between brothers, and among citizens of society from the highest position to the lowest.

Though all the festivals have Hindu civilizational roots, Dr Hedgewar deliberately didn't celebrate them as religious festivals.

He was more concerned about the renaissance of a united Hindu society. If I may say so, more as a socially united society than as a religious sect. He was clear that he did not want the RSS to become a *sampradaya* (sect) within Hindu society. He wanted it to be an organization of Hindu society. As its oath indicates, the pledge is more about materialistic goals for the nation and the society, not self-liberation or mukti. The RSS provides no comfort of personal mukti or nirvana. It only talks of karma yoga. This might explain why modern-day gurus and sects gain quicker following than the RSS. The element of nirvana provides the emotional cushion in most of the bhakti or yoga inspired sects and *deras*.

Vijayadashami is the other festival in the RSS that also happens to be its foundation day, being celebrated from the first year. It is the day when RSS swayamsevaks take out their parade in full uniform with its musical band across Bharat. The Sarsanghchaalak always celebrates the day in Nagpur and gives his keynote address. In absence of media briefings and press conferences earlier, this speech was taken as a direction for the RSS in the coming year. *Shastra poojan* or worshipping the arms or tools of production on this day is an ancient tradition. Incidentally, to celebrate Vijayadashami, some enthusiastic Punjabi traders got real swords from Vardha. But Dr Hedgewar refused to use them. His explanation was this:

> Pandavas hid their arms when the situation was adverse, they brought them out at the right time. For Sangh too, the time is not yet ripe for use of arms or show of aggressive strength against the British. Right now, there is need to first unite the Hindus, make the society disciplined and harmonious. We should focus on this work first. (Palkar 2000, 176)

A musical band or *ghosh* was introduced in 1928 to satisfy the urge to do something innovative. It would make the march past look more spectacular. The first training for the formation of the band was done under the guidance of a Christian teacher. It is notable that Dr Hedgewar refused to allow the use of *ghosh* for any personal or private purposes, even to raise funds when a few people suggested that route to overcome fund shortage (Palkar 2000, 186 and 198).

As the RSS grew, it required more funds. Many supporters and workers suggested use of the RSS band to raise funds by playing in public programmes. But, Dr Hedgewar would never agree to any suggestion that went against the objectives and working methodology of the RSS. He was clear that all the organization's expenses should be met through guru dakshina alone (Palkar 2000, 198). Some swayamsevaks suggested arranging special drama shows to raise funds by selling tickets. He did not agree to that either. He explained to his colleagues, 'The Sangh work should be dependant only on guru dakshina [from the swayamsevaks] from the contribution of well-wishers that is done with a smile and sense of sacrifice (Palkar 2000, 1999).

Though Doctorji had appointed Sanghchalaks who were the guides, philosophers and public face of the RSS in an area, he had not designated a post for himself. It needs to be noted that the Sanghchalaks of different regions were not necessarily shakha-going members. They would be some notable personality and could be from any organization with no exposure to RSS work, but agreed to Dr Hedgewar's request, understanding his dedication and objectives. In November 1929, he called a meeting for training of all the Sarsanghchaalaks from different places where the Sangh had begun its work. Though there was a resolution in a meeting that Doctorji is the ultimate authority of the RSS, he did not have an official designation. Senior colleagues, led by Appaji Joshi who were part of the founding team of the RSS decided to name Dr Hedgewar as Sarsanghchaalak on the first day of the meeting. The next day, on 10 November, while he was in the shakha at Mohite Wada, Appaji Joshi called out the order, 'Sarsanghchaalak pranaam 1-2-3', just the way the *Bhagwa dhwaj* was saluted! And this is how the title 'Sarsanghchaalak' was publicly announced on that day (Palkar 2000, 194). Dr Hedgewar later complained to Appaji Joshi that he didn't like the idea of being saluted by people who were his seniors. He felt that his declaration as Sarsanghchaalak was not a good idea.

Appaji Joshi was the eldest in the RSS team. He could be called the alter ego of Doctorji. He was a family man and a dedicated Congressman. But, he gave his entire life and energies to RSS work, working closely with Dr Hedgewar. He worked till his death in 1975 and courted arrest during the Emergency though he was very weak. He could not survive the hardships of prison life at the age of 81. I was fortunate to have listened to his emotionally charged lectures in the RSS training camp in 1973.

During this time, Vitthalbhai Patel visited the RSS office on a Vijayadashami festival. Madan Mohan Malaviya too visited an RSS shakha in the presence of Dr Hedgewar. He had high praise for its discipline and energy. When Malaviyaji offered to collect funds for the RSS, Dr Hedgewar said, 'We don't need funds, your blessings are what we need' (Palkar 2000, 191). Though the RSS did in fact need funds at the time to continue its fast expanding work, it was not the way Doctorji worked. There was a time when he had to cancel his tour as there were no funds.

While he was in Wardha, Gandhiji visited the Wardha camp on 22 December 1934 and stayed for 1.5 hours. There were 1,500 youth in that camp and he saw flag hoisting ceremonies and physical drills. Putting his hands on Appaji Joshi's shoulders he said, 'I am really happy to see this. I have never seen such an impressive scene in the entire country so far.' He did, however, tell him that this work is only for Hindus; if it were open for others it would have been even better (Karandikar 1999, 235). He also met Dr Hedgewar the next day and had a lengthy discussion with him. He recounted this visit when he addressed swayamsevaks in an RSS rally that was held in Delhi on 16 September 1947 on his request (Gandhi, Vol. 96, 380). Incidentally, Dr Babasaheb Ambedkar had also visited the first RSS Sangh Shiksha Varga of Maharashtra Prant at Pune in 1935. Then he visited the local Sangh shakha and had a candid conversation with the swayamsevaks. In 1939, Babasaheb had visited Sangh Shiksha Varga in Pune and interacted with the swayamsevaks along with Dr Hedgewar (Thengdi 2015, 153–54). In Bhandara by-elections in 1954, Dattopant Thengdi, a prachaarak, was his election agent.

As the Sangh's work expanded, there was a need felt to train teachers, so that they went to the field ready with basic instructions and intellectual inputs. The first training camp for senior workers was conducted during summer vacations in 1929. Swayamsevaks would stay at the ground from morning till evening for physical training and then the intellectual training would be conducted by Dr Hedgewar. Even though Doctorji had much experience as a revolutionary and as a Congress worker, he would never speak about that experience. It was as if he had started afresh with a clean slate. He used all his experience in public life to design the structure of RSS work and for creating networks. His focus was Hindu unity and raising a disciplined harmonious Hindu society.

Finally, an idea came to him for a four-week residential training. This was initially called Officers Training Camp (OTC), and later renamed Sangh Shiksha Varg. Then, it evolved into a three-step training programme. For the first three years, it was held at Nagpur. After this, the second training camp began in Pune. Later on, it was conducted separately for each state (Karandikar 1999, 154). Recently, another primary course called Prathamik Varg of one-week duration has been added to this training syllabus. This course prepares a new swayamsevak to become a worker by giving them a basic idea about RSS methodology and philosophy. Once he starts taking responsibility, he is sent for one-month training workshops. All other training workshops now have different levels of responsibility and maturity to qualify a worker for the next-level training.

Dr Hedgewar had clear long-term and short-term goals, what many call his 'bifocal vision.' For him, offering satyagraha or going to jail was a short-term objective. Building up the RSS as an organization and training people for any duty to the nation was the long-term goal. In his speech before going for satyagraha in 1930, Doctorji said, 'You should be prepared to die for the country, but live doing the organization's work all the while. Unless you take such a pledge our nation will not see good days' (Karandikar 1999, 193–94).

When he decided to offer 'Jungle Satyagraha' in 1930, he spoke to his swayamsevaks on the Guru Purnima festival day (12 July 1930) in the RSS shakha. He shared his decision to participate in the satyagraha and resigned as the Sarsanghchaalak of the RSS. His view was that the freedom struggle must be fought under one organization, that was Congress at that time. He handed over the reins of the RSS to Dr L.V. Paranjape. In his speech, Dr Paranjape said,

> Those who wish to participate in the agitation must do so. Others should work for this young organization. This current movement is to take our nation forward, there is no doubt. But, this is just one step towards freedom. The real work is to organize such people who will give their lives for the freedom of this nation. (Palkar 2000, 205)

The RSS leadership was clear that the 1930 agitation was a step towards freedom, but was not decisive, yet. Once when a swayamsevak showed his urge to go to jail by offering satyagraha, Dr Hedgewar reiterated that going to jail did not mean one has done his bit for the freedom of the country. This was similar to the views he had expressed in 1920. According to him, a short-term goal would be going to jail for satyagraha and a long-term goal would be organizing the society to expel the British from India. Obviously, his statement of asking a swayamsevak to dedicate more time to the organization (than going to jail) has been misconstrued. The oath of the Sangh clearly stated that a swayamsevak was joining the Sangh to work towards the full freedom of the Hindu Rashtra.

One can also see that RSS leaders had no delusion that this agitation would be the last. Their goal was to create dedicated swayamsevaks who would be able to stand for the nation in the times to come. It was also an option for young members to choose satyagraha or to keep working for strengthening the organization that had long-term goals of freedom and reforming the Hindu society. Doctorji was imprisoned for this 'Jungle Satyagraha' for nine months. Hundreds of swayamsevaks and other colleagues too participated in this satyagraha (Palkar 2000, 204–05).

In 1931 after his release, he also visited Kashi and was there for some time. He conducted many meetings. During these meetings, he would express his pain at the Hindus' loss of historical memory and pride. He said, 'Why is there a mosque atop Kashi Vishweshwar temple? Why is there an Islamic tower on the Ganga ghat? Why do these questions not rise in Hindus' minds? Why does it not disturb them? Don't forget that the Sangh is there to change this situation' (Palkar 2000, 229). It is notable that the RSS passed a resolution for the return of Kashi Vishwanath temple to Hindus in 1959, much before the resolution on Ram Temple was passed. The first resolution on Ram Mandir was passed in 1986.

An incident tells us the dispassionate bipartisan view that guided Dr Hedgewar. A felicitation function was organized for Dr Munje on his return from a roundtable conference where he had gone as a representative of the Hindu Mahasabha. Dr Hedgewar was present in it though he did not agree with the position of the Hindu Mahasabha. In his short speech before Dr Munje's long keynote lecture, Doctorji presented his views about defining the quality of a leader.

> To flow with the public opinion is not a sign of leadership but of backwardness. One who changes the scenario and pulls people's opinion into his thinking is a true leader. Leadership is not in following popular view but to influence those views. If situation demands, to not hesitate in going against public opinion is true loyalty to truth. On this test, one can't find a better truthful leader than Dr Munje. (Palkar 2000, 234)

This openly expressed respect for a person with whom he was not always in agreement and showed his conviction in the spirit of democracy. He had refused to toe the Hindu Mahasabha line and instead joined the 1930 'Salt Satyagraha' as part of Civil Disobedience agitation or *Savinay Avagya Andolan* in the form of 'Jungle Satyagraha.'

First Alarm Bells for the RSS

By this time, the British were worried about the growth of the RSS. They could no longer neglect it as a minor phenomenon. They began to keep a sharp eye on the RSS. On 15 December 1932, a circular was released by E. Gorden, chief secretary of the Madhya Prant government, banning the participation of government employees in RSS work, claiming that it was a communal organization and increasingly participating in political movements (Palkar 2000, 250). Doctorji wrote to the workers explaining that the Sangh was not communal as it was not against any other community. He said that uniting one's own fragmented society cannot be called communal. In January 1933, he invited an ex-home minister of Madhya Prant, Moropant Joshi, for the Makar Sankranti festival of the RSS. In the function, he said,

> We challenge the MP government to show if the RSS has taken part in any political movement, or if we have troubled any other community? You can call an organization communal only if it runs a campaign against another community. But, coming together for self-organization without any envy or insult to any other community cannot be called communal. (Palkar 2000, 252)

Seeing virtually no effect on Sangh work, the British government released another circular in December 1933 adding that teachers of government schools and employees of local bodies too couldn't take part in RSS shakhas (Palkar 2000, 255).

Nashik and Vardha district councils, under pressure from the British government, too, released directives disallowing their employees and teachers from taking part in RSS activities. But, with the vigorous public contact programme of Dr Hedgewar, many newspapers came out criticizing this ban, many other local bodies passed resolutions opposing such a ban and welcoming RSS work (Palkar 2000, 257).

The matter was finally presented as a cut motion in Madhya Prant assembly in March 1934. It proved to be an eventful session and showed Dr Hedgewar's skills in people management. He had launched a massive personal contact program prior to this cut motion and met various Congress leaders and newspaper editors. The newspapers protested strongly against calling the RSS communal and efforts to suppress its activities. Public opinion also began building up against these orders. Babasaheb Kolte brought in a cut motion against this background. The government was questioned and ridiculed by various speakers. Though there were many factions in the Congress, on this particular issue, almost all Congress representatives took a strong line in favour of the RSS. They questioned the basis of calling an organization for Hindus communal but not question organizations that worked for other communities. A Congress leader, Rehman, also gave his support to the cut motion, raising questions about the definition of communalism. Dr Hedgewar was present all through in the visitors' gallery, enjoying this spirited debate. Finally, the government lost the cut motion, losing face in the process. Though the government did not withdraw the notification, it just faded away(Palkar 2000, 265–67). This episode shows the length to which the British government went and how self-rule elected bodies of Indians fell in line to create difficulties for the RSS. It is disturbing that the arguments of Hindu communalism unleashed against the RSS by the British are the arguments still being raised while its own leaders had rejected these arguments at that time. This is the original order that is still being cited in various forms to stop government servants from joining the RSS.

Building a Young Dedicated Team for Expansion

To expand the Sangh outside Vidarbha, Doctorji encouraged the youth to go for studies outside their state. He also encouraged well-educated youth to go out for jobs. He would send out young boys to go to other villages to start Sangh work during holidays. Some would work full-time. Arrangement for their stays would be made at homes of people known personally to Doctorji. These families would take care of their basic day-to-day requirements. He would keep a tab on their work and behaviour by writing letters to the hosts and locals Sangh contacts. He was highly conscious of his swayamsevaks' behaviour, both at a personal and organizational level, and cautioned them where required (Karandikar 1999, 264).

Dr Hedgewar used to keep in touch with people through letters. While recuperating from a sickness in Indore, he wrote five letters to his young colleagues—most of whom were students—about his grand vision about Hindusthan and the RSS. Most of them were hardly twenty-five years old. The first to act on his appeal for giving more time to the Sangh was Krishnarao Mohril who gave his entire life to the organization after completing his B.A. The next was Govind Sitaram Paramarth alias Dadarao Paramarth, and the third was Babasaheb Apte, the senior-most. While Dadarao was hardly twenty-five at that time, Babasaheb was twenty-six years old (Karandikar 1999, 179–80, 185). This was the first team of the RSS that worked full-time for the Sangh till their last breath. This was the team that laid the foundation of the institution of prachaarak within RSS. Interestingly, Dadarao was one of the youth whom Dr Hedgewar had chided for playing cricket on the day that Lokmanya Tilak had passed away. From the first day onwards, he was committed to the RSS.

Krishnarao Mohril became the fulcrum of the central office of the RSS in Nagpur, who kept thousands of people, swayamsevaks and karyakartas in touch. He worked there for his entire life while the Sangh work expanded in leaps and bounds. Dadarao Paramarth went all over India from Assam to Kerala and from Punjab to Tamil Nadu to set up RSS work. He was a brilliant and aggressive speaker. He travelled extensively for nearly sixteen or seventeen years. Babasaheb Apte was not a graduate but was an avid reader and gained knowledge on his own. He was the eldest in the group. He introduced Sanskrit in the RSS. He was instrumental in setting up the Itihas Sankalan Samiti, the body that was instrumental in the search for the vanished Vedic river Saraswati. His book, *Hamaare Rashtra Jeevan ki Parampara,* first published in 1950, can be considered the first attempt at decoding the story of 'Dashavatar' or the ten incarnations of Bhagwan Vishnu from the Puranas, as an interpretation of ancient Indian history in a definable timeline. This novel attempt was the precursor to later studies.

Bhaiyyaji Dani, who took the RSS to Banaras Hindu University (BHU) as a student and brought Shri Guruji to an RSS shakha, was another key member of Doctorji's team and later Guruji's team. He was the first one to go out of Nagpur as a student to spread RSS work. He was a Sarkaryavaah during the most critical years of the RSS from 1946 to 1956. He was Sarkaryavaah again from 1962 to 1965. He was eighteen years old and present in the meeting when the RSS was founded. He was the first married full-time worker or prachaarak of the RSS (Karandikar 1999, 208). Many other young men who were first-generation RSS prachaaraks spread its work across India. They all used to meet and discuss issues with Dr Hedgewar at his home. This group included Nana Bhishikar, Manohar Oak (brother of Vasant Oak) and P.R. Khandekar (Karandikar 1999, 186).

The senior generation colleagues of Dr Hedgewar were Vishwanath Kelkar, Appaji Joshi, Balaji Huddar, Appa Sohoni, Tatya Kalikar, Bapurao Muthaal, Babasaheb Kolte, Martandrao Jog and Devaikar, among others (Karandikar 1999, 170). As noted earlier, of these, Huddar and Sohoni had left Doctorji due to differences of opinion. Another key person in the scheme of things was Babasaheb Ghatate, who was a Nagpur Sanghchalak and a very successful prosperous lawyer (Karandikar 1999, 329). He was very helpful in the growth of the RSS for nearly fifty years during both Doctorji's and Guruji's time. We see the sterling quality of a great organizer and leader in Dr Hedgewar, that he built such a dedicated team of workers from varied social and educational backgrounds, at a time when the RSS was in its infancy and faced the toughest of times.

These first pioneer RSS organizers were not called prachaaraks at that time, as this idea was still germinating. But this was the small beginning for the idea of the prachaarak. These people had no resources as students except their love for the motherland. An urge to spread RSS work under the guidance of Dr Hedgewar motivated them.

Many of these swayamsevaks were given a letter of introduction to a local person by Dr Hedgewar from his wide contact list. There was no other support. When the host was generous, he would take this prachaarak into his home and provide basic facilities such as lodging and boarding. Beyond this, the condition of the prachaarak was like a *bhikshu* or sanyasi. He would move around on foot and meet people to start a shakha in that area. If he was lucky he would be offered food, if not, he might have had to sleep on an empty stomach, sometimes tying a towel tight around his stomach. Due to the negative propaganda of the then ruling party, they would not even be offered water in some places. Yadavrao Joshi and his colleagues in Karnataka faced such a situation. Sometimes, these new guests would even be asked to sleep outside the homes of their hosts. Cycles were a luxury. At times, they would have to walk miles, at night, to reach their destinations. Despite all the hardships, these brave first-generation prachaaraks soldiered on.

Since the RSS did not have resources, many of these RSS workers had to find ways and means to take care of their own expenses. Many of them took up small jobs. Bapurao Moghe took tuition. Bhaurao Deoras had to often sleep on a half-empty stomach that led to his ill health later in life. This could be the reason why many of these prachaaraks ended up with chronic diseases such as diabetes and weak digestion or cardiac issues. Dr Hedgewar himself undertook strenuous travels on shoe-string budgets that led to his deteriorating health, once an envy of many.

As Sangh work expanded, prachaaraks had a better support system. They could have local conveyance like cycle or scooter and travel third class to distant places. Swayamsevaks who became part of the RSS would provide better support to prachaaraks and they became part of those families. Most of the prachaaraks would have one foster family to take care of their minimum requirements. Close affectionate relationships created a culture of close familial relations that made the RSS such a close-knit family despite being such a huge organization spread across the country. This family atmosphere has served RSS work in a big way through its history, including helping underground workers during the struggle for democracy against the 1975 Emergency.

Yadavrao Joshi met Dr Hedgewar in a musical programme where he had won the Kumar Gandharva prize. Dr Hedgewar, who was a special guest due to the insistence of the organizer, wanted to hear him again. He felt that transmitting the feeling of patriotism through music was so much easier compared to a dry lecture. That is how the mutual affection grew. Finally, Yadavrao Joshi decided to give up his highly promising singing career to dedicate himself to the nation under the guidance of Dr Hedgewar (Karandikar 1999, 402–03). He was the one who undertook the tough task of nurturing the seed of RSS work in Karnataka. Doctorji's deep sense of patriotism mesmerized him. Such was Yadavrao Joshi's talent in singing that even Bhimsen Joshi used to respect him hugely; even his guru, Sawai Gandharva, appreciated Yadavrao Joshi's singing. But Yadavrao Joshi gave up fame for the nation (Karandikar 1999, 405). This was the general thinking of the prachaaraks.

All these workers later rose to high ranks in the RSS. Many a prachaarak like Bhaurao Bhuskute was from a rich landed family but he remained a prachaarak in Madhya Pradesh and Orissa Karandikar 1999, 375). Eknath Ranade, the builder of Vivekanand Rock Memorial, began his life as a prachaarak in Mahakoshal (part of present-day Madhya Pradesh) after his B.A. (Karandikar 1999, 390).

Since Dr Hedgewar's time, RSS workers were trained to stay away from the limelight. One of the songs sung at that time had the following lyrics.

> *Vrittpatra mein naam chhapega, pahnunga swaagat samuhaar,*
> *Chhod chalo yah kshudra bhavna, hindu rashtra ke taaranhaar.*
>
> Meaning,
>
> That my name will appear in newspaper, that I will wear welcome garlands,
> Forget such petty thoughts, O' propagators of Hindu Rashtra. (Swaroop 2017, 267)

By this time Bhaiyyaji Dani, who had gone to BHU as a student to expand Sangh work, had managed to get a teacher, Madhav Sadashiv Golwalkar, interested in the RSS. He might have given his assessment of the impressive personality of Golwalkar, popularly called Guruji in BHU, to Doctorji. To give him a better exposure to RSS work, Guruji was invited as a special guest along with Prof. Sadgopal for the Vijayadashami utsav in 1932 by Dr Hedgewar. He was taken around to some other shakhas in the neighbouring areas to give him a better exposure to RSS work. He was also taken around to a few places around Nagpur to give him a good understanding of RSS functioning. From that time onwards, he began to take more serious interest in RSS work (Karandikar 1999, 286). After finishing his temporary assignment in BHU in 1933 he returned to Nagpur and got involved in RSS work in a small way, while enrolling himself for a degree in Law. Bhaiyyaji also did his Law with him during this time. This studying together brought them closer. His journey within the RSS began as a karyavaah of a local shakha. But, he was not yet fully committed as we shall see later that his prime focus was spiritual enlightenment.

Word of RSS work had spread across India. On 3 October 1935, the son-in-law of Bhai Paramananda, wrote a letter to Doctorji asking for his help to begin the work of RSS in Punjab where the situation was very grave. He wished to visit Nagpur and understand the work done by the RSS. In January 1936, Bhai Paramananda also wrote to Dr Hedgewar asking him to visit Punjab and stay there for a year to expand Sangh work. Giving due consideration to these requests, Doctorji began sending more karyakartas to Punjab (Karandikar 1999, 279). We see that there was demand and expectations from the regions where the RSS had not reached, as the name of the RSS as a disciplined patriotic organization spread. Later, Madhavrao Muley was sent to Punjab, which was his land of action for nearly thirty-three years.

Birth of Rashtra Sevika Samiti

Another significant development took place during this time. Smt Laxmibai Kelkar met Dr Hedgewar to request for women's participation in Sangh work. Her son was a swayamsevak. She had seen swayamsevaks maintain very good, warm relations with families and their colleagues. So she understood the Sangh work to some extent. When she met Doctorji, she asked him, 'Why don't you provide it to girls and women?' He explained that considering the intensity of physical exercise and games, it wouldn't be prudent to put boys and girls together in a single shakha. He himself had no experience of dealing with women's organizations. His said, 'So far we have kept this work limited to men. But, if you are ready to take the responsibility of working with women, Appaji Joshi will surely support you in this endeavour.' Thus, on 25 October 1936 on Vijayadashami day, Rashtra Sevika Samiti was formed (Karandikar 1999, 260). The organization runs independently of the RSS, and only a few senior workers assist it wherever required. Incidentally, Sevika Samiti, following RSS methodology, has sustained itself and grown, but Hindu Mahasabha's women's wing inspired by Veer Savarkar eventually closed down after some years.

Decline of strong Hindutva organizations like Hindu Mahasabha (and its women's wing) founded by the brilliant scholar and leader Veer Savarkar, but sustained growth of the much less flamboyant RSS is a matter of serious research. It also throws light on the organizational science developed by the RSS.

Changing Equations between the RSS, the Hindu Mahasabha and the Congress

When Veer Savarkar was released from his house arrest in Ratnagiri in 1937, he travelled extensively. He was received and heard by huge crowds wherever he went. When he came to Vidarbha, he was accompanied by Dr Hedgewar in Nagpur, Chanda, Vardha, Bhandara, Akola and Umred, among other places. Doctorji felt privileged that he was able to be with Savarkar (Palkar 2000, 311).

When the Hindu Mahasabha conducted its session in 1938 December, Savarkar was the Chairman. RSS swayamsevaks provided volunteers and supported it whenever required. Doctorji was also present on all three days as a member of the local reception committee. During this time, there was a camp of the RSS where 2,500 swayamsevaks participated. Savarkar was invited for a visit and he was very happy to see the large, disciplined gathering. Savarkar gave a brilliant speech, where he also suggested that all swayamsevaks should have arms in their hands, as just doing parade and waving a lathi was of no use. As was the custom, swayamsevaks heard him silently and so did Dr Hedgewar, but it showed the chasm in the thinking of the Hindu Mahasabha and the RSS (Karandikar 1999, 315). The RSS kept working in its peaceful way. One may recall that Dr Hedgewar had to remove Balaji Huddar for his violent approach. After Savarkar's speech, Dr Hedgewar delivered a speech to young swayamsevaks to realign their thoughts to the fundamental work in his review lecture on the completion of thirteen years of the RSS, titled *Trayodash Varshik Simhavalokan*. However, Savarkar again visited an RSS camp after another year in Pune. He had come on his own, after telling his followers, 'One doesn't need an invitation to visit one's own home.' He gave a lecture there and said,

> Our work is like heavy rain showers. The water collects for a short time but flows out without seeping into the fields. Doctor's work is like that of a skilled farmer, who utilizes each

> and every drop of water for his farming. You all should follow Hedgewar's work and follow his path. (Sinha 2004, 217)

This gradual change in attitude of a great philosopher revolutionary like Savarkar showed how Doctorji's humility and calm working style affected people's attitude.

The Hindu Mahasabha had hoped that the RSS would work as its volunteer force during its programmes and as its arm. However, Dr Hedgewar had different ideas and kept a distance. Thus, the Hindu Mahasabha had to set up Ram Sena, which was its armed wing, and took orders from Dr Munje (Karandikar 1999, 344). Dr Munje was clear that the RSS was to be a non-political organization that wished to unite Hindus. He was the mentor and supporter of Dr Hedgewar since his youth. He had taken care of his studies and Dr Hedgewar had stayed in his home for a long time. But, on the question of aims and objectives of the RSS, Doctorji never compromised. Dr Munje too respected him and they did not have a falling out because of their differences, even though Dr Munje was unhappy.

It was not just the British government that was getting worried about the RSS. The Congress leadership also became jealous of the RSS for reasons unknown. Criticism of the Sangh had begun in 1935 within the Congress. One of the major reasons was the working style of the RSS. Congress had misunderstood the definition of ahimsa propagated by Gandhiji. In a bid to show their faith in ahimsa, they started criticizing everything that entailed discipline—be it physical exercise or uniform or military discipline. They also felt that the work of uniformed volunteers was only to spread durries, arrange for water and milk, be the guard of honour, and so on. Looking at the organization from the outside, they mistook the RSS for a non-thinking organization that was against Gandhiji's ideal of non-violence (Swaroop 2017, 22).

For reasons unknown, the Congress also began to get jealous of the RSS's growth as a disciplined organization and its rising appreciation from all quarters. It was perhaps due to the insecurity of losing its monopoly on the socio-political front. Around this time, the Congress committee of Madhya Prant sent out a letter to Doctorji saying that the Congress wished to decide about its relation with the RSS. So, they asked for more information regarding its objective, programmes and missions. Since Dr Hedgewar had worked in the Congress for many years, its office-bearers knew him well. Jamnalal Bajaj had also visited the RSS and Dr Hedgewar a few years back. They had witnessed RSS work for twelve years by now. Doctorji simply replied, 'RSS programmes are taking place in the open for the last twelve years in Nagpur; people know about them. Our lectures also clear our aims and objectives. We have nothing more to inform.' When Dr Hedgewar returned from his tours, there were three letters on his desk from the office-bearers of the Congress that complained that his response was unsatisfactory and dismissive. Again he wrote, 'It is quite puzzling that staying in the same city you are not aware of Sangh work' and stressed that the Sangh 'was never or is opposed to the Congress' (Karandikar 1999, 316). That Dr Hedgewar carried no bitterness or animosity towards any person, could be gauged by the fact that after the Congress passed a resolution for 'complete freedom' in December 1929 and asked the nation to celebrate 26 January 1930 as independence day, Dr Hedgewar welcomed it wholeheartedly and sent out a communication to all the shakhas to celebrate the day in shakhas, unfurl the proposed national flag (that was a saffron flag with a blue charkha in the upper corner which had been finalized by the flag committee at this time). He directed them to explain the goal of freedom to the swayamsevaks.

Another incident showed the strange thinking of Congress leaders of that time. During the Congress session in December 1936 in Faizpur in Maharashtra, the tricolour got stuck half-way up an eighty-foot high flagpole in the presence of Nehru. People were petrified. A young swayamsevak, Pardesi, climbed up the pole, untwisted the flag and unfurled it. Congress members literally lifted him on their shoulders and it was decided that he would be felicitated by Nehru. However, once the word spread that he was an RSS swayamsevak, the programme was quietly buried. When Dr Hedgewar came to know of this incident, he applauded the young man and invited him to a nearby town where he was on a visit. He appreciated Pardesi for his service to the motherland and presented him with a silver bowl (Karandikar 1999, 319). Dr Hedgewar didn't utter a single word against the Congress.

This kind of quibbling led to many other issues later for the nation and other organizations. When Dr Hedgewar went to BHU, socialist youth distributed pamphlets accusing it of having a capitalist agenda and supporting Hitler's dictatorship (Karandikar 1999, 317–18). Communist critics, those who had called Netaji a fascist and 'running dog of Tojo', accused Doctorji of learning and importing his working style from Hitler, an accusation that had no basis at all (Swaroop 2017, 23). However, Dr Hedgewar soldiered on silently, without any bitterness.

RSS Expansion Outside Central Provinces

While Dr Hedgewar was grooming highly capable workers like Guruji, from 1937 onwards he started sending young people to different parts of the country; he sent Bhaurao Deoras to Lucknow, Digambar Paaturkar Munje to Lahore, Krishna Joshi to Sialkot and Moreshwar Munje to Rawalpindi to study and organize Sangh work there. He had also sent Narahari Paarkhi and Bapu Diwakar to Bihar, Vitthalrao Patki to Bengal and Gopalrao Yekuntwaar to Bombay as full time workers. Apart from this, he used to send out Dadarao Paramarth and Babasaheb Apte for tours to different places depending upon circumstances and requirements. Thus, he had set up well-planned activities to spread the Sangh's work all over Bharat even though the organization was still mainly limited to erstwhile Central Province, United Province, Punjab and Bombay Presidency. In other places, only seeds had been sown. This was the capital that Sangh had when Guruji was appointed Sarsanghchaalak of RSS (Ranga Hari, 2018).

By 1939, RSS work had reached Punjab, Delhi, Sindh, Bihar, Bengal, Madhya Prant, Uttar Pradesh and Tamil Nadu. Doctorji was so focused on the organization's growth that he would tell his lieutenants that 'We were organizing for organizing sake'. That was the prime objective. This focus was the reason he was against any publicity as it diverted attention. When young Vasant Oak reached Delhi for Sangh work, there was a news report. He immediately wrote to him, 'One should not publicize when work has just begun. As the work grows, work by itself gets publicized (Karandikar 1999, 280–81). Interestingly, even as the RSS moved into other social activities, this guiding principle of 'organization for organizing's sake' remained rooted in Sangh working even till the 1960s.

When RSS swayamsevaks had reached across India, Doctorji advised them to take care of the culture and language of that region and be sensitive to their regional pride. He would encourage them to learn and converse in the local language, adopt their dressing sense as far as possible and connect with them with pure love (Karandikar 1999, 271). Prachaaraks learnt local languages. Since the Sangh's work began in Maharashtra, the initial batch of prachaaraks was from Maharashtra and most of them from Nagpur, which was the fountainhead of the organization. They also learnt Tamil, Gujarati, Punjabi, Malayalam, and any other language of the place where they worked. For example, Shri Shivram Joglekar, a prachaarak in Tamil Nadu, went on to write books and articles in Tamil. Vegetarian prachaaraks changed their food habits depending on areas they worked in. In a short time they would integrate themselves with the local milieu completely. It was based on such sacrifices that the foundations of the RSS were laid. The great organization that we see today was founded by the sacrifice of these prachaaraks who worked tirelessly, expecting no recognition or rewards in return. There used to be an RSS song with the following words:

Uchch hai wah shikhar dekho,
Main nahin wah sthaan loonga,
Poojya hai matri mandir,

Neenv ka main rajkaran hun,
Pujya maa kee archana ka ek chhota upkaran hun.

Meaning,

See that high spire,
I will not take a place there,
That temple of mother is worthy of worship,
I am just a speck of dust in its foundation,
I am just a small tool for her worship.

Refining Methodology and Systems for a Growing Organization

By 1939, the RSS had spread to many states. Doctorji's health had deteriorated badly. Till that time RSS work was primarily rooted in Maharashtra, the RSS prayer had its first stanza in Marathi (taken from Swami Ramdas's seminal work *Dasbodh*) and a stanza from an Arya Samaj prayer. It was fine till then. But, as the organization spread to other parts of the country, people would complain of their inability to understand the prayer. The mode of imparting physical training and giving it a standard format and syllabus was also felt. In short, the team found it necessary to reconsider Sangh work and methodology as it was already fourteen years old. To tackle such issues, a week-long meeting with a small key group of RSS office-bearers was held in Sindi, a small village near Nagpur in 1939 (Karandikar 1999, 334). Guruji had already been appointed as Sarkaryavaah before this meeting.

There were wide-ranging open discussions. The team had selected workers amongst its founding seniors like Appaji Joshi to young firebrands like Balasaheb Deoras. The effort was to create methodologies and systems that would be suitable for the forthcoming expansion of the RSS as it was on the verge of becoming a truly all-India organization. English orders for drills were changed to Sanskrit terminology as it would be acceptable across Bharat as the mother of all Indian languages. A new prayer was also created with the help of Sanskrit scholars (Karandikar

1999, 343). The Sarkaryavaah formally became the No. 2 man of RSS, with full responsibility for the growth of shakhas and related work. The systems and protocols set at that time are still working in the RSS with very little change. Only new ones have been added with changing times and new dimensions of RSS work. These systems and protocols formed the basis of the written RSS constitution that was formed on demand from the government in 1948.

We can say that this workshop saw the rise of Guruji as a prominent thinker and organizer within the RSS. The decisions taken in this prolonged meeting had a far-reaching impact. The overall methodology followed by the Sangh still flows from this meeting.

After ten days of this milestone meeting, Dr Hedgewar asked his close associate, Appaji Joshi, 'How would Guruji be as Sarsanghchaalak?' Appaji immediately agreed to the idea (Karandikar 1999, 335). Dr Hedgewar felt relieved as he finally had an answer to who would succeed him. He already knew that his days were numbered.

From this time, Dr Hedgewar began sending Guruji on tours. His first assignment was Calcutta where he started a shakha. When Guruji was first sent to Calcutta, he had only ₹20 to take care of travelling and local expenses. He used to walk 12–15 miles daily to save money. When he returned, he handed back three paise at the office. Later he was sent on a tour to Punjab during training camps (Karandikar 1999, 323).

Around this time, World War II (WWII) broke out as Dr Hedgewar had foreseen. He was highly pained that he could not raise the RSS to the level where it could exploit this opportunity to directly fight for freedom with a strong Hindu society. At that time, he articulated his idea of how strong the RSS should have been to take this plunge. In March 1940, when WWII was already on, he felt that it was the time to engage in the battle for freedom. He had certain organizational targets to fulfil the objectives of the RSS in terms of fully trained swayamsevaks. What should be the ideal numbers for RSS swayamsevaks for this purpose? In a letter dated 18 March, he wrote:

> To make our Sangh effective, I put forward a suggestion that in the coming three years (from 1940 to 1942) each state should have young uniformed swayamsevaks in the ratio of 1% in rural areas and 3% in urban areas. How will it happen? I think, if all of you take it up with positivity and hard work, we can do it in three years easily. I pray to God that he gives you success in this work. (Palkar 2000, 374)

Thus, it is clear that Dr Hedgewar had seen 1942 as the decisive year for gaining freedom. This prediction proved correct when Gandhiji gave a call for 'Quit India' in August 1942 and Azad Hind Fauj was founded in September 1942.

Undying Focus of a Freedom Fighter

The depth of Dr Hedgewar's angst for freedom and his anguish at his inability to finish this task due to his failing health can be seen in an incident quoted by ex-Sarkaryavaah H.V. Kulkarni.

> One night Doctorji called me home. After everyone else had gone to sleep, he told me, 'I fear that we might miss this golden opportunity of the World War. We needed our organization to be very strong before this war itself. I had full idea of this war. But if this huge nation had a Dr Hedgewar in each of its villages then I could have seen my dream of a free Hindu Rashtra in reality. But, it seems God wills something else.' Saying this, Dr Hedgewar became emotional and tears rolled down his eyes. (*Dr Hedgewar Smriti,* special edition, 1962, 76)

This angst seems to have inspired Guruji to speed up the organizational growth of the RSS at a frenetic pace when he took over.

In the Pune officers' training camp in 1940, Dr Hedgewar again stressed that the RSS would not put energy into articles or publicizing its views through newspapers. It would focus on groundwork completely. He also explained that all the political parties of India, like the Congress, the Hindu Mahasabha, and the Socialist parties were formed by 'our own people', so the relations with them should be as with friends. He said, 'Even if our views didn't match, there should be no sense of animosity. We must treat all the citizens of India with love and win them over' (Karandikar 1999, 347).

He returned to Nagpur in poor health with a high fever and back pain. It was at this time on 20 May 1940 that Dr Shyama Prasad Mukherjee met him. He was deeply disturbed by the atrocities against Hindus in Bengal. Dr Hedgewar suggested that Hindu society become strong keeping in mind the needs of the future. Mukherjee assured him of his full support for RSS work in Calcutta. Dr Mukherjee suggested that the RSS should get into politics, but Dr Hedgewar again made it clear that the RSS would not take part in day-to-day politics (Palkar 2000, 388).

The final programme for Dr Hedgewar was a short lecture at a valedictory event of a one-month RSS training camp. This officers' training camp (now called Sangh Shiksha Varg) saw participation from all provinces of India. Dr Hedgewar had felt a great sense of satisfaction. He said in his lecture, 'I can see a small microcosm of Hindu Rashtra today.' He sent them off with a message that there should never be a time when you would say, 'I *was* a swayamsevak' (Karandikar 1999, 354). He added, '[The] Sangh shakha may be organized on grounds, but RSS work is in the society. There is an important area of work outside the RSS shakha, in the society' (Karandikar 1999, 355). Deendayal Upadhyay was one of the students who heard this last lecture as a participant of the 3rd year Sangh Shiksha Varg of that year.

A young swayamsevak, who had been taking care of him, had asked, 'If a senior RSS leader dies, would you carry out his last rites with military honours?' Remember, military and physical training was a very important and visible impression of the Sangh. Dr Hedgewar explained, '[The] Sangh is a large family; it is not a military organization. Therefore, just as we perform the last rites of a head of the family, we should be taking care of these rites with traditional simplicity.' He had left behind a guiding principle (Karandikar 1999, 356).

The Opposition had hoped that what they thought was a one-bamboo tent, would collapse after Doctorji's death. There was speculation that Appaji Joshi being most senior, would be the next Sarsanghchaalak. However, he declared the name of Guruji (Karandikar 1999, 360). Sangh swayamsevaks, especially in Maharashtra, were surprised as Guruji, at that time, was not very well known in this region though he had travelled to many other regions. But, over time, with his dedication, regular tours and meeting the workers, he overcame the resistance of a small section of the organization and became one of the most towering figures of the RSS for the next thirty-three years.

Doctorji: The Leader

The biggest contribution of Dr K.B. Hedgewar was the creation of an unorthodox organization with a methodology that was never tried earlier or later in the world. His idea of contributing at least one hour every day for the society and nation-building is a unique out-of-the-box concept. We have seen how this idea of selfless dedication has inspired people to even sacrifice their lives for the nation, as they grew within the organization. Even his idea of funding the organization through totally voluntary 'guru-dakshina' was a unique idea that has served the organization well and helped it stay independent of any outside influences.

He founded an organizational science that evolved over time but remained grounded in the principles he set. He created an organization of Hindus that spoke of material well-being and not spiritual upliftment. It was possibly the only organization with no religious underpinnings, no religious rituals or promise of spiritual upliftment. He inculcated pure karma yoga in his swayamsevaks and the organization, with no expectations of any returns or personal gain. It is an unprecedented action. For him, Hindu dharma was an enlightened way of life for the society, not to be seen through rituals. This has been the way most of the reformers of Indian society have worked.

He was able to lay down an organizational structure that could overcome the inertia of individualistic Hindu society. Hindus were to be brought out of their ritualistic, inward-looking, defeatist and divisive mindset. It was not against anybody, but it was to address the ills of Hindu society.

His practice of coming to any decision after due consultation with other members—though he could have easily dominated the decision-making process—created an organization that ensured that its members always work on the basis of consensus and not just a majority view. This has created a unique organization that has never split in nine decades.

Dr Hedgewar presented a new vision about raising an organization, taking along the simplest of people and nurturing them, according to their capabilities, to take on higher responsibilities. Explaining the nature of Sangh work, he said,

> Ninety per cent of the people in the society are of average intellect and capability. It is boring work to cultivate the culture of service to the nation, but someone has to do this work as it is necessary. Every mother does it for years to rear her child. The intellectually capable may open new horizons of ideas, similarly very few workers can continuously work for nurturing others. Just as intellectuals don't give up an idea because of criticism, a worker who moulds the swayamsevaks should also not get bored or judge a person quickly. (Karandikar 1999, 274)

This ability to work with the simplest of people patiently, irrespective of their qualifications, intelligence, station in life, caste or creed, and raise them to extraordinary levels separates him from all other social leaders. This is an important factor behind the success of the RSS in augmenting its cadre and its expansion in a sustained manner. Patience, compassion and perseverance is the key.

From the beginning, he focused on teenagers and youth.

He clearly saw this work as a long-term project. He utilized the services of elders for stabilizing the organization and nurturing young talent. It may be noted that when the Indian government tried to put a condition of age limit on young boys entering the Sangh before lifting the first ban on the RSS, the RSS leadership simply refused to accept that condition. Patience and vision were key factors.

He underlined the importance of compassion in organization-building and paying minute attention to the problems of all his swayamsevaks. Yadavrao Joshi stayed at his home as he had no other support system. There are many others stories that speak volumes of his help to his colleagues and juniors.

The culture of non-publicity began during the early years of the RSS when Dr Hedgewar felt that till enough strength was gathered to fight for freedom, work should be low key. He emphasized that the RSS work was purely towards consolidation of Hindus. If somebody asked him about the criticism of his work in newspapers or periodicals, Doctorji would simply say that he felt amused (Karandikar 1999, 276).

Dr Hedgewar also understood the importance of EQ, as it is understood in organization-building theories today. He utilized EQ for building a sensitive organization and a compassionate band of workers. Dr Hedgewar's message to his followers was clear—the RSS is a family organization and not a para-military or a military organization, and a family runs on emotions and love.

He was also unorthodox. His organization was thoroughly nationalist but he did not choose a khadi uniform, instead he opted for a Western uniform. He wished to project a modern, disciplined India with youth at the forefront. He was rational about this choice.

He did more for the upliftment of oppressed classes and he did this without discrimination. It was not to show off but to erase practices that created caste rifts. His approach in the organization was that nobody would talk about caste or ask anyone about their caste. Being Hindu was the only identity. He followed Swami Vivekananda's practice of reforms with persuasion and setting practical examples rather than being confrontational.

With his hard work, he could reach out to all the provinces in a small and big way in fifteen years. The seed he nurtured with his own blood and sweat had become a young plant with a presence across India within these fifteen years. And in this period, he could create a structure that still provides a solid foundation for this massive organization.

Dr Hedgewar was so merged with the objectives of the RSS and the ultimate goal of independence that he insisted that he didn't wish to celebrate twenty-five years of the foundation of the RSS. He wished to see a free Bharat with his own body and his own eyes—*yaachi dehi, yaachi dola*. Unfortunately, he put his body through such rigour that he couldn't live beyond fifty years, of which fifteen years were totally dedicated to building the RSS into a strong organization. Dr Hedgewar had the satisfaction of seeing trainees from all the provinces of Bharat and he expressed it in the valedictory session of his last training camp. He emphasized that shakha may be organized on the grounds, but real work is outside in the society. This vision fructified later, but his direction was carried by his successors all through.

The smooth transition of leadership from Dr Hedgewar to Guruji—as well as similar transitions in the future too—tell us about the success of the organizational model that Doctorji created. Indeed Dr Hedgewar maybe the only leader who is lesser known than the organization he built. This deliberate exercise of self-abnegation is another lesson for social movements. All the Sarsanghchaalaks and senior leaders of the RSS followed in the same path. Such was his self-effacement that when someone requested Dr Hedgewar to write his biography, he said there is nothing great about his life that would be helpful in writing a biography. His first small biography came after his death in 1940. This edition did not have an author name, and it appeared only in the next edition. The author was Babasaheb Apte, the first generation, eldest of the prachaaraks. Then, his colleagues published two memoirs titled *Hamaara Aadarsh* and *Smriti*

Kann. Finally, the first proper biography appeared only in 1960 written by a very senior prachaarak, N.H. Palkar, after painstaking research. No other biography of his has provided more authentic information (Swaroop 2017, 133).

I would like to quote an incident narrated by veteran RSS prachaarak, Shri Dattopant Thengdi, about the greatness of the leader who was hardly known till a few years back. He described this incident in his book, *Karyakarta*.

The incident took place sometime between 1966 and 1968. Thengdi had been a prachaarak in the Communist stronghold of Kerala. He was a Rajya Sabha member at that time. A Communist colleague, while chatting in the Parliament canteen, asked him the name of RSS founder. When he said 'Dr Hedgewar', his colleague had a questioning look on his face saying he hadn't heard of him. Thengdi kept quiet. But, another Communist member of Palghat, Balchandra Menon, spoke out, 'You should not speak about great people in such an insulting manner.' His friend said that was not his purpose. Menon then said, 'I would ask you two serious questions. Give me serious answers. When did Nehru die?' The response was 1964. 'How popular was he at the time of his death?' His friend asked, 'What are you asking? We know he was famous the world over as one of the triumvirate of the three top leaders of the Non-Aligned Movement. Gamal Abdul Nasser, Josef Broz Tito and Jawaharlal Nehru?' Then, he asked Thengdi, 'When did your Dr Hedgewar die—June 1940? How well was he known at that time?' Thengdi responded by saying, 'Not much. Only people in the Central Provinces knew about him.'

He then went on to say,

> Nehru died only recently. Dr Hedgewar died twenty-four years back. Nobody knew him beyond his state at that time. Nehru was a leader of a global level. Now, I will ask you one question, if one were to appeal to people to be ready to put their lives at stake for the principles that Nehru expounded

> then how many people will come forward? And if I ask the same question about Dr Hedgewar, how many people would be ready to give their all for his principles?

He again addressed his Communist friend, 'Not even fifty people will stand up for Nehru, but for Dr Hedgewar you will find lakhs of young people ready to come forward. You know it well.' Thengdi then asked Menon, 'What is the criterion of one's greatness?' Menon immediately responded, 'The length of one's shadow on the future.'

It is notable that one of Dr Hedgewar's good friends was Comrade Ruikar. Similarly, Dattopant Thengdi too had excellent relations with Communists. Later, other leaders of the RSS too had good relations across the political spectrum. This thinking was nurtured by Dr Hedgewar by his own example.

Dr Hedgewar had a clear view about the role of the RSS in the national scenario. When the Sangh had become big enough to be noticed, critics had asked him, 'But, what will the RSS do?' His answer was, 'The Sangh will do nothing; swayamsevaks will do everything.' He had indicated that the role of the RSS was only in making simple men into men of high calibre who would then work in society based on their own understanding of the requirements of the time. We will see later how his vision was transformed into reality in subsequent years.

Shri Guruji: Nurturing RSS into a Massive Organization (1940–1973)

Madhav Sadashiv Golwalkar, the second Sarsanghchaalak got his more famous sobriquet 'Guruji' at Benaras Hindu University (BHU), where he was teaching for a few years. Contrary to popular perception, he was not 'The Guru' of the RSS, but a popular guru of his students. However, this became a part of his persona.

The roots of the Golwalkar clan lay in a small, remote village called Golwal in Ratnagiri, Maharashtra, where his ancestors had moved from Kashi as Upadhyayas or priests (shortened to Padhyes in Maharashtra). His family had a strong lineage of scholarship. Born in 1906, he was the only surviving child out of eight that his parents had. He was a precocious reader with an extraordinary memory. The young Madhav excelled in elocution and won various prizes including in English. He had memorized major parts of *Ram Charit Manas* at a very young age as he was fascinated with it. So good he was at his studies that he once proved his teacher wrong when the teacher referred to a guide. Madhav was admitted to English High School in 1919. He received a princely scholarship of ₹4 per month on winning the high school entrance and scholarship exam after standard VII. In Hislop College he got into an argument with his Principal, Gardiner, over a reference in the Bible. Again he was proved to be correct (Ranga Hari 2018, 20). He had also learnt Malkhamb, the famous Maharashtrian form of gymnastics, in Nagpur.

Madhav Golwalkar went to BHU in 1924 to pursue a degree in BSc in Zoology. He was there till 1928 and finished his MSc from BHU. Being an avid reader, he devoured books on every possible subject available in the huge university library.

He had a friendly nature and loved meeting people. He was equally adept at fun and games. He played hockey and tennis too. He also got lessons in flute once in a while from Sanwalaa Ram, and learnt to play the sitar as well. During exam time, he put his heart and soul in studying. When a scorpion bit him, he put his leg in water and kept studying. When his friends questioned him about how he could study with the pain, he said, 'Brother, scorpion has stung me on my leg and I am reading by using my head. Let both of them do their respective jobs.' This spiritual strength of detachment could be seen time and again, when he was being treated for cancer in his last stages of life. He could keep chatting in a light manner even when the doctor was dressing his painful surgical wounds.

Madhav went to Chennai for his PhD in fisheries. However, he couldn't complete the thesis as his father had retired as a teacher and he couldn't get a scholarship because the person who could offer it was on travel constantly and the deadline for the fee had passed. Even so, he gained other experiences, including spiritual experiences, from his time there. His biography tells us that it was a kind of turbulent period in his life when he had self-doubts, philosophical experiences and wide-ranging thoughts about the independence struggle.

Madhav Golwalkar's spiritual proclivity in his life was visible since childhood. It got further strengthened during his secluded life in Chennai. He wrote to his close friend Babu Telang, who was married by then–

> Can I not stay aloof from the world even while staying within it? Surely it can be done. It is not necessary to get married to follow a worldly path. As per religious texts, marriage may be a duty, but a person decides on it based on his or her own situation. Getting married may be ideal, but even if one doesn't get married, nothing is lost [...] Earlier my thought of going to Himalayas was a negative thought. I am trying to

> achieve *sanyaas* for life while staying in this world, braving vicious attacks from people and carrying out the duties expected of me as a part of this society. Now, the Himalaya is within me and solitude is within me. No need to go anywhere. (Ranga Hari 2018, 36)

Incidentally, his friend Baburao Telang had become an RSS swayamsevak by that time. But, Guruji was not quite convinced about the RSS at that time. He wrote to him,

> If you keep talking and working for Sangh then it will be stupidity. It is good to be part of Sangh [...] But, you don't know how to serve four members of the family and you wish to serve the whole Hindu society! It is meaningless. Still, please do what you deem fit. I have presented my views to you. (Ranga Hari 2018, 37)

It is interesting to see how the wheels of time moved in his life later. It was his characteristic style to present his views without getting attached to them; he would then abide by what his friends or colleagues finally decided, all through his life.

After his return to Nagpur, he got an appointment for a temporary job as demonstrator in the zoology laboratory in BHU. He quickly became popular amongst the students because of his happy, straightforward and helping nature. He would go out with students to play hockey and tennis, swim in the Ganga. He would not like to be seen in dirty clothes and this habit was there throughout his life. He would not give advice easily, but would share his experience if asked. He was just twenty-five at the time (Ranga Hari 2018, 41, 42).

He would help any student on any subject. If he didn't know the subject, he would study the subject in the night and offer the student the right solution next day. He would arrange for books for poor students. Major part of his salary would get consumed in this and he would make do happily with whatever was left for him. The students began calling him 'Guruji' out of respect. This was the phase in his life that transformed Madhav Golwalkar into 'Guruji' and this became his popular name (Ranga Hari 2018, 43).

He never showed off his intellectual prowess. He loved every kind of knowledge. He was a storehouse of every possible kind of knowledge. He could recall the entire speech of Mark Antony in the death scene of Shakespeare's *Julius Caesar*. He had memorized *Ekach Vyala* of Marathi dramatist Gadkari. He read the complete works of Swami Vivekananda in Kashi and used to narrate stories of Vivekananda to his students (Ranga Hari 2018, 44). He would play and chat comfortably with kids and intellectuals with equal ease.

As mentioned in the previous chapter, Dr Hedgewar began nurturing Guruji by inviting him to Nagpur for a Vijayadashami programme and sending him around to see Sangh work more closely. He visited Nagpur in the summer of 1932 where he met Dr Hedgewar for the first time during this visit. Dr Hedgewar came and stood before him and straightaway enquired, 'Are you Madhavrao Golwalkar?' This was their first direct introduction. He went his way after a brief conversation.

This was the beginning of a deep affectionate association between the two. While speaking of his own experience of this meeting, Guruji said,

> 'I was humbled before that great man. His transparent passion and struggle for the nation with no show of brilliance of intellectualism and total surrender to the nation made me bow before him. And this surrender was a pleasure (Karandikar 1999, 310). This Nagpur tour was highly inspirational. They talked of these energizing experiences after their return to shakhas in Kashi.

An outing to Sarnath was organized by the Kashi shakha in the last week of December, in which forty swayamsevaks with Guruji took part. He narrated the history of Sarnath to other participants there and the historic, philosophic and global importance of Bhagwan Buddha. This picnic was the turning point in the history of Kashi shakha. Guruji also started going regularly to shakha after this.

He began taking more interest in physical programmes. He would remove his coat and tie after the shakha and learn *dand* (practice with the wooden stick) from teachers (Ranga Hari 2018, 47).

Guruji used to practice his favourite *raagas* on sitar or flute before sunrise or after sunset in his room. Other music-loving friends would also join in many a time. Once, some of his friends found him tense and immersed in deep thought. When asked the reason, he didn't say anything. He rose silently, brought out his sitar and handing it over to a friend he said, 'That's it. Now, the music of life is going to be different.' He never touched the sitar or flute after that day (Ranga Hari 2018, 48). This was an indication of his deepening commitment to social causes.

Guruji returned to Nagpur in 1933 in February after the teacher he had substituted for returned, and decided to do law from the Law College of Nagpur. He became a teacher again in his uncle's coaching centre to be self-reliant. He never practised law. His first case proved to be his last as his client wanted him to speak untruth, which he refused, and decided that this was not his profession (Ranga Hari 2018, 53 and 55).

His friend from the university, Raghuvir Dhongdi, lived in Shri Ramkrishna Ashram hostel (Ranga Hari 2018, 56). This connection proved to be life-changing as we will see later. Guruji used to deliver lectures on Sundays at this shakha. Later Dr Hedgewar appointed him as General Secretary (kaaryavaah) of Nagpur shakha in 1934.

His mother used to pester him to get married like all fond mothers. One day he finally told her,

> *Tai,* don't tell me about the continuity, damage or disappearance of our family name. If this society around us has to survive and remain united, it would be imperative that many other families also lose their family names, not just ours. I am not unhappy at all about it. (Ranga Hari 2018, 55)

That was the end of the conversation about his marriage. It was an indication that he had decided the future course of his life.

His spiritual quest hadn't cooled down. He finally left for Sargachhi in 1936 with his friend Raghuvir Dhongdi without informing anyone. Swami Akhandaananda was guru bhai (disciple of the same guru) of Swami Vivekananda. After staying in the ashram as a disciple of Swami Akhandaananda doing various chores as directed by the guru, he finally received the blessings of his guru and was initiated into the order of the Ram Krishna Mission monks in the early morning of 13 January 1937. It was a huge cataclysmic event in his life. He said,

> I can never forget those moments. The look in the eyes of Gurudev, his affection, his overpowering presence; the way he kindly bestowed upon me that luminous joy—I think and hope that I will never forget all this. Every atom of my body was tremulous. I experienced my transformation. I was no more the person I was a few moments earlier. (Ranga Hari 2018, 67)

However, the guru had understood his disciple. He told him, 'Madhav, this is not your area of action, it is somewhere else' (Karandikar 1999, 301). Unfortunately, Swamiji left his body within a few days on 7 February 1937, leaving his disciple distraught. Madhav Golwalkar, an ordained sanyasi now, finally returned to Nagpur with some items of his guru as his sacred memory. He carried his *kamandalu* (wooden water vessel carried by sadhus) till the end of his life (Ranga Hari 2018, 70). All his life he was guided by the basic philosophy of Guru Akhandaananda '*Main nahin, tu hi* [not me, you come first].' He carried on his *saadhna* and other rituals throughout his life as he was trained as a sadhu. But he never asked others to follow any rituals.

On why he preferred Sangh work over Ram Krishna Mission work, he said in an interview, 'I think that my decision to take up this work is in line with Swami Vivekananda's ideology, his teachings and working. No other great soul has had as much impression on me' (Karandikar 1999, 285). Swami Vivekananda had written to his disciples in Madras from the US, 'For the next fifty years, consider this Bharat rashtra and its society as your only God. Even if you keep other gods away for some time, it is fine' (Karandikar 2018, 308). Here we must recall the letter he wrote to his friend, in which he talked about staying back to serve society instead of going away to the Himalayas in search of peace.

During this phase, he translated the famous letter written in Persian by Shivaji to Raja Jaisingh into English. His lecture on this topic used to be the highlight of any RSS workshop. Later, he translated *Rashtra Mimamsaa* into English. It was a book written in Marathi by Babarao Savarkar, elder brother of revolutionary Vinayak Damodar Savarkar. During those risky days, Babarao misplaced that translation. Golwalkar, then just thirty-two-year-old, had been highly impressed with that book. So, he wrote a monograph based on this book. It was titled *We or Our Nationhood Defined*. This is the booklet that is bandied about by the critics as the perennial views of the RSS, though the RSS never refers to it as its foundational document. The preface to this sixty-seven-page booklet was written by a top-ranking Congress leader of the Central Provinces M.S. Aney. Aney mentioned his differing opinion in the preface. At the same time, he appreciated the sincerity and honesty of the author. He wrote, 'This creation is a scientific exposition about nationalism. But, I would like to say that the strong vituperative language used by the writer against those with whom he doesn't agree, crosses the fine line of civility [...] This book is, perhaps a necessary and much desired response against the *blank cheque* mentality of Mahatma Gandhi and people like him.' Extending what Aney wrote in the preface, Madhavrao Golwalkar in his dedication wrote, 'To the memory of those noble martyrs who despite ignominy, calumny and contempt at the hands of their own undeserving brethren, have kept the flame of true Nationality burning in our Land.' It is important to note that in the changed post-Independence scenario, Guruji himself had said, 'Forget "We". It is outdated now' (Swaroop 2009, 108). This was in response to Devendra Swaroop's question to him about the definition of nationality based on this book. Swaroop writes that he was reminded of Gandhiji's sentence, 'Only my latest views on any subject should be taken as my views at that time, not my earlier views' (Swaroop 2009, 108). After this booklet, Guruji seemed to have found no time to create literature as Doctorji got him involved deeply in RSS work. All his subsequent works and quotes are transcripts of his lectures, not written by him. This discarded book still remains the pet reference point for defining this towering personality, instead of his later work as RSS head.

I have talked about the Sindi meeting in 1939 in Chapter 2. It was considered a milestone in the evolution of the RSS. Here I would elaborate a little further. The people invited for this meeting did not fall into any particular category like experience, organizational responsibility and years with the organization. Attendees included Doctorji's colleagues Appaji Joshi and Nanasaheb Talaatule, along with people from the younger generation like Balasaheb Deoras, Tatyarao Telang, Vithalrao Patki, Babaji Saalodkar and Krishnarao Moharir, as well as a comparatively new entrant Madhavrao Golwalkar. Discussions went on for eight hours every day for ten days. In-depth discussions encompassed the Sangh's systems, methodology, orders, oath, prayer, hierarchical structure, official festivals of the Sangh. After thorough all-round discussions, the final responsibility for taking a decision was left to Doctorji. The current Sanskrit prayer, orders in Sanskrit, basic state-wise organizational structure, regular management systems for the Sangh Shiksha Varg, etc., are all the outcome of this historic meeting. Nearly all the decisions about new systems and processes set there about running of RSS shakhas are still followed with very few modifications.

All the participants had noticed Guruji's highly analytical intellect, logical approach, sharp focus and strong ideological clarity. At the same time, his spiritual nature enabling him to take a detached view once a decision was left to Doctorji and then moving on to the next subject was also noticed. The incident of Doctorji seeking his senior colleague Appaji Joshi's advice about nominating Guruji as the next Sarsanghchaalak and immediate approval by Appaji has been described in one of the articles in Appaji Joshi's memoirs. In the words of Yadavraoji Joshi, 'Keshav had perceived Madhav' (Ranga Hari 2018, 76).

Youngest Sarsanghchaalak Takes Over

To overcome chronic and severe backache, Dr Hedgewar went in for a risky lumber puncture procedure. However, there was no other way out. Doctorji called Guruji urgently to his room and told him in front of all the people present in the room, 'Time has now come to carry out lumber puncture. If I am saved, it would be fine. Otherwise, please take over the whole responsibility of Sangh work.' Guruji exclaimed in deep grief, 'Doctorji, what are you saying? You will be alright very soon.' Doctorji smiled on hearing these words and said, 'That is alright, but do remember what I have told you' (Ranga Hari 2018, 80).

These words were uttered on 20 June 1940 in the presence of Krishnarao Moharir and Yadavrao Joshi and were conveyed to the core team members. From there on, the news spread rapidly that Madhavrao Golwalkar is the new Sarsanghchaalak. The official pronouncement had not been made so far. A meeting was convened on 30 July in Akola by the senior-most Sanghchalak Appaji Joshi. Among those present were, Nagpur Sanghchalak Babasaheb Ghatate, Vidarbha state Sanghchalak Bapusaheb Sohoni and Maharashtra state Sanghchalak Kashinath Limaye. Everybody accepted the last wish of the late Sarsanghchaalak solemnly without any discussions (Ranga Hari 2018, 82).

While stating his decision for a traditional funeral to Dr Hedgewar, Guruji said, 'Ultimately, the Sangh is a big family, not a militarist organization. For us, Doctorji was the head of this family and like a father.' Therefore the last rites were conducted in a normal, family tradition (Ranga Hari 2018, 85). This was in line with what Doctorji had told the young swayamsevak before his death that he should be cremated like the head of a big family. Despite the image of the RSS as a para-military organization at that time, it was, primarily, Dr Hedgewar and Guruji who underlined that the RSS was a family organization.

After taking over the mantle of Sarsanghchaalak, he said,

> People have been asking various questions about our organization. People even raise questions about the direction that Sangh will take in future. Actually, the goal and work of Sangh are clearly defined. Vision of Sangh is steadfast, there is no reason for it to deviate in future. What will happen to [the] Sangh after Doctorji? Such doubts rise in many hearts. The truth is that there is no reason for such questions to arise. There is no doubt at all that Sangh will always march forward bravely on its well-defined course, crushing all types of hazards. (Ranga Hari 2018, 86)

He used to say,

> While we sleep it is Kaliyug, when we are awake it is Dwaapar yug, when we stand up it is Treta yug and when we begin walking, the age of action, Krita yug is created.

It was to be Krita yug for him from then on. He circumambulated Bharat sixty times in thirty-three years—non-stop, continuously, untiringly, without break or rest—from the Himalayas to the Indian Ocean. This was done in most ordinary methods of travel. (Ranga Hari 2018, 87). Of these, the last three tours were after the detection of cancer and its treatment.

It is not known to most people that it was not smooth sailing for Guruji initially. He was not known well in Pune or in southern Maharashtra. He was only thirty-four-years-old when he was made Sarsanghchaalak. There were some harsh reactions to his nomination. 'Who is this Guruji?' some people asked (Karandikar 1999, 360). A couple of seniors resigned when he was made Sarsanghchaalak. Realizing the huge respect that people had for Dr Hedgewar and his own relative inexperience and late entry, Guruji knew that he had an uphill task to measure up to the swayamsevaks' expectations. He, therefore, said after his nomination as Sarsanghchaalak, 'The post of Sarsanghchaalak given to me by Dr Hedgewar is a huge responsibility. But this is Vikramaditya's throne. If you make a shepherd sit on it, he will give proper justice' (Ranga Hari 2018, 84). It took him some time to win over seniors, who looked at him as an outsider, by working calmly during this period.

He travelled across India three or four times in a short spell to get to know RSS workers better and establish warm relations with them. While Doctorji was a hardcore social and political activist who consciously decided to keep the RSS out of politics, Guruji by his innate nature was never well disposed to politics. He had experience in the spiritual field but not in social or political fields. Many swayamsevaks who were close to the Hindu Mahasabha, didn't like his attitude. So they would raise questions in meetings, sometimes insolently. But true to his nature and training received from Doctorji, he refused to bite the bait and kept silent (Karandikar 2018, 361). It was only as days passed that such elements in the RSS began appreciating his energetic and serious leadership and the voices of criticism slowly died down.

Heady Expansion of Sangh Work and British Efforts to Curb It

Guruji had a clear worldview and a good understanding of the historic period. Before leaving for spiritual pursuit in Saragachhi, he had written a letter to his BHU colleague and swayamsevak, Dr Sadagopal, on 7 July 1936:

> World politics is changing at a rapid pace. Who knows that a situation may emerge that we may have to jump into it (to gain freedom)? If we do not catch hold of such a moment, it is possible it may never come again. We may have to keep waiting in disappointment and pain in dark till the next ray of hope emerges [...] We should not give an opportunity to our future generations to say that we lost a chance, the way we blame our previous generation that they lost a chance during 1914 [Wold War I]. Therefore, we should spread a strong network of RSS shakhas all over the country, so that

> we can strike hard and gain independence as soon as such an opportunity arises. (Swaroop 2009, 142)

This was much before he had joined the top echelons of the RSS. This view was quite close to what Doctorji had been saying since the formation of the RSS. As noted earlier, Doctor's major regret during his last days was that he couldn't reach his organizational target before World War II.

Taking this as a guideline, Guruji took up rapid expansion of the RSS in all earnestness. He hoped to have a ready organization to take advantage of the British getting weaker after WWII. His emotional and spiritual pull saw huge increase in the ranks of prachaaraks and huge growth during 1940–1942, especially in the north and north-west of the country. His appeal to young swayamsevaks was, 'We need prachaaraks [...] we need prachaaraks. This is the demand rising from all directions. We must fulfil this demand.' He would say,

> Karyakartas don't fall from heavens. For this we will have to make efforts ourselves and create karyakartas from amongst ourselves. We will have to walk the path of duty with firm resolve and austerity by giving up all thoughts about our personal lives [...] the mission before us is enormous with very little time in hand. But do not worry. The question is of just bringing about a little revolution within our hearts. Just one revolution of hearts and our lives will see unprecedented changes and we shall see the gateway of hope [...] Let us close all the doors of our personal lives and take a pledge of concerted efforts. Let us become sanyasins for one year. (Ranga Hari 2018, 94)

Remembering those heady days, ninety-four-year-old prachaarak Thakur Ram Singh said proudly, 'Forty-eight prachaaraks came out just from Lahore in 1942. Of these, ten were M.A., two doctors, fourteen shastris and others were B.A. and above Matriculate. Prachaaraks also came also from other towns. Fifty-two prachaaraks came out of Amritsar city; of these, there were four doctors' (Ranga Hari 2018, 95).

On the day of *shraddhanjali* (homage day), twenty-two karyakartas had become prachaaraks in Nagpur. Many prachaaraks joined in from Vidarbha and Maharashtra. Guruji and Balasaheb Deoras appointed these people in different states of the country strategically (Ranga Hari 2018, 95). The year 1942 was literally a year of comprehensive transformation in the history of the Sangh. These developments were the biggest signs that the RSS was not going to be a personality-oriented organization. This intellectual clarity saw the organization weather many storms and grow strong.

Within two months of his appointment, the British government released a circular that no organization can have a uniform similar to the armed forces in any way. It was targeted at the RSS, of course. Guruji changed the uniform to a less military-like outfit. English words such as drill were changed and many military-like exercises were also diluted. For him, long-term goals were more important than short-term issues and he refused to get provoked. He somehow managed to persuade young elements of the RSS to keep their cool (Karandikar 1999, 371).

It was not that there were no challenges from within where swayamsevaks went to work. Hindu society has varied customs and traditions. When RSS work began in Punjab, the society was in a flux. There were mainstream Hindus, Arya Samaj followers who didn't believe in murti puja, and Sikhs. The Arya Samaj had a very strong impact on Hindu society at that time, and there were still Arya Samaji purists who had seen it at its peak. Not many of them would come to shakha. Those who came would not bow down to the saffron flag nor would they say '*Bharat mata ki jai*', as she was a symbolic idol of the motherland. Madhavrao Muley, the prachaarak there, allowed all this and did not get into any argument. Because of the use of the word 'Hindu' many Sikh youths too would avoid the RSS. He would give the example of strong blood relations between Hindus and Sikhs, giving example of Guru Tegh Bahadur, Bhai Dayala and Bhai Matidas who were beheaded in Chandni Chowk. He would quote Guru Gobind Singh often. After two to three years of discussions, youths from the Arya Samaj and Sikh youths began to join in big numbers. By 1947, their numbers increased multi-fold (Karandikar 1999, 379–80).

When a senior Hindu Mahasabha (HMS) leader in Punjab asked Madhavrao Muley why the RSS and the HMS couldn't work together in Punjab, he explained that the HMS ran a strong political movement that was tied to current issues, while the RSS was working on Hindutva that loved and respected Bharatiya culture as the basis of its work. The RSS was not interested in short-term movements; rather, it was looking at eternal inspiration for Hindutva, divorced from politics (Karandikar 1999, 379).

Slowly, new systems emerged. Regular weekly, monthly and quarterly meetings of the RSS began getting organized from the local level to state and regional levels. They would review the growth of Sangh work, discuss any problems faced by workers and local issues. Sangh Shiksha Vargs (called Officers Training Camp [OTC] at that time) also became regular features in all the states.

Guruji would attend two-day state level meetings in every state. He could recognize thousands of workers by name because of his photographic memory. Some prachaaraks would return home for normal domestic life and more would join the ranks. The meetings would take place at the homes of swayamsevaks and prachaaraks too would stay at some or the other home depending on the situation in that place. Mostly, there were only state-level offices called *karyalaya* in the Sangh at the time. These karyalayas later also worked as the resting place for retired prachaaraks as they aged. They would not like to return home but preferred to stay with their swayamsevaks with whom they had spent their lives. People would come from distant places to meet them. This was the scenario till 1945, before things took a turn for the worst. The RSS also made deep inroads into the southern part of India during this period.

By this time the British government became acutely aware of the expansion of RSS work. The central government came out with a gazette on 5 August 1940. As per its sections 56–58, private organizations were prohibited from giving army training or wearing army uniforms. There was no mention of the RSS, but its target was clear. Guruji's tactical response was to not react against the government, but find ways to blunt the attack. After ten days, he wrote on 16 August to Professor Malkani in Sindh, 'Our purpose is not to raise an army. We believe firmly in an organized society. Our goal is to generate a sense of unity in the Hindu society.' He wrote in similar vein to Vasantrao Oak in Delhi,

> You know it well that we are not bound by any specific type of programme. We are not shackled by any methodology and we modify our programmes and come up with plans for new programmes keeping in mind our core objective. With this view, we had given up that part of our training syllabus in our programmes that was based on military terminology keeping in mind restrictions imposed by the notification issued in August 1940. Today, now that this department has lost its utility, we have decided to dissolve it totally. We have removed these posts from our organizational planning. It is unnecessary to say that this system of command has effectively ended by itself. (Ranga Hari 2018, 95)

Guruji had sent notifications with similar content from Nagpur central office to all the states, knowing well that these letters will be scrutinized by the British police. The idea was to remain under the radar till the Sangh was strong enough to challenge the might of the British, without any compromise to its core objectives. That the British were flummoxed by these moves is clear from the report sent by the Central Police Intelligence Department on 13 December 1943, which noted,

> It is not possible to create a case for banning Sangh. But, it is equally clear that Golwalkar is creating a strong organization at a rapid pace that would obey the orders, maintaining confidentiality and jump into any activity of sabotage or of any

> other type whenever required as per their leader's orders. The structure of this organization looks superficially like that of *khaaksaars*. But the fundamental difference between the two is that the leader of *khaaksaar*, Inayatullah, is a big mouthed imbalanced lunatic, while Golwalkar is a very cautious, crafty and much more capable leader. (Ranga Hari 2018, 96)

Clearly, there were never any compromises in the foundational objective of uniting and strengthening Hindu society and its work for freedom. There is not one correspondence or any piece of evidence in the pre-independence history of the RSS to show that it had in any way, cooperated with the British.

Quit India Movement and Subsequent Developments

When the Sangh was growing at such a frenetic pace, August Kranti (Quit India Movement) of 1942 rose in India. The year 1942 was a major test of Guruji's political acumen—whether to participate as the RSS or voluntarily as individuals, was the question. There have been conjectures that if it were Dr Hedgewar, he might have jumped in directly. Why didn't the RSS jump into 1942 in full strength but let individuals take part and give underground support to the movement? According to Dattopant Thengdi, a young prachaarak at that time, he had discussions with Guruji after meeting some senior Congress leaders with his young team. The main reasons that he enumerated were that the Congress leadership did not have a clear strategy or fall-back plan once the agitation was launched. Unlike in 1930, the Congress leadership did not reach out to the RSS to take part in the movement and share with it its plans. The Sangh was strong only in Central Provinces. In other places, the organization was present but it was still weak. There was lack of clarity from the Congress leadership about the course of the agitation. If it failed, it would have a big impact on this small organization and the morale of its workers. Finally, after due deliberations, it was decided to let swayamsevaks take part in the agitation as individuals under the Congress umbrella and support it wherever and in whichever way possible (Swaroop 2009, 149). This had been the principled stand of Dr Hedgewar during earlier agitations too.

The Vidarbha region had a strong RSS network. Naturally, the fiercest agitations took place in Bali (Amravati), Ashti (Wardha) and Chimur (Chandrapur). News about the Chimur agitation was broadcast from Berlin Radio. This agitation was led by Uddhavrao Korekar of the Congress and RSS leaders Dada Naik, Baburao Begade and Annaji. A young swayamsevak, Balaji Raipurkar, was killed brutally in police firing when he was trying to raise the Tricolour. Sangh swayamsevaks took part in the Chimur agitation in 1943 along with the Congress and the Tukdoji Maharaj-led Shri Gurudev Seva Mandal.

This encounter became famous in the history of this movement as the Chimur Ashti episode. RSS swayamsevaks had established a parallel government in Chimur. A total of 125 satyagrahis were put on trial and handed imprisonment and thousands of swayamsevaks were imprisoned. Dada Naik, head of RSS Chimur branch, was sentenced to death. Hindu Mahasabha leader Dr N.B. Khare, a member of the British Viceroy Council, took up his case with the authorities and got the sentence commuted to imprisonment. Later, Sant Tukdoji Maharaj became one of the co-founders of the Vishwa Hindu Parishad (Vaidya 2018, 30).

Hemu Kalani, a swayamsevak of Sakkhar town in Sindh, got arrested while removing fishplates from railway tracks with his colleagues to frustrate plans to move forces to suppress the struggle in various areas. Hemu was arrested while his friends managed to escape. Hemu was handed a death sentence by the Army Court in 1943 (Ranga Hari 2018, 99). He has a memorial in his name constructed by local Sindhi swayamsevaks and maintained by 'Hemu Kalani Yadgaar Mandal' in Chembur, Mumbai. His statues have been erected in other Indian cities in Rajasthan and Gujarat too. This story is also recounted by late Gobind Motwani in his book (Wadhwani and Motwani 2006, 58). A stamp was released by the Government of India in 1983 to commemorate his contribution to the freedom struggle.

On 11 August 1942, Patna saw a successful attempt by young boys to hoist the Tricolour above the government secretariat. Six agitators were felled by police firing. Of these six, two, Devipad Chaudhary and Jagatpati Kumar, were swayamsevaks. The first Sanghchalak of Bihar and senior journalist Krishnakant Ojha confirmed their RSS connection. A felicitation programme to honour them was organized during the fiftieth anniversary celebrations of Independence in 1997, under the chairmanship of renowned litterateur and revolutionary Shri Vachanesh Tripathi in the presence of the then regional prachaarak, now Sarsanghchaalak, Dr Mohan Bhagwat. Their kin too were invited to the programme.[2]

Swayamsevaks plunged into the Quit India Movement wherever they were in India and were imprisoned in many places. Some of the well-known senior swayamsevaks were Dr Annasaheb Deshpande (Aarvi, Vidarbha), Ramakant Keshav (Babasaheb) Deshpande in Jashpur (Chhattisgarh) who went on to establish Vanvasi Kalyan Ashram, Shri Vasantrao Oak (Prant prachaarak of Delhi), Narayan Singh known as Babuaji in Bihar who later became Bihar Sanghchalak, Shri Chandrakant Bhardwaj (who received a bullet in his foot that couldn't be removed). Bhardwaj became a famous poet and wrote many poems which are sung in the RSS. There were Madhavrao in East UP, who became prant prachaarak later and Dattatreya Gangadhar (a.k.a. Bhaiyyaji) Kasture, who too became a prachaarak later (Vaidya 2018, 30–31).

Apart from such activities, many swayamsevaks also helped underground leaders of the movement when the overground agitation went awry. House of Sanghchalak of North East Lala Hansraj was the secret place of stay for Aruna Asaf Ali. Renowned Vedic scholar Pandit Shripaad Damodar Satavalekar, Sanghchalak of Aundh, gave asylum for many days to the revolutionary underground leader Nana Patil, who had experimented with the novel idea 'Patri Sarkaar'. Nana Patil's colleague Kisanveer

[2]Taken from an email from Sanjeev Kumar, from Patna, on 10 December 2018.

had stayed at the house of Satara Sanghchalak in Wai while working underground there. Famous Socialist leader Achyutrao Patwardhan had stayed at many Sangh swayamsevaks' homes when he used to work underground and change places according to circumstances. Not only these people, but even the life-long bitter opponent of [the] Sangh, Gandhian Sane Guruji, used to stay at Pune Sanghchalak Bhausaheb Deshmukh's house secretly. (Ranga Hari 2018, 99–100)

Ganesh Bapuji Shinkar, a 1942 Congress veteran, later resigned from the Congress in 1948 and took part in the RSS satyagraha to press for the removal of ban on the Sangh in 1948. He issued a statement,

> I had participated in Bharat Chhodo [Quit India] movement in 1942. Capitalist and agrarian community was scared of the government at that time, therefore we were not offered safe haven in their homes. We had to stay in Sangh workers' homes to work underground. People from Sangh used to help us happily with our underground work. They also took care of all our requirements. Not only this, if someone from amongst us fell sick, Sangh swayamsevak doctors used to treat us. Sangh swayamsevaks who were advocates, fought our cases fearlessly. Their patriotism and value based living was undisputable. (Ranga Hari 2018, 100)

Guruji's big worry as Sarsanghchaalak was how to guard this young plant of the RSS in the storm. His tours were organized in various places where he met swayamsevaks and took careful stock of his work. During this time, his correspondence with nearly all the senior prachaaraks continued (Ranga Hari 2018, 101).

Guruji took decisions in 1942 reflecting upon how Dr Hedgewar might have thought in a particular situation. He felt that the RSS needed to be expanded much rapidly first as per Doctorji's dream and then strike when the opportune moment came. The British too had taken serious cognisance of Guruji and the RSS during 1942–43 as their intelligence reports indicated. In hindsight, we can understand that the RSS could not have served the nation in 1946–47 period of serious violence perpetrated on Hindu-Sikh brethren, or defended Jammu and Kashmir against the Pakistani attack in 1947 had it not reached the strength it did under Guruji's calm and confident leadership.

In spite of pressure and the keen watch of British intelligence and police, he kept expanding the organization in a sustained manner. The CID report of 30 September 1943 noted that the ultimate goal of the RSS was freedom of India and it was increasing its strength so that it could attack the British at the right moment. Till then, it was avoiding any direct confrontation with the British (Swaroop 2009, 56). The British government was alert about the RSS. It had kept a sharp eye on every activity of Guruji. The CID kept sending reports about him regularly. The report on 30 December 1943 said,

> RSS is moving ahead rapidly towards building a highly significant all India organization. Spokesmen of [the] Sangh kept saying that the basic goal of [the] Sangh is to achieve Hindu unity... In a programme in November 1943 in Lahore, M.S. Golwalkar declared that [the] Sangh's objective is to remove the feeling of untouchability and weave together all sections of Hindu society in a single unifying thread. It is clear that [the] Sangh is bent upon expanding its area of influence and this year it has been able to bring on board, the famous religious saint Sant Tukdoji Maharaj from Central Province for spreading its message [...] Membership of [the] Sangh is swelling continuously. In Central Provinces, membership has increased from 32,000 to 33,344. It has reached 20,476 from 18,029 in Mumbai and 14,000 from 10,000 in Punjab [...] A new dimension to their growth is their efforts to gain entry in the villages. M.S. Golwalkar laid a lot of stress on this aspect in the winter camp of Vardha—that Sangh should expand into villages [...] Sangh office-bearers from its head office are touring the shakhas in remote areas continuously, so that they

> can heighten the interest of swayamsevaks in Sangh work, give them secret directions and strengthen the local organization. We can see the recent well spread out tour of the present Chief of Sangh, M.S. Golwalkar as an example of such efforts. In the last month of April he was in Ahmedabad, in May he was in Amravati and Pune. In June he was in Nasik and Benaras. He toured Chaandaa in August, Pune in September, Madras and Central Province in October, and Rawalpindi in November.

Guruji's biographer, Ranga Hari points out,

> If one were to read this report carefully, one interesting fact emerges. All the places mentioned in it are situated north of Chandrapur, with exception of Chennai where work was begun by Sanjeev Kamat of Chennai who was present in the valedictory function of 1940 Sangh Shiksha Varg due to personal relationship and efforts of Sangh founder Dr Hedgewar. Guruji had taken initiative to expand Sangh in Southern states using this contact and undertook a special tour of South. Under this plan, he had sent English-speaking prachaaraks from Mumbai presidency and Central province to South in 1942. Dattopant Thengdi went to Calicut in Kerala. Yadavrao Joshi was sent from Jhansi to Belgaum. A gold medallist Shivram Joglekar from Pune was sent to Chennai. Shivram Shankar alias Dada Apte, who became General Secretary of Vishwa Hindu Parishad twenty five years later, was sent to Tiruchirappalli in Tamil Nadu. Narhari Parkhi was sent to Andhra region of Madras Presidency. Anna Shesh and Babu Telang reached Mangalore and Thiruvananthapuram, respectively. This is not the complete list but only a representative one. Guruji used to visit major cities of South to strengthen the newly launched expansion programme that began in 1941–42, and to be in close touch with young committed prachaaraks. (Ranga Hari 2018, 101, 102)

Assertive, Calm Leadership during the Disturbing pre-Partition and Partition Days

In the meanwhile, the situation was deteriorating fast. Congress had opposed partition of Bharat in 1945. Jinnah had managed to turn the political narrative in such a way that even the Congress used terms like Muslims and non-Muslims in a country where the majority was Hindu. This suited the Muslim League well. Dr V.R. Karandikar notes that the Muslim League told the British, 'Gandhi and Congress have no right to speak about Muslims, they represent Hindus.' Nobody asked Jinnah where was he during the freedom struggle, nor pointed out that he never went to jail even once. The Muslim League launched Direct Action on 16 August 1946 in which 5,000–10,000 Hindus lost their lives and over 15,000 were injured within a week. But no one from the Congress said, 'We will not talk to murderers of Hindus under duress.' Savarkar who had opposed the Muslim League for months from the platform of Hindu Mahasabha was labelled communal and was isolated, while the person who got thousands butchered was honoured as 'Qaid-e-Azam' by Gandhi ji (Karandikar 1999, 434–35). According to Devchand Jha, Partition ultimately led to the killing of six lakh people including children and women, 1.5 crore were displaced and became refugees (Karandikar 1999, 439).

In 1946, Congress had passed a resolution that it stood for united or *akhand* Bharat. Sardar Patel had claimed, 'sword will be met with sword.' Jawaharlal Nehru said, 'Pakistan is a fantastic nonsense.' Mahatma Gandhi had written in *Harijan* on 6 April 1949 and 13 April 1949, he said, 'Two nation theory is a baseless falsehood. My conscience abhors this very idea [...] Division of Bharat is a scenario that is worse than anarchy. It is unbearable chopping-off of limbs. Cut me down before you divide Bharat.' The Congress was shaken to the core due to the 'Direct Action' movement and abandoned the battle ground (Ranga Hari 2018, 104).

Many people ask, 'Why didn't the RSS oppose Partition?' The question that arises is this—what could have been done and what could have been achieved? Could they offer satyagraha and go to jail? Should the RSS have hit the road and gone violent? At that time, there was the interim government of Congress led by Nehru at the Centre. Could it have disturbed its own government? The Sangh was still sure that Gandhiji would stand by his word and not allow partition of the country. Guruji is quoted by his biographer having shown full faith in Gandhiji. And looking at the danger of the Muslim League-led violence, should the RSS have put its energies to protect Hindu society or lead an agitation against its own interim government that would leave entire society exposed to violence? These are questions that don't have easy answers.

In this uncertain and disturbing scenario, Guruji took up the responsibility of keeping the morale of common people high. He also sent a message across to people to conserve their energies and build up their strength to face the disaster looming ahead. Criticizing the 'weakness in action' of the leadership at that time, he said during the Vijayadashami festival on 5 October of 1946, 'Like Arjun, Hindu society finds itself mesmerized with the dilemma of action versus non-action, doing duty or not doing duty...' He went on to rouse the conscience of Hindu society,

> There is a lot of talk about not picking up arms and not taking revenge. But, I cannot agree with this current language of not reacting. This talk is not arising out of bravery. It is nothing but cowardice and fooling ourselves. It is 'adharma,' that is, immoral to inflict pain upon self.

He affirmed,

> It is our firm belief that every individual has a natural right to self-protection and the society made of such individuals also has the same right. I had read a bizarre statement in newspapers which said, 'An individual or society does not have the right to defend itself, only the government has this right, and a person should not take law unto his hands even if he is attacked.' Only Law has the right to defend an individual

> and society. Does it mean that we should sit quietly and wait for police if somebody attacks us? Should there be no attempt for self-defence? How far can this be justified? Right of self-defence is a right endowed by nature to every individual and society. (Ranga Hari 2018, 105)

This criticism and aggressive language of Guruji irked top Congress leaders no end and fuelled their animosity further.

Prominent leaders of the RSS including Guruji, Babasaheb Apte and Balasaheb Deoras along with Punjab prachaarak Madhavrao Muley toured troubled areas. Hundreds of young men and middle-aged people began joining the Sangh. Hindus and Sikhs in cities and villages of Punjab like Rawalpindi, Lahore, Peshawar, Amritsar, Jalandhar, Ambala, and so on organized themselves confidently. The *English Tribune* wrote, 'Punjab is the sword arm of Hindustan and RSS is the sword arm of Punjab.' (Ranga Hari 2018, 105)

Guruji addressed meetings in Sindh that had around eighty shakhas and fifty-two prachaaraks that also included L.K. Advani. The Head of Shri Ramkrishna Ashram, Swami Ranganathanand Maharaj was present in the huge public meeting held in D.B. High School grounds on Bunder Road of Karachi that Guruji addressed. Perturbed with the assertive growth of the RSS, the mouthpiece of the Muslim League, *Dawn*, wrote, 'If Congress leadership wishes to receive cooperation from Muslims, then it must ban [the] Sangh immediately.' India saw the nature of 'cooperation' when a train full of corpses and raped women carrying a taunting message reached Indian borders later.

There is an interesting anecdote about Pandit Nehru's visit to Hyderabad, Sindh around the same time. Muslim League supporters had threatened to sabotage Nehru's meeting openly. Fearing this threat, two local Congress leaders Chimandasji and Baba Kisanji met city Sanghchalak Hotchand and asked for the Sangh's support for a trouble-free meeting. The Sanghchalak agreed with open heart. Many swayamsevaks attended this meeting and it was conducted peacefully without any trouble (Ranga Hari 2018, 105, 106). This again highlights how the RSS always cooperated with the Congress with open heart.

Apart from the Muslim League, the Communist Party was also in favour of Partition and had passed a resolution in its favour. Under a political settlement, a coalition government of the Congress and the Muslim League formed a government in Delhi in September 1946. The League began showing its true colours again. The first day witnessed unruly scenes both inside and outside the assembly. They decided to repeat this show on the second day too. A top leader of Delhi state Congress, Lala Deshbandhu Gupta, came to the Sangh office in Kamla Nagar and met state prachaarak Vasantrao Oak. As a result of these talks, hundreds of swayamsevaks surrounded the assembly hall from the morning. League ruffians lost their nerves and the assembly took place. In spite of all these efforts, Partition of India was announced on 3 June 1947 (Ranga Hari 2018, 107).

Relations between Hindu and Sikh brethren were very close as both had been fighting to save their lands and their people from marauding Muslims. When Guruji was touring Punjab, members of the gurudwara committee of the holy Mastuana Sahib Gurudwara visited the camp to invite Guruji to the gurudwara. Many Jathedars (heads) of Gurudwaras of Pepsu region had also been invited. Chiefs of Gurudwaras gave him a heart-warming welcome. The chief of the Gurudwara said,

> It is our immense fortune that we have amongst us a great soul today who has tied the sacred thread of protection for defending dharma. He was offered *saropaa* [a sacred piece of cloth blessed by Shri Guru Granth sahib] after his short speech. (Ranga Hari 2018, 108)

Considering the grave situation in Punjab, the Sangrur and Phagwara training camps were disbanded before schedule and swayamsevaks were asked to go back to their homes and prepare plans for defending the society. They were also told that they should leave their posts only after safe passage of Hindu brothers and sisters to Hindustan (Ranga Hari 2018, 107). Swayamsevaks honoured this call till Partition-related violence abated and as many people as possible were brought back safely.

The situation had deteriorated so badly that even Sardar Patel had to admit, 'It won't be possible for the government to defend everybody. Each person will have to try to defend self.' In these tough times, swayamsevaks took up the responsibility of securing the society at risk to their lives. Sangh leaders including Guruji and Balasaheb Deoras were on the battlefield to guide the self-defence teams. Security camps filled up fast and additional arrangements had to be made in this emergency scenario. Middle-class swayamsevaks made arrangements for fifty to sixty displaced people in their homes. Nobody cared about the caste, sect or profession of these people (Ranga Hari 2018, 108).

One incident that shows the steely commitment of Guruji to the nation is worth sharing here. It was shared by Madhavrao Muley who headed the Sangh operations in those times.

> Guruji had to reach Ludhiana from Jalandhar but there were very heavy rains. Roads and normal train services were suspended. Railways told the team that they could arrange for a trolley. Muley sat on the trolley with Guruji and Shri Dharmavir but there was a huge nullah in Chahedu that had washed away one pillar of the railway bridge, leaving the railway track swinging freely with rail sleepers. Trolley-pullers refused to take the trolley over this track. Without seeking suggestions from others, Guruji stepped onto sleepers of swinging tracks without a second thought. Water was gushing ferociously just two–three feet below the loose railway tracks. Others had to follow him as there was no choice left. From Chahedu they found an engine that was to go to Goraya. The driver, upon hearing Guruji's name, promptly agreed to take them with him. Guruji and team reached Goraya, sitting in that engine. They finally reached Ludhiana by 5 p.m. after

> starting from Jalandhar at 7 a.m. Ludhiana programme was as per schedule. (Ranga Hari 2018, 109)

Apart from securing the lives of thousands of Hindus and Sikhs, the RSS also organized a large number of relief camps in nearly all districts of Punjab, parts of Jammu, and also in the east in Bengal. I have written a small book *The Sangh and Swaraj* in which I have summarized the massive efforts of the RSS in Sindh, Punjab, and Jammu and Kashmir. During these trying times, Guruji was most disturbed if someone called these displaced brethren as refugees. 'Guruji, after all, we are refugees.' On hearing these words, Guruji said immediately, 'No, you are not refugees. This nation belongs to each and every individual. All of you have the same rights over her. How can somebody be a "refugee" in one's own home?' He had unshakeable faith. 'Bharat is one, unbreakable [*akhand*] and all her citizens are children of this unified nation.' He felt that the word refugee was an obscenity used to insult those unfortunate fellow beings (Ranga Hari 2018, 110). While the nation celebrated Independence Day, Gandhiji was moving in riot-hit Bengal, and swayamsevaks were busy saving refugees from Punjab and taking care of them. None of these souls had any time to celebrate the day.

It is said that there is not one family in Punjab or Sindh who can forget the Sangh's role in saving them. Some years later, when renowned litterateur, P.L. Deshpande was chatting with Lieutenant General S.S.P. Thorat and his wife and Dr V.R. Karandikar, the author of *Teen Sarsanghchaalak*, about the RSS and was criticizing it, Mrs Thorat said, 'Whatever you may feel about the RSS, we cannot forget the work of RSS swayamsevaks in Punjab during Partition who fearlessly worked to save the honour of women and protect refugees' (Karandikar 1999, 454).

There is an almost forgotten chapter about Shri Guruji's role in the accession of Jammu and Kashmir to India that is not much discussed. He had paid a personal visit in October 1947 to persuade the Maharaja to accede to India. He did not believe in publicity or broadcasting the work of the Sangh so he never spoke about it.

His team on this visit included Vasantrao Oak and Barrister Narendrajeet Singh, as well as the regional prachaarak of that area, Madhavrao Muley, and four to five state-level workers of Jammu and Kashmir. On 18 October 1947, Guruji went in a private car to Karn Mahal to meet the Maharaja. After an initial informal chat, formal discussions began at 10:30 a.m. Nobody was present from either side during these discussions, so no one knows what transpired during the discussion. When the Maharaja came out to bid farewell to Guruji after the discussions, he came near his car and said, 'I will definitely weigh your suggestions carefully.' Before leaving, Guruji urged Maharaja, 'It may be a good idea to send the prince to Jammu and you should remain in Srinagar so people's morale will not dip' (Ranga Hari 2018, 112). This incident was corroborated in a signed statement by Captain Diwan Singh who was his ADC at that time and remained so until his death. This is also corroborated by Arun Bhatnagar, once a close aide of Sonia Gandhi, in his book, *Shedding the Past, Embracing the Future, 1906–2017*.

It is worth noting that Guruji repeatedly travelled through the western sector during very tense times. He conducted his last meeting on 7 August 1947 in Hyderabad, Sindh, which was attended by 35,000 (out of a population of 65,000) Hindus. This took place a week before Independence. Guruji directed a group of twelve select swayamsevaks to stay back in Karachi till their brethren were taken back to the safety of Bharat. They stayed back for nearly a year. This group was led by a Jhamatmal Wadhwani who later became a veteran leader of Jan Sangh, later BJP, in Mumbai. Rajpal Puri, state prachaarak of Sindh, led the refugee rescue and rehabilitation in Jodhpur. L.K. Advani was the karyavaah of the Karachi branch of the RSS at that time (Motwani and Wadhwani 2006, 108). The head of the Rashtra Sevika Samiti, Laxmibhai Kelkar, with her colleague, Venu Tai, also visited Karachi to boost the morale of the sisters there. They addressed a gathering of sevikas. She made arrangements to take as many women as possible back to safety (*Karmayogini Mausiji* 1996, 51–52).

Dawn of Independence and Oppression of RSS by Nehru-led Congress

Independence Day for the millions of Hindus, Sikhs and Bengalis meant nothing but disaster. For them it was the beginning of a dark night which they had never dreamt of. While Congress leaders escaped to the safe environs of Delhi and began preparing for the new government, the RSS cadre were fighting for the security and rehabilitation of their brethren on both sides of the new border and in Kashmir. Many of them had lost their own families and business, hearth and homes in the process. Ironically, many Congress leaders who had sought RSS help in this period, later spoke against the RSS.

Seen against the background of what happened from 1946 to August 1947, it is true that Guruji did not accept the Partition of the country till his last days. For example, in his lectures, he always said, 'Part of our country is called Pakistan today.' However, he never spoke in a critical way like the Communists who used to say things like, 'this independence is not true independence' or 'Independence Day is a day of fraud.' Guruji accepted the bitter truth, even if with anguish. Speaking on 9 August 1947 in Ahmedabad, he said, 'Members of a family don't celebrate birth of the first child if the mother dies during the birth of her son. A deep sense of grief envelopes the family... For me, the pain of getting separated from my brethren is unbearable' (Ranga Hari 2018, 117). Being a Punjabi, and having met many in our families who suffered and many whom I met later, I can very well identify with this emotion.

While the nation was going through these turbulent times, the Congress was busy playing political games. Rather than recognizing and appreciating the sterling services of the RSS to the nation, the leadership was trying to put it down. It was nothing but the fear of losing a monopoly built on a struggle for which the Congress was treated by all the freedom fighters as the common organization for a united struggle, where people represented political views right from Hindu nationalists to socialists. Dr Hedgewar too had underlined this time and again.

Nehru loyalists in the Congress opened the front against the RSS in Maharashtra. According to a report in the daily *Dainik Kaal,* dated 13 October 1947, the Satara Congress committee in Maharashtra passed a resolution and asked Chief Minister B.G. Kher to 'uproot Rashtriya Swayamsevak Sangh.' The committee boasted, 'otherwise we would destroy Sangh ourselves using 1942 type of terrorist methods.' The chief minister advised them, 'Don't take up an action in a mood of pessimism, or else you would be totally destroyed' (Ranga Hari 2018, 123). A big state-level camp of the RSS, to be attended by Sardar Patel and over 100,000 swayamsevaks in November 1947, was cancelled at the last moment. The excuse given was of a 'law and order situation.' Madhya Pradesh's home minister, Pandit Dwarika Prasad Mishra, made a statement that was soft towards the Sangh. Treating allegations of the opposing camps lightly, he told *Nagpur Navbhaarat* in a report dated from 19 December 1947,

> The very idea that [the] Sangh can overthrow government on the strength of lathis is laughable. It is surprising that this allegation was not made against the local DSP. I cannot believe at all that [the] Sangh is a political organization and that there is a possibility of it overthrowing Pandit Nehru's government (Ranga Hari 2018, 125).

Ram Madhav notes that D.P. Mishra later admitted in his autobiography,

> That Mahatma Gandhi's assassination gave a handle to unscrupulous politicians to defame and if possible to pull down their rivals is difficult to deny. The attempt was made in Delhi to bring Patel, a non-Brahmin, himself into disrepute and to cause a breach between him and Nehru is well known.[3]

[3]https://www.outlookindia.com/website/story/the-worst-that-the-rss-can-do/224844.

Next month, in November, a meeting of chief ministers was called in Delhi. The increasing popularity of the Sangh and the challenge arising out of it was the focus. The problem facing them was how to bridle the Sangh. Around this time, accusing swayamsevaks of fomenting riots in Kandaale in Uttar Pradesh, the Congress government there put up cases against them. These accusations were proven incorrect later on and they had to be released. Such evil ideas were floated in other places also. On 17 January 1948, a meeting of the All-India Congress Committee in Delhi passed a strongly worded resolution against the Sangh. It demanded state governments also to take anti-Sangh steps. The lowest units of the Congress were asked to follow this policy. During this time, the central government also released a circular that made it illegal for a government servant to be a member of the RSS. The leader of this anti-Sangh front was the UP minister Rafi Ahmed Kidwai (Ranga Hari 2018, 123).

In a public meeting on 6 January 1948, Sardar Patel said,

> Congress people in power should behave in a different way of dealing with [the] Sangh rather than laying stress on their own rights and powers. It is not possible to suppress an organization with the power of penal action. [Members of the] Sangh are not the type [of people] who will fight for selfish interests. They are patriots who love their motherland.

Within a few days, Nehru, as if in response to this speech, said in Amritsar, 'Sangh and Hindu Mahasabha people have insulted our national flag. They are traitors. I will crush them' (Ranga Hari 2018, 124).

Guruji responded to Nehru's threat in his speech in Amritsar indirectly in the public meeting saying, 'We shall face any disaster that befalls [the] Sangh successfully. This work has not grown with somebody's courtesy nor will it shut down if somebody stares at it with anger. It was not created by a paper resolution. Therefore, it can neither be dissolved by paper resolution' (Ranga Hari 2018, 127).

It was clear that the RSS would be the envy of others and suffer because of it and the internal politics of the Congress. Imagine the disappointment and sadness of the swayamsevaks who saw this happening despite their service and sacrifice in the wake of the Partition.

Assassination of Mahatma Gandhi and Persecution of RSS

At this difficult juncture, Mahatma Gandhi was assassinated by a Hindu, Nathuram Godse. On hearing that the person who fired at Gandhi ji was a Hindu, Guruji's immediate reaction was, 'Sangh work has suffered a setback of twenty years' (Karandikar 1999, 461). As the situation unfolded, we find that he was prophetic. The following is a brief account of events in the ensuing months of the assassination that proved momentous for the RSS.

Guruji was in Chennai in a small gathering of prominent citizens when the news of the assassination came in. He cancelled the meeting immediately. He passed instructions from Chennai to all the shakhas on the very same day, 'To express our grief due to sad demise of respected Mahatmaji, shakhas will observe condolence period for thirteen days and all daily programmes will be put on hold.' (Ranga Hari 2018, 128). It was an unprecedented move. Never in its history has the RSS ever suspended its daily shakha. It was not done for Dr Hedgewar or for any of its other top leaders. Guruji left for Nagpur on 31 January by air.

The strong language used by Guruji in his condolence messages tells us how anguished he was. In separate letters written to Pandit Nehru and Sardar Patel (in English to Nehru and in Hindi to Patel), he wrote,

> I was in Madras yesterday when I heard about the tragic news that has shaken the whole of humanity. Such an evil and condemnable incident should never have taken place in history. Heart is distressed with unbearable pain... It is difficult to find right words to condemn the person who has carried out this despicable act. One cannot even think of such

> a senseless evil act. What can one say of a person who has stunned the whole world into silence? (Ranga Hari 2018, 128)

Nehru used this incident to wreak vengeance on the RSS by naming it immediately without a shred of evidence. Crowds of goons surrounded Guruji's home on 1 February and stoned it. Uneasy swayamsevaks created a protective ring around his home (Ranga Hari 2018, 130). He counselled them to be patient and did not allow for deterioration in the situation. Guruji was picked up under the draconian sections 120, 307 and 302 on 3 February 1948. It was only on 7 February, realizing its foolishness, the government withdrew these sections and put him under the Defence Act (Ranga Hari 2018, 133). He asked his swayamsevaks to keep their cool even while their homes, their businesses and they themselves were being attacked. He did not want any division in the society that the Congress wished to create.

The court case for Gandhiji's assassination was conducted in the Red Fort in Delhi for two-and-half months. All accused, except two fugitives of Gwalior, had been arrested. The chargesheet of the case did not mention either the Sangh or any Sangh swayamsevak. Thus, people and rulers knew clearly that the Sangh had no involvement in this incident. But there was another bitter truth behind this Congress drama that lay hidden in government files for many years. A high-ranking police official in charge of the Gandhi assassination case, Sanjeevi, had submitted his report within one month of the incident. He had completed his job in seventeen days and handed over the complete report in writing to the home minister. Based on this report, the home minister had written a long letter urgently to the prime minister on 27 February 1948. (Das 1973)

- All the materials received through known-unknown, true-untrue, named and unnamed sources have been sifted thoroughly. 90 per cent of these are baseless speculative reports. Most of the allegations are about activities of RSS—that they distributed sweets, held celebrations. All this was found to be false upon investigation.

- Strong opponents of Bapuji's policies and thoughts, many of whom were members of the Hindu Mahasabha and RSS did welcome this murder. But, beyond this, there is no way one can drag RSS and Hindu Mahasabha members into this conspiracy on the basis of available evidence. The RSS may be responsible for some other disturbances but not for this one.
- Confessions of the conspirators prove that the RSS was not a party, in any way, to this conspiracy.

Thus, it is clear that when the Sarsanghchaalak was writing letters to the prime minister and the home minister about providing evidence of the RSS's involvement in Gandhiji's assassination or to lift its ban, they already knew the truth about the Sangh for months (Ranga Hari 2018, 140). This was horrible cynical politics that made thousands of Indians suffer for months and some for years because of irreparable damage to their professions and businesses. Many lost their jobs, especially government jobs.

Guruji was released in August 1948 as there was no ground to keep him under arrest. He wrote a number of letters to Nehru and Patel, visited Delhi a number of times to reason with the government, and asked them to produce evidence of RSS involvement—or lift the ban. He was arrested again on 12 November at night from Delhi where he had gone to demand either an evidence of the involvement of the RSS in Gandhiji's assassination or a lifting of the ban (Ranga Hari 2018, 147).

Since all their efforts fell on deaf ears, it was decided to launch a satyagraha for lifting the ban on the RSS. Guruji wrote a letter from jail to rouse swayamsevaks for the satyagraha. It was handed over to each satyagrahi. It was so inspiring that many swayamsevaks in jail had learnt this letter by heart. The last line of this famous said, 'So, arise with a victorious roar for Bharat Mata's glory that would reverberate from the horizons of the heart to the horizons of the universe and rest not till work is accomplished.'

The satyagraha that was devised was very simple. The leader

of a team would inform the police station in advance that he and the team were going to have a shakha in a particular place. At the appointed time, the shakha would be held. The police would swoop down on them and take them to jail. Nehru had dismissed the satyagraha saying, 'What will these urchins do?' But, the urchins were able to build up a huge satyagraha across India. The final number of arrests in this forty-five-day satyagraha from 9 December 1948 to 22 January 1949 was 77,090—more than the numbers arrested during the 1942 agitation (Ranga Hari 2018, 156). At many places the police were very rough and beat up young boys. Various newspapers and eminent personalities began criticizing the government for their oppressive behaviour. There were atrocities in jails too.

A strong reaction to the oppression of RSS youth was expressed by an ex-advocate general and renowned liberal leader T.R. Venkatram Shastri. It was published in a local daily.

> It is not a crime to express an opinion that Sangh swayamsevaks are innocent and it is not right to run this campaign of oppression against them. I have been told that infamous Moplah police has been brought to Madras to teach a lesson to these agitators of [the] Sangh. Some years back the British government had brought this same police to crush Congress agitators. I had agitated against this cruel oppression of British government. This agitation of mine was not taken as a crime, though there was a foreign government at that time. (Ranga Hari 2018, 153)

The government had no reason for the ban on the RSS as neither the accused nor the police or the courts had named the RSS anywhere. They needed a face-saving device, so the RSS was asked to produce a constitution. As mentioned in a letter by Guruji to the prime minister and home minister, the fact that the Congress did not have a constitution for fourteen years after it was founded was conveniently forgotten.

Venkatram Shastri became the mediator and went to meet

Guruji in jail. As he came out of Seoni Jail after meeting Guruji, he told Eknath Ranade, 'To make your Guruji agree to anything is like moving a mountain. Still, due to his respect for me, he agreed to my views with open heart. Now, provide me with the necessary material to help me prepare the constitution.' Eknath Ranade and Deendayal Upadhyay sat together to put together the working methodology of the Sangh that was already being practised. After discussions with other seniors, a primary draft was handed over to Shastriji. A legal authority, Shastriji, shaped it into a proper constitution and sent it to Barrister M.R. Jaikar in Pune for the final finishing touches. He gave it the required finishing touches and sent it back very soon, and the constitution of the Sangh took form (Ranga Hari 2018, 157). However, at the last moment, the Nehru government refused to accept the constitution on a flimsy pretext of Shastri not having been authorized and did not lift the ban. The stalemate continued. The idea was to split the young RSS leadership while the Sarsanghchaalak was in prison.

Guruji kept writing to the government. Fed up with the government's games, in one of his letters Guruji wrote,

> In a matter like this, a suggestion of an independent enquiry committee can come only from people who do not understand even the basics of governance—I am obliged for being told about this. I accept my ignorance on this subject. Not just an ordinary human being, but even Mahatma Gandhi, himself, had a right to this ignorance, so I consider this a matter of pride for me. If this is how your government basically thinks then it is dangerous. (Ranga Hari 2018, 161)

Support and sympathy was building up for the Sangh. The Bhaiyyaji Dani–Balasaheb Deoras duo took an aggressive stance. When a government-appointed anonymous person met Bhaiyyaji Dani to get the Sangh's opinion, Bhaiyyaji showed him the typewritten copy of the document about the formation of the proposed political party. Vasantrao Oak also followed the same strategy. When these details reached various ministries, many chief ministers started saying, 'We shall have to reconsider the proposal of April about ban on Sangh.' Many ministers expressed the opinion that if the Sangh entered politics, it would be transformed from *'brahmin'* to *'brahmraakshas'*, that is from a peaceful person to a righteous demon. It seems Nehru had also seen the writing on the wall. We can conclude so because the chapter covering this issue in the words of Nehru was titled 'the less of these bans the better' (Ranga Hari 2018, 165).

There was lot of pressure on the RSS to join politics right from the freedom struggle days. There was an intellectual struggle between Nehru and Sardar Patel. Patel wanted a patriotic and nationalist organization like the RSS to join the Congress and strengthen it. He expressed this wish during backroom talks with RSS leaders during its ban in October 1948. While rejecting this suggestion in November 1948, Guruji at that time had said,

> It has been suggested that [the] Sangh should become part of a political party. This would mean that apart from political parties, no other organization or activity including cultural work would have any right to be alive. It is an unacceptable situation and it doesn't behove people who give this advice. Cultural activities should be free from political running around. (Tapasvee 2001, 530–32)

Pandit Moulichandra Sharma, an eminent personality, was finally drafted by the government to break the stalemate and get out of the self-made mess. He met Guruji in jail. He was warned by young leaders led by Balasaheb Deoras and Eknath Ranade that the Sangh wouldn't budge and was ready to form a political party if any more games were played. After the meeting, he shared his experience and showed his amazement about Guruji's conduct when he went to meet him.

> His carefree countenance, generous heart and sense of affection created an impact on me with every passing moment. I could feel in my heart that I was sitting in front of an extraordinary divine personality. I kept the documents in

> front of him after taking tea [made personally by Guruji]. He said, 'Give these to me, I will sign them.' I told him, 'First read these letters properly, think over them. It is possible that some words in them may not be of your liking. He wrote that letter on a letter pad with his name, signed it and gave the letter to me. (Ranga Hari 2018, 166)

This quote shows a *sthitpradnya* personality, that is, one who is not swayed easily by circumstances. It also shows his complete trust in his young colleagues.

Moulichandra Sharma the document to Bhaiyyaji Dani and Balasaheb Deoras first and then gave it to then chief minister Dwarika Prasad Mishra who read it out to Sardar Patel in Dehradun on telephone. Sardar Patel was recuperating after a heart attack, but gave it his acceptance and directed that the letter be sent directly to the Delhi office. The Dehradun-Nagpur-Delhi hotline did its work on the midnight of 11 July and before sunrise on 12 July, the ban on the Sangh was lifted (Ranga Hari 2018, 166). Ironically, the ban, which was not lifted earlier on the flimsy pretext that Shri Venkatram Shastri did not have written authority, was lifted on the basis of a mere telephonic conversation.

A New Beginning

A new challenge now faced the RSS leadership—to kick-start the organization that had faced serious damage due to corroding struggle during Partition and the ban. Thousands of swayamsevaks had been uprooted, their businesses destroyed, jobs lost and studies disrupted. This is the scenario that Guruji faced. On his release, Guruji received a huge response from the people across Bharat. He did not let the bitterness of the past few months affect the Sangh's work. In his first talk, after restart of shakha activity and its offices, he said,

> Our work is beginning again today. A person waking up from sleep feels refreshed and energetic. We too have to get down to work with [the] same enthusiasm... We have to make this

> work magnificent by developing it. Purity of the work depends on the purity of heart. Heart cannot be pure without pure emotion of love... Whether one is a friend or an enemy, our approach should always be 'maa vidvishaav hai' [animosity towards none]... Bharatvarsh represents the colossal form of our nation and we are all arms, limbs and parts of this body, we have to develop this gigantic magnificent work, winning over everybody with allegiance to the goal and our affectionate behaviour. (Ranga Hari 2018, 171)

This imagery of the nation as *'Virat Purush'* and its citizens as its limbs and its cells was in consonance with views of Aurobindo. He followed this principle of 'animosity towards none' all through his life.

He wrote more than twenty letters in a day to leaders like Gopalswamy Iyengar and Shyama Prasad Mukherjee in English, to Sardar Patel and Purushottamdas Tandon in Hindi, and to B.R. Ambedkar in Marathi. He met Pandit Nehru and Sardar Patel in the first week of August (Ranga Hari 2018, 171). The only thought behind these efforts was to put an end to the mindset of conflict that had erupted in the interregnum and create an environment of mutual co-operation and friendliness once again in the country.

In his letter to Pandit Nehru, showing his readiness to forget the past and move ahead in nation-building, he wrote,

> I am trying hard as it requires uncommon efforts to wipe away bitter memories from the hearts of my co-workers. There is no sense in remaining lost in memories of the past. I am doubtlessly sure about receiving co-operation from the government that will help generate a healthy atmosphere based on mutual affection, respect and co-operation that would result in a helpful environment of goodwill. (Ranga Hari 2018, 171)

Responding to him, Sardar Patel wrote back within three days on 21 July. 'As you have said in your public address, [the] situation in the country is such and things are happening in such a manner, that we should all look at the present and the future rather than [looking] into the past' (Ranga Hari 2019, 171).

His urge to work together with people of all shades of opinion and bring back normalcy, showed in his speech at the felicitation programme in Pune,

> It is true that there are differences between [the] government and us, but is there any place where there are no differences? There are differences even within families. Nurturing unity in diversity is the real test of democracy. We have proven true to this test... Our own desire is that this nation, like sacred Ganges, should flow uninterrupted, with fulfilment of all the desired traits. For this, responsibility is upon each of us. Let us re-initiate our work with renewed energy, but while doing this let us not have mentality of jealousy or animosity... It is but natural to feel angry, but in not letting it overpower us is our greatness. Attaining the highest stage is humanity. It has been well said, '*Beeti taahi bisaar de, aage ki sudhi ley*' [forget the past, take care of the future]. (Ranga Hari 2018, 174)

At another time, he told swayamsevaks, 'You don't break your teeth, if they bite your tongue by mistake. This entire society is ours.'

His conduct throughout the crises and his readiness to wipe out the bitterness showed a statesman who was interested in national good and was ready to pay any price for harmony. Instead of diminishing, his popularity soon reached dizzying heights. *Amrit Bazar Patrika* printed on 28 August noted:

> When Shri M.S. Golwalkar reached Delhi station and the way he conducted himself when he was greeted by huge crowds; one could see that he had all the qualities of a winner... It seemed that his standing was in no way less than Pandit Nehru or Sardar Patel. When there was need for silence, such would be silence that you could hear a pin drop and when there was

> an occasion to exhibit enthusiasm, then claps and cheers rose from the thousands of throats in unison... People seemed to have as much faith in the swayamsevak wearing black caps as they had in members of army and police managing the programme. (Ranga Hari 2018, 178)

The BBC, which was considered the most prestigious radio station of that time, noted,

> Who after Nehru and Sardar Patel? The answer to this question is not Leftist leaders but Sangh chief Golwalkar. When he came to Delhi 250,000 people were present to hear him. Only Nehru can attract such a big crowd. Such a grand welcome of the chief of an organization banned for nineteen months and such a mammoth meeting is an example by itself. Propaganda has been unleashed [by] showing [the] Sangh as [a] Nazi organization and [the] Sangh chief as a dictator. But, one could not discern anything in Shri Golwalkar that could be compared to European dictator Hitler or Mussolini. (Ranga Hari 2018, 178)

Guruji had once said, 'Train is my home.' During his unending travels, he used to stay in one of these four places: first, the train bogey as he had said; second, at Sangh camps with swayamsevaks, third, with Sangh workers, sympathizers or office-bearers while on tour; and fourth, at Hedgewar Bhavan—the Nagpur Central Office of the Sangh (Ranga Hari 2018, 87). In fact, this culture of staying with families began with the founder of the Sangh. Guruji converted this into an arrangement and a part of Sangh's system of working. This arrangement is still prevalent.

People used to wonder how young boys whom they saw playing on grounds or doing parade could achieve extraordinary feats during Partition and satyagraha against the first ban. An army officer once asked him the secret behind the daring feats of RSS swayamsevaks. Stressing upon the working methodology of the Sangh, Guruji said,

> There are only two secrets of our work—First is that there is no secret. And, second is, Kabaddi. This programme, even today, has the same character. Motherland below, God created skies above, and Hindu society all around us. Based on these elements, Kabaddi has been successful. So much power was generated by this kabaddi; power that saved lives, honour and wealth of lakhs of people during partition of Punjab... From where did we get this power? Did we have manifestos at that time? Did we have rosy pictures of the future? Or did we organize conferences or publicized our views? We only played kabaddi. This is absolutely true. The foundation of our unified soul, in that kabaddi came to signify 'organization.' We need to understand this well. (Ranga Hari 2018, 188)

There were many attacks on Guruji after the ban was lifted in Maharashtra in the name of anti-Brahmanism, even though he was being feted all over India. Swayamsevaks would guard him in uniform, but he always kept his calm. The RSS cadre and leadership saw to it that there was no violence or retaliation despite provocations (Karandikar 1999, 480). One needs to put in a small reminder that there were widespread vengeful riots targeted against brahmins and RSS swayamsevaks in Maharashtra, which were made especially bitter in Pune, Sangli and Kolhapur by Congress members and Congress-inspired goons after Gandhiji's assassination. Many swayamsevaks and a large number of brahmins lost their homes, businesses and jobs. It is estimated that hundreds, if not thousands, lost their lives. However, no enquiry was done by the government. Koenrad Elst dwells on this issue in his book *Why I Killed the Mahatma: Uncovering Godse's Defence.*[4]

Just as the Sangh was settling down to its work, Bengal saw a repetition of Punjab. A heavy inflow of persecuted and oppressed refugees began flowing in from 'Pakistani Bengal' to

---

[4]Refer to https://www.indiatoday.in/lifestyle/what-s-hot/story/this-author-s-book-debunks-several-myths-associated-with-mahatma-gandhi-s-assassination-1186885-2018-03-11.

'Bharatiya Bengal.' Hindu organizations like Ramkrishna Ashram and Pranavaananda Ashram also fell prey to such Islamic attacks. Guruji rushed there as soon as he got the news and met Hindu leaders personally. The Sangh work here was not as strong as it was in Punjab. Even then Vaastuhaaraa Sahaayata Samiti (Displaced People's Relief Committee) was constituted under the chairmanship of Barrister Ranadev Chaudhary on 8 February 1950. Additional prachaaraks were deputed from nearby states to help it out. Responsibility of the whole exercise was put on the shoulders of Eknath Ranade. After reaching Delhi from Kolkata, Guruji appealed to the people to send relief material to Bengal. He gave a detailed statement informing people of the tragic situation of Bengal. He stated, 'I believe absolutely that it is of utmost importance to help Hindus there. It is not possible to describe the horrible condition of people there. Piercing the steel wall put over East Bengal, we are getting news regularly about inhuman killings, robbery, arson, rapes and religious conversions.'

> It would not serve any purpose if we forget that atrocious condition of these people is a result of our leaders' acceptance of religious based division of our country. It is paramount that our leaders should free themselves and people of this delusion that Partition is not based on religion but on geography. Reality is clear and we should face it. It will not do any good if people who control the reins of power do not accept this truth. [...] This confused thinking about Partition along with distorted ideas about secular [*vidharmee*] state being presented before the nation on and off, is proving to be a major hurdle in resolving the problems faced by the nation. What will you call these one and half crore unfortunate brethren—foreigners or locals? The rehabilitation minister has concluded that they are foreigners and they have become an unnecessary burden on us. But is this view right? Using softest possible words, one can only say that this view is absolutely inhuman. Not only is this view their condemnable insult but

> also something because of which they are being deprived of their right of Bharatiya nationality and being sacrificed at the altar of Pakistani cruelty. (Ranga Hari 2018, 189)

Appealing to the government he said,

> It is my request to the government and especially to the Prime Minister is that he should find a solution to stop these bestial atrocities of Pakistan and rescue our brothers and sisters on the other side of the border. If our policy is going to be vague, confused and weak then the government will be accused of the sin of complete devastation of one and half crore innocent Bharatiyas and its esteem will be reduced to dust. It may be [through] taking police action or it may be [by] sending Muslims to Pakistan and get Hindus back to Bharat in exchange. Any stern action must be initiated immediately, so that our one and half crore brethren of our own flesh and blood should be able to lead a secure life. (Ranga Hari 2018, 190)

Shri Guruji appealed to people that they should not exhibit their anger in a way that would create hurdles in government's working. Everyone should come forward to serve with body, soul and funds and open their hearts to give place to their miserable brothers and sisters. More than five thousand swayamsevaks joined the relief work. Guruji wrote a letter that was like a report on the prevailing scenario and the state of relief work to Sardar Patel on 5 April. He also met him on 12 April and informed him about his efforts. Patel expressed hope that Sangh work would also expand in north east region of Bharat (Ranga Hari 2018, 190).

There was a disastrous earthquake in Assam around the Independence Day of 1950, resulting in immeasurable losses. Sangh swayamsevaks rushed to help the affected people. Sarsanghchaalak Guruji also reached there. A Relief Committee with its centre at Dibrugarh was set up under the Chairmanship of retired Justice Kamakhya Ram Baruah. After reaching Calcutta, he sent out an appeal to all the countrymen to help unfortunate victims of the earthquake. The response to this appeal was also good (Ranga Hari 2018, 191). The RSS was fighting on various fronts during these years even as it rebuilt the organization.

Thus, the new beginning was not easy. On one hand, it was about recreating the confidence in swayamsevaks who began putting together their broken lives, and on the other, motivating them to the task of helping their brethren in distress. There was too much on the plate.

Testing Times and Serious Churn within RSS

The period after lifting of the ban was the toughest period for the RSS. In spite of the best efforts, number of shakhas dropped in next five or six years, as did attendance. Swayamsevaks were busier with family issues and self-sustenance. The number of prachaaraks was reduced by about forty per cent. Bhaiyyaji Dani as Sarkaryavaah played a major role in keeping the morale of swayamsevaks high in initial two years after the ban was lifted. Guruji was not perturbed, or didn't show it, if he was. He kept working with focus. The situation changed slowly by 1965 (Karandikar 1999, 483-484). Recall that Guruji had said after Gandhiji's assassination, 'Sangh work has gone back by twenty years.'

Devendra Swaroop notes that actually the real pain within the RSS was that it lagged behind the timeline-based goals set by Dr Hedgewar. Guruji expressed this anguish in 1960 in a meeting of RSS prachaaraks,

> Someone will ask when will our work get over. Dr Hedgewar had expected it to reach a certain stage in fifteen years. Unfortunately, he died fifteen years after he began this work. In his last stage he had given a time limit of three more years to complete this work. Why this limit of three years? I believe that Dr Hedgewar was a visionary. If things had moved the way and efforts aligned in the troubled year of 1942, then the future of this nation would have been different. But, people

> don't think in this way about this period. (*Shri Guruji Samagra Darshan,* Vol. 4, 2005, 43)

He further noted in this lecture how the black shadow of Partition sucked away the energy of the organization followed by the struggle to get the RSS ban removed, sapping the organization further. In all, from 1946 to 1949, the RSS had to continuously struggle on these two issues. Then, there were disasters noted above that hit the nation and the RSS put in a lot of efforts. The Sangh lost these years of struggle at a huge cost to its cadre. It is equally true that if the RSS and its swayamsevaks had not been involved in saving Hindu and Sikh refugees and then in the satyagraha to get the unjust ban lifted, the picture would have been different (Swaroop 2009, 84).

This intellectual churning was also reflected in its own periodicals. *Organiser* in 1949 carried editorials by K.R. Malkani and articles by Prof. Balraj Madhok that urged the RSS to join politics. One of the earliest prachaaraks of the RSS, Dadarao Paramarth, who began work with Dr Hedgewar from 1930 during the Non-cooperation Movement as a young boy, also supported this idea. Balasaheb Deoras wrote an article in *Yugdharm* titled, '*Sangh ka agla kadam*' (next step of RSS) that stated that the Sangh would now work in every area of social life. This article was discussed widely during those days. We will see in Chapter 4 that he was called a living image of Dr Hedgewar by Guruji himself and was Sarsanghchaalak for twenty-one years after Guruji left this world. Delhi state prachaarak, Vasantrao Oak, a prominent figure of the RSS who had begun RSS work in Delhi and expanded it successfully, was also a vocal supporter of the RSS joining politics (Swaroop 2009, 127).

There were two different streams of thought in the Sangh. One that wished to move away from the present working methodology of the Sangh and work for the reformation of society in a non-political creative way. The second viewpoint was to enter politics and work towards rebuilding the nation. Many believed that it was not just the last two years, but the RSS working style needed rethinking since its last five to six from 1942. In those intense debates about utility of Sangh, someone asked, what if karyakartas leave and Sangh work crumbles, Guruji said, 'Well, if everything crumbles down, I will begin from the beginning' (Pachpore 2011, 51). Common swayamsevaks believed in Guruji's intellect and strategic thinking. Slowly, they turned to the idea propounded by Guruji that a shakha-based system of the RSS was the best way to move forward.

The most serious upheaval took place in Maharashtra. A group of dedicated RSS swayamsevaks and prachaaraks who had worked for long years in the RSS believed that the organization's work should take a new direction now. They were from Pune, Bombay and some other parts of Maharashtra. They believed that the oath they had taken in the RSS to gain freedom had been fulfilled. With time, people were also coming out of the pain of Partition. These idealist senior workers felt that there were new challenges before the nation and the RSS was not giving enough attention to current issues affecting the society. Entire efforts of the Sangh with a large number of dedicated swayamsevaks were going only in one direction. Such youth felt that despite raising these issues, the seniors had not responded to them (Karandikar 1999, 480–81).

Such disaffection had also arisen in other states but senior workers and praacharaks managed to handle them tactfully. Those regions had also begun many other activities, not associating them directly with the RSS. However, in Maharashtra, the situation worsened as the then seniors, probably, did not handle such concerns sensitively. There was one meeting headed by Dadasaheb Apte, the much-respected senior prachaarak, who handled their questions sensitively. After the meeting he told one of the upset workers, 'Have faith in me, whatever you are saying, will happen soon' (Karandikar 1999, 490–91). But the disatisfied workers had probably already made up their mind.

Guruji was of the view that major work of the RSS was to create patriotic people with character. Unless this work reached a certain stage, getting into other fields might be counterproductive. He believed that the Sangh had not reached that stage. In fact, the Sangh was highly weakened due to the energy-sapping episodes of Partition and the RSS ban. He felt, 'On one side people's expectations from [the] Sangh have increased multifold, on the other hand [the] Sangh work itself has weakened. Therefore, to say that we can reform society [by] undertaking other work is meaningless' (Swaroop 2009, 128).

Another meeting with Guruji took place in Nagpur, which was attended by unhappy seniors like Madhukar Rao Deval, D.V. Gokhale (who later became a renowned journalist) and G. Majgaonkar. Later they met Dattopant Thengdi, a young but experienced prachaarak who was then about thirty-one years old and stayed at the Nagpur RSS office. Deval was very aggressive even while talking to him. He told Dattopant, 'You must be complimented. You are working among students and labour—much different from RSS work. But you are staying in RSS central office.' Dattopant told them, 'But, I am not doing anything on my own; whatever I am doing, is on the directions of Guruji!' But, somehow, this evolution in the RSS work did not strike Deval. His ego perhaps did not allow him to understand the changes taking place in the RSS (Karandikar 1999, 491).

It seems that those who left in a hurry did not have the patience to see the changing facets of the Sangh's work. As noted above, activities to expand Sangh work beyond shakhas had already begun. But Guruji believed in talking about any new idea only after it had struck roots.

Later when Balasaheb Deoras became the Sarsanghchaalak, he went to meet his old friends to fill the chasm of years and see the progress of Dr Pendse and Deval's projects. Many of his other friends of that time also joined in (Karandikar 1999, 494).

After years, a need for a personal assistant (*niji karyavaah* in RSS terminology) to the Sarsanghchaalak was felt. This is because his engagements had become more widespread. For this, Dr Abaji Thatte was deputed to help Guruji during this period. He was a prachaarak from Bombay and practised medicine before he was assigned the responsibility of being Guruji's assistant. He was with Guruji for nearly twenty-two years like his shadow. Only people close to him knew about his knowledge and understanding of the Sangh. He was witness to Guruji's meetings with RSS swayamsevaks and outsiders, social and political leaders. After Guruji passed away, he was given some all-India responsibilities, before he retired due to ill health. Till his last breath, he never spoke of or boasted about what he had witnessed or shared. It was the highest form of self-abnegation. When somebody asked him to write a biography of Guruji, he said, 'Hanuman did not write Ramayan. Rishi Valmiki wrote it' (Karandikar 1999, 548–49). This practice of assigning a prachaarak as personal assistant to the Sarsanghchaalak was extended to Sarkaryavaah and became a regular practice.

Expanding Horizons of RSS: The Gradual Unfolding

Understanding the serious situation by the end of 1946, Guruji found it necessary to reach out to people and explain the Sangh's point of view in Punjab and Delhi. The weekly *Organiser* started publication in July 1947. The publication *Panchjanya* had Atal Bihari Vajpayee as its first editor, while *Rashtrashakti* in Maharashtra was edited by C.P. Bhishikar. Both of them were prachaaraks. Nearly all states had their own regional periodicals over time. Dailies such as *Swadesh* from Lucknow and *Bharatvarsh* from Delhi emerged. The news agency *Hindusthan Samachar* serving regional languages came up in 1958, and was led by Dadasaheb Apte. He was then practising law but stopped after his third Sangh Shiksha Varg. Inspired by Guruji, he became a prachaarak. He also wrote many books (Karandikar 1999, 499–500). An English daily *Motherland* was launched in the 1970s, but folded up during the Emergency period.

The direction for swayamsevaks in media was (and it continues to be till this day): 'There should not be propaganda for propaganda's sake. The objective should be to provide people with information, and that information should never be inflated to make [the] Sangh look good.'

The first steps towards an organization outside the RSS were taken with Akhil Bharatiya Vidyarthi Parishad (ABVP). It was founded during the RSS ban of 1948. A key strength of the RSS is youth. During the ban, they couldn't attend daily shakhas. To keep them engaged, the first get-together happened in Delhi University. It was followed by Punjab University and more colleges. In the second half of 1948, Vedprakash Nanda and Acharya Giriraj Kishore, both prachaaraks, began this activity. In July, more workers came together in Delhi and ABVP was born. Dattopant Thengdi and Dattaji Didolkar played key roles in its growth. Prof. Yashwantrao Kelkar from Bombay later took full responsibility of the organization and took it to great heights (Karandikar 1999, 501). We should note that Guruji was in jail at that time. This initiative took place through his senior workers, showing the synergy between him and his colleagues. It reflects on the unity of purpose of the Sangh workers, wherever they are.

ABVP gained domination in the student world. However, the most notable project of ABVP was to bring in young teenage boys from tribal areas of the Northeast and host them with families for a few years and educate them in schools in Bombay, Pune, and other cities. This initiative was called Students' Experience in Interstate Living (SEIL). By 1966, this idea picked up well and nearly 400 students came to different cities to stay with host families like their family members. Similarly, students from different places used to visit the Northeast for two-four weeks and stay with locals where possible and interact with them. A part of the results one sees in the Northeast now can be attributed to this idea. As a general rule, Maharashtra was assigned the role of the guardian state for the Northeast in general—whether it was sending out a prachaarak or raising resources for schools or hostels or health facilities. Any keen observer who has studied the RSS will find most of the prachaaraks from Maharashtra have been prachaaraks in the Northeast at some stage or other. Even

Dr Mohan Bhagwat has served in Northeast as a prachaarak.

In 1946, a swayamsevak from Punjab, Jagdish Chandra Sharda Shastriji, on his way to Kenya to work as a teacher decided to offer the Sangh prayer to the motherland on board the ship in the evening. Hearing him reciting the prayer, another Gujarati swayamsevak, Manek Rughani, joined him. By the time the ship anchored in Mombassa in the third week of September, this group had expanded to seventeen—many of them having no earlier connection with the RSS (Shastri 2008, 27). Officially, the first shakha inspired by the RSS began in Kenya on 14 January 1947. It was named Bharatiya Swayamsevak Sangh (BSS).

Shastriji had to take up a teaching job in Kenya because of financial constraints. He met his senior prachaarak Chamanlal, and expressed his unhappiness at leaving Bharat. Chamanlalji advised him that he would not be able to resolve his financial issues unless he took this chance. Upon his advice, he assured Chamanlalji, 'Wherever I go, I will take the Sangh with me' (Shastri 2008, 20). This was the inspiration. It is typically the way various organizations inspired by the RSS or affiliated to the RSS have come up.

Dr Mangalsein, who later became a minister in the Haryana Cabinet, had started Bharatiya Swayamsevak Sangh (BSS) with some friends in then Rangoon in 1950. But during this period, countless Bharatiyas had to leave Brahmadesh (now Myanmar) and come to Bharat due to political upheaval there. Sangh activities were stopped because of the disturbances. After five years, Shri Ram Prakash Dhir, a Burmese citizen when it was part of Bharat, was sent there to re-organize Sangh work. He had become a prachaarak when he came to Bharat for studies and joined the RSS in 1942 in Jalandhar. Ram Prakashji restarted the work based on his experience in Punjab. He undertook many experiments to spread Sangh work among Hindus and Buddhists of Brahmadesh in those trying times (Ranga Hari 2018, 223). In the process, he developed warm relations with the highly respected U Chhaan Thun, who was the then president of World Fellowship of Buddhists, writer of the Burmese Constitution and chief justice of its Supreme Court.

U Chhaan Thun expressed a wish to meet Guruji whenever an opportunity arose. He came to Bharat with his wife in 1959 to take part in the World Jurist Conference (Ranga Hari 2018, 224). He also took part in Bombay's Makar Sankranti festival of the Sangh and was on the stage with Guruji for some time. He suggested many constructive ideas for spreading BSS work in Myanmar, including a change in its name to suit the religious and social environment there. Guruji readily agreed to most of his suggestions, including changing the name of BSS to Sanatan Dharma Swayamsevak Sangh (SDSS). The first stanza of the SDSS prayer is the panchsheel prayer of the Buddhist religion (Ranga Hari 2018, 227).

Different RSS-inspired organizations came up in different countries over the years. Later, coordinators of such Hindu organizations decided to have a common nomenclature and the name Hindu Swayamsevak Sangh (HSS) was coined. Each HSS is registered locally in that country and has its own constitution and office-bearers, with some basic coordination between them. It was in 1990 that HSS from various countries came together in India in Bangalore in a camp called Vishwa Sangh Shivir (VSS). It was meant for having closer coordination between the organizations and to work out some common ideas for Hindu communities abroad. This is now a regular feature and these VSS camps take place every five years. HSS can be said to be the first Indian citizens' body that represented Hindu interests locally as an umbrella organization for many other Indian organizations and also to talk to the Indian government through local embassies and consulates. HSS organizations exist in nearly forty countries.

Chamanlalji, a prachaarak stationed in Jhandewalan, was the single point of contact since 1946 for the swayamsevaks who went outside Bharat. They would make it a point to visit Jhandewalan to meet him and re-energize their spirits. He maintained relations with thousands of swayamsevaks overseas through letters and personal meetings. Laxmanrao Bhide was later deputed to BSS in Kenya around 1957 as the first prachaarak of Sangh associated work outside Bharat (Shastri 2008, 49).

I was fortunate to meet and work with both these prachaaraks; they were very simple and humble. They never displayed any ego that they had raised Hindu organizations across the world. A graduate with impressive academics, Chamanlalji came from a wealthy family from Punjab. He had never travelled overseas but his knowledge of foreign affairs was amazing. A law graduate, Bhideji was an acclaimed kabaddi player. He was senior prachaarak in UP with Deendayal Upadhyay, Bhaurao Deoras and Nanaji Deshmukh before he went to Kenya. He travelled to nearly eighty countries.

The Vishwa Hindu Parishad (VHP), founded later in 1964, has connections in some more countries. Hindu communities are thus organized on the common theme of working for the well-being of Hindus in nearly eighty countries. They are well-integrated with the local communities and carry out social work there for the local as well as the Indian community. When some of them asked Guruji what their organizational goal should be, he said,

> While staying in another country, as we leave behind our country even for a short period, we carry a sombre responsibility. People of those countries are going to judge our country through our behaviour [...] Taking care of many distracting issues, we should keep in touch with our other brethren and exchange thoughts. As we observe the wealthy life of those countries, we should commit ourselves to creating better life in our own country. Without sacrificing our self-pride, our special character and being firm about keeping our best qualities intact, we should absorb the best qualities of the host country. (Golwalkar 2008, 326)

On another occasion guiding a team from an African country, Golwalkar said,

> The society there is awakening. It has awakened to a large extent, but progress in the vital fields of education, commerce,

> industry etc. leaves much to be desired. It should be highly valuable for us to put in our strength [and] intelligence to help them achieve this progress comprehensively. It seems right to be a citizen of a newly independent country and be seen as one of them in this endeavour for development. (Golwalkar 2008, 329)

This guiding principle has led to these Hindu organizations integrating well with the local society and working for it whenever needed. Many Hindu organizations began *sewa* in host countries too and this practice carries on.

It was the effort of these bodies that resulted in Pravasi Bharatiya Divas under the NDA government led by Atal Bihari Vajpayee. It was a major shift from the days when Indian governments used to look at Indian diaspora as a liability and a community for whom India had no obligations. They treated all of them as people who had migrated to other countries out of choice, which was not wholly true. Treating our brethren as assets and not liability was another success of RSS-inspired Indians settled or working outside India. Overcoming US sanctions after the Pokhran nuclear tests was the first illustration of the power of People of Indian Origin (PIO). Now during Narendra Modi's leadership, we have seen how this soft power has been leveraged to provide more heft to India's diplomatic efforts.

The birth of Vanvasi Kalyan Ashram also has the stamp of Guruji's inspirational personality. Ramakant Keshav (Balasaheb) Deshpande who had struggled hard against the British during the independence struggle was appointed as the regional officer in the Madhya Pradesh government. Observing his capability, honesty, dedication, courage, strong willpower and grip over administration, missionaries took him as their biggest enemy. The reason was that he had ably assisted the Niyogi Commission set up by Madhya Pradesh's Congress government, headed by Ravi Shankar Shukla, which laid bare the machinations of the Church for converting the gullible tribals. They began harassing him with their clout in bureaucracy. Balasaheb Deshpande once went to the capital city,

Nagpur, for some official work and met Guruji. He apprised him about dishonest bureaucrats and cunning missionaries. Guruji's advice was,

> If you think that you can serve the society by being a government servant then you will never get rid of this problem. You are a lawyer by training. Why don't you get rid of this weight of government off your shoulders? You can work as a lawyer without any help from anybody. You will get sufficient time for this work and earn respect and power in the society. *Apna haath Jagannath.* [One's own hand is the hand of God]. (Ranga Hari 2018, 245)

Saying so, Guruji reminded him of their meeting in the Dhantoli shakha in 1938. This reminder and guidance created a warm bond. Balasaheb gave up his government job and began his law practice in Jashpur in 1951. In 1952, Guruji sent a thirty-seven-year-old prachaarak of Khandwa region, Moreshwar Ketkar, to assist him. Both of them worked very closely. The Maharaja of Jashpur, Shri Vijay Bhushan Singh Judeo, was their pillar of strength. The confluence of this triumvirate resulted in the birth of Vanvasi Kalyan Ashram, and they were joined in by nine more locals on 26 December 1952 (Ranga Hari 2018, 245).

By this time, the bittersweet relations between the RSS and the Hindu Mahasabha had matured to mutual respect. Veer Savarkar had decided to dissolve Abhinav Bharat on 9 May 1952 as he believed that its goal of freedom had been achieved. Guruji also received special invitation for this massive conference. He gave a short speech and paid tributes to all the revolutionaries and showed his respect for Savarkar (Ranga Hari 2018, 196). It would be apt to recall here that Gandhiji's views about dissolution of the Congress were also the same but were not accepted by his followers.

In a significant move to motivate swayamsevaks to contact and reach out to society, Guruji initiated the movement for cow protection by harnessing the religious pull of sadhus. Guruji was pained that except for their relations with their followers, sadhus and *maths* were cut off from the society in general. Guruji used a meeting of Bharatiya Sadhu Samaj in 1952, where he had been invited, to convey his message. He tried to raise their national consciousness and exhorted the sadhus to reawaken the spirit of Bharat. He said,

> When the British conspired to enslave Bharat intellectually, a tradition of sadhus was born to spread the light of brilliance. Swami Vivekananda, Swami Ramteerth, Maharshi Raman and Maharshi Aurobindo awakened the nation. Bharat came face to face with its greatness that resulted in an awakening amongst people making it impossible for the British to stay in Bharat for long. The credit for this goes to those great sadhus who were working selflessly inspired only by noble thoughts of making people's lives better. (Ranga Hari 2018, 197–98)

The RSS had taken up the sensitive issue of cow slaughter and Akhil Bharatiya Pratinidhi Sabha (ABPS) (National Committee) had passed a resolution in Nagpur just a month earlier in 1952 asking for a ban on cow slaughter across Bharat. This resolution asked for cooperation from everyone—individuals, organizations and institutions. Guruji raised this subject in his discussions with sadhus. There was all-round acceptance of this idea and the offer for full cooperation. But the sadhus requested Guruji to use his organization to take this message to the entire country, 'Only you can give it a pan-Bharat shape' (Ranga Hari 2018, 198).

It was decided to collect signatures of adult citizens of the country, from north to south, and from west to east. It was also decided that all swayamsevaks and well-wishers would visit people door to door to explain the importance of the subject and take their signatures while keeping daily shakha work undisturbed. Signatures were not to be collected in places like markets, offices and stations where people crowd together for their routine work. Every state published pamphlets in its own language based on an illustrative sample sent from the central office. The period for collecting signatures was from 26 October to 22 November. 26 October was the day of Gopashtami. A large number of booklets, handbills, and a stamp with a picture of a mother cow suckling her calf were printed. Apart from this, Guruji's statement was printed, to be distributed in every home. Guruji also wrote letters to political leaders, editors, and religious heads individually. Though the subject was cow protection, the content of the letter differed depending on whom it was addressed to. Teams of swayamsevaks went from house to house to warmly greet residents. Commuting by foot and by cycles, they collected signatures from 94,459 villages and towns. The complete accounts reached the centre on 5 December. The total count of signatures was 17,989,332! It was a massive effort in public advocacy never tried anywhere in the world. The number of signatures collected was probably a world record for that time (Ranga Hari 2018, 199–200).

At the end, Guruji presented a complete account of the campaign to swayamsevaks. Shakha remained his prime focus. He said,

> The central point and foundation of our work is the daily programme of Sangh. I cannot think of neglecting it. I do not know the art of keeping a tree green after cutting the roots. A tree can survive only if there is a root, knowing this, we only believe in watering the roots. This is the reason why we have collected these signatures without neglecting daily Sangh work. (Ranga Hari 2018, 200)

He was able to achieve the dual objective of stirring up the RSS cadre, which had felt dispirited for reasons enumerated above, and also awaken Hindu society. He formally presented the signature collection to the president. The president assured him saying, 'I will see to it that the government looks at this memorandum sympathetically.' Humming the mantra, '*karmanye vaadhikaaraste*', Guruji returned. This cow protection campaign of 1952 rejuvenated the Sangh. The despondency that had gripped swayamsevaks for months earlier due to the electoral debacle of the nascent Bharatiya Jan Sangh was finally dispelled (Ranga Hari 2018, 201).

Politics and Guruji

The process that led to the birth of Bharatiya Jan Sangh began in 1950 when Dr Shyama Prasad Mukherjee resigned from the central Union Cabinet in 1950 due to strong differences with Nehru over the Nehru-Liaquat pact. He felt that the party ought to look after national interests and Hindu interests. A similar idea had been discussed within the Sangh circle during this period. Four articles in the *Organiser* under the pen name of *Kamal* (lotus) had been published by its editor K.R. Malkani in November and December of 1949. He argued that the Sangh could not leave the issue of nurturing Indian cultural values in the hands of politicians, as politicians were more worried about their standing before the voters. It was imperative for the Sangh to defend itself from attacks from other political parties. So it was necessary to get into politics. It was during this time that prachaaraks like Vasantrao Oak and Balraj Madhok, a prachaarak from Kashmir, were insisting that Dr Mukherjee launch a political party. Many RSS workers, especially displaced people from Pakistan wished that the RSS should get into politics. In fact, such was the heat of the moment that Guruji felt that Vasantrao Oak was too eager to join politics, which didn't suit a swayamsevak. Bhaiyyaji Dani, the then Sarkaryavaah, felt that the Sangh should not deviate from its main objectives (Karandikar 1999, 509–10). Guruji took a harsh decision to transfer Vasantrao to another region, a decision that had serious repercussions. Vasantrao quit Sangh work. Both kept their relations alive even after this incident. He finally returned to Sangh's fold after some years during the Goa liberation struggle and offered satyagraha there.

During this time, the situation in East Bengal was turning for the worse. Guruji and Dr Mukherjee met thrice during these times. Unfortunately, Sardar Patel, considered helpful by Hindus, passed away. Finally, in a meeting in 1951 held at Lala Hansraj's house, who was the then Delhi Sanghchalak, the Bharatiya Jan Sangh was launched. Guruji had two points in mind that he felt must be addressed. One was the issue of Hindu nationalism and the other was that the Sangh would not get involved in politics (Karandikar 1999, 510). While this development took place, the fact that no political leader took up the issue of the RSS ban despite nearly 77,000 swayamsevaks offering peaceful satyagraha might have weighed on Guruji's mind too.

Once the decision was taken, Guruji deputed some of the best prachaaraks to Jan Sangh. They included Nanaji Deshmukh, Balraj Madhok, Dharmavir, Sunder Singh Bhandari, Jagannathrao Joshi and L.K. Advani. Atal Bihari Vajpayee was sent a little later and was appointed secretary to Dr Mukherjee. Deendayal Upadhyayji was chosen by Guruji to take on the onerous responsibility of organizing the party and he was made the general secretary of the party (Karandikar 1999, 511). He held this post till he was persuaded to take up the responsibility of party President in 1968. Even today, nearly all the organizing secretaries of centre and state come from the RSS prachaarak lineage.

Deendayal Upadhyay came from a poor family and was orphaned quite early in life. He was raised by his maternal uncle. He was a brilliant student and a very simple person. He was initiated as a prachaarak and nurtured by Bhaurao Deoras (younger brother of Balasaheb Deoras, the third Sarsanghchaalak) from 1937 to 1938 (Karandikar 1999, 512). He finished his third year RSS training in 1940, the last training workshop that Dr Hedgewar attended and spoke at before he passed away. Upon his return from Nagpur, he told Bhaurao Deoras that he would not marry and dedicate his entire life to the Sangh.

He was very dear to Guruji due to his sharp intellect. He was very calm with an amiable nature. Such was his brilliance that Dr Mukherjee had said, 'If I had two more Deendayals, I could have changed the entire picture of Bharat' (Karandikar 1999, 515). It is said that one of the rare times Guruji was seen emotionally disturbed was when he saw the body of his precious protégé after he was killed in 1968 during a train journey. He had just been appointed as the president of Jan Sangh in a highly successful national conference in Kerala. At his condolence meeting he said, 'Deendayal had become a big name in India already. But, in coming times he would have been a celebrated name in the world. But, before this could happen he had been suddenly pulled away from us by cruel fate' (Karandikar 1999, 515). Sadly, the government of the time never carried out a serious investigation and a foul political murder was left unknown.

The 1952 defeat of Jan Sangh in elections was another shock for swayamsevaks, already in a state of self-doubt. Many Sanghchalaks had entered the electoral arena either on Bharatiya Jan Sangh tickets or independently with energy and optimism. Their misplaced optimism may have been fuelled by the way they had served the displaced people of Punjab and Sindh, huge response to the Sarsanghchaalaks' nationwide tour that seemed like a victory march and comments by news media like BBC. But Guruji himself was not moved by such expectations. He had clearly told the participants that such expectations would prove to be a mirage and it would only result in disenchantment. There were over-enthusiastic people who believed that they were good at crystal gazing and had taunted Guruji about his non-political wisdom or lack of it. Guruji's analysis turned out to be closer to the truth. All the candidates lost elections, many of them losing their deposits. Despondency plumbed to the depths after sky high expectations (Ranga Hari 2018, 195).

In keeping with his apolitical nature, Guruji had left for Raigad to take rest where he spent a few days while elections were going on (Ranga Hari 2018, 194). When a question about this crushing defeat was raised in front of Bhaiyyaji Dani, he asked, 'Have we forgotten why [the] Sangh was founded? Did we save our brethren at the risk of our own lives to win elections? Did we do it to get power?' He went on to reprimand everyone saying, 'It would be ideal for those who have longing for power and are looking at Sangh with this attitude, to stay away from the Sangh' (Karandikar 1999, 485–86).

But Guruji tried to comfort the frustrated swayamsevaks. He held get-togethers, intellectual discourses, discussions, Q&A sessions and had dialogue with people in many places. A famous lawyer of Punjab who had lost his deposit, spoke out with aggrieved heart, 'These people are ungrateful.' Guruji showed his strong disapproval at such a thought. Looking directly at him, he asked him,

> Dear friend, do you consider your demand for fruits of your services and accuse others of ungratefulness? Is this what [the] Sangh has taught you? [....]It is unjustified and wrong to blame [your] countrymen if your expectations are wrecked. Our disease has much deeper roots, and it is necessary to treat it from the roots. To uproot this fundamental disease, [the] Sangh has developed the system of daily training, instilling qualities, sacrifice, discipline and patriotism in a sustained way every day—that leads to creation of an organized, unified and progressive nation. (Ranga Hari 2018, 195)

In fact, in that post-election period, Guruji took extra care that politics should not encroach into the RSS. He would opine on the matters of the Jan Sangh team only if they sought his advice. The only time he spoke with them on his own was on the issue of Punjabi language in Punjab. This was because he was upset by the stand taken by the Jan Sangh.

Guruji had to face an unexpected disaster in the beginning of the new working year of 1953–54. The founder of Bharatiya Jan Sangh, Dr Shyama Prasad Mukherjee, died on 23 June in a prison in Kashmir under suspicious circumstances. Guruji had conveyed his feelings to senior workers of Jan Sangh that Dr Mukherjee shouldn't go to Kashmir. But Dr Mukherjee's decision to enter Kashmir had been announced all over the country. The expectations that Guruji had with the birth of Jan Sangh, seemed to have been destroyed suddenly. He was in Secunderabad when this news reached him. His face turned ashen on hearing this news. He went inside a room and shut the door for some time (Ranga

Hari 2018, 204). It was a huge setback for the national movement.

Though not much is discussed in RSS circles, the political approach versus purely organizational approach saw many seniors sitting at home for a long period after the 1952 debacle. Many seniors were dispirited. Guruji had to pick up and rebuild the organization that had become a shadow of its former self. He tried to keep a balance between the two views.

Another round of unpleasant experience of similar type for political workers and swayamsevaks in Maharashtra followed in 1961. There was a rare but huge flooding of rivers Mula-Mutha. Swayamsevaks worked day and night to provide relief to people. Jan Sangh karyakartas working with RSS karyakartas were quite sure that this work could fetch them handsome returns. However, Jan Sangh lost the next elections. Many swayamsevaks were bitter. But Guruji offered them solace and explained that one shouldn't expect returns from good deeds.

During this period, Guruji asked Deendayal Upadhyay to find an alternative political economic theory (*arth shastra*) since both Capitalism and Socialism did not suit Indian genus. Rajju Bhaiyya in his biography talks of this development. Guruji explained that both the theories were based on materialism with no place for spiritual side of the human being. Both believed that material fulfilment could satisfy an individual. The critical difference was only in who owned the means of production. They are not complete. So, we need to find a Hindu way for development. Deendayalji then did deep studies and came up with the philosophy of *Ekatma Manav Darshan*—the philosophy of integrated human life, that in English, for want of better words, is known as 'Integral Humanism.' While '*darshana*' (closest word is philosophy) is open-ended, 'ism' becomes a tight-bounded ideology (Sharda 2018, 80). Thus, Jan Sangh and its later avatar, the BJP, got its indigenous socioeconomic philosophy based on Bharatiya genius. He presented it at a three-day lecture in a workshop. After his untimely demise, Dattopant Thengdi expanded the philosophy with his genius. His exposition remains the prime reference source to this day.

Entry in Labour Field

The birth of Bharatiya Mazdoor Sangh (BMS) is an absorbing story of the intelligence of RSS leaders in creating an organization with patience. Immediately after independence, leading dignitaries like Guruji, Bhaiyyaji Dani and Balasaheb Deoras had done a detailed study and analysis of organizations working in different fields of the society. The ban led to an interruption to this activity. After removal of this ban, their attention was again drawn to this activity, namely, labour unions. Coincidentally, the Sangh prachaarak, Dattopant Thengdi, received an invitation from the president of Indian National Trade Union Congress (INTUC), P.Y. Deshpande, in 1949, to work for that organization. Balasaheb Deoras asked him to accept it immediately. Guruji added,

> Follow the discipline of the organization for which you are going to work. When its discipline and your ethical intellect lead to any conflict, it would be ideal to resign at that time. But, as long as you are in that organization, you should always consider its discipline as your yardstick. (Ranga Hari 2018, 18)

Thus, Thengdi went to a labour organization that had very different ideology and would be a competition later, in a bold move. Finally, on 23 July 1955, BMS was born in Bhopal. Its flag was saffron. The entry of saffron in the field of labour was a major historic event. BMS declared Vishwakarma Jayanti as the Bharatiya Shramik Din (Indian Labour Day). Thengdi had gone to Nasik once to discuss various issues with Guruji. He asked Guruji, 'Do we have an honoured labour day in our traditions that would be acceptable to all, could inspire everybody and also weave them together in a common thread of unity?' Guruji told him, 'Yes, there is such a day and it is Vishwakarma day' (Ranga Hari 2018, 210–11).

The first national convention of BMS was held only in 1967 after twelve years on the field. For twelve years, it had worked silently to build a strong base. At the time, the number of its affiliated unions had reached 541 and total membership was nearly 250,000. It is instructive that people of opposing ideologies could work together and be friends during those times. BMS opened new avenues of trade unionism in unorganized sectors like farmers and marginal workers like domestic helps that were overlooked by traditional trade unions. Its approach was not adversarial but of cooperation. It guided its members not to destroy properties when on strike as it was their source of income. This was in line with Dr Hedgewar's views, when he had corrected his friend Balaji Huddar saying that Hindutva doesn't believe in conflict between owner and the employee—it is a family.

S. Gurumurthy notes that though it was the youngest all-India trade union (formed in 1955), BMS over took INTUC (the largest trade union), in just three decades. In 1989, the strength of BMS was more than thirty-one lakh. That was more than the combined strength of CITU and AITUC, the two monopolists in the labour field. Yet Dattopant Thengdi was not a Communist. He actually opposed the communists, stormed their citadel and captured it. Never a socialist, but, he defeated them in their own territory. He waged an open war, an ideological war, against them, and defeated them in a straight war, not in guerrilla warfare. Also, he never used his strength, never called for a bandh, the normal weapon of large trade unions, and never brought any city to a standstill. His unions never indulged in violence. He never made his unions the wing of any political party.[5]

Dattopant Thengdi was a multi-dimensional thinker. Way back in the late 1960s when communism was at its peak, he had predicted the downfall of communism and the break-up of the USSR. I had the occasion to hear him on this topic in 1973. Later, he founded Swadeshi Jagaran Manch, his last creation. He was quite close to Dr Babasaheb Ambedkar. Guruji was concerned about Dr Ambedkar's decision of leaving the Hindu religion and conducting *Dhamma pravartan* on 14 October 1956. He sent Dattopant Thengdi to discuss

---

[5]Refer to https://hinduway.wordpress.com/2017/07/16/dattopant-thengadi-a-tapasvi-dies-unnoticed/

it with him. However, Dr Ambedkar did not change his mind. It is also worth noting that Dattopant Thengdi was the chief election agent of Dr Ambedkar in Bhandara elections in 1954. He even wrote a book on him, *Dr Ambedkar aur Samajik Kranti ki Yatra.*[6]

In a blog paying homage to Dattopant Thengdi, S. Gurumurthy tells us about Dattopant Thengdi and Dr Babasaheb Ambedkar.

> He [Dattopant] said 'I was eyewitness to Babasaheb's tensions and problems.' He recalled 'Babasaheb wanted the Hindu saints and religious heads to declare openly that untouchability did not have the sanction of Hindu religious scripts.' RSS efforts in this direction were not bearing fruit. Babasaheb told Thengdi that time was running out. His health was deteriorating fast in 1954. Babasaheb told Thengdi, 'I have faith in the process of the RSS in removing untouchability. But that is too slow. I cannot wait because I will not live to see the end of the problem.' Thengdi also recalled what made Babasaheb embrace Buddhism, in Babasaheb's own words thus: 'If I did not show the way for this helpless community they would be hunted down by the Christian church and the Communists.' What Babasaheb wanted the Hindu religious leaders to do in 1954, RSS could persuade them to do only a decade later, in 1965, in a conference of Hindu religious leaders in Udupi organized by the Vishwa Hindu Parishad. This made many, myself included, insist that Thengdi write on his days with Babasaheb. A couple of months before Thengdi passed away he did this too, and his book on Babasaheb Ambedkar was also released.[7]

Considering the expansion of the Sangh and shortage of resources, RSS leaders decided to celebrate Guruji's 51st birthday in 1956–57,

---

[6]https://www.indiatoday.in/magazine/cover-story/story/20160425-rashtriya-swayamsevak-sangh-rss-sangh-parivar-mohan-bhagwat-828762-2016-04-14.

[7]Refer to https://hinduway.wordpress.com/2017/07/16/dattopant-thengadi-a-tapasvi-dies-unnoticed/

despite his reluctance as he never celebrated his birthday. He accepted their request with humility as an 'order' from his colleagues. The RSS had never celebrated any leader's birthday earlier, nor did it do so again. Another important reason behind it was to undertake another mass contact programme (Ranga Hari 2018, 214). The target for contacting people was two percent of the population, that is, 3.6 million. Ultimately, the total number of people contacted was 4,103,411. The target for a purse to be gifted to Guruji was ₹21 lakh. The actual purse collected was ₹20,75,105,5 anna and 6 paise! (Ranga Hari 2018, 215) This is another example of RSS swayamsevaks' dedication to work, working to a plan and achieving targets with sincerity.

His speech on the occasion opened a new dimension to Sangh work. He made a special appeal to Christian and Muslim communities of the nation. He expressed the same views publicly in these meetings that he had expressed in an article he wrote on 25 October 1955 in the weekly *Rashtra Shakti*.

> We have a large number of people who have become Christians and Muslim in our country. A large majority of them are progenies of the people who have been living in this very country for many generations. They did not convert to the religions of the rulers out of any devotion to their rulers, but out of fear from the attacks of aggressors, rape and greed when there was no other way left. If they wish to make use of freedom then all Muslims and Christians who were Hindus earlier, should give up the religions and sects that symbolize insulting foreign pillage and rape and return to the original faith of their forefathers. Only then the freedom of this nation will attain its completeness. (Ranga Hari 2018, 216)

He requested the traditional Hindu members of the society who represented the other side, 'We should accept all of our own people into our families with open hearts very happily. Their return is coming back to their self-faith *(ghar wapsi)* and is not a conversion.' He went on to give many examples.

> Shri Madhavacharya, who later became Vidyaranya Swami, was the person who motivated Shri Harihar and Bukka to give up Islam and return to their own faith. Shri Madhavacharya had inspired them to accept their self-faith and establish Vijayanagar Empire. Shivaji Maharaj accepted famous Maratha commander Shri Netaji Palkar back from Islam into his original faith. He also accepted Shri Bhalji Nimbalkar back into self-religion and got his own daughter married to him to reinstate his prestige in the society. These were the people who became protectors of Hindu society later on. If we had not given them our respect and status after bringing them back to self-religion, history would have taken a different shape altogether. (Ranga Hari 2018, 216–17)

This was the first call for *ghar wapsi* or returning to the roots. He did not just give a call but gave guidance on issues that would rise when a person returned to his/her faith. But, even a personality like Guruji had to wait for ten years—till the 1966 Kumbh Mela in Prayag—to get his revolutionary ideas accepted by the religious leadership at that time.

Very few citizens of India, including political leaders were agitated that million of Indians were still facing slavery under the Portugeuse and French for years after India gained Independence. Pondicherry (now Puducherry) was returned to India by the French on 21 October 1954, but, Goa, Daman, Diu, Nagar Haveli continued to be under foreign control. Apart from the RSS and like-minded organizations, only Dr Ram Manohar Lohia spoke about it. The RSS had a major role to play in the liberation of Goa, Daman and Diu as the Government of India was dithering to show its liberal face to the world. In April 1954, the RSS formed a coalition with the National Movement Liberation Organisation (NMLO), and the Azad Gomantak Dal (AGD) for the annexation of Dadra and Nagar Haveli into the Republic of India. On 2 August 1954, a team of hundred swayamsevaks led by Vinayak Rao Apte, Sanghchalak of Pune, stormed the enclaves of Dadra and Nagar Haveli. They attacked Silvassa, forcing hundred-and-seventy-five Portuguese soldiers to surrender and the national Tricolour was hoisted and handed over to the central government. They were felicitated on 2 August 1979 in Silvassa as freedom fighters (Seshadri 2000, 28).

In 1955, RSS leaders demanded the end of Portuguese rule in Goa and its integration into India. When Prime Minister Jawaharlal Nehru refused to provide an armed intervention, RSS leader Jagannath Rao Joshi led the satyagraha with a group of around 3,000 members straight into Goa. He was imprisoned with his followers by the Portuguese police. The non-violent protests continued but met with repression. On 15 August 1955, the Portuguese police opened fire on the satyagrahis killing thirty or so civilians. Rajabhau Mahakaal of Ujjain led the batch from Ujjain. He died in the police firing while he held the Tricolour aloft even after a bullet had pierced through his right eye (Sharda 2019, 80). Jagannath Rao Joshi went on to become one of the prominent leaders of Jan Sangh later in the south. Past state prachaarak of Delhi, Vasantrao Oak was also the leader of one team. The Congress government's attitude about people's agitation for Goa's liberation was that of disinterest and non-cooperation. Guruji expressed his strong displeasure about this attitude (Ranga Hari 2018, 210). Finally, Goa was liberated by Indian forces on 18–19 December 1961.

Coming Up of Some More Major Projects

Bharatiya Kushtha Nivarak Sangh was registered in Champa in Madhya Pradesh on 5 May 1962. Leading this organization was a team comprising a lawyer from Bilaspur, Jamunaprasad Verma, as its president; Sadashiv Govind Katre as its general secretary; and six other members. This organization was born out of a whirlpool of emotions created with social under-current of revulsion, scorn, non-acceptance, neglect, the indefatigable urge to live, capacity for struggle, deep faith in society and the readiness to surrender self for the good of others. There was a good deal of support from respected Guruji in helping this idea evolve.

Katre had suffered from leprosy and went to missionary hospital for treatment. He was appalled at conversion tactics of those missionaries in the name of social service. An agitated Katre complained to Guruji about these missionaries. Guruji advised him,

> Such protests are meaningless. They will only result in discord. A person whose heart is agonized will have to get involved in this kind of work. You are a swayamsevak who has been a victim of this disease. Why don't you think that God may have planned to make you work for this neglected field. (Ranga Hari 2018, 243–45)

This motivation saw the birth of Kushtha Nivarak Sangh with the help of the state prachaarak.

Another landmark event that took RSS work in a new direction was the celebration of Swami Vivekananda's birth centenary in 1962. It was deemed fit that a compact compilation of Swamiji's thoughts be made to mark the centenary year, so people can easily understand his thoughts. Guruji gave responsibility for this activity to Eknath Ranade. He compiled a 200-page book named *Swami Vivekanand's Rousing Call to Hindu Nation*. It was translated in all the Bharatiya languages. A total of 21,000 copies of the English edition were sold in the first month itself (Ranga Hari 2018, 260). At that time, there was no plan for a memorial for Swami Vivekananda on the rock in Kanyakumari in the sea where he had meditated before embarking on his plans to rejuvenate Hindu society. Construction of the memorial is a long and fascinating story. One can read the entire story in the book *The Story of the Vivekanand Rock Memorial* as told by Eknath Ranade. Here is a gist of the story.

Plans were afoot to build a memorial on the Vivekananda Rock from January 1962 itself as it was the beginning of the centenary year. The move had begun as a local initiative but somehow, political resistance and Christian opposition to it had stalled it for months. Finally, the local team went to meet Guruji. Eknath

Ranade had just been relieved of the post of Sarkaryavaah of the RSS after a six-year stint and people knew that he had written the book on Swamiji. They suggested to Guruji that he be given the task of leading the memorial initiative. It is a wonderful account of how an RSS man was able to bring around politicians of different political parties across the entire spectrum of ideologies to get 323 Members of Parliament (MPs) to affix their signatures in one month to present a petition as a first step to urge the government to build a Vivekananda Rock Memorial. It is a story of how a one man army of an intelligent prachaarak could persuade people from different walks of life, from different ideologies and parties to support this project. How he could keep politics out of it in spite of pulls and pressures from politicians. It was not at all easy.

Another interesting aspect of the Memorial was the second phase of the construction. One Rupee coupons were released to collect money from citizens of Bharat. Funds of approximately ₹3,000,000 were raised through this route. More funds were collected from various sources. The third surprising part was that hurdles from different quarters were raised till the end when the memorial was finally inaugurated on 4 September 1970. But ultimately Bharat saw a wonderful graceful memorial to Swami Vivekananda inaugurated by the President of India and also visited by the then Prime Minister Indira Gandhi (Ranade 2013, 79–81).

Courage to be Politically Incorrect

Guruji never shied away from speaking the truth which might be politically suicidal or unpalatable; for example, his views on linguistic states. Tempers ran high on linguistic and regional issues during the latter half of the sixth decade. Guruji was the chief guest of a conference against regionalism on 23 May, in Bombay in a surcharged atmosphere. Barrister Jamunadas Mehta chaired the meeting. Sanghchalak of Mumbai city, Dayabhai Patel inaugurated the conference. Guruji spoke bluntly to the advocates of linguistic states that could make them rethink. He said,

> Due to the wicked strategy of the British, we have begun to believe that difference in language leads to difference in culture, but this assumption is wrong. This thinking has even forced its way into the Bharatiya constitution. We have called our country a 'Union' in our constitution which is incorrect. Union actually means sticking together some fragmented pieces to make them stand together. Ours is a nation with a unified soul, and it is not fragmented. Some people call themselves supporters of 'United India.' But from where has this term 'United India' come? This idea itself contains an unconscious thought of differences, which is spreading like an epidemic across the nation.

He asked the supporters of linguistic states, 'Why should those people who talk of the whole world being one single state, be afraid in their hearts about making of Bharat into one state?'(Ranga Hari 2018, 208)

At the same time he supported the demand of Akali Dal for Punjabi Suba on the ground that if other states were organized on linguistic lines why was it denied to Punjab? This view shocked the media and political establishment. A *Hindustan Times* despatch notes that the RSS chief's views on Punjabi Suba were similar to Akali stand. The report says,

> Surprisingly, somewhat abruptly, the Akalis and RSS, bitterest foes in the present day Punjab politics, have moved to nearly identical positions on the Punjabi suba issue... During an informal talk in Jalandhar yesterday, Mr Golwalkar, RSS Chief, did not see any justification in denying the formation of a Punjabi suba when the linguistic state principle had been accepted in the rest of India... Personally, however, he was opposed to redistribution of the country on linguistic lines. He did not mind a Punjabi suba if it covered all the genuine Punjabi speaking people. (*Hindustan Times*, 4 Nov 1960)

Guruji had criticized Arya Samaj and chastised misguided BJP leaders who had supported the demand for non-Sikhs to enter their mother tongue as Hindi during the census of 1951. (*Hindustan Times*, 4 November 1960)

Deendayal Upadhyayji had gone to Punjab in 1956. Opinion was that language based states were being formed. A very serious Deendayalji told karyakartas, 'We should not oppose Punjabi. You may fight for Hindi, you may keep opposing Punjabi Suba, but in ten years Punjabi Suba will be reality.' He was upset about the scenario in Punjab. Incidentally, Punjabi Suba did become a reality in ten years as predicted by Deendayalji. It was created in 1966.[8]

Ultimately, Punjabi Suba was created but the delay in forming the state of Punjab led to lot of heartburn and accentuated the feelings that Sikhs were not treated at par with other citizens of India. This feeling of injustice could be considered as the seeds of latter-day extremist agitations.

Reformist Guruji

Critics of the RSS and Guruji have tried to paint Guruji as an orthodox Brahminical leader who supported outdated religious ideas and traditions. One couldn't be farther from the truth. In the tradition of Dr Hedgewar, he was a reformist, not an agitationist. He believed in upward evolution *(utkranti),* not revolution *(kranti).* He understood the psychology of the people of ancient Hindu dharma. Some of the examples of his anti-fatalist and modern reformist approach are mentioned below. He once said,

> Pushing great people out of the ranks of normal human beings shows a weakness in human thinking. What right does an individual have to call out to God for even his petty affairs, while he sits back passively, as if God has no other business and would come running whenever he calls Him. (Golwalkar 2005, 116)

Guruji was in Palghat on tour once. A group of four or five Brahmins

[8]Taken from an interview with Krishanlal Dhall recorded in Jalandhar on 25 May 2017.

was waiting there to meet Guruji. Among them was a brilliant scholar Anantkrishna Shastri who had published a book called *Shatabhushani* that contradicted a book *Shatadooshani* written by a Vedantic scholar Venkatanaath. Shastriji spoke to Guruji in Sanskrit, 'Guruji, you are a religious scholar; you also know the religious protocols. Can a non-Brahmin present a critique about Shruti scriptures and teach them?' Shri Guruji responded with humility,

> Gentleman, I am not a religious scholar, nor do I have an authoritative knowledge of religious protocols. I will not even dare to say that I know Sanskrit. But, I do know a little about Sanskrit... Some doubts do rear their heads in my mind too about this subject once in a while. Was the visionary of great Gayatri mantra a Brahmin? Valmiki, who gave us Ramayan, was he a Brahmin? One who rendered Gita and the one who heard it—were they both Brahmins? I have similar doubts about the dialogues in Upanishads. The problem is a little complex. So, what do I do? You are the right people to search for an answer.

Naturally, this dialogue came to a halt there itself. The team went back after presenting a copy of *Shatabhushani* to Guruji. (Ranga Hari 2018, 230–31)

Around the same time theists of Maharashtra had a difference of opinion. Many ritualistic people wished to sacrifice animals as a part of Vedic rituals for a Vajpeya *yagya*. This led to a chaotic situation in Maharashtra, a leader in social reforms. In Guruji's view, it was undesirable to use Shastras as a shield to resurrect stale outdated systems and rituals. Guruji talked of refashioning ancient value systems and not uprooting them, which was contrary to the intellectual confusion created by orthodox or progressive elements. The outcome of these efforts was encouraging. The conscience of the brethren of Maharashtra was awakened on Guruji's appeal. The programme was held without any disturbance. (Ranga Hari 2018, 231)

Dattopant Thengdi in his Hindi book, *Dr Ambedkar aur saamajik kraanti* gives another example of Guruji's reformist approach without being aggressive. In 1960-61, Guruji had gone to meet Swami Karpatriji at his place of residence in Delhi. He was president of the Ram Rajya Parishad at that time. He was a strong supporter of *Chaaturvarna* (basic four fold classification of society). During discussions, he asked Guruji, 'Golwalkarji, do one thing. You have so many swayamsevaks all over the country; ask them to work according to their varna (loosely and wrongly translated as caste by Westerners and their followers). They will listen to you.' Guruji said politely,

> I am chief of Sangh, but all these people are not my disciples, they are my brothers. I don't give them orders. Still, since you are directing me, I will ask them. If they like it, they will surely follow this idea. But there is total disorder in our society today. Therefore, if they were to be shown an example, then we can tell them that this is the type of society that we wish to build. You can do this job very well since you have thousands of disciples and you are their Guru. They should surely listen to you. You ask your disciples that they should set an example by working according to their varna. I will see, what I can do.

Swamiji could understand the underlying message of polite refusal. He was upset and said, 'You are trying to push things on me. If you do not wish to do this, tell me frankly.' Guruji said,

> Please don't be displeased. Please tell me what is left of *varnashram*? Is there anything left of caste system? It is waste of energy to try to resurrect this highly decayed system. Time has come to demolish all this completely and create a new 'varna.' Only that will lead to creation and development of a new social order, and that would be apt too. This is what Sangh is doing. It is Sangh's view that everyone should be brought together on the eternal foundation of society and nation to

> build an orderly society. There should be no other differences. (Ranga Hari, 232)

There couldn't be a stronger negation of *varna vyavastha* while critics wish to show him as a supporter of this outdated decayed system.

Guruji never shied away from criticizing undesirable mentality rising within religious leadership of Hindu society, and recounted his experience quite frankly about an incident that occurred during the formative years of Vishwa Hindu Parishad. We have many different sects. Vishwa Hindu Parishad organized a conference to create some harmony between them. Some workers met the heads of various sects to invite them for the conference. When they presented the invitation to one such head, he accepted it and asked immediately, 'What is the seating arrangement?' When workers informed him about the arrangements, he said, 'How can I come? Will all others sit with me? What kind of arrangement is this? After all we too have certain protocol with limitations and a concept of senior and junior. Therefore, make arrangements accordingly, only then will we (I) come.' When Guruji was informed about this, he was surprised that a person wearing saffron had not been able to get rid of petty thinking about honour-insult. Next time when he met him, he reconfirmed if the gentleman had made such a statement. He confirmed saying, 'How can they make us sit with junior people?' Guruji told him,

> Please take off your saffron clothes. I am ready to give you my kurta, please wear it. Then talk like this. I am not even ready to listen to you in these clothes. Even I have not accepted fourfold ashram concept. But, my life has been spent among sadhus. It has been spent in company of such divine souls about whom one can say, 'Guruh sakshat parabrahma.' On basis of that experience I am asking you to remove your saffron clothes.

He was a great soul. He was not upset. He looked at Guruji for a moment and said, 'Brother, what you say is correct' (Ranga Hari

2018, 336–37). His own humble but scholarly personality made even revered sanyasins listen to him.

An unexpected event also took place in Guruji's life that shows how deeply he was respected by the saints and gurus of Hindu tradition. Head of Govardhan Peeth of Jagannathpuri, Shrimad Bharati Krishnateerth, left for his heavenly abode before he could ordain his successor. However, he had left behind a list of possible successors in a document. It also had the name of Madhav Sadashiv Golwalkar. He had handed over the responsibility of setting up a proper system to the Head of Dwarkadhish Peeth. Guruji received this information. He wrote to Dwarka Peeth head in Sanskrit, politely declining the offer. He also visited the Acharya of the Peeth and explained to him his commitment to Sangh work and requested to excuse him and let him keep working for Sangh (Ranga Hari 2018, 236–37).

Birth of the Vishwa Hindu Parishad

One of the most important organizations that brought different sects and *sampradayas* on a single platform and set the pace for reforming the Hindu society was nurtured with personal involvement by Guruji. It was Vishwa Hindu Parishad, the birth of which has its own background story. Guruji was in Belgaum in Karnataka on 24 November 1963, when a parliamentarian from Trinidad, Shri Shambunath Kapildeo met him, tracking his schedule from the RSS office in Delhi. In the eighteenth century, when European imperialists established their different colonies in Caribbean island nations, thousands of poor Indians were exported there as indentured labour or *girmitiyas* with conditions that virtually made them bonded labour. After years of hard work, people there had joined the mainstream in their respective societies. However, they were worried about maintaining their culture and nurturing it. They expected support from Hindustan for the purpose. He had brought a delegation of select parliamentarians in search of an answer. The delegation knocked at the doors of many leaders but they disappointed him with their response that 'this is a secular country'. There was one sympathetic leader who told Shambhunath, 'You should meet Guruji Golwalkar for this work, only he can do your work' (Ranga Hari 2018, 262).

He explained to Guruji the reason behind his visit and his disappointing experience in Delhi. Next morning he met him again before leaving. Guruji pondered over the expectations and problems of Hindus living abroad and sought the views of Laxmanrao Bhide (a prachaarak who travelled around the world to organize Hindus) and Deendayal Upadhyay (who also toured the world). They gave detailed ideas about the expectations and requirements of overseas Hindus.

During the same period, Swami Chinmayananda had expressed his views in his Ashram's monthly magazine *Tapovanprasad*.

> A vague idea is taking seed in my heart, that a global Hindu conference should be organized. An appeal should be made to Hindu brethren spread all over the world to send their delegates to the conference. There should be discussions in this conference about the development and spread of Hindu culture. Problems that may come up should be discussed. There is a need to ponder over how the spiritual base of Hinduism can be strengthened and stabilized. A plan should be built to give a practical shape to the conclusions drawn from these discussions. This global conference should be held in Delhi or Calcutta.

Guruji contacted Swamiji immediately. To accomplish this work, a talented prachaarak Shivram Shankar (Dadasaheb) Apte was given its responsibility. Dadasaheb Apte met over 200 religious preachers and visited forty to fifty religious institutions. His contacts were widespread among religious sects. Finally, the VHP was established on 29 August 1964 in Sandipani Ashram of Swami Chinmayanand in Mumbai. This act saw the rise of a global movement for resolving religious, social and community issues of Hindus (Ranga Hari 2018, 263–64).

Major decisions of this first meeting were: (i) There should be a Global Hindu Conference (Vishwa Hindu Sammelan) on the occasion of Kumbh Mela in Prayag from 22 to 24 January 1966; (ii) it should have a religious parliament with participation of all religions and sects; (iii) there should be programmes in that conference that would propagate 'unity in diversity'; and (iv) an exhibition should be organized there showing the continuity of Hindu dharma from Vedic times to present times (Ranga Hari 2018, 264).

The world conference of VHP, Vishwa Hindu Sammelan, took place on 22–24 January 1966 in Prayag, during the Kumbh Mela there. A religious parliament was organized in 'Dharma Nagar' on the huge Saikati banks of the holy Triveni Sangam. One religious parliament had been organized in the times of King Harshvardhan in AD 680, nearly thirteen millennia back. After that, Hindu society chained in slavery could not even think of such an attempt. Eleven resolutions relating to Hindu society and religious sects belonging to Sanatan Dharma were passed in the conference (Ranga Hari 2018, 275).

Of them, the most important resolution was about reconversion to original faith (*paraavartan*). Second name of paraavartan was 'returning home' *(ghar wapsi).* Swami Vishwesharteerth, head of Madhav sect of Udupi declared, '*Na Hindu patito bhavet*' (No Hindu is sinful), thus ruling out untouchability. The large congregation sitting there gave wholehearted support to it. Guruji's quest that had begun in 1956 had concluded successfully that day (Ranga Hari 2018, 275).

Guruji remained in the background and did not sit on the dais in the entire conference. He was requested to give his concluding remarks. His concluding remarks showed his deep empathy for the downtrodden and alienated sections of Hindu society,

> All religions and sects are mine, all castes are mine, people living in hills and forests are mine. If they are unhappy then it is only because of our weaknesses. Our tribal society, lying neglected because of a big section of Hindu society that

> considers itself wise; is my inalienable part. I will do whatever is necessary to correct the wrongs perpetrated over years, awakening within all this kind of strong resolve. Hindu society will stand up in a unified way; a strong society that would stand in its place of birth, in its own land from Himalayas to Oceans with its head held high in the world (Ranga Hari 2018, 275).

This was a path-breaking speech and launch of a path-breaking movement for reforms in the Hindu society that showed the broader vision of Sangh work.

The first regional convention of VHP was organized on 2 October in Guwahati. Guruji was the chief guest. It showed the focus and concern RSS leadership had for the Northeast, the hotbed of conversions and separatist movements. With hard work put in by local leaders and swayamsevaks for four to five months more than seventy delegates took part from the foothills, forests and mountainous regions. There were representatives from tribes of Daflash, Aksa, Naga, Neka, and many others. There were also brethren from Mikir, Jayantiya, Khasi and Kachari communities. It was after many years, perhaps for the first time, that seventeen anointed disciples of Shri Shankardev had come together (Ranga Hari 2018, 281).

The British, with the help of various churches in the Northeast, had labelled the local tribals as 'animist' and 'nature worshippers'—not Hindus. Guruji as the chief guest explained how the British tried breaking our society by labelling them as indigenous, hilly tribes, uncivilized, backward, etc., and created separate identities, calling worshippers of inanimate objects or nature as non-Hindus. Actually all Hindus were nature worshippers. He elaborated that Hindu philosophy is to envision unity in diversity; therefore, Shankaracharya had weaved together all the prevalent sects into a unified thread through *panchaayatan upaasana* (worship of five elements). He said, 'There is no division between believer and non-believer. But, it is not in our nature to bind everybody in a single form of worship or belief. There is an absence of close relationship between heads of *maths* and their disciples. Acharyas of Shaiva and Vaishnav sects do not come together even in times of difficulties, then how will we face disasters like religious conversions?' (Ranga Hari 2018, 281) This speech gave direction to the entire Sangh and affiliates' work in the Northeast that slowly and steadily changed the course of this region.

In 1966, many Hindu organizations organized another agitation for cow protection. A big rally of sadhus, lawyers and common people took a march to the Parliament on Gopashtami day. This rally is remembered for the brutal oppression and led to Gulzarilal Nanda's resignation as the home minister. Tear gas shells were lobbed, followed by reckless firing by the police on sadhus. A report in the *Organiser* (dated 25 November 2007) put the figure of martyrs at 375. The cow slaughter issue subsequently forced Indira Gandhi to set up a panel under a retired Supreme Court chief justice A.K. Sarkar to see if a nationwide ban on cow slaughter was feasible. In an unconventional move, she nominated Guruji as a member of the panel, along with the Shankaracharya of Puri, V. Kurien of the National Dairy Development Board, economist Ashok Mitra and others. The committee's initial mandate was to submit a report in six months' time but nothing came of it. It was dismissed in 1979 by the Morarji Desai government.[9]

The next regional conference of VHP was organized in Udupi in 1969. It was huge, with over 15,000 delegates. Such was the rush that delegates were accommodated in the homes of the welcoming citizens of Udupi. A resolution to eliminate untouchability was to be passed in that session. The chairman of the session was a retired IAS officer from a scheduled caste, R. Bharaniayya. After discussions held against the background of social spirit of oneness, equity and unity a resolution was passed unanimously. Head of Madhav sect *math*, Swami Vishweshwar Teerth stood up and raising both his

---

[9]Refer to https://www.news18.com/news/opinion/rajasthan-assembly-election-2018-forget-whatsapp-rumours-here-are-the-facts-about-1966-cow-slaughter-agitation-1958749.html.

hand, pronounced, '*Hindavah Sodaraah Sarve*' that is 'All Hindus are born from same mother,' meaning, they are brothers. Bharanaiyyaji, overwhelmed with emotions, shedding tears of happiness, said, 'Guruji, all this is due to your efforts.' Guruji promptly said, 'No, all this has been due to all of us and our mother-like society's willpower.' This pronouncement read with the pronouncement in Prayag of '*Na Hindu patito bhavet*' were the boldest statements made by leaders of Hindu society in centuries. According to Yadavrao Joshi, who was witness to that moment, it was a moment of ultimate joy in Guruji's life (Ranga Hari 2018, 302).

To make people understand the difficult path ahead, Guruji stated,

> This resolution about untouchability authorized by scholars, religious gurus, heads of *maths* and other saints will not become a part of our lives so easily and simply. Beliefs that have taken firm roots over centuries will not be uprooted simply by words or resolutions. We shall have to publicize it by contacting people, cities to cities, villages to villages and house to house...We wish to transform hearts, religious and emotional transformation through contact and practical behaviour. Our goal and work is not only for achievement of economic and political equality. We wish to see right kind of change, we wish to envision the spirit of unity... We shall have to blow outdated orthodox views to smithereens with hard blows. We shall have to take it to jungles, caves and plains... we shall have to expect conflicts, opposition and hurdles... We should not expect show of gratitude or any miracles! Please give up this expectation also. We shall have to work untiringly with clear understanding of harsh realities with extreme compassion.' (Ranga Hari 2018, 303)

This was a clarion call for reforming the Hindu society with empathy, expecting nothing in return except renaissance of our nation. This was the biggest announcement of the resolute Hindu societies led by its leaders to end the scourge of untouchability.

Guruji: An Idealist Democrat

As an observer from the outside, Guruji had a clear idea about how politics should be done and how politicians should conduct themselves. The year 1967 was a politically significant year. Breakdown of the unchallenged monopoly of the Congress over power also began that year, leading to many political changes. Guruji gave advice in an unattached manner with a true liberal spirit. Lohiaji had met Guruji to urge that non-Congress parties should come together. The first thaw in opposition parties' relations with the RSS occurred during the by-elections held for three seats that were fought jointly by the opposition. The candidates were Ram Manohar Lohia, Acharya Kripalani and Deendayal Upadhyay. RSS workers pitched in and worked for all the three candidates. Lohiaji and Kripalaniji won but Upadhyayji lost as he refused to appear on public platforms as a 'brahmin' to woo the dominant Brahmin community in his constituency Jaunpur. He was a reluctant candidate anyways and told his workers that he was happy that he lost so he could keep working for the organization. This experiment led to the first non-Congress governments called Sanyukt Vidyayak Dal (SVD) in states like Madhya Pradesh, Rajasthan etc. (Sharda 2018, 146 and 155).

Guruji was clear that RSS swayamsevaks must not expect to get favours from their political colleagues in Jan Sangh. Addressing a state level meeting after the formation of the government in Punjab in Delhi on 22 July, he advised swayamsevaks not to seek any favours from their elected representatives for whom they worked, even though there would be an urge to help others. Sangh work is God's own mission (*Eeshwareey karya,* as RSS leaders refered to it) and for its workers to stretch their hands in front of political workers for petty things is condemnable. He pointed out that if the representatives fail to deliver they could be rejected by the people (Ranga Hari 2018, 285). He drew a sharp line between the RSS and Jan Sangh; between social obligations and politics yet again. These guidelines have helped the RSS steer clear of factional politics and political shenanigans, and to keep growing irrespective of which party was in government.

During this period, *The New York Times* carried an interview of Guruji by its reporter Lucas that throws light on relations between the RSS and Jan Sangh/BJP as he perceived it. He suggested that they should not publish interviews and articles on the BJP and the RSS together in the same issue as that would create further confusion. His response to the question about Sangh and Bharatiya Jan Sangh was,

> Sangh swayamsevaks are free to join any political party. Till 1937–38, our swayamsevaks used to be in Congress and Hindu Mahasabha. Whatever be their political differences, they could work together quite well in Sangh. Congress shut its door on Sangh swayamsevaks later on. Hindu Mahasabha has become very weak and it does not even have presence in many places. Therefore, those who wish to join politics, seem to get into Jan Sangh. But, number of swayamsevaks who are not in any political party is substantially higher. It is our belief that our nation can progress only if the society is unified and organized in a thread of unity, and its ethical and spiritual association remains unbroken. (Ranga Hari 2018, 297)

To another question he said, 'No nation can live in isolation. There is no way that it can remain unaffected by industrialization and such similar developments. But, it is possible to achieve growth without sacrificing national character.' Clearly, he did not believe in an insulated nation and expected Bharat to absorb what was good elsewhere too. These views are quite similar to the views Dr Mohan Bhagwat expressed in his three-day Delhi lecture series last year.

Guruji's commitment to democracy and democratic norms was not superficial or based on convenience; nor did it depend on the politics of the time. It can be seen from a little known episode of Kerala in 1959 when the first democratically elected Communist government in the world was sought to be thrown out by Indira Gandhi and other opposition parties by hook or by crook.

Panchjanya had planned a 'Kerala special' issue in the light of anti-Communist agitation led by Congress under Indira Gandhi to dismiss the Communist government there. Devendra Swaroop was editor of the weekly. He thought Guruji will give his support to the efforts to bring down the Communist government. Guruji sent him a long confidential letter, not for publication, dated 29 June 1959. He disclosed this letter much later in his book. Extract of relevant portions of the letter say:

> Friend, Pandit Deendayal Upadhyay and others are discussing this issue. You would have received analysis from them. So, it would not be right for me to present my views. But, one thing is clear that if we consider democratic system and consider our constitution then it may be said that the agitation going on there should not be supported. If someone is trying to remove a ruling party using forms of satyagrah, but basically use of muscle power seems incorrect, it would be disrespect for the constitution. People who believe in the principle that might is right, for them all these activities are right. Unless the Centre and Constitution declare the current government as anti-national, people who believe in the constitution cannot support this agitation, I believe. (Swaroop 2009, 103)

One notes that though Guruji considered Communist ideology as non-Indian and inspired from outside and Communist movement as anti-national, he was not ready to support an agitation that was inspired only by party politics. In the same letter in the first para he had noted that the meeting will be held under the directions of the Sarkaryavaah and he will follow the tour plans and any other decision that was to be decided in that meeting on 11 July. The letter also shows that though people believed that he was the all-in-all, the supreme leader of the RSS, he considered himself only an obedient member of the organization when he clearly indicated that the decision would be taken by Deendayal Upadhyay and his colleagues, his juniors, showing his belief in internal organizational democracy. Those who raise doubts about his commitment to the Indian constitution and democratic values would do well to study this incident.

Devendra Swaroop goes on the note that Jan Sangh and Panchjanya didn't go by his advice and celebrated 18 July as 'Kerala Divas' as per decision taken in all-India meeting of Jan Sangh on 8 July and supported the agitation. Guruji did not reprimand the people involved in Kerala matter about this, but he just let his views be known (Swaroop 2009, 105). This incident illustrates the democratic nature of collective decision-making in the RSS and Jan Sangh.

Against this backdrop, it is ridiculous to keep calling him a supporter of Nazis and Hitler, for years without a shred of evidence. Critics quote 'We—Our—Nationhood defined', a 1938 publication which we noted above, he had disowned as no longer valid. He took over as Sarsanghchaalak in 1940. His views on minorities were enunciated well in his last interview published in 1972. Even if taken at face value, the horrors of gas chambers had not yet reached the world. World War II ended around 1942 and horrific facts came into public domain around 1945. There were many politicians who appreciated Hitler till these horrors burst upon the world. The worst charge against him, was he advocated that no group should have any special privileges (which the Leftists translate as the minorities being given a status of second-class citizens). This is the basic premise of a secular polity.

Koenrad Elst, in his book *Saffron Swastika*, says, 'Even if this view is taken at its full face value, it is not in any way different from the stated Islamic rule (evident in all Muslim majority states) that gives status of second class citizens to non-believers—claiming it to be as per 'The Book'. If this is acceptable to supporters of Semetic religions, will critics accept that Islamic rule is fascist?' (Sharda 2018)

When people try to relate Nazism or Fascism to Hindu organizations, they forget that both the Hindu Mahasabha (born in 1906) and the RSS (born in 1925) came into existence before anyone in India knew of Hitler. Savarkar's *Hindutva* (1923) was published three years before Hitler's *Mein Kampf*. The Communists opposed the British in 1940 (under Stalin's pact with Hitler) and supported them after 1941, yet after independence they have not been branded as collaborators with either fascism or colonialism. But calumny continues. Contrary to Congress and Left propaganda, Dr Hedgewar never went out of India and never met Mussolini or Hitler. As we have seen earlier that he had basic differences with the HMS leader Dr Munje and did not follow Munje or Savarkar's advice many times.

Another extract often quoted by the critics is from the chapter titled 'Internal challenges: Christians, Muslims and Communists' from *Bunch of Thoughts,* is mentioned. Dr Manmohan Vaidya, Sahsarkaryavaah of RSS, analyses Guruji's views in the present context in a recent article. He says,

> In today's context it should be interpreted as Christian evangelism, jihadi Muslim fundamentalism and Naxalism or Maoism. Their activities are a threat to the very idea of Bharat envisaged by the Constitution makers. Not all Christians, but some churches and missionaries are involved in evangelical activities and wrongful conversions and they have been successful in getting the tacit support of certain members of the Christian community in the name of religion. The first anti-conversion law was enacted in 1967 in Madhya Pradesh and Odisha when they were ruled by Congress. The clause simply said that conversion by force, fraud or allurement will not be permitted, which was vehemently opposed by Churches and missionaries. Similarly, not all Muslims in Bharat but some Muslim organizations are involved in propagating and spreading jihadi fundamentalism in the name of Islam and they succeed in getting support from some members of the Muslim community in the name of religion. The subversive and divisive activities of Maoists and urban Naxals are now exposed to the public. Have you ever heard of

> a Communist organization condemning the brutal attack and killing of Bharatiya security forces while combatting Naxals and Maoists, performing their duty to protect the people and the state? The same people create a hue and cry when Bharatiya security forces are successful in nabbing or curbing the subversive activities of Naxals and Maoists. Warning Bharatiya citizens about these three anti-national activities is important and necessary. (Vaidya 2019)

In essence, if one sees the violence perpetrated against the opposition by the Communist regimes in Bengal, Tripura and Kerala, it is easy to judge who is fascist or totalitarian in reality. In comparison, there is hardly any persecution or atrocity on people who oppose BJP governments in the states ruled by it.

Criticism with Cooperation

We see Guruji and the RSS criticizing Congress government policies on many occasions in lectures or through RSS resolutions in ABPS and Kendriya Karyakarini Mandal (Central Working Committee). However, it is equally true that the RSS always supported the government in every war and every kind of difficulty including natural disasters. Criticism has always been constructive.

The government accepted that Bharat had been attacked by Communist China on 20 October 1962. Guruji while on his tour of Rajasthan for ten days from 10 to 23 October had also indicated this possibility. At a public programme in Chittor on 16 October, he had said, 'I have definite information that China is going to attack Bharat. Our country's leaders are shouting slogans of "*Hindi Chini bhai bhai*" and welcoming the Chinese prime minister in Red Fort in Delhi. But China will attack us.' He repeated this statement in Alwar again on 18 October. There was strong reaction in newspapers to these statements. A so-called progressive columnist commented, 'What kind of irresponsible leader is he?' One columnist declared, 'Golwalkar's statement is nothing but his imagination run wild.' However, when All India

Radio announced this imagination as actual news, everybody was astonished. Now, newspapers had a new question, 'How did Golwalkar get this information?' Upon reaching Delhi at the end of the tour, seven to eight leaders of the ruling party met Guruji at Lala Hansraj Gupta's home where he was staying. All of them had the same question, 'From where did you get the information that China will attack us?' Unhappy with the events, he responded calmly, 'Anyone who wishes to see honestly, can see everything. My eyes are not covered with any glasses of politics or power therefore I can see everything. Even political leaders can see all this, but they do not speak out due to political compulsions. They are worried about what will happen to the high-sounding principles that they had been talking about.' However, Guruji went to meet President Radhakrishnan the same afternoon to express his solidarity.

Much earlier, he had countered journalists on 2 February 1960 in Bombay with his own query and explained, 'In that period, Shri Mirajkar had written in the monthly *Kalyan* published from Gorakhpur, that there are army posts on the way to Kailash and Mansarovar pilgrimage route where belongings of the pilgrims are thoroughly checked before they are allowed to proceed further.' It is therefore clear that he could surmise his views from very diverse sources. When asked, 'Will you co-operate with the government if it decides to counter Chinese attack?' Guruji's answer was, 'Definitely. We have made an announcement. Other parties will also co-operate. Only one party will oppose it and that is the Communist party' (Ranga Hari 2018, 250–251). He gave a statement on 29 October in which he requested all the citizens, especially swayamsevaks, to give unquestioned support. Guruji stated,

> Most important job is to protect common populace from fear, panic and sense of terror. Government should get full support from people to be alert and stop such possible incidents at their root. It is our duty to organize in every village and every town with self-motivation and pay attention towards maintaining peace and order.

Clearly, for him every citizen of the country had a role in protecting and serving the country. Next day, on 30 October, he sent a written letter of support to the prime minister, 'All us brothers will spare no effort to carry out our natural duty to free the nation from this danger with all our strength. I feel highly fulfilled in giving this unconditional assurance to you as the person heading the government' (Ranga Hari 2018, 251).

The Sangh organized a huge rally in Delhi on 23 December in Ram Lila ground to spark self-confidence, dedication, willpower and feeling of cooperation. Instructions were passed on at the organizational level to cooperate with and help the government as and when required. Teams of swayamsevaks gave full support to government officers in different places as required. In north Assam, even the morale of para-military forces was maintained by Sangh swayamsevaks. When the myth of the Chinese brigade moving south of Assam after crossing Bondi Valley spread and government servants began fleeing their posts, hundreds of swayamsevaks stopped them courageously, putting their own lives at stake. The president and prime minister too received such information from time to time from the armed forces (Ranga Hari 2018, 252).

Republic Day was celebrated on 26 January 1963—two weeks after the cease fire. To reinvigorate the national morale, the government came up with plans to get people's participation in Republic Day parade. Invitation for this parade was also received by Sangh office in Delhi. The Sangh being ever ready, 3,000 swayamsevaks got ready in full uniform in that short time of less than a week to take part in the grand republic day parade, coming up behind the formal armed forces (Ranga Hari 2018, 253). There are newspaper reports carrying photographs of the RSS batch in full uniform. The RSS documentation centre has also been able to video record some of the surviving members of the group who were present in the parade.

Nehru never hid his poor view of Nepal while Guruji saw Nepal as a natural ally. He did his best to see better relations between the two spiritual brothers. On 24 February 1963 on Maha Shivratri day, Guruji visited Pashupatinath temple and was in Nepal for two days. He met the prime minister of Nepal Dr Tulsi Giri during these days and also King Mahendravir Vikramshah. The King of Nepal shared his anguish in the meeting. Discussions were held for nearly 60 minutes. The pain of Nepal, to summarize, was that:

> Nepal's people were economically and socially backward. Leftist extremists took shelter in Terai area of Bharat after their attacks. There was a natural affinity and affection between the two countries because of religious and cultural commonality that Communists hated and China was a giant that couldn't be displeased. Nepal's request for import through Calcutta was not granted, so they had to take help of Pakistan to get their goods via Chittagong to which it had agreed easily. Clearly, Nehru didn't like Nepal as a Hindu state. This bias needed to go.

Guruji responded, 'I suspect that your views and feelings do not reach Pandit Nehru. There might be some confusing perspectives too. It seems Bharat will have to do some rethinking about Communists because of Chinese aggression.' He assured the King that when Home Minister of Bharat, Lal Bahadur Shastriji would arrive on 1 March 1963 in Nepal, he could speak to him on the basis of religious and cultural unity of Nepal-Bharat. He felt this could be the basis for strong and congenial relationships with Bharat. He assured his support for better relations by talking to senior leaders in India (Ranga Hari 2018, 253 and 254). We can see how Nehru's ideological prejudices overshadowed diplomacy and embittered a good but weak neighbour.

Guruji and his personal assistant Dr Abaji Thatte returned to Varanasi on 27 February. With just two days left, Guruji immediately wrote letters to Pandit Nehru in English and to Home Minister Shastri in Hindi and sent it by hand through a responsible swayamsevak. The Nepal tour of the home minister was a success. When Atal Bihari Vajpayee met Shastriji after two and half years in 1965, he noted with pleasure, 'While talking to the King of Nepal, I realized that three fourth of my work has already been done by Shri Guruji by preparing a favourable background for strengthening Bharat-Nepal friendship' (Ranga Hari 2018, 256).

In spite of such a cooperative environment, the central government had stopped the Nepal King's tour and aborted his plans of attending the Makar Sankranti festival of Sangh where he had been invited as the Chief Guest on 14 January 1965. Dr Abaji Thatte read out the speech of the Nepal King sent through his consul (Ranga Hari 2018, 257). On one hand, Shastriji had admitted that three-fourth of the work had been done by Guruji, on the other hand, this was the reward the RSS received from the prime minister of Bharat! But, Guruji never held any grudges.

In the current scenario of strong antagonism between the Communist regime of Nepal and the Indian government, we can see how big the blunder was, to keep snubbing Nepal's kings in the name of secularism and encouraging Communist rebellion in the name of democratic struggle. India's governments did their best to push Nepal into China's lap.

In the wake of the war with Pakistan in 1965, the prime minister had called for an all-party meeting to seek co-operation in war efforts from the top leaders of different political parties. He requested Guruji to be present in this meeting, the only non-political leader (Ranga Hari 2018, 272). Guruji said in that meeting, 'I will speak of only one thing, that is, we have to win this war. For this we should be ready to put in whatever efforts are required. There should be no political groupism.' Chiding an opposition leader for repeatedly saying, 'your army', he said that saying so is like treating the forces defending the country as outsiders. Even when it is clear that we have to defend ourselves when we are at war with the aggressors it is astonishing to say, 'let us define our war aims.' Let those who attack us define it. We don't need to. Our 'objective' is very clear. That is to gain victory while defending our honour and teaching right lessons to the aggressor (Ranga Hari 2018, 273). He put national interest above politics.

After the meeting he went to the border state of Gujarat straight from Delhi, where he spoke from the Akashvani station of Vadodara on 19 September. Essentially, he appealed to the society to stand with the army and the leaders in the war and keep up the moral fortitude of society. He then went to Punjab. He spoke before the army jawans and officers in Ambala cantonment on 15 October. He met the prime minister the second time on 12 November. He also met defence minister Yashwantrao Chavan. He spoke on 14th from the Red Fort grounds in a public meeting organized by the Sangh (Ranga Hari 2018, 274).

Guruji sent his comprehensive views about the possible accord with Pakistan in writing to Shastriji. He did not send it to the press, as he had written it as a citizen, not as a politician. He received the news of the sudden death of Shastriji while he was on tour in Assam. He rushed to Delhi the same day from Guwahati to pay his floral tributes to Shastriji (Ranga Hari 2018, 274). It showed his deep commitment to the nation irrespective of political differences.

In 1971, there was another decisive war with Pakistan that saw its dismemberment and birth of Bangladesh. Preceding this event, Pakistan had started throwing out Buddhist-Christian-Hindu brethren from East Pakistan across the borders on false pretences since many months. According to official sources, more than seven million refugees had already come into Bharat. According to information received by Intelligence Bureau, massive preparations for an attack from both East and West wings of Pakistan were afoot. In this complex scenario, a meeting of the Central Committee was presided over by Sarkaryavaah Balasaheb Deoras and attended by Sarsanghchaalaks. A resolution to awaken the people, maintain their morale and keep them ready to face the danger was passed. The resolution contained unconditional support and co-operation to the central government (Ranga Hari, 324).

He addressed the swayamsevaks in Kerala and cautioned, 'It will be wrong to think that danger is only in the north-west parts. It will be wrong to escape the fact that the enemy can smuggle arms through seas. We shall have to be alert day and night.' One can imagine that he must have been seen as an alarmist in those times. But, his views on coastal security are relevant even now. He toured Bengal, Gujarat and Rajasthan subsequently (Ranga Hari, 325). He prepared the swayamsevaks and society to face the situation with courage. In spite of his criticism of the government, he supported the government fully and praised Indira Gandhi on the decisive victory in the war and the creation of Bangladesh.

But, Guruji was a realist too. While the nation was celebrating the birth of Bangladesh and going ecstatic, he was careful and cautious, though even he too was pleased with the developments. He was in Calcutta from December 31 to 2 January 1972. During a discussion, a swayamsevak asked Guruji on a lighter note, 'What is the meaning of "saavdhaan" in Sangh?' (saavdhaan is an order in physical drills) Guruji answered, 'Be cautious.' Picking up that thread, Guruji noted,

> We should be cautious in the life of our nation too. Fervour should not overpower us, nor should we overpower fervour. Do not forget that Bangladesh is that land where Muslims are in majority. When the Vijayanagar Empire was prosperous by virtue of its own strength, five Muslim states surrounding it had come together to attack and destroy it. Possibly, in future, two enemy nations instead of one may confront us. (Ranga Hari 2018, 326)

This was his analysis within two weeks of Bharat's victory when there was euphoria all round. Subsequent developments proved that he was not off the mark.

It is a measure of his dedication that he was working at this hectic pace when he had already been diagnosed with cancer in the chest.

Untiring Work despite Terminal Illness

The cancer could have been actually detected in 1969 when he embraced a monk, his old time friend of RK Mission, and experienced searing pain when his pen touched a small boil on his chest. But, he did not pay any attention. Finally when the boil became too apparent, his cancer was confirmed in Pune Sangh Shiksha Varg in May 1970. Doctors told him not to postpone it as it could prove dangerous. Guruji said after a pause, 'Let us do it after completion of training camps by June end.' His tours from one Sangh Shiksha Varg camp to another began again. He never betrayed any anxiety and worked through these months as if nothing had happened (Ranga Hari 2018, 309). The operation was done on 1 July.

Another round of turbulence was about to hit the RSS and Indian politics. At the peak of her popularity, Indira Gandhi was busy strengthening her power further and trying to finish any opposition. She saw Sangh too as her enemy. Again the idea of a ban on the Sangh was floated. Old stale arguments were played out again. But Guruji was unmoved. His appeal was to double the number of swayamsevaks and he directed the swayamsevaks to keep working, keeping their cool.

He held a press conference in Delhi in June. Responding to a question about a ban, he said, 'Such a threat would not work. Such an action would prove to be dangerous for them. Let them remember their earlier experiences' (Ranga Hari 2018, 310–11). Later, while he was in hospital, the Delhi government did ban holding of shakhas in public grounds but nothing came of it (Ranga Hari, 313). Another round of experiments in controlling the RSS had begun, though they did not succeed.

He was under Ayurvedic treatment when the Vivekananda Rock Memorial was finally inaugurated by the President on 4 September 1970. Naturally, his heart ached at his infirmity and his chats indicated that he wished he were there. He must have recalled the struggle that went into building the memorial (Ranga Hari 2018, 316). Finally, he was able to visit the memorial on 15 January 1972.

During one of his post-operative chats with the doctor, he asked the doctor about the time left with him. The doctor replied honestly that it was around three years. 'Good enough. I will be able to do a lot,' was his answer. (Ranga Hari, 316) He seemed not at all worried with the imminent painful culmination of his life.

Eight years after the celebration of the Swami Vivekananda Birth Centenary, the centenary year of Sri Aurobindo came up. But the government was not in a mood to participate in it with an open heart because Aurobindo Ashram refused to accept a government suggestion of removing a map of 'Spiritual Bharat' exhibited in the Ashram that represented an undivided Bharat or modify any of Maharshi's literature. The Sangh filled in the breach and organized celebration committees till the level of villages in entire Bharat. Shri Aurobindo's speech given in 1909 May in Uttarpada was translated and published in nearly all regional languages. Shri Aurobindo Centenary was celebrated far and wide throughout Bharat under the guidance of Guruji (Ranga Hari 2018, 323)

Last Interview about Minority Issue

In December 1971, Guruji gave an interview to Arabic scholar and journalist Dr Saifuddin Jeelani that covered a lot of ground on Sangh's views on minorities. This being his last interview, it should be taken as his views on the minority issue. It was published in *Organiser* weekly in January 1972. Guruji presented clear views on Muslims that were quite different from how he is presented.

In his response to the solution to Hindu-Muslim problem, Guruji said, "I do not differentiate between Hindus and Muslims when it is a matter of working for the nation. A solution to it is possible if leaders stop looking at it as a political bargaining point.' He explained that political parties only work for power, they don't think of the nation. He clarified, 'I work for the Hindus because I think for the nation. If Hindus begin to go against national interest, I will not keep any relations with them' (*Samadhan* 1998, 66). Muslims should get their share, but it does not mean that they should ask for special rights and privileges. When their leaders talk of unfurling their flag on Red Fort, and the top leader doesn't deny the statement, it upsets people who think about the nation (*Samadhan* 1998, 67).

He pointed out that Pakistan celebrated the 5000th anniversary of Panini who was born in that part of the land. 'If Pakistanis can remember him as their forefather, why can't our local Hindu Muslims do the same? I call them "Hindu Muslims". They can also consider Panini, Vyas, Valmiki, Ram and Krishna as their forefathers. Many Hindus too don't consider Ram and Krishna as avatars but consider them as great persons. So, if Muslims don't consider them as avatars, it doesn't matter,' he said. He went on to stress that Muslims should follow their religion honestly but this should be with deference to national interest. Nobody can claim privileges at the cost of the nation. He said, 'We do not say that only they have a right over Bharat as Hindus. We never say that. If some people come forward and say they want a state within a state and a separate existence, I cannot bear this argument. Everybody today is trying to be declared a minority because special rights have been granted to minorities.'

Jeelani asked Guruji why Hindus and Muslims should not come together as people who believe in God to fight Communists who don't believe in God. He shared his experience with a Kashmiri Muslim, claiming to be from the Sufi tradition, who came up with the same suggestions but after some discussions about Dharmic religions believing in so many different forms of God, he finally said, 'Why don't all of you convert to Islam?' (*Samadhan* 1998, 69) The discussions ended.

He went on to say, 'I don't like the word "tolerance" because it means tolerating someone. Higher emotion is to respect others' views. We do not believe in tolerance, we believe in respect.' To another question, he said that wherever there is a communal problem in the country, the politician is the villain there. Unfortunately, the politician has become the people's leader. He went on to say that people should stop following men of straw and follow people with high character and a large heart.

On the question about what could be the way for creating affection between the two communities, he said, 'We should not have non-religious education, but education that gives knowledge about all the religions at a broad level. We should also not tell a distorted history. If Muslims from foreign lands plundered Bharat, our Muslims should say that such an attack is not their tradition as they are from Bharat. No leader seems to have the courage to say so' (*Samadhan* 1998, 71).

The Bharatiya Jan Sangh had introduced a concept of '*Bharatiyakaran*' or 'Indianization' during this time. Jeelani asked about it. Guruji said,

> Indianization call was, no doubt, given by Jan Sangh. But, Indianization does not mean converting everybody to Hindu. As I have said, we should understand and believe that we are all the sons of this land that we indeed are. We should believe that we are part of this same society. Our aspirations are also the same. This is the meaning of Indianization. It does not mean leaving your ways of worship. We don't support it, nor can we think like this. We believe that no single way of worship is ideal for the entire human kind.

On Jeelani's suggestion whether this was the right time to meet Muslim leaders who wish to remove communal misgivings and find a way out of it, he said, not only did he like the idea, but he welcomed it (*Samadhan* 1998, 72).

Dr Jeelani wrote about this extraordinary interview,

> This meeting with Shri Guruji proved to be a highly inspiring and unforgettable incident in my life. I have met all the big personalities of world from Hitler to Col. Nasser, but I have not come across any person as pleasant, confident and impressive as Shri Guruji. I honestly feel that Shri Guruji is the only person who can provide the desired guidance to solve the Hindu-Muslim problem. (Ranga Hari 2018, 321)

Last Workshop

Considering Guruji's health, it was decided that a special national-level intellectual workshop would be conducted that year at a suitable time. The last such workshop was organized in Indore twelve years back. In this passage of time many dimensions of Sangh movement had grown in multiple ways (Ranga Hari 2018, 339). The idea, obviously, was that he should put forth his views to the top rung of RSS workers one last time, share his vision about the RSS and Bharat. He would also clarify any query from his colleagues.

This was the last workshop Guruji attended and this was also the last Diwali of his life. The meeting took place from 23 October to 3 November 1972 in Thane in the premises of Swaadhyaay Parivar. Guruji exhibited exemplary willpower yet again. He would go from Chembur (where he stayed during this time at the local Sanghchalak, Anantrao Deshpande's house) to Tata Memorial for radiation therapy, then travel to Thane for the workshop, attend it for the entire day, take active part all through and return to Chembur. Considering the quality of cars, roads and distances, one can imagine that it would be a tough call even for a normally healthy person. Ranga Hari notes in his biography of Guruji, 'Guruji never seemed exhausted. His face reflected same happiness, his voice had same sweetness, his presentations had same logical clarity, his conclusions carried same sharp intellect. Only difference that he spoke in sitting posture and cough used to disturb him once in a while' (Ranga Hari 2018, 340). His almost super-human control over his terminally sick body showed the strength of his spirituality and it left a deep impression on all the RSS swayamsevaks.

He explained to the participants that this workshop was to reinforce some of the ideals and ideas and discuss them in current perspective. Some of the points he made during these discussions are noted here. He said,

> Hindu philosophy and living systems have been present in this country, when Islamic and Christian communities did not even exist in this world. One may ask, then, how can Hindu mean to be anti-Muslim? Similarly, Sikh and Jain sects etc.

> come within purview of Hindu. If one were to have a feeling of opposing them when one speaks of 'Hindu' it would be akin to cutting one's own limbs. Then, how is Hindu against them? Undoubtedly, these allegations are born out of petty mentality and confusions resulting from it. There is no truth in this. All these are falsehoods. 'Hindu' is not against anybody. This is a completely emotional thought, against anybody at all.

He asserted,

> We must say with complete resolve that, yes, we are Hindus. This is our dharma, our culture, our society and built from all this is our nation. Our birth is only to build a powerful, capable, grand, effulgent independent life for it. It is paramount to have such a strong belief in our hearts. Therefore, we must motivate other people for this purpose. There is no need to be embarrassed or be afraid in expanding this view. (Ranga Hari 2018, 340–42)

In the workshop he shared his thoughts on democracy and electoral process. He said,

> Of all the types of systems of governance in the world, it is accepted that democracy has the least shortcomings. Entire populace gets representation in this system. But, for system to succeed it is mandatory that common people should be well educated. Not only well educated but they should have good knowledge about economics, politics, international relations etc. so that they are capable of selecting the right representative. If it does not happen this way and common people are illiterate and have no information then they can chose ineligible representative due to some selfish motive or inducements. Such a society repents for the next five years, wondering what it has done. Lack of education and awareness of voter means a bleak scenario for democracy as capable representatives are not elected. There are other negative fallouts too because of this and then basic thought

> about democracy is lost. [....] Difficulties arise in democratic structure. How can we find a way out of these? One view that comes up in this regard is that current system is to elect people on territory and population based on census etc. This can be kept as it is and in addition system of having representatives of industry and other segments should be followed. All other professions and businesses should be represented in a structured manner this way. It is called 'Functional Representation.' It is already implemented in some countries. If it can be linked to the present electoral system, then the assembly which is made up of uninformed people and takes responsibility of running the government will also have some knowledgeable people. They would be able to provide novel thoughts about any subject when required. (Ranga Hari 2018, 342–43)

When some participant raised some queries about Communism and Socialism, he surprised the audience with an entirely new perspective. He talked about a rarely known book, *Sukhdaayak Rajyaprakarani Nibandh*. None in the audience knew about it. He elaborated,

> This is a Marathi book written by Shri Vishnubua Brahmachari in 1867. As the name indicates, it is an essay about a system of governance that would result in happiness. The writer had sent out 10,000 copies of the book translated in English in 1870 within and outside Bharat. The book became a subject of discussion everywhere at that time. It was also translated in Hindi and Gujarati. The same year also saw publication of Karl Marx's *Das Kapital*. It is beyond imagination that both of them could have met by any chance. Still their direction of thinking and its conclusions are quite close to each other. Surprisingly, both books are original and revolutionary thoughts about political, economic and social thinking. Both sages give directions about progress of human society with their own intellectual prowess. The only key difference in their

> presentations is that Brahmachari took both material and spiritual aspects into account, therefore accepted dharma as the power that holds society together. Marx said that religion is opium of the mind. He found it obligatory to criticize religion and he did so successfully. There was solid reason behind it. It was not possible for him to think of 'Dharma' the way this concept is understood in Bharat. What he had in front of him were outdated semetic forms of religions. On the other hand, Vishnuji was a celibate follower of Dattatreya sect. Because of this background, his analysis was based on Bharatiya experience and ethics. This scripture of Vishnubua being inspired by swadeshi talent, can be more valuable and helpful for the labour movement in this country. (Ranga Hari 2018, 343)

This interaction showed the depth of Guruji's studies. A booklet titled *Dishabodh* was published subsequently, carrying the proceedings of this workshop. This again showed the vast storehouse of knowledge that he carried in his mind and used it discreetly to guide people, not to impress anyone.

His commitment to social cause defied even serious sickness. He went out during his terminal days on December 27 to unveil a life size statue of Dr Munje in Sitaburdi, Nagpur. Guruji was the Chairman of its organizing committee. Members included Jagjivan Ram and C. Rajagopalachari. The chief guest was General Cariappa. This was his last public programme (Ranga Hari 2018, 349).

Guruji had developed a second cancer boil, still he went on a last tour of seventy-five days. He left this world on 5 June 1973 while the Sangh Shiksha Varg was going on. He murmured his last Sangh prayer the evening before his atman left his body. He was only sixty-seven at that time.

Shri Guruji: The Leader

Guruji was the longest serving Sarsanghchaalak and the youngest to be nominated for this post. He saw the RSS and the nation through the most turbulent periods. He took charge in 1940 when the RSS had just struck roots and comprised very young swayamsevaks and karyakartas and leaders. Recall that when the Satyagraha against the RSS ban in 1948 was announced, Nehru had dismissively said, 'What can these urchins do?' The organization was, indeed, very young. The young all India-level leaders of the RSS were in their twenties.

His ability to keep himself above political bitterness and keep the good of the nation as the ultimate goal led the organization out of its worst phase. He could inculcate this habit of not carrying any animosity in his heart despite routine persecution, political untouchability and RSS-bashing and spread it across the organization to help workers across rank and file conserve their energy for positive work. He never let ideological differences cloud personal relations, just like Dr Hedgewar. He would jokingly call the BMS founder, Dattopant Thengdi, 'our communist in the Sangh.'

He nurtured that sapling left behind by Dr Hedgewar into a massive banyan tree of hundreds of small and big organizations that reached every nook and corner of the nation, and touched nearly every aspect of social life.

Over time, the RSS recovered from internal self-doubts, despite weakening of the organization after strenuous period from 1946 to 1949. It was his calm and encouraging guidance and intense travelling that made it happen. Any other organization would have collapsed under the strain of the painful and self-sacrificing work done during Partition along with sustained persecution by the the Congress and a struggle get the ban lifted over one-and-a-half-years, followed by turbulence within the organization.

It is no small sacrifice to give up on the goal of 'nirvana' and move back into the society. Though he forsook the bhagwa clothes of his sanyasi persona, he lived the life of an ascetic. Even during Badrinath pilgrimage he did not use any special food or clothing. He didn't wear socks and shoes though he made arrangements for them. He said, 'There are many people in mountains who manage to live without special clothes to ward off cold, then why should I need so many clothes to protect myself from cold?' He had stopped taking even tea. He would not take dinner in the evening or milk at night. He used to take food only once in a day, and that too very little (Ranga Hari 2018, 293). Earlier in 1967, he had told an Ayurvedacharya that he had hardly slept for nearly ten to twelve years and ate frugally, when he had gone for treatment to Kerala. Surprisingly, all his other indicators were fine. This was the life of a true mendicant, who carried on his life's mission without any outward show of spirituality.

In spite of politically adversarial positions and objective criticism of the government for lack of vision and strategy, the RSS always helped the government and stood by the nation through all the wars. He would write letters to various prime ministers anytime he felt like sharing an idea, not letting egos come in the way. He had his eyes firmly on national security and foreign affairs too, especially neighbouring countries. He cautioned the government time and again about Pakistan's infiltrations and China's aggression. He tried to make the government see reason and treat Nepal with warmth and give it the respect it deserved. He raised alarms about infiltration from East Pakistan, Christianisation of the Northeast, and linguistic reorganization of states and how this could lead to fissiparous tendencies (Karandikar 1999, 521). However, despite his differences, when attacks did take place, he got the entire RSS might behind the government's war-time efforts.

During the years of anti-RSS feelings, political untouchability and ostracization of the RSS, Guruji travelled across Bharat continuously to create an atmosphere for Sangh thought, nurtured leaders, helped create new organizations. He overcame all this negativity and defied all attempts to marginalize the RSS. It was through this untiring labour of love, that the society at large changed its view about the RSS and the RSS grew from strength to strength in all the fields of national life.

He stabilized and institutionalized the working of the prachaarak system that was informal when he took over as the RSS Sarsanghchaalak. He extended the feeling of the RSS being a family organization over time by guiding workers on how to build relations with families. He himself stayed in homes, many of which did not have basic amenities and identified with every member of the family. His example went a long way in creating a culture.

Dr Hedgewar created a system of taking decisions collectively, not letting a person become bigger than the organization, beginning with himself. He fine-tuned the consensus-building process that had been initiated by Dr Hedgewar.

His acute attention to details, words and deeds saw a healthy growth of the RSS into a mature organization with a balanced approach to all the issues. His deep knowledge and erudite enunciation was fact based, not rhetoric or emotion based, though his speeches had a strong emotional appeal. As seen in the previous pages, he was a true democrat both inside the organization and outside in the socio-political field.

In today's world, his disinterest in publishing literature about the Sangh and its philosophy and abhorrence to any kind of publicity, even of the right kind may look anachronistic. But, he firmly believed in person to person contact for spreading Sangh work like his predecessor. He believed that publicity could disturb positive work and distract workers. Person-to-person contact is still considered the life-blood of the RSS.

He explained that the *Bouddhik* (or intellectual activities) in Sangh falls under this classification of 'shruti.' This is not an exhibition of one's intellect, but a radiation of emotions of the heart (Ranga Hari 2018, 93). Many people take this as his disdain for intellectualism, though he himself was an intellectual of the highest order. But, his advice to swayamsevaks not to argue hard to win a debate had a different reason. 'You may win a debate but will lose a person who could be yours in future,' he said.

His personality affected organizational behaviour of most of the RSS workers, especially prachaaraks. They looked at the entire service to the motherland as a spiritual exercise. When he went to Kerala to recover from physical weakness due to his incessant tours he was asked to light a lamp and pray before the treatment began. Guruji said, 'Me? Oh friend, I have never prayed to God for this physical body. I have prayed a lot no doubt, but never for my body.' After two-three seconds pause he added, 'Doesn't mother understand more about the demands of the child? For me it is just *karishye vachanam tava* [carrying out thy orders]. For everything else, I have faith in Him' (Ranga Hari 2018, Chapter 36). This sense of submission to the motherland as a living God percolated throughout the organization.

Though the critics feel that Guruji was an inward-looking purist who focused only on the RSS shakha work, they forget that it was his time that saw maximum diversification in nearly all the fields of national life. He was a guardian to all the RSS-inspired organizations—national as well as regional. Even as he nurtured his most favourite organizational work of RSS and its shakhas, he inspired and guided RSS-inspired organizations to bloom in almost every field—students, education, empowering tribal brethren, politics and religion and beginning of Hindu consolidation even outside Bharat. If we were to look carefully, except VHP that is focused on religious renaissance, all other organizations that grew under his eyes and guidance were focused on the material well-being of people—basically focused on *param vaibhav* as mentioned in the RSS daily prayer—that is prosperity. His approach to social well-being was spiritual in an elevated sense, but work was rooted in reality of all-round development of the society and inviduals.

I have quoted him earlier showing that he believed that the men required to take up various projects and head organizations are created in RSS shakhas; if they go weak, the required organizers will not be available. Dr Hedgewar used to call RSS shakhas as the power house that supplied power to the society. It was incumbent that the generator should not trip.

His faith in the cultural unity of India came from his actual experience across India during his endless travels. Witnessing diversity radiating out of the same unity, Guruji had said,

> I had the great fortune to traverse whole of Bharat from Himalayas to Indian Ocean. I have gone to Kashmir and also to Kanyakumari. I have literally travelled across Bharat many times over, to the extent that I have reached smallest places in remote parts of our nation for prolonged periods. I have reached the conclusion that, actually there is no difference between people of this country at individual level in real sense. They have similar strengths and similar weaknesses. Then, that person may be a Tamil-speaking person, or Marathi or Bengali or Punjabi-language-speaking person. The lesson that this mission has taught me, makes me see all these people as one. (Ranga Hari 2018, Chapter 17)

Though focused on Bharat's rise, his mind was not closed to the world. Far from it, he was of the view that Bharat has a lot to learn from the world and a lot to be gifted to the world. Guruji was clear about larger canvas of Sangh work. He once said,

> RSS has not come into being to run riot with a lathi in hand. Our next goal is to achieve peace in the world. Spreading the spiritual message and create the feeling of brotherhood is our real work. But when will it happen? When we are able to bring together lakhs of people who have imbibed the cultural values only then can this goal be achieved. This should be our thinking when we do Sangh work. (Karandikar 1999, 465)

He used to say, we are organization specialists. He not only created a strong closely knit organization but also an organizational science that clearly demarcated the borders and limitations of different spheres of social organizations that came out during his time. He created a stable organization structure that was so flexible yet so strong that it could absorb varying personalities, run organizations in different, sometimes competing social spheres, growing within the same fold. He left behind this open flexible structure that has endured after his passing away for nearly fifty years, with no signs of inadequacy. This was his biggest contribution to the RSS and organizational science.

Balasaheb Deoras: Moulding RSS into an Activist Movement (1973–1994)

Madhukar Dattatrey Deoras (aka Balasaheb Deoras) was a swayamsevak of the first shakha of the RSS that was started by Dr K.B. Hedgewar. Balasaheb's family hailed from a small village called Chennur in Andhra Pradesh on the banks of the Godavari, and migrated to Nagpur via Chandrapur about 200 years back. Born in December 1915 in Nagpur, in a family of five brothers and four sisters, Balasaheb was the eighth child. Being one of the youngest in the family, his pet name 'Bal' (in Marathi, it means 'child') became more popular than his real name, Madhukar. Two years later the youngest sibling Murlidhar, better known by his pet name Bhaurao, was born (Hebalkar 2000, 2).

Both the brothers joined the RSS shakha in 1926–27 at a young age and went on to become prachaaraks. They loved carrom and cricket, but both brothers would drop any game when it was time for shakha. Recognizing his brilliant calibre, Dr Hedgewar made Bal the leader of a team of talented young teenage swayamsevaks. The team was called Kushak Pathak. This group had members such as Eknath Ranade, Yadavrao Joshi, Bhaurao Deoras, Bapurao Divakar and Narhari Parkhee, among others. All of them went on to lead various RSS activities throughout their lives (Hebalkar 2000, 8).

Balasaheb trained under the guidance of Dr Hedgewar from being a teenage swayamsevak to become a talented karyakarta (worker). He was an expert organizer. When Dr Hedgewar decided to extend Sangh work in Itwari area of Nagpur, which was basically an area of traders, Balasaheb was given the responsibility. It had nearly one-fifth of the Nagpur population but the shakha there was weak. Realizing the difficulty of tradesmen to come to shakha in the evenings, he started experimenting with new timings. Morning (*Prabhat*) shakha, annual functions, weekly meetings, and so on, were introduced. Due to this, the Sangh work struck roots in this area. His talent for innovative solutions was noted by Dr Hedgewar. (Pachpore 2011, 35) Considering the expansion of shakhas, he also directed that swayamsevaks coming from different localities should start shakhas in their own locality. This led to a big growth in shakhas.

Balasaheb passed his graduation in Sanskrit and Philosophy as well as his LLB with distinction. His father was ambitious that he should take the Indian Civil Service (ICS) exams (and he could have done so easily), but he refused. His heart was already made up. He wished to devote his life to society and work for it through the Sangh. His excellent academic record was a big achievement considering that he studied only for almost twenty-four hours without much sleep for fifteen days. The reason was that he was busy with RSS work all the time and also teaching boys English in an orphanage for one and half years during this period. (Hebalkar 2000, 36)

Right from childhood, Balasaheb had a reformist's zeal. As a young boy he told his mother that all his friends, irrespective of their caste, must be served together. His mother happily agreed (Karandikar 1999, 550).

An Untiring Karyakarta

An informal system of prachaaraks had already come up by the time he was given some responsibilities in the Nagpur shakha. As a young RSS karyakarta, he came up with an idea of *Vistaarak* that would be full-time RSS work for a short duration. A swayamsevak was to work for limited periods (during his holidays or take short leaves from work for a few months) and expand the shakha network. This led to a spurt in shakhas in Nagpur (Pachpore 2011,

38). He had attended Sindi baithak in 1939 (see Chapter 2). He was the youngest member of this group.

When Balasaheb Deoras was asked to go as a prachaarak to Calcutta in November 1939, his father was highly incensed. He rushed to the station when he came to know that his son was catching a train. Playing hide and seek, Balasaheb evaded his father and left for Calcutta. Some years later when their father went to Kashi, arrangements for his comfortable stay were made by swayamsevaks who spoke highly of both his sons. His father then realized how big they had become and the respect they had earned. He felt proud of his sons. After he returned to Nagpur, he would speak proudly of his sons, who had certainly earned more respect than what an ICS officer would have received (Pachpore 2011, 47–48).

Bhaurao never returned to Nagpur after going to Lucknow. He worked as a prachaarak in the north after graduation, and spent a major part of his life in UP. He nurtured wonderful leaders such as Pandit Deendayal Upadhyay, Atal Bihari Vajpayee, Ashok Singhal, Prof. Rajendra Singh, Murli Manohar Joshi, Baleshwar Agrawal and Laxmanrao Bhide. He also played a crucial role in the expansion of the Sangh's work in Assam, Bihar and Bengal (Pachpore 2011, 36). Both the Deoras brothers played a big role in the expansion and evolution of the RSS. A very senior prachaarak told me that the only reason Bhaurao Deoras did not agree to be Sarkaryavaah—though he was eminently suitable for the post—was that two brothers at the top could have sent a wrong message to the swayamsevaks and to people at large.

Balasaheb was a quintessential swayamsevak. He was self-effacing and a disciplined organizer who would speak only when required. He had a great quality of nurturing karyakartas and prachaaraks. There are stories about this strict disciplinarian who had a soft heart for the swayamsevaks that would make him run to their home in case of any sickness or problem. I have seen this myself, how he would pay personal attention to each karyakarta with empathy and patience. Dr Sharad Hebalkar mentions an insightful incident about his encouragement to Baburao Chauthaiwale, who was then a karyakarta, in his biography.

After giving the Intermediate exam, Baburao showed his willingness to go as a tehsil prachaarak somewhere in Vidarbha, and he informed Balasaheb accordingly. However, after talking to Eknath Ranade who was looking after Mahakoshal prant, he was appointed as district prachaarak of Chhindwara. From the Sangh's point of view, it was a tough place. He told Balasaheb, 'I can't speak Hindi. I don't know how to give lecture in *Bouddhik* varg. I don't have enough experience to run a shakha independently. That is why I request you to send me to a small tehsil place.' Balasaheb told him, 'Oh! You have become a big man!' Baburao, with his head bowed, replied, 'No, it is not like that.' Then Balasaheb explained gently,

> Arrey, one who comes to know himself well, is called a big man. Are you telling me what you are? No karyakarta in [the] Sangh comes completely polished. Even I was not, right? But, we have to mould ourselves according to the need. You will learn Hindi, since you don't know it. Watch how an experienced and intelligent prachaarak like Eknathji works and talks to leading persons. Watch how he takes baithak, and practise. You will be successful.

Baburao ultimately proved to be successful. Infact, Eknath Ranade once told Guruji, '*Babu, achcha kaam karta hai* [Babu does good work].' Balasaheb was mature beyond his years (Hebalkar 2000, 69).

Balasaheb was given the responsibility of a camp of 10,000 held in 1947 in Pardi near Nagpur, of which he made a grand success in every sense. He was an organizer par excellence and this could be seen in whichever responsibility he was given. He added new dimensions to RSS methodology. For example, he introduced collective singing of patriotic songs in shakha and RSS programmes (Pachpore 2011, 82). No one remembers when the solo song was introduced before an intellectual lecture; it had become a part of the standard process earlier. Working closely with Guruji, he was also involved in changes made to the RSS uniform (Karandikar 1999, 552).

A Disciplined Disciple of Dr Hedgewar

Guruji had huge respect for Balasaheb. Maybe he was aware of the expectations Doctorji had from Balasaheb, and knew he would have liked to see Balasaheb take on bigger responsibilities as he matured in the organization. He was hardly twenty-five years old when Doctorji passed way. Guruji used to introduce Balasaheb thus, 'If you wish to see Doctorji, and understand how he worked, look at Balasaheb.' In an OTC camp in Pune in 1943, Guruji told participants that if they had not seen Dr Hedgewar, they could look at Balasaheb Deoras to understand how he worked. Though not recorded in his biography, a story that many prachaaraks recall (and I have heard it too), is that Guruji called for him from the kitchen to give his introduction to the participants. Balasaheb was in charge of the kitchen arrangements. He came to the meeting room with his hand behind him as they were wet with the flour he was kneading. Guruji asked him to give a *Bouddhik* (lecture) there itself, not realizing that his hands were not clean! Balasaheb gave a lecture for forty-five minutes without batting an eyelid—not one person could guess his condition!

Balasaheb played a key role along with other young leaders like Eknath Ranade in the satyagraha for the lifting of the ban on the RSS in 1948. Guruji was in jail and had given full authority to Balasaheb to take decisions on satyagraha and also hold discussions with the government. When talks on the ban were frustrated by the obdurate approach of Jawaharlal Nehru, the RSS took a tough stance. Balasaheb wrote a letter to Guruji about floating a political party and deliberately leaked the letter. The government got worried and it was one of the reasons behind lifting the ban. Moulichandra Sharma was sent for negotiations. He told Moulichandra clearly that Guruji will not make any appeal to Nehru for lifting of the ban. When the documents were finally prepared by Balasaheb and Eknath Ranade, Guruji signed them without getting into details, so much was the trust between the team. Moulichandra was amazed on realizing the trust between the two (Karandikar 1999, 554).

During the time of the RSS ban, Nagpur University elections were held in 1948. Vasantrao Sathe, who went on to become a minister in the central government, approached the RSS leadership for help in the elections, harking back on his earlier time as a swayamsevak. But Balasaheb motivated the RSS youth to fight on their own considering the strong presence of swayamsevaks in the colleges. Finally, the swayamsevak won the elections beating the united challenge of Students Congress and Communist-inspired Students Federation. This was before ABVP had been launched. (Hebalkar 2000, 82) One can thus see his keenness and his visionary approach for the RSS to foray into other segments of society.

When it was decided to enter the publication field for proper dissemination of national news and views, Balasaheb took on the responsibility of running the daily *Tarun Bharat* as well as the management of the trust Shree Narkesari Prakashan, which was established in 1949. He was the chairman of the trust (Pachpore 2011, 52). Even when he was inactive in the Sangh for a few years, he continued to take care of the management of the trust. After *Tarun Bharat*, other periodicals began to be published from different states.

There are people in the RSS who believe that Guruji leading the RSS and Balasaheb leading Jan Sangh in politics would have been the best possible solution in 1951–52. However, Guruji was of the firm opinion that the RSS needed Balasaheb for its growth (Pachpore 2011, 58). His repeated pronouncements of Balasaheb's importance in the scheme of things showed his conviction time and again. This was perhaps dictated by his understanding of what Doctorji's expectations from Balasaheb Deoras as well as the image of Doctorji that he could see in him.

However, Balasaheb was not actively involved in the Sangh from 1950 to 1960. According to his biographer, Dr Hebalkar,

Balasaheb was unwell at this time. Diabetes had struck his young body. Despite this, he gave his full energy to resolve any issue sent to him by Guruji during this period. Guruji deputed a poor swayamsevak Nathuprasad for his care, who stayed with him for ten years. When he was fit enough, Balasaheb would go to his village to enjoy farming. At other times, he stayed at the Sangh office (Hebalkar 2000, 108). He kept a close watch on the arrangements made for prachaaraks and nurtured them carefully.

His family farm was in Karanja in Balaghat district in Madhya Pradesh. He would go there whenever he found time, as he took personal interest in farming. He also took care of the entire village, getting it electricity and other infrastructural help. Later he, along with Bhaurao, sold the farm and donated the entire amount to the RSS for sewa projects (Hebalkar 2000, 107).

When he began taking up responsibilities on his return, many people wished him to join politics. He simply said, 'I will do whatever Guruji tells me to do' (Hebalkar 2000, 110). He began his activities again in 1960 as a Nagpur karyavaah. In 1962, he was appointed Sahsarkaryavaah of the RSS when a memorial for Dr Hedgewar was inaugurated. When Bhaiyyaji Dani, his close friend left this world, he was appointed Sarkaryavaah. It was during this tenure that he introduced the concept of each shakha doing some socially relevant programme in its neighbourhood (Pachpore 2011, 53).

When Guruji passed away in 1973, Balasaheb was in Hyderabad. He rushed to Nagpur. When his appointment was announced as Sarsanghchaalak, he was stunned. He exclaimed, 'Was he not aware of my weak health?' But since he was given this responsibility, he gave his all to it (Pachore 2011, 63). In fact, fifteen days before these developments took place, he had fallen unconscious due to complications from diabetes. However, he had not told Guruji about the incident when he came to Nagpur fearing he would be worried.

In his acceptance speech Balasaheb said,

> I am not knowledgeable like Doctorji or Guruji, or nor am I a speaker like them. I just have some capabilities as a manager and a competent administrator. But, Guruji has created a team of rare workers [he used the word *dev durlabh*—that even Gods would find difficult to get]. Therefore, I have belief that with their cooperation, I will be able to succeed in the responsibility I have been given. (Hebalkar 2000, 137)

He told his colleagues, 'Since Guruji believed that I am fit for this responsibility despite my sickness, please fix my tour programmes as required. Don't worry about my health' (Hebalkar 2000, 138). He worked incessantly for twenty-one years till his body simply refused to cooperate.

M.G. Vaidya notes that people wouldn't have been surprised if Dr Hedgewar had nominated Balasaheb as the Sarsanghchaalak before he passed away. But, he perhaps felt that the strong spiritual and intellectual base of Guruji was more important at that delicate time of the RSS's growth (Pachpore 2011, 57).

Balasaheb knew that he was going to be compared to Guruji who had a huge divine persona. He was a non-traditional yet dedicated reformist Sangh worker who had imbibed all modern philosophies and theories. He never did a regular morning ritual or evening puja. But because he did not want to disappoint swayamsevaks, he began to read the Bhagavad Gita regularly every morning after his bath, although he never talked about it (Pachpore 2011, 68).

On becoming Sarsanghchaalak, one of his first visits was to Madhukar Deval, who had left the RSS in 1949 to start his own project among Dalit brethren. He saw and understood the project at length and appreciated it wholeheartedly. He then went on to declare that it was also an RSS project. He didn't stop at this. He would talk about this project for the upliftment of Dalits in all his speeches in Bharat. He also visited Gyan Prabodhini of Appa Pendse in Pune. He went to meet all the ex-prachaaraks and swayamsevaks who had left the RSS during the tumultuous period of 1949–52. He could see the idea of social harmony in the project run by Deval and the next step he had in his mind was, therefore, to work consciously for social harmony (Pachpore 2011, 114–15). Thus, he was able to bring back nearly all the dissatisfied elements who had left the RSS in 1949–50, increase the presence of Sangh in other social fields and also strengthen its organization.

Assertive Reformer

When he was invited to deliver a lecture at the prestigious Vasant Vyakhyanmala, he agreed to speak there. He had a specific reason for this. His speech there on 8 May 1974 is considered historic. It removed many cobwebs from the mind of people about the RSS, and its approach to social inequality and casteism. The topic given to him was one he was very passionate about—social harmony and Hindu organization. He put forward the Sangh's point of view in a forthright manner. It is a classic lecture in the way it is structured, and one that set the tone for social discourse on casteism, untouchability and role of the RSS in resolving this conflict.

The background to this lecture was constant sniping at the RSS by vested interests. Probably that is why he had decided to take on the subject head-on. A few years back, Guruji had an academic informal chat followed by an interview with the editor of *Navakal*. During the chat, he expressed his opinion on *chatur varna* vis-à-vis caste system based on his vast reading and understanding of the subject and its irrelevance. He had gone on to call it *avyavasthaa*, (not order but chaos) as we noted in Chapter 2. We also saw that he had opposed ritualism as well as a traditional view of the caste system practised by Hindus and was instrumental in getting nearly all sadhus, gurus and sampradaya (sect) chiefs together under the banner of the Vishwa Hindu Parishad. He had pursuaded them to declare that all Hindus were born of the same mother, hence no Hindu could be untouchable. However, because of the way *Navakal* had presented the said interview, it stirred up a huge controversy in the heated politics of Maharashtra, known to run on the steam of caste politics. Witnessing the uproar due to this misrepresentation, Guruji had issued a statement and reasserted that whatever be the *varna vyavasthaa* of old times, it was not valid anymore and should be abolished. Simply put, it was out of sync with the present times. However, he was quoted out of context for years and is being quoted even now in public debates (Ranga Hari 2018, 296).

Balasaheb Deoras decided to take the bull by the horn and present the views of the RSS on this serious issue in a crystal clear manner. He had a reformist zeal from his younger days and followed it up with action on the field. We have seen that he had a highly scientific approach to social and religious issues. This logical and scientific approach clearly shows in his speech.

He began his talk by stressing on the greatness of Hindu culture and traditions, and then went on to chastise Hindus who continued to follow tradition just for the sake of it. He said,

> It is not true that all that is old is good. We don't keep drinking water from a salty well just because our forefathers drank [from] it. If new way to get sweet water is found, we should drink sweet water. Our scholars called such people who refuse this logic, cowards. We speak with pride about our old knowledge about astronomy, solar and moon eclipse. However, to explain these phenomena, the *Puranas* talk about Rahu-Ketu biting into Sun and Moon. Should we believe the stories word by word and publish them in our children's books? We should look at systems built by earlier societies as per their requirements of those times. We say, God has said that I take avatar again and again when there is harm to dharma. But, does it mean that when he/she is incarnated, he/she keeps the system or situation as is? We can say that God also makes changes as required. Every race and religion, except Islam have revised and relooked at their knowledge and made changes as per new situation. He gave example of Jews and Christians. (Deoras 2014, 10–11)

He continued,

> Somebody has said, any system entails classification. But, it doesn't mean there has to be discrimination. We don't have to have a varna system based on birth. Can we say feet are better than hands, or thighs are better than heart? They are all critical parts of our body that makes a complete person. There were no aptitude tests. There were checks and balances. In absence of checks and balances, new classes rise. In his book *The New Class*, Milauvan Djilas tells us how a new class has developed in Communist countries. If this can happen in Communism in fifty years, we are thousands of year old—distortions and vested interests would rise. There are directions in our scriptures that say, a Shudra with his actions can become a Brahmin and a Brahmin who is actionless is Shudra.

He challenged the very concept that some systems have been handed over to us or have been created by God. He said, 'When God takes an avatar, does he carry on with the old system? No. He changes the existing systems and structures and creates new ones.'

Balasaheb also gave examples of Rishi Shring, Vashishtha, Vishwamitra and Agastya, who became Brahmins because of their meditation. A Shudra woman's son Mahidas became a Brahmin. Jaabaal, whose father was unknown, was made Brahmin by his guru. Thus, our system was flexible. Slowly, as population rose, checks and balances became weaker, and children who learnt skills from their parents simply followed in their footsteps. It became hereditary. But, still there was no discrimination. To say that these qualities come from genes is incorrect. He went on to show how this theory has been proven wrong. He gave the example about the Japanese who were thought to be a martial race, but that isn't true. Therefore, to create a whole theory about genetics to justify *varna vyavasthaa* or caste system is laughable. Now there may be castes, but they are only for the purpose of marriage, as most people do not strictly follow in the professions of their varna.

> What was a system [*vyavasthaa*] earlier is no more a system. It is no more for organizing the society. It is *avyavasthaa*. It is distortion; it has nothing to do with social system. It is on the way out. All the society can think is how it can be banished in a proper manner. This is my view. However, dealing with each other [across castes] for marriages between our sons and daughters has not yet picked up. We must accept it frankly. We must [also] get rid of this constraint in marriages. Good matches shouldn't be on caste but on matching qualities of boys and girl, their education, their living style, etc. This can [remove] social inequality and discrimination.

Then finally he came to the topic he wished to speak about very strongly.

> The saddest issue today is that this social inequality has led to untouchability. Many scholars claim that it was not there earlier. But, it is there for centuries now. Everybody agrees that it is a grave mistake. It must go lock, stock and barrel. It should be destroyed completely; there is no doubt in anybody's mind. Abraham Lincoln when talking about slavery, had said, 'If slavery is not wrong, nothing is wrong.' We should also say, if untouchability is not wrong, nothing in the world is wrong... This inequality must go because it leads to breakdown of the society, makes it weak. All of us should explain this to people and find ways to stop it. This will lead to removal of inequality, and hurdles against Hindu unity will be removed. (Deoras 2014, 18–19)
>
> For this, we should take help from dharma gurus, sants, great leaders, scholars as they have great impact on society. There are gurus who stick to old ideas; [they] are orthodox. We can pray to them [so they can] see what is perennial and what is changeable as per [the need of the time]. Teach people accordingly. We should tell them, please do not sit in your *maths*—protecting the society is your duty. You can choose the way you wish to take the message to the masses.

He did not mince words in this bold lecture nor did he try to avoid any issue. He gave an example of how leaders of the Vishwa Hindu Parishad and Guruji persuaded acharyas to move among the deprived sections of the society. He also spoke of how through the work of the RSS, people who wished to return to their original faiths (*ghar wapsi*) were able to do so.

He talked about how Dr Hedgewar, through Sangh camps and programmes, could change people's conduct regarding caste divisions and idea of untouchability without being too harsh. He did not throw out people who behaved in a casteist manners; instead, he got them to change through love and patience.

He stressed,

> Our Dalit brethren have suffered a lot for centuries. They have borne with exploitation and atrocities. They carry this pain in their hearts, this pain is in our hearts too. Now we have to find way out of this situation. This inequality must go. All of us want this. We have to find ways to stop this injustice. For this, our behaviour should give strength to these efforts. Our language and our conduct should be such. This is my request to my Dalit brethren too... I am sure our Dalit brethren don't want pity or piety. They want to be equals. We should think on these lines. For this they need some facilities—they have a right to ask for these. How long they wish to keep these, it is their decision. Ultimately, they wish to prove that they are equal due to their talent. I know about this because I have talked to many of them. But, that day should come when all of us in society can say we are all equal now. (Deoras 2014, 26)

He went on to underline how the world has accepted the richness of our culture. But, to bring forth the wonder of our culture and knowledge, we still have to get over social inequality in the Hindu society. We need to do it in a persuasive way by taking everyone along.

With this timeless lecture, he not only smothered the casteist attacks on the RSS but also added a new dimension to RSS work. It set the tone of his term as Sarsanghchaalak.

Another incident in his life illustrates his strong feelings and sensitivity to this subject. His commitment to social harmony and removal of caste inequality was not limited to words. This incident took place much later in his life during his last years as Sarsanghchaalak. The stir for renaming of Marathwada University to Dr Babasaheb Ambedkar University was simmering for two decades. Only the Sangh had given its total support to it, while political parties were busy playing politics. During this period, the atmosphere came to a boil due to the sudden decision to implement the Mandal Commission report that had been lying dormant for years. The issue of the extension of reservation for SC/ST also came up in the Parliament during this time.

During these disturbing times, the Akhil Bharatiya Pratinidhi Sabha (ABPS) was discussing the issue of reservation, and a resolution to support the act was proposed in 1990. A heated debate ensued for the entire day. It is a tradition in the RSS that every resolution is debated upon and amended till a consensus can be reached. This debate had been quite agitated. It disturbed Balasaheb immensely. He was not well and was lying in his bed in a separate room and listening to the debate. He called the then Sarkaryavaah, Rajju Bhaiyya, and told him that he wished to go down to the meeting. His was so weak that it would have been very painful for him. However, he was adamant. He intervened in the debate and simply said, 'Imagine for a moment, you were born in a Dalit family. Put yourself in that position. Then, discuss whether reservations should continue or not' (Pachpore 2011, 119). The tone and tenor of the debate changed totally after his intervention and Rajju Bhaiyya steered it, so a harmonious message could be sent to society.

There was a tradition of some shlokas being recited in morning shakhas, which were a celebration of Bharatiya culture. To update it and make it more inclusive, Balasaheb set up a group in the 1980s. Sudarshanji was the *Bouddhik* pramukh at that time and he headed the group. This team added names of prominent leaders and saints. Not all were Hindus, and there was representation from other communities and professions as well—traditions and faiths like Jains, Sikhs, Boudhha, artists, scientists, political leaders, and so on, were added. It had Parsi and Muslim names too. There was an attempt to forge a national identity beyond all religious paradigms (Karandikar 2000, 556–57).

He brought in another huge and critical change in the Sangh's thinking. He set up the Prachaar Vibhag or media division. It was a major departure from the RSS philosophy of 'no need for media'. And though the media was used occasionally even in the past, it was more of a grudging use, with an unstated policy of avoiding use of media. The fact that this happened after almost seventy years of its existence indicates how big a change it was.

Balasaheb also decided to be more open to media and held discussions with them. He did not shy away from talking on politics too. In a press conference in Bangalore in 1974, he talked about the relation between the RSS and Jan Sangh.

> We gave our support and strengthened Jan Sangh of S.P. Mukherjee because we don't want to be isolated from the society or politics. Vallabhbhai Patel wished the Sangh to work with Congress but Nehruji was against it. Therefore we did not go to Congress. But our workers are free to join any party. At least political untouchability would go because of it. (Pachpore 2011, 115)

When asked how the RSS can think of a prosperous nation without 'Akhand Bharat', he said,

> Yes, it is our ambition to have Akhand Bharat. We still dream about it. How it will happen we can't say today. But, everyone agrees that Partition of India was not a good idea either culturally, geographically or from the point of view of security. This mistake can be undone only if we keep this dream alive. (Pachpore 2011, 115)

At another time, Balasaheb talked about forming a federation of nations from Iran to Singapore. The reason was that Bharat had long cultural relations with all these countries. By coming together, they could become a powerful block that could limit the influence of Russia, the US and China. This was an alternative practical view of Akhand Bharat (Pachhpore 2011, 116).

RSS Joins Anti-Corruption Movement and Fights for Democracy

The next life-changing decision for the RSS was a landmark decision in the history of the RSS. It was his direction to RSS swayamsevaks to participate in the anti-corruption movements that erupted in 1973 in Gujarat and then spread to Bihar. Though RSS's name was not officially a part of the movement, it was open enough about its people supporting this struggle. Balasaheb deputed Nanaji Deshmukh for this job. Nanaji Deshmukh was instrumental in persuading the highly respected Jaiprakash Narayan, a veteran socialist turned social worker who had given up politics, to return to politics and take the lead of this anti-corruption agitation. ABVP worked on the field wholeheartedly and in close cooperation with Jaiprakashji (Karandikar 1999, 558).

Nanaji Deshmukh had become a swayamsevak in Uttar Pradesh at the age of eighteen. He was a close compatriot of Bhaurao Deoras. He had lost his parents at a young age. He would work, collect money and then study. By the time he had collected money for his graduation, Dr Hedgewar left this world. Bhaurao told him, 'We need prachaaraks, give up studies.' So, he gave up his studies and became a prachaarak. He worked as an editor for *Swadeshi*, *Rashtradharma* and *Panchjanya* and was also a part of the team that started Rashtradharma Prakashan. He was instrumental in starting the Saraswati Shishu Mandir primary school project with Bhaurao and Rajju Bhaiyya (Karandikar 1999, 559). He was one of the key prachaaraks deputed to Bharatiya Jan Sangh and was considered a sharp political mind. We also know of his detached view of politics. He resigned from the Union Cabinet of the Janata Party and decided to work for the party. He later retired from active politics at the age of sixty to devote time to social work and set a benchmark. He was made the secretary of Lok Sangharsh Samiti headed by Jaiprakash Narayan. Lok Sangharsh Samiti was created by all opposition parties coming together, and with Morarji Desai as the chairman and Ashok Mehta as treasurer.

When a journalist in a press conference accused the RSS of supporting the Navnirman Andolan of Gujarat (anti-corruption agitation), Balasaheb said,

> If our organization was so strong to run and control such an agitation, I would have been very happy. Is [the] Sangh swayamsevak not a citizen of this nation? The problems of corruption hurt him like any other citizen. If these problems are solved then his life too would be much better. Then, why shouldn't he take part in such an agitation? (Pachpore 2011, 116)

By 1973, the anti-corruption agitation had picked up a lot of steam and the Congress was worried. It had realized that the RSS would be the main force behind this agitation as only it had the required strength.

On 8 January 1975, Indira Gandhi's legal advisor Siddharth Shankar Ray submitted a letter to Indira Gandhi for a government notification that could be released to ban the RSS. He also sent out the pro forma of such a government resolution. However, this news was leaked in *The Indian Express* on 20 June 1975. The idea had to be dropped due to the ensuing uproar (Pachpore 2011, 125). On 21 January 1975, Balasaheb addressed a press conference and cleared the RSS stance. He said,

> Due to influence of the Communist lobby within the Congress, the central government is trying to end democracy and take all the rights as a dictator to set up a one-Party rule. The effort to ban RSS is a step in that direction... The reason for this is clear. The people who are opposed to Bharatiya national life and Bharatiya sanskriti are aware that a nation-wide disciplined

> organization like [the] Sangh that guarantees freedom for the Indians and their security, will not bear this oppression and will resist it strongly. (Pachpore 2011, 125)

ABPS passed a strong resolution on 30 March 1974 against the attempts of the government to ban the RSS and called it politically motivated. The RSS leadership was clear about the danger of a ban and began planning strategies accordingly. It was decided that even before the ban was declared 1,000–2,000 prachaaraks would go underground and work under the guidance of the then Sarkaryavaah, Madhavrao Muley (Pachpore 2011, 128).

To get a proper perspective of the scenario before Emergency, we need to go back a few years. India had faced three years of draught in 1969, 1971 and 1972. Indira Gandhi had nationalized banks in 1969 and abolished privy purses of the erstwhile princely states. In 1973, the Gulf War happened and prices of fuel went through the roof. During all this came up another grave crisis. Elections in Pakistan witnessed the rise of a leader from East Pakistan. Sheikh Mujibur Rahman gained majority but in 1971 the Pakistani military regime and politicians refused to allow a Bengali leader to take power. This led to huge unrest and oppression by military and its cohorts in the then East Pakistan, which ultimately saw the birth of Bangladesh. But India too got embroiled in these disturbances as nearly ten million Bangladeshi refugees poured into India for nearly nine months. There was lot of agitation in society. However, under Indira Gandhi's leadership, India won the war and Bangladesh was born. This historic episode and her slogan of 'Garibi Hatao' led to a huge victory in the mid-term general elections she called at that time. Corruption during this time had plumbed to unforeseen depths. She was quoted as saying, 'Corruption is a global phenomenon, not just an Indian problem.' At the same time, a new effort to create a cult around Indira Gandhi also began.

During this period, students in Gujarat rose against the highly corrupt regime of Chimanbhai Patel, the Congress chief minister.

It was named Nav Nirman Andolan. It spread to Bihar under the auspices of Chhatra Yuva Sangharsh Vahini and Lok Sangharsh Samiti. Jaiprakash Narayan came out of political retirement on persuasion of many leaders and took the lead with all opposition parties joining him. He called for 'Samagra Kranti.' Society was in foment.

Unfortunately for Indira Gandhi, the Allahabad high court declared her election null and void and disqualified her from her Lok Sabha seat. On the eve of the stay order of the high court in implementing its decision, internal Emergency was declared on the midnight of 25 June 1975. The Sangh was banned on 4 July. Though a total of twenty-seven organizations were banned, the target was obviously the RSS, as the others were too small or ineffective on the ground.

Balasaheb was arrested on 30 June after declaration of Emergency and sent to Yerwada Jail. It was decided to keep the centre of the struggle against Emergency in Bombay for easy communication with Balasaheb. While Nanaji Deshmukh was secretary of the Lok Sangharsh Samiti, Moropant Pingley was the point man for the RSS. Four senior prachaaraks were given responsibility of four zones. For the South, it was Yadavrao Joshi; West, Moropant Pingley; North, Prof. Rajendra Singh and East, Bhaurao Deoras. Various activities from village, town and state levels would reach Balasaheb twice in a day even while he was in jail. This was ensured through proper communication channels and reports of any activities on ground. Eknath Ranade was to keep in touch with government officers. Two platforms were floated to spread information about atrocities and curtailment of democratic rights through RSS swayamsevaks there. One was Indians for Democracy and the other Friends of India Society International (Karandikar 1999, 560-561).

Opposition leaders in jail are said to have asked Balasaheb Deoras, 'You are in jail, how come work outside is happening so smoothly?' He responded, 'They have arrested one Sarsanghchaalak. There are four Sarsanghchaalaks working outside' (Karandikar 1999, 562). This statement clearly shows that a particular post in the RSS is merely a matter of convenience and collective decision. All senior workers and leaders are equally capable and there is no sense of competition, rivalry or politics among them.

The impact of the close interaction between the RSS and Bharatiya Jan Sangh (BJS) leaders with Jaiprakash Narayan during the anti-corruption struggle can be seen in 1975 when at a meeting of BJS in Delhi, he said,

> I have worked closely with Sangh and Jan Sangh since last year. My experience tells me that the accusation of fascism and orthodoxy thrown at them by communists and supporters of Indira Gandhi are clearly false.

He went on to say, 'If Jan Sangh is communal then I too am communal' (Karandikar 1999, 558). This change of heart of many leaders, and influencing the outcome of that dark period decisively and restoration of democracy was a result of clear long-term vision of Balasaheb Deoras, who went beyond immediate worry about his own organization.

Master Strategist but a Humble Leader

During Emergency when Balasaheb was in prison, he would give guidance to swayamsevaks and others. He told senior workers that it was a war of nerves. One who doesn't budge from one's ground and nor gets dispirited and has stamina, will win this war (Sharda, 2018, 164). He would tell them that Emergency could last even fourteen years. Hence, energy must be conserved. People and nations that conserve their spirits and energies rise back to gain their place again. He gave the example of Israel. It was the willpower of the Jews that led to the rise of Israel.

Such were the arrangements that swayamsevaks who were outside, would take care of families of swayamsevaks who were inside jails, and especially those whose primary income-earner was in jail and whose families were impoverished.

During Emergency when there seemed to be a stalemate, Balasaheb sent out a letter from Yerwada Jail. It read, 'To bring about a change in the current situation, it is necessary to take some strong steps. Therefore, I have decided to fast unto death. I am a diabetic patient, so I will not last for more than four or five days. I hope you will find this plan useful.' All the six senior RSS leaders who were working outside were stunned. They couldn't even imagine how serious the implications of this decision could be. They did not accept this and told him accordingly. It was decided to follow the non-violent path afresh (Pachpore 2011, 141). While this struggle was on and he was in jail, the movement was directed by Shri Madhavrao Muley, who was Sarkaryavaah at that time with other key leaders of the RSS like Rajju Bhaiyya, Bhaurao Deoras, Moropant Pingley, Dattopant Thengdi, and others. There was no dearth of leadership in the RSS—designations didn't matter. I had a chance to ferry the underground leaders for their meetings in Mumbai during that time and had met nearly all the top leaders in different get ups. Since their faces to the outside world were not very familiar, even a slight change in the get up could make a huge difference to an outsider.

In this atmosphere of total pessimism, Socialist leader Achyutrao Patwardhan said, 'Sangh is the only ray of hope.' *The Economist* from London wrote on 4 December 1976:

> The underground campaign against Mrs Gandhi claims to be the only non-Left wing revolutionary force in the world, disavowing both bloodshed and class struggle. Indeed, it might even be called Right wing since it is dominated by the Hindu communalist party, Jan Sangh and its 'cultural' [some say paramilitary] affiliate the RSS. But its platform at the moment has only one non-ideological plant; to bring democracy back to India. (Pachpore 2011, 142)

This newspaper also took note of Achyutrao Patwardhan's views. He said,

> The ground troops of this operation [underground movement] consist of tens of thousands of cadres who are organized to the village level into four men cells. Most of them are RSS regulars, though more and more new young recruits are coming in. The other underground parties which started out as partners in the underground have effectively abandoned the field to Jan Sangh and RSS. (Pachpore 2011, 141)

Readers will note that the tag of communalism attached to the RSS by the British in 1932 is still the standard phrase used by West and West-influenced intelligentsia in India. This is despite a much better understanding of it. While the British had an ulterior motive as a colonial power, one fails to understand why our own intelligentsia refuses to modify its viewpoint.

Many accept that if there was no Sangh, it would have been next to impossible to see the return of democracy in India. Prof. Arvind Rajagopal wrote in *The Hindu* in 2003, 'Indeed the RSS literature describes the Emergency as the second freedom struggle, with Sangh at the head of it. It was RSS that saved democracy' (Pachpore 2011, 131).

All this happened due to the indomitable spirit and guidance of Balasaheb Deoras. He wrote to Indira Gandhi during this time that instead of repeating old accusations, she could search and collect all documents from the RSS offices, which were under her government's control and come up with something new, if they get any evidence against the RSS (Pachpore 2011, 139). It was like a challenge. As a part of tactics to keep Indira Gandhi engaged, he also offered cooperation from the RSS for national reconstruction while his entire organization was working to dismantle the totalitarian regime. There is a lot of talk about Balasaheb's letters as conciliatory messages to Indira Gandhi. These people forget that even Shivaji had written conciliatory letters to Adil Shah, Aurangzeb and Jai Singh at different times to work out fresh strategies of counter attack and protect his kingdom. In the final count, the ultimate truth remains that the RSS was the main force that fought for democracy and gave ground support to the Opposition in the elections of 1977 when entire Opposition and leaders of society were in disarray and deep pessimism.

There are many chronicles and complementary documents about the RSS's role in defeating Emergency, including that of the famous Kannada writer Shivram Karanth (Pachpore 2011, 138).

Balasaheb was one of the earliest political prisoners picked up by the police after 25 June 1975 when Emergency was declared. His interactions with leaders of other political and religious bodies were a revelation for most of them. He had excellent relations with Socialist leaders as well as those of Jamat-e-Islami.

Jail is a place where the best of people are exposed to tough conditions. One can make out the mettle of a person in that situation. Balasaheb's colleague in jail, Prof. Sharad Wagh, notes,

> He did not allow, even by oversight to show people that he was somebody separate from the others. He would use the same utensils used by the others, used same water of the jail like others. He never asked his colleagues from Pune to bring him separate set of utensils. He would bathe and wash his clothes like all others. He could have stayed in a separate room comfortable as he was the Chief of RSS, but he didn't. His ideal of simple life and high thinking was an open book. [He further stated] He would have open hearted discussions with other opposition leaders like Prof. G.P. Pradhan, Bhai Vaidya, Dr Saptarshi, and so on. But, there never used to be bitterness or animosity. None would get upset with criticism. This led to optimist atmosphere and people felt charge. (Swaroop 2017, 156)

Prof. Sadanand Varde wrote in the weekly *Manohar:*

> As the head of a huge nationwide organization, there was not a trace of ego or throwing his weight. Once he told me in the barrack in a very natural way, 'I am the head of an organization; it is just a coincidence. I don't feel for a moment that I have a

> special scholarship, nor have I done something great due to which I have got this responsibility. All these things are just coincidence. This is also a coincidence, I feel.' But, behind this statement was his humility and egoless personality. He had reached his post due to his skill in connecting people with the organization, working in a sustained manner, maintaining his character and hard work day and night that inspired people. (Swaroop 2017, 157)

Plans of forming the Janata Party were already under way in jail. The MoU between different opposition parties including the Jan Sangh was being discussed. Balasaheb played an important role in finalizing this MoU in Yerwada Jail. This was four months before elections were declared.

Dattopant Thengdi wrote the rough draft of the proposed Janata Party and sent it to Morarji Desai, Madhu Limaye, S.M. Joshi and after their remarks, it was sent to Balasaheb in Yerwada Jail. There were 8–10 reputed lawyers in jail. Balasaheb discussed the final draft with them over four months' time. This final draft was sent to Moraraji Desai, who along with other merging parties, gave it his approval. This message was received in jail. This entire exercise was completed in about six months before Emergency was lifted. The jailed leaders felt that chances of victory were better as and when elections took place, due to this advance planning and coming together of the parties. Balasaheb played the role of key advisor. This information was shared by a senior cooperative sector leader Bapusaheb Pujari who was also in jail at that time (Pachpore 2011, 149).

Indira Gandhi's intelligence agencies gave her the idea that she would win elections hands-down if elections were held. She was also under pressure from the international community to prove her credentials as a democratic leader due to lobbying done by people aligned to the RSS philosophy. An organization, Friends of India Society International (FISI), was floated for the sole purpose of exposing atrocities and suppression of democratic rights. They were doing a lot of work to expose the anti-democratic face of Indira Gandhi through dissemination of news and conducting seminars. Dr Subramanian Swamy's attendance in Lok Sabha and his subsequent disappearance to the UK was a high drama conducted with great skill by RSS swayamsevaks under the guidance of veteran prachaaraks. While overseas, he was taken care of by the FISI group, largely made up of swayamsevaks of Hindu Swayamsevak Sangh.

On the eve of the declaration of election results, Indira Gandhi tried to play politics with the RSS. A message was sent to the RSS leadership, and senior government officers met Madhavrao Muley. The officers offered truce with a suggestion of a subtle threat that if the RSS was kept away from elections, the ban would be lifted. And, that if the RSS did not agree, their people in jail would get demoralized and their families would suffer. They claimed that people were against the Sangh, and ultimately, the Congress would win. All the underground leaders would be arrested and put in jails. So, the only way out was to break its relations with Janata Party and promise to keep itself away from the elections. However, the Sangh leaders were not scared. Muley said,

> Our leader Deoras ji had extended a hand of co-operation but you did not pay attention. Now that time is gone, nor is it possible. Any understanding with the government would be a betrayal of the nation. Swayamsevaks had resolved to finish this issue through elections. We cannot ask them to retreat from this position. If the election results go against us, we will keep the struggle going. Morale of our brothers in jail is very high, we are in contact. We know them better than you. They will not collapse if they have to live in jails for a little more time. Underground workers are also ready for a long drawn fight. On the contrary, the underground movement has become more popular and people's sympathies are with us. We will not let this sacrifice go in vain. (Pachpore 2011, 141)

An important aspect of the struggle of 1975 was that the RSS did not focus on its ban and chose to fight for democracy instead. When the Janata Party wished to put forward a proposal in its manifesto for lifting the ban on the RSS, Balasaheb refused. The focus was on ridding the country of dictatorship and restoring democracy. It showed the sagacity of Balasaheb to work for a larger objective, rising above organizational selfishness.

Balasaheb was an intelligent fighter. In fact, he had once confessed during his speech, 'If I had not got in touch with Doctorji, I would have become a commander of armed forces.' He was a true commander who won battles on social front (Pachpore 2011, 66). As noted in the chapter on Guruji, he was instrumental in persuading Guruji to support the formation of Jan Sangh. He had intelligent understanding of politics.

Opposition leaders were pessimistic and demoralized. Many didn't even want to fight elections. Balasaheb motivated them to fight elections. He stressed that their absence would be misconstrued as support for Indira Gandhi. He said, 'Even if you are out of prison, consider that you are still not free. So you must fight strongly [and] give it your all. The Sangh will support you fully' (Pachpore 2011, 144). It was the first election where the Sangh took part directly.

The ban on the RSS was lifted on 21 March, though there was no demand for it from the RSS. The demand for the re-establishment of democracy was the main motive. This single step raised the level of discourse from a political fight to one geared for saving democracy.

Primacy of Organization

In this entire trying period and in the euphoria of the Janata Party's victory, Balasaheb remained rooted in the Sangh's shakha work. As inmates began to be released from jail from 22 March, he called for a meeting of RSS workers. He said,

> All of us were in jail for twenty-one months. Many would have wondered what will happen to our families, our businesses,

> or our jobs? What will happen to our farming? We must have realized that while we were in jails, the world outside worked just fine.' He quoted a Tukaram *abhang* (devotional song) to underline the point. He then added, 'We will go out in the evening. I request you all—don't make the excuse, 'I have no time for Sangh work now' (Pachpore 2011, 151).

Now the prison ward where he was imprisoned, has been named 'Deoras Yard,' and this is where RSS workers go to pay homage on his death anniversary on 17 June. There are other yards in the campus carrying names of 'Gandhi Yard' and 'Tilak Yard.'

As Virag Pachpore observes succinctly, 'This revolutionary movement was not inspired by Marx; rather by Gandhi and Jaiprakash. It strengthened human civilization, democracy, abolished political slavery and nurtured brotherhood' (Pachpore 2011, 144).

After the ban was lifted, he and other released prisoners received a tumultuous welcome everywhere. For the first time, a non-Congress party came to power in the thirty years of independence. Despite paying a heavy price for this fight, RSS swayamsevaks never boasted about it and went back to their regular business of organizing the Sangh and related activities.

Speaking in Delhi on 20 April 1978, after the successful defeat of dictatorship and the lifting of the ban on the RSS, Balasaheb said,

> The first Sarsanghchaalak sparked a fire for freedom and patriotism in the hearts of swayamsevaks. The second Sarsanghchaalak gave the great mantra of organization. Now, I am giving a message of service to the society, Sewa. Hindu society doesn't talk of just equality but of *samarasataa* [harmony]. [The] Sangh will work in all the segments of social life to bring about this harmony now. (Pachpore 2011, 76)

At this high point in RSS history, he gave an indication that RSS work needs to go beyond shakhas and connect with society directly through sewa (service) at local level. There were sewa projects run by swayamsevaks, but he exhorted swayamsevaks to make this a part of their regular life. This idea was further evolved by him in 1989 during the centenary celebrations of Dr Hedgewar. His next statement showed his self-abnegating nature.

> This is a felicitation of Dr Hedgewar and Shri Guruji. Swayamsevak is the Sangh. Swayamsevak is the strength of Sangh and my strength is these swayamsevaks. If Sangh swayamsevaks had not stood up with forbearance and patience, nobody would have bothered about me. This felicitation is of the common people who stood up against injustice and threw away the government representing this injustice with great courage. I am just a medium. (Pachpore 2011, 153)

Emergency also offered him the opportunity to closely interact with Muslim leaders of the Jamat-e-Islami while in jail. He had open cordial discussions with them that removed many misgivings about the RSS. There were ten leaders of Jamat-e-Islami there. Before they left jail, they came to meet him and met him again after he was released. When journalist M.J. Akbar asked him if he would take food in a Muslim's house, he responded immediately, 'Wherever I go, I meet my Jamat-e-Islami friends, especially those who were in jail with me and I go to their homes too' (Pachpore, 2011, 157). Such was the trust of these Muslim leaders that they went and met him when the Janata Party government was about to collapse. He would give the example of Indonesia where the majority converted to Islam but they did not give up their Hindu culture. They still celebrate Ramayana and Mahabharata with dance dramas, they named their airways 'Garuda', their President's name was Sukarno and wife's name was Ratnadevi. The way of worship can change but not the culture. He felt that this can happen in Bharat too.

He went further and declared that the Sangh shakha gates are open to all those Muslims who believe that Bharat is their country—those who believe that their past is rooted in this country and who are ready to follow discipline in the shakha, they are welcome to join (Pachpore 2011, 157). Thus, he expanded the definition of Hindu and showed his willingness to open up the Sangh further. This thought was taken forward later by Sudarshanji in a big way.

Promoting and Inspiring Affiliate Organizations

Disaster management during 19 November 1977 after a cyclonic storm in the coastal area of Andhra Pradesh proved to be a major talking point within and outside the RSS, because it was the biggest and most ambitious rehabilitation programme undertaken by the RSS so far. An entire village was built in record time under the guidance of the Deendayal Research Institute. It was named Deendayal Puram. Balasaheb dedicated it to the nation and the entire world took note of it (Pachore 2011, 159). Thus, not just rescue but rehabilitation too, was taken as a part of disaster management by the RSS and its affiliates. It is generally seen that though help pours in from various organizations to provide immediate relief, but it dries up soon and most organizations leave the field after the initial help is provided. This was a different approach.

Another initiative he took was to bring the work of Nanaji Deshmukh in Gonda to the nation's notice. He invited the then President Neelam Sanjeeva Reddy and many other Cabinet ministers there. The entire nation watched as top national leaders of different political thoughts sat on the ground together with local tribals and had lunch (Pachpore 2011, 160). It was a strong message of social equality and harmony.

He motivated Saraswati Shishu Mandir during this period to host a national convention of its students in Delhi. As noted earlier, this project was begun by his younger brother, Bhaurao Deoras in Gorakhpur in 1952 with other senior RSS prachaaraks. The convention saw 1,60,000 girls and boys coming together to present dazzling drills and songs. The chief guest of the programme was Jagjivan Ramji. He proudly said, 'Shishu Mandir work is RSS work.' After this programme, Shishu Mandir began activities in Orissa, Assam, West Bengal, and others. In Assam, the local workers established the Shishu Shiksha Samiti and schools in the state were named 'Shankerdev Shishu Niketan.' We find mention of these schools even nowadays when top rankers from these schools come into the limelight for various activities. Vidya Bharati became an umbrella organization to coordinate all these activities (Pachpore 2011, 160).

On 19 October 1977, the then prime minister, Morarji Desai came to Jashpur and stayed for twenty minutes in Kalyan Ashram. Balasaheb met the prime minister four months later in February 1978 in his office. The prime minister asked him, 'How can I help you? What is the policy of Kalyan Ashram regarding government grant?' Balasaheb responded,

> The policy of Kalyan Ashram is not to accept any government grant. When you visited Kalyan Ashram, I could not express my gratitude to you due to my busy schedule. Therefore, when I came to Delhi this time for some work, I thought I should meet you personally to express my gratitude.

The prime minister told another social worker sitting with him in this meeting, 'Look Shrikant, this is the secret; it is completely self-reliant.' This was the thought that Guruji had expressed about how a Sangh-affiliated organization should be run. It is difficult for a lay person to understand the policy of the RSS that forms the core of its work (Ranga Hari 2018, 247)

Balasaheb reiterated the separation between the Sangh and politics but reminded people that there needs to be synergy between social and political efforts. There was a certain fine-tuning to the firm line between the Sangh and politics drawn by Guruji. He said,

> [The] Sangh believes in this view from beginning, therefore [it] has kept itself away from electoral politics. But, it doesn't mean that it negates the importance of politics in economic and social reconstruction. We can present analysis and solutions for problems in their multifarious forms in the national life and suggest solutions. But, implementation of those thoughts

> and solutions will have to be done by political power. We can say that in this journey of socio-economic reconstruction, political and non-political efforts are complimentary. (Swaroop 2017, 171)

Regarding the efforts put in by the Sangh for social reforms and economic development, he asserted that swayamsevaks are present in all spheres of social life. They are government servants, farmers, labour, traders, teachers, lawyers, doctors, engineers, journalists and writers. Therefore, the effort of the Sangh is that first they should behave ideally in their respective professions, present an example worth following. One notes that his response always used to be measured, logical and open.

> I am a farmer, I keep experimenting with new seeds and other inputs to raise productivity. I am also motivating other villagers to do the same. Many swayamsevaks in our area do the same. Second part of this effort is that there are many organizations running in different areas of social life by people inspired by [the] Sangh and swayamsevaks. They study problems of their particular community and try to find solutions with studies. We will work more in this direction in future. (Swaroop 2017, 170)

Collapse of Opposition Unity: Firm Response of an Astute Leader

The artificially created controversy by the Socialist group that saw the collapse of the Janata Party was initiated by senior Socialist leader Madhu Limaye in the name of dual loyalty of Jan Sangh constituents of Janata Party. He was the same man who was ready to wear an RSS uniform when he was in Yerwada Jail with Balasaheb. While leaving the jail, he had told Balasaheb, 'You just order me, I will come running to you like a swayamsevak' (Pachpore 2011, 169).

Limaye was joined by the well-known 'young Turk' Chandra

Shekhar. They were obviously scared that due to the RSS's better organization, they would dominate the Janata Party as this constituent had the highest number of seats in the new Lok Sabha (about 94) within the party. They insisted that the mass organization affiliates of the RSS like Bharatiya Mazdoor Sangh and ABVP should become fronts for Janata Party. Balasaheb told them clearly, 'All the trains leaving New Delhi station need not necessarily leave from Platform No.1' (Pachpore 2011, 170).

However, they didn't give up. The three letters Balasaheb wrote to Indira Gandhi, as a part of his tactics to help keep the organization working, were quoted as surrender to Indira Gandhi. In this political skulduggery, they forgot that the entire period of underground resistance rested on the Sangh's shoulders. Finally, the dispute reached Balasaheb. Chandra Shekhar came to Nagpur. Balasaheb himself went to receive him though it was not necessary. He did this merely to show respect to him. Nobody knows exactly what transpired in this ninety-minute meeting. But some points were revealed after the informal meetings. Balasaheb clearly put down four points:

1. The RSS will not change its foundational principles.
2. It will keep working as the fully conscious national watchdog to keep an eye on national security and national interest. It will not allow any political party or component of ruling party to do anything anti-national.
3. Except RSS office-bearers, all other swayamsevaks were free to join any political party or organization as per their inclination. The RSS will not stop anyone from doing this.
4. The erstwhile Jan Sangh members and workers should follow the discipline of the party and work there. They can decide what they wish to do about the Sangh. The Sangh will not interfere in their decisions. They have very old relations with the RSS and it will not ask them not to take part in Sangh activities.

Still the Socialist group kept insisting that Jan Sangh leaders must sever their ties with the RSS as if it was their sole duty to keep Janata Party together. Balasaheb went to the extent of writing a letter to Chandra Shekhar to propose that the elected members of Jan Sangh would be free to not attend RSS programmes. Many colleagues told Balasaheb that it won't serve any purpose as Socialists were bent upon insulting the RSS and isolating its members in the Janata Party. But he felt that if such a letter satisfies them there was no harm in trying. But, the Janata Party leadership revelling in its ego never responded, leading to its split and final eclipse (Pachpore 2011, 173).

The entire episode did prove that the RSS was now capable of giving direction to the national polity with its rising strength. The return of Indira Gandhi showed the intellectual bankruptcy of the so-called big leaders of the Socialist movement. After this the Socialist movement went downhill, never to recover. Over the years it has become a caricature in the hands of family-run parties. The arrest of Indira Gandhi despite Balasaheb's suggestion to forget and forgive gave her career a new lease of life just when she had touched the bottom of her political career. Thus, his call to forget and forgive was not just an extension of Guruji's advice after lifting of the ban on the RSS in 1949, it was also a sane political viewpoint.

The Janata Party split and the Bharatiya Janata Party (BJP) was born on 6 April 1980. When BJP adopted Gandhian Socialism as one of its founding principles, many felt that it had faltered on its foundational principles that included '*Ekatma Manav Darshan*' (Integral Humanism) as espoused by Deendayal Upadhyay, their biggest ideologue. Balasaheb watched all this but did not interfere. He possibly decided to let them experiment.

When some people asked him about this ideologically confusing stand, he simply said, 'Don't worry. In the coming two or three years BJP will become totally Hindutvavadi and will promote Hindutva' (Pachpore 2011, 175). He took the line of 'wait and watch' as he kept faith in the political understanding of Vajpayee and L.K. Advani. He explained on another occasion that both of them were dedicated life-long swayamsevaks of the Sangh, so they must have taken such a decision keeping in mind the current political situation. Once they had taken a decision, it would be wise to let them review it rather than criticize them or force them to change. Thus, he laid guidelines about how to treat large affiliate organizations within the Sangh umbrella, give them due respect and autonomy, and let them take their decisions. He never showed impatience or criticized them. Yadavrao Joshi too echoed the same sentiments. They eventually returned to their Hindutva base with the Ram Janmabhoomi agitation.

Response to National Issues

Another key initiative of Balasaheb was organizing a VHP convention in Assam for the Northeast region in 1981. It was attended by the renowned Naga freedom fighter Rani Gaidinliu, Rajmata Vijaya Raje Scindia and many prominent Hindu saints of various sects and leaders of local indigenous faiths. It strengthened the hands of followers of indigenous faiths to stave off conversions by Christian missionaries (Pachpore 2011, 161). The movement of indigenous faiths picked up steam over years as the converts to Christianity realized that it meant cutting off from their roots. There is a yearning to return to their traditional faiths.

The following decade witnessed a highly disturbed national scene with more rebellion raising its head in the Northeast, Kashmir getting into its worst-ever spot, and Punjab burning with the Khalistan movement. Balasaheb provided his guidance during this disturbed period and activated the RSS and related organizations to resolve conflicts. Various resolutions in ABPS on these issues show the deep concern the RSS had on these issues.

A senior prachaarak, Krishnarao Sapre, prepared a report on rampant conversion activities in the Northeast through networks built by the Church. This report was presented to the then Home Minister Shankarrao Chavan. He told the delegation, 'What you say is true and the Indian government is aware of this information, we also get regular updates. But we can't take any action as it will go against our political interests' (Pachpore 2011, 179).

Later, an ex-prachaarak of Vivekananda Kendra, Virag Pachpore, wrote a book on conversion activities of the Church after intensive study while working there for fourteen years. The book is titled *The Indian Church*. It was released by the then RSS Sarsanghchaalak Sudarshanji. This led to a dialogue between Christian groups and the RSS.

In 1979, Assam went up in flames due to agitation against illegal immigrants in Assam. It was led by Akhil Assam Students Union (AASU) and Akhil Assam Gan Sangram Parishad (AAGSP). By the 1980s, Punjab too had huge disturbances in the name of Khalistan. Nagaland, Manipur and other states in the Northeast too were disturbed with separatist movements. Sri Lanka and Bharat had serious problems because of LTTE violence.

The RSS had been worried about infiltration issue from the time of Partition. It had been warning the nation from time to time through its resolutions. However, in the 1980s, the situation became extremely grave. At the time of Partition, Jinnah was able to get Sylhet district into the then East Pakistan but could not take over all of Assam as he had desired due to alert Congress leader Gopinath Bardaloi. But, Jinnah had told his secretary Moinul Haq Chaudhry, 'We won Sylhet, we shall merge Assam with Pakistan with our strength.' The slogan of the Muslim League in Bengal at that time was '*Sylhet nelaam, ganabhote, Assam nebo latheer chote*'. Meaning, 'we got Sylhet using democracy, we shall win Assam with force of our lathi' (Pachpore 2011, 180).

Indian governments never paid attention to Assam and the entire Northeast for years. Such was their pathetic understanding that when China overran the area now-called Arunachal Pradesh, all Nehru could do was to say, in his 'farewell' radio address, 'My heart goes with the people of Assam.' The people of Assam still have this pain in their heart; they haven't forgotten how they were abandoned.

Balasaheb in his 1981 meeting in Shivsagar in Assam stressed the need to differentiate between infiltrators and genuine refugees. It was not a popular stance but he educated people that in case of atrocities in neighbouring countries, where would Hindus go? He went on to caution that if Muslim-majority districts went increasing like this, all of Assam could become a Muslim-majority state. Assam could break away from Bharat (Pachpore 2011, 183).

In a 1981 public meeting in Shivsagar he asked people not to call everybody a foreigner. To solve the problem we need to define, who is an infiltrator and who is a refugee. He reasserted this view in the VHP sammelan organized in Guwahati in 1982. Sudarshanji was the kshetra or regional prachaarak at that time. He had studied the entire issue thoroughly and worked hard to change the force of the agitation from anti-outsiders that included Hindus too, to illegal foreign infiltrators. Thus, anger against Hindu Bengalis could be diverted and these genuine citizens of Assam and refugees from East Pakistan could be taken out of the firing line of agitators (Pachpore 2011, 183).

These efforts from that time have finally seen the result today in the form of the Citizenship Amendment Bill. The RSS and Balasaheb Deoras were criticized heavily for their stand and called communal but he was firm that sooner or later people would understand this viewpoint.

Balasaheb used to say that it is very important to conserve and preserve the unique features of tribals and their lifestyle. But by calling them tribals, we are separating them from mainstream Hindu society. The RSS prefers to use the term '*janajatis*' and '*vanvasis*'. No one has tried to solve their problems. Christian missionaries provide them services in education and health but in return they convert them. It is the business of missionary organizations to convert *janajatis* or tribals through sewa and use it to change their loyalties away from their nation. The way out is to win their confidence and raise their self-respect, awaken their faith for their culture and belief system, and take them along with Hindu society (Pachpore 2011, 185).

In 1982, there was a huge upheaval in Hindu society and

the government was badly shaken too. An entire village in Meenakshipuram had been converted to Islam. It disturbed the RSS and the VHP very much. Their efforts in bringing deprived brethren from SC/ST closer and provide them a respectable place in society did not seem to have worked. Many *dharma sansads* (religious parliaments) were organized in various parts of the nation. The next step was the Ekatmata Yatra. Three main and 312 smaller *raths* (chariots) were designed, and each had an idol or large photograph of Bharat Mata along with large containers of *gangajal* (water from the Ganga). Smaller containers of *gangajal* were also distributed at places where the *raths* stopped. The man behind this idea was Moropant Pingley and inspiration, Balasaheb Deoras (Pachpore 2011, 190).

Moropant Pingley was a veteran prachaarak of the first generation who had worked with Balasaheb Deoras since their first shakha in Mahal, Nagpur and was a member of the '*Kushak Pathak*' created by Dr Hedgewar. Not many people outside the RSS know about him. He was an organizer par excellence. He had a knack of picking up new projects wherever he went and giving the responsibility to local RSS swayamsevaks. Bharat has some or the other form of sewa project across the country that was promoted by him. He had a great sense of people and their issues. He was a person who could bring a smile to any person's face. His meetings used to be full of laughter. He would say that the Sangh's work is serious but you must do it with a smile. He toured all over India. Not all workers were convinced with the idea. But he told them confidently, 'This yatra will succeed, whether you become part of it or not.' And actually the yatra was successful beyond anyone's imagination. These veterans really had their ears on the ground. I have been a witness to this phenomenon, which saw at least eight crore Indians participate in this pan-India programme.

To further struggle for social harmony and stop conversions, a new organization called Hindu Munnani was established. In Karnataka, the '*Hindu Samajotsav*' came up. They worked vigorously to awaken an atmosphere of Hindutva and were able to reconvert many of the converted back into the fold of Hinduism. Many sadhus, heads of *maths* came out of their temples and *maths* and went into the areas where Dalit and oppressed Hindus lived. They did this to gain their trust. The RSS did some huge programmes in Karnataka, Kerala and Tamil Nadu. Bangalore saw a huge gathering of 21,000 swayamsevaks in 1982. Kerala saw renewed rise in number of members from SC/ST in the RSS (Pachpore 2011, 189).

The Tamil Nadu VHP organized *Gyan Rathams* to awaken Hindus. This yatra or pilgrimage went to 900 villages—mainly in those in which Dalit and backward Hindu brethren were in high numbers. This *rath* had an idol of Bhagwan Murugan. Six lakh people worshipped it (Pachpore 2011, 190).

This was a precursor to the biggest mass movement of post-Independent India—Ram Janmabhoomi agitation. Again the person who was key to its success was Moropant Pingley. Like all prachaaraks, he remained behind the scene and worked silently without any urge for self-promotion.

The RSS gave unqualified support to renaming of Marathwada University after Dr Bhimrao Ramji Ambedkar even though various political parties were fiddling with the issues and letting the issue simmer, leading to massive unrest. To bring out harmony in various sections of Hindu society, Balasaheb inspired a Phule Ambedkar Yatra under the auspices of the newly formed '*Samajik Samarasta Manch*', which was founded in 1983 in Maharashtra by a prachaarak. The occasion chosen for the purpose was the birth anniversaries of Dr Babasaheb Ambedkar and Dr K.B. Hedgewar, both falling on the same day as per Christian and Hindu calendars (Pachpore 2011, 189–90). It also supported the extension of reservations under the Constitution.

His commitment to social harmony (*samarasataa*) was underlined by the touching incident. I have described earlier in the chapter, when he went down to the meeting hall despite his ill health and changed the tone and tenor of the debate on reservations (this incidence has been described in the same way earlier in the chapter).

It was during his time that RSS-inspired teams persuaded Guruvayur Temple to allow Dalits to dine together with other so-called high caste devotees. It was February 1983 when Dalit brethren had taken out a 200-mile march from Trivandrum to Guruvayur to put an end to discriminatory 'Brahmana Bhojana' inside the temple. RSS swayamsevaks were directed to welcome them along the entire route. Communists had expected this event to put Hindu organizations in a quandary but swayamsevaks' rousing reception to them en route and taking care of their food and shelter turned the whole event into a positive programme. People of all castes ultimately dined together inside the temple premises. Vishal Hindu Sammelan, Kerala (VHS, Kerala) had also celebrated fifty years of successful Dalit entry into the temple with reception and felicitation of thirty-two surviving satyagrahis inside the Guruvayur temple in 1982 (Sheshadri 2000, 137–38). Many such programmes of social harmony are recounted in the book *RSS: Vision in Action* written by the then Sarkaryavaah H.V. Sheshadri. It was under the guidance of Balasaheb Deoras that this exercise in social transformation picked up momentum.

A few words about Shri H.V. Sheshadri need to be added here. He was born in 1926 in Bangalore. He completed his master's degree in chemistry from Bangalore University. Having being inspired by the ideals and principles of the RSS from childhood, he became a prachaarak of the RSS in 1946 and would play a pivotal role in the growth of the RSS in Karnataka. He held various responsibilities in the RSS such as prant prachaarak, kshetra prachaarak and finally became Sarkaryavaah of the RSS in 1987. Due to his failing health, he retired as Sarkaryavaah in 2000 and was henceforth the organization's Akhil Bharatiya Prachaarak Pramukh, a post he held until his death.

An excellent writer, he received the Karnataka State Sahitya Akademi Award in 1982 for his work *Torberalu*. He also wrote several articles for *Vikrama, Utthana, The Organiser, Panchajanya* and other periodicals. He wrote many books on the RSS and played a key role in setting the intellectual discourse of the Sangh.

After the Khalistani agitation began, Balasaheb Deoras toured Punjab twice and took public meetings in Jalandhar and Ludhiana. He said clearly that Sikhs are a part of Hindu society. The names of Ram, Krishna and Durga appear hundreds of times in the sacred *Guru Granth Sahib*. Words of Sant Namdeo from Maharashtra also find place in it. He opined that politicians should not use religion to fight a political battle. Hindus and Sikhs should agitate together regarding issues of Punjab.

A major opposition and strong dislike for the RSS in militant Akali parties is due to the fact that the RSS proclaimed that Sikh Panth is a distinct off-shoot of the Hindu dharmic family, while the most important project of Khalistanis and militant Sikhs has been to create a separate political identity by establishing that Sikhism is a separate religion. The Sikh clergy and militant Sikhs resented the RSS view and feared assimilation into the mainstream Hindu society. It was an imaginary fear whipped up by vested interests. It also feared the dilution of its puritanical code of conduct in the new generation influenced by Western culture.

Over time the Sangh also modified and fine-tuned its terminology to make room for Sikh leaders' sensitivities. However, it insisted that the relation between Sikhs and Hindus is that of nails and skin. They cannot be separated. Political expediency makes it difficult for hard-line Sikh groups to accept this truth even though there have been strong blood relations for centuries. There was a tradition of offering the eldest son to the 'Gurus' that is, to the Sikh Panth. It is still common in families to have a Sikh member as well as a non-Sikh member. The RSS is not alone in propagating that Sikhs are part of larger Hindu society. When Akali leaders approached the then prime minister, Morarji Desai and deputy prime minister Charan Singh to declare Sikhs a minority community, both turned down the request on the grounds that they regarded Sikhs as a part of the Hindu community.

The RSS had passed sixteen resolutions related to Punjab.

Of these, two were on the Punjabi Suba—in 1961 and 1966 and fourteen were related to Khalistan terror. There is mention of the Punjab issue in a few other resolutions too when issue of internal security or inter-religious harmony arose.

The RSS joined the battle for bringing back unity of hearts in Punjab. Jaikrishan, an ex-prachaarak and a senior RSS worker at that time, had raised concern in an RSS meeting in the presence of the Sarkaryavaah Prof. Rajendra Singh about the rising sense of animosity between Sikhs and Hindus and people leaving Punjab due to fear. Within a month, he was invited to Delhi for a meeting to discuss what could be done to repair the social relations and restore people's confidence. Bhaurao Deoras, the kshetra prachaarak Thakur Ram Singh, Indreshji, Vishwanathji and Bhagwat Singhji sat with Jaikrishan and discussed the matter and decided that a movement to stop the exodus from Punjab and stop the divide between Sikhs and Hindus had to be initiated at any cost. He was assured that the whole organization will work with him. In fact, he recounts, 'I was asked, "Do you know what it means?" Yes, I said, "Bullet. I am ready for it."'[10]

Thus, the 'Punjab Rashtriya Suraksha Samiti' was born. Their slogan was '*Hindu Sikh ko jo ladave wo desh da bairi hai. Hindu Sikh nu ladan ni dena, San 47 banan ni dena* [One who tries to make Hindu Sikh fight is an enemy of the nation. We will not allow Hindu Sikh to fight and we will not allow repeat of year 1947].' Jaikrishan recounts, 'Soon, conferences began and big public meetings took place. The exodus from Punjab slowed down. Nearly thirty-two full-time workers without any remuneration joined us and said they will go to any extent to maintain peace and brotherhood in Punjab.'[11]

When the Samiti movement was going on, Bhaurao called a meeting of intellectuals in Amritsar in 1986–87. It was then decided that a national body be created. This body was named Rashtriya

---

[10]Taken from an audio recording of Jaikrishan on 21 April 2017.

[11]Taken from an audio recording of Jaikrishan on 21 April 2017.

Sikh Sangat, and it was created approximately at the same time when the Ekta Sammelans were taking place.

Considering the problems created because of the murders of innocent citizens of Punjab under influence of our neighbouring country, the RSS state unit decided to form a 'Punjab Peedit Sahayata Samiti' on 2 November 1986. Huge programmes such as Ekta Sammelans were organized on directions of the then General Secretary Prof. Rajendra Singh aka Rajju Bhaiyya, who became the Sarsanghchaalak later on.[12]

> To raise the morale of RSS swayamsevaks and Hindu society in general, Sarsanghchaalak Balasaheb toured Punjab in December 1983 and laid down guidelines for swayamsevaks about their work in Punjab to preserve unity between Sikhs and Hindus. He criticized Akali leadership for creating a fear psychosis in the Sikh community. He stressed that Sikhs are part and parcel of Hindu society. He cited hymns from Guru Granth Sahib, Guru Gobind Singh's banis where names of Ram, Hari and Chandi are taken hundreds of time. He talked of Sant Namdev's bani in Guru Granth Sahib. He stressed that no religion in Hindu society has lost its identity, giving example of Jains. He differentiated between territorial political demands and religious demands and asked them not to mix them up. Balasaheb explained at length that similar cultural differences have existed in the world and even within India, but people are living together happily. He said the key to resolving problems in Punjab is trust and mutual love. He asked people to apply restraint in their talk and behaviour. He also underlined the role of the press in normalizing the situation *(Punjab Problem and its Solution, Balasaheb Deoras* —Suruchi Prakashan, Delhi, March 1984).

The RSS also brought out a booklet, 'Agony of Punjab' in July 1984 stressing the oneness of the nation and Punjab and common

[12]Taken from documents sourced from the RSS Documentation Centre.

heritage of Sikhs and Hindus. Many such publications were released.

When terrorists attacked RSS shakhas and many swayamsevaks died, he advised swayamsevaks and Hindus to keep calm in that violent atmosphere and be patient. He reiterated that they should be optimistic as the entire Sikh society was not supporting Khalistani terrorists. He told reporters in a press conference in Jaipur in November 1987 that there was not even one communal disturbance in the entire period of Khalistani agitation and this possible confrontation was avoided because of the RSS (Pachpore 2011, 186–87).

After the assassination of Indira Gandhi and horrific large-scale killings of Sikhs and the Congress' victory with 400 seats in 1984, Balasaheb spoke openly about Hindu unity and vote bank to counter destructive forces. In that year's Vijayadashami annual lecture he said, 'The strength of this nation is Hindu society and if we wish to change the situation, we need an awakened, proud, patriot Hindu vote bank, so the political parties are forced to talk about taking care of Hindu interests' (Pachpore 2011, 191).

When serious incidents in Jammu & Kashmir increased after 1986, he toured Udhampur. After listening to the woes of local Hindus, he told them that it was very important to save the Jammu region. He told them not to fall into the trap for getting minority status. That was not the main problem. The entire Hindu society and RSS will be with them. He also appealed to Hindus of Kashmir not to flee from Kashmir Valley. This was a fight for respect and rights and the entire society would be with them. The solution was to remove Article 370 (Pachpore 2011, 188). He wrote to Governor Jagmohan that he should study Article 370 thoroughly and find a legal solution.

Formalising Social Service and Expanding RSS Reach

Balasaheb used Dr Hedgewar's centenary-year celebrations in 1989 in a way that gave a new direction to RSS work. The founder of the RSS was strictly against any type of programme for birthdays and so on. He had also said that the Sangh should not celebrate jubilees and said, 'The Sangh will merge into society.' The day the goal of Hindu unity and creation of people of character for nation-building is achieved, the utility of Sangh work will end, the dream of the RSS will be achieved and the Sangh will merge into society. This was Dr Hedgewar's dream under whom Balasaheb had trained. Yet, he decided to celebrate it with a specific purpose.

During this period, many of the large organizations born out of the Sangh's inspiration had become quite big. Vishwa Hindu Parishad had grown big after the Ekatmata Yatra. Bharatiya Mazdoor Sangh had become the No.1 labour union. BJP was still confused about Hindutva and was trying to distance itself from Hindutva. Overall, as organizations became bigger, they seemed to have overlooked the collective objective of the Sangh's philosophy. They were also becoming egoistic about their own organizations. Balasaheb perhaps felt that the founder of RSS Dr Hedgewar's centenary could be a major cause of bringing in better coordination and shedding organizational egos. His powerful personality could help remind them that this great person had founded an organization of which all were a part. Thus, it was decided to celebrate it in a big way (Pachpore, 192).

Swayamsevaks went out to contact citizens and tell them about Dr Hedgewar and RSS. When one such team went into a village in Mizoram, Christian Mizos, after listening about the RSS and Doctorji, said, 'Had you reached us twenty years back, none of us would have deserted our religion' (Pachore 2011, 193).

In 1989, Sewa Bharati was also established, and 5,000 new sewa projects were started. This was also the year of Nehru's birth centenary. But while his centenary was celebrated by the governments, Dr Hedgewar's centenary was celebrated not only in India but also abroad by the common people.

Somewhere around 1982, Balasaheb attended a *shibir* (camp) in Prayag. During an informal chat, he asked the local workers whether there was a lock on the Ram Janmabhoomi temple. On receiving an affirmative answer, he turned serious and asked,

'When will this lock be removed? (Pachpore 2011, 193). This question acted as a spur for the Ram Janmabhoomi movement.

This movement saw many innovative programmes emerge such as Karseva, Shila Pujan and Rath Yatra that lay the foundation of the temple at the hands of a Dalit, which surprised the Left 'progressive' intellectuals. The architect of this extraordinary, phased strategy was Moropant Pingley, again. They had no answers except criticism and rhetoric. This agitation was also termed 'Mandal vs Kamandal' in the wake of the implementation of the Mandal Commission report by Prime Minister V.P. Singh in 1990. The timelines clearly establish that the Ram Mandir movement had begun way before the implementation of the Mandal Commission. This struggle, sustained by the RSS and its associate organization from 1986 to 2018, ended in a successful, non-violent resolution to the Ram Mandir issue. It shows the tenacity and ability of the RSS to sustain movements over long periods. Not an easy task.

His scientific temper saw him promote a science that was rooted to the soil. Vijnan Bharati, an organization to promote scientific temper and bring it to the common people, was launched in 1992 with eminent scientists as part of its team. I was involved in the first poster exhibition of Ancient Science and Technology in India, which was prepared by eminent senior scientists in year 2000. These posters were later converted into a poster book.

A new sewa project was launched by a prachaarak, Girish Prabhune, in 1992 for the most marginalized and ill-treated community—the gypsies and groups such as '*Pardhis*' (hunting and gathering communities who live in forests). This was the Bhatke *Vimukt Vikas Pratishthan*. Its school saw the first batch of Pardhi children passing SSC examinations.

In 1992, in his Vijayadashami speech on 5 October, Balasaheb exhorted swayamsevaks working in various social service projects to speed up their activities and spread the work, as social harmony was the most important aspect of a Hindu organization. He went on to stress that wherever there were RSS shakhas, in those villages, there should not be more than one cremation ground, temples should be open to all and everyone should be able to fetch water from the same well or pond. Such an atmosphere should be built naturally without any aggressive action. It should be evident from a swayamsevak's own behaviour (Pachpore 2011, 162). The current Sarsanghchaalak, Dr Mohan Bhagwat, is also stressing upon this point.

Unintended destruction of the Babri structure led to great upheaval in social life of India, including riots, dismissal of BJP governments in three states and another ban on the RSS. After all this turmoil, an RSS swayamsevak, Atal Bihari Vajpayee, finally came to power. By this time, he had handed over the reins of the RSS to Prof. Rajendra Singh in 1996, but he was there to witness this historic day and it was the fulfilment of a vision that he had about politics of India.

When the government decided to abandon the hybrid license raj wrongly called the Socialist economic model and liberalize the economy, there were many misgivings about Indian industry, especially small and medium-sized enterprises (SMSE) being destroyed by laws that favoured large multinational corporations. Dattopant Thengdi floated the Swadeshi Jagaran Manch to canvass for a level playing field and the protection of the SMSE segment, which provided most jobs in the Indian economy. It was a movement that especially touched people in the SMSE segment and in trading. The relevance of the idea is being felt now, in the post-COVID-19 world order and the Modi government has relaunched this idea with new dimensions.

The demise of his younger brother on 13 May 1992 left a deep pain in his heart. It was only the incident of 6 December 1992—the Babri structure destruction—that energized him to continue for the sake of Hindu society for a few more months before he retired from his post.

He retired due to ill health and nominated Prof. Rajendra Singh as his successor after due consultations with other senior RSS leaders. This was another first. He started a new trend in the

RSS, that the organizational head could give up responsibility if health did not permit him to put in his best. His instructions to cremate him in a public crematorium, neither to create any memorial nor to put up his photograph in RSS programmes was another lesson in self-abnegation. It was also a clear guideline to keep away from any form of hero worship.

Balasaheb Deoras: The Leader

Balasaheb was an organizational scientist trained in Dr Hedgewar's school of thought. One can say, he was the first Sarsanghchaalak born out of the process of the RSS shakha. His thoughts on the role of shakhas were as uncompromising as his predecessors. But, he further expanded its scope of work.

He trained under Dr Hedgewar while Guruji got trained under his guru, Swami Akhandananda of the Ramkrishna Mission. Guruji may have ended up as a great sanyasi, while Balasaheb could have become a military commander, if they had not got in touch with Dr Hedgewar.

Like all Sarsanghchaalaks, he had a brilliant academic record. And like all RSS leaders, he was deeply compassionate and had deep love for swayamsevaks. He insisted on going to Madras to meet the families of eleven swayamsevaks who had died in a bomb attack on the RSS office in 1993. He did so despite strong medical advice against this, because of his frail health.

His view about an effective shakha was crystal clear. Describing the role of an effective Sangh shakha, Balasaheb said,

> Sangh shakha is not just a place to play games and do physical drills. It is to promise to provide protection to civil society, nurture values in youth to keep them away from undesirable activities. It is a centre of optimism that would reach out to people in case of any disaster. A shakha is an affirmation that women can move around fearlessly and none can misbehave with them. It is an obstacle to animalistic and breaking India forces. And while doing all this, it is a university that educates

> people to become qualified workers out in national life in different areas. And to achieve all this, we play games in shakha as a medium to achieve all this. (Pachpore 2011, 81)

Balasaheb was one of the senior-most RSS leaders who had seen all the bans and fought against them as a leader—first as a member of the core team that organized and planned the 1948 Satyagraha for lifting of the ban after Gandhiji's assassination. He was a RSS Sarsanghchaalak when the RSS was banned in 1975 during the Emergency and in 1993 after the Babri structure demolition. His sagacity can be understood from his magnanimous comment, 'Let us forget and forgive.'

His stance on untouchability and the outdated caste system famously enunciated in Pune had changed the paradigms of public discourse earlier. After Emergency was over and he was quizzed by many journalists at different times, he openly said that Muslims and Christians are welcome to join the RSS if they believed that Bharat is their motherland and its culture was their culture. He encouraged interactions with various groups regularly.

Virag Pachpore notes that without much fanfare, he brought about decentralization of the Sangh as an organization. He probably sensed that the number of swayamsevaks in shakhas may decrease as a natural trend. So, he decided to take the Sangh to people through various allied Sangh activities. From co-operative banks and small savings groups, to tribal and student communities and to women as well as in the education sector, in agriculture, in labour and sewa activities, he gave the mantra of Hindu organization.

The seeds sown by Guruji in different organizations like Vanvasi Kalyan Ashram, Deendayal Shodh Sansthan, Samajik Samarasata Manch, Sanskar Bharati flowered and bore fruit during his term. Though the activities of the RSS were being criticized as being limited to the middle class, they actually went deep into remote areas in villages and tribal belts. Vanvasi Kalyan Ashram too was working since 1952. He gave it an all-India reach with more prachaaraks deputed for its work and his own personal interest.

Though Sewa projects had already begun under Guruji, he gave this activity an organized thrust. As Sarkaryavaah he made sewa a part of shakha activity by directing that each shakha should take up a sewa project in its own area.

By saying that membership of the RSS was open to all religions, he widened the dimensions of Hindutva; all Indians who respected the land and culture of Bharat were welcome to the RSS. His openness to support even those actions which did not fit into the objectives of the RSS led to its rising influence in politics too. However, while doing all this, he remained rooted.

His move to voluntarily retire from his post due to poor health was also adopted by future Sarsanghchaalaks Prof. Rajendra Singh and Sudarshanji.

Guruji was an overpowering personality. He was approachable and charming, but his persona and intellectual height did not make it look easy. Balasaheb was totally down to earth, and seemed very approachable. But his intellect couldn't be denied. His Pune address is a classic lesson in public speaking and erudite presentation of historic issues in a lucid manner.

Shivrai Telang, a senior prachaarak and a great literary person, wrote in *Tarun Bharat* after Balasaheb Deoras's demise,

> Sangh received the right kind of leadership as per prevailing circumstances, it is blessing of the Supreme Being. All the three Sarsanghchaalaks had the same vision of the nation and they presented it to the society as per situation of those times. For this purpose, all three worked as per demand of the times in tune with their respective personalities. Sangh have never encouraged production of clones. No one is alike another, still all of them are same. (Pachpore 2011, 64)

The creation of a media cell in the RSS was a bold change and made the Sangh look more friendly and approachable to people. Till he came to the fore, there was a feeling in the society that the RSS was a good organization but it was something remote. There was a kind of veil around it. Balasaheb removed that veil and connected it directly to society, just as Dr Hedgewar would have wanted.

His initiative of starting the *Samarasta Manch* to propagate harmony and equity within Hindu society was a major initiative. To defeat casteism in the society, he supported inter-caste marriages. He said if caste differences were to be overcome, *beti-beta* exchange (through marriages) outside of ones caste should be encouraged.

Balasaheb Deoras was not shy of politics as we saw in 1948–49—the period of its first ban. He was also clear that while the RSS was not interested in power or electoral politics, it would not shy away from entering politics if the situation demanded. This was a major departure from the earlier stance of the RSS not getting into politics that Guruji had followed. The merger of Jan Sangh with the Janata Party was a big sacrifice and a bold move. It changed Indian politics forever. His open support to the anti-corruption agitation, RSS's fight against Emergency and his support to the merger of political parties changed the RSS in a big way. From its introverted organizational approach, it became an extroverted outward-facing movement.

In his presence, a new platform *Sarva Panth Samadar Manch*—equal respect to all faiths—was created by Dattopant Thengdi. It was an effort to have honest interfaith dialogue. Maulana Wahiduddin was there for its inauguration in Nagpur in 1994. This initiative was later taken forward with courage and conviction by Sudarshanji.

The idea of Dr Hedgewar that society and the Sangh would merge into a single identity and that would be the ultimate success of the RSS was brought into the RSS as the central paradigm of its working during his term. Balasaheb Deoras said that whatever happens and doesn't happen in India would be the responsibility of the RSS. Whether these things happen through Sangh or through its associate organizations was not important. Ultimately all of it would be connected to the root that is Sangh.

He worked like a balance wheel between the RSS and associate organizations. Shrikant Joshiji, his personal assistant and a very senior prachaarak, said, 'Balasaheb brought in the idea of "Applied RSS" that would bring "Pure RSS" philosophy into practice' (Pachpore 2011, 215). This idea of applied RSS further evolved in later years under different Sarsanghchaalaks as different activities within the RSS framework increased and expanded.

In a programme at the completion of sixty years of the RSS in Nagpur in 1985, he said,

> The Sangh has completed sixty years. It will complete seventy-five years and then hundred years too. If this does not benefit the society and the nation, then what is the use of such celebrations? As RSS shakhas increase and the Sangh expands, swayamsevaks must create impact in all the areas of nation and make their presence felt. A swayamsevak's work doesn't end by coming to shakha but he must create an impact in his area of interest. We must spread and be present in all the areas of social life. (Pachpore 2011, 84)

This concept of having an impact on the society was brought to the fore time and again by him.

Acceptability and respect for the RSS in mainstream politics and the media began in his period. The transformation of the RSS from an organization to an activism based movement began under Balasaheb Deoras.

Rajju Bhaiyya: A Fine Political Mind Guiding RSS through Renaissance of Hindu Spirit (1994–2000)

Professor Rajendra Singh aka Rajju Bhaiyya was born in Banaul village of Bulandshahr to Kunwar Balwir Singh, the first Indian chief irrigation engineer in Uttar Pradesh (UP). His father was a stickler for discipline, fiercely honest and always played by the rule book. He lived a frugal life, never allowing his high post to affect the behaviour of his children. This discipline and frugal nature of his family left its mark on young Rajendra Singh in life. Because of the nature of his father's job with the UP government that saw him stationed at various places, Rajju Bhaiyya received his education in different parts of the country. The family finally settled in Allahabad (Prayag). His final studies and subsequent career as a teacher was in Prayag. He had two younger brothers and two sisters. All of them did well in life. (Sharda 2018, 1).

He used to give the example of how he initially scored poorly in his exams due to continuous transfers between schools and how he finally came into his own with hard work and reached the top as years went by. His brilliance and mastery over his area of expertise, physics, was phenomenal. He scored full marks in the practical examination in Physics for illustrating the Raman Effect. His examiner was C.V. Raman himself. Raman invited him to Bangalore to work as his assistant. However, the young Rajendra Singh politely declined the offer saying that he wished to do research with his guru, Prof. Krishnan. Raman told Prof. Krishnan, 'I have not seen such a practical boy in my life!' (Sharda 2018, 44–45)

Professor Rajendra Singh rose very fast from being a teacher to a professor due to his diligence and keen interest in teaching. He proved to be an excellent and very popular teacher. He would teach those students who needed help in both English and Physics (Sharda 2018, 53). It was at this time that he became Rajju Bhaiyya to all the students and then to the entire society. He had a deep commitment to harmony and equity. He would affectionately tell his students who brought him gifts, 'Why don't you give a gift to your poor friend in the class. It would not hurt their ego and create affectionate bonds' (Sharda 2018, 55).

From a Swayamsevak to a Karyakarta and Prachaarak

Like Guruji, his entry into the Sangh was quite late in his life. He joined the Sangh in the final year of his BSc. Before this, he was a regular visitor to Anand Bhavan and was connected with the 1942 Quit India Movement. Poor planning and the unsuccessful end of this agitation disturbed Rajju Bhaiyya. Regarding 1942, he said,

> I came into Sangh very late, therefore there was not much discussion whether [the] Sangh contributed to 1942 movement or not. But, it seems whatever decisions [the] Sangh took was correct. Congress leaders passed the 'Quit India' resolution. All the leaders were caught and put into jail. Not one leader remained out of jail who could guide the nation, the society or the people about the next step. All the big leaders like Nehruji, Tandonji and Kripalaniji were members of the working committee. To imagine that the British wouldn't ban Congress or would not send people involved to jails could be excused only as a thinking of a common person with limited short-term thinking. There was no plan for the people who may not have been arrested and were out of prison. Only Ram Manohar Lohiaji and Jaiprakashji did something outside.

Rajju Bhaiyya met many leaders and asked them about their future plans, but nobody had any clue. He was very disappointed to see this lack of direction in an organization like the Congress (Sharda 2018, 40). His view of the 1942 Quit India Movement was that of a youth, who had no relation with the RSS at that time. During this time, his friend took him to an RSS shakha and his lifelong relationship with the RSS began.

He was attending a camp when his MSc results came out. As noted above, he had done very well. Guruji asked him what he would do after post graduation. He told Guruji he would become a teacher and do research. Guruji gave his blessings to this idea. This was his first meeting with Guruji and also the beginning of his journey as a teacher and an RSS worker (Sharda 2018, 42).

Ashok Singhal, who later became the president of VHP, was a prachaarak too. He was junior to Rajju Bhaiyya and had close family relations with him. He joined the shakha because of Rajju Bhaiyya. He was a great singer and won many awards. Later, he completed his degree in mineral engineering and became a prachaarak who was inspired by Bhaurao Deoras (Sharda 2018, 36). In all-India-level meetings, he would be asked to sing a Sangh song. I have heard senior prachaaraks saying that Guruji would sit with closed eyes listening to his beautiful renditions.

The RSS was a very young organization, mostly with very young members. Many older Congress members joined the RSS after 1942. Some of them went on to become BJP leaders such as the ex-chief minister of Uttar Pradesh, Ram Prakash, and Mahadevi Prasad. Many students joined too. During those days, mostly young people joined the RSS as older people felt that it was not meant for them (Sharda 2018, 41).

Lal Bahadur Shastri too used to go to Anand Bhavan. He was working with Purushottamdas Tandon for an organization formed by Lala Lajpat Rai called the Peoples' Society of India. Rajju Bhaiyya found him to be very gentle. In 1945, when he stood for elections, such was his relation with him that he requested him to depute a prachaarak who could sing patriotic songs at his meeting. He readily agreed, saying he wished for Shastriji to win from his seat with a big margin (Sharda 2018, 135). It shows that the animosity that the RSS experienced later did not exist in Congress as a party. It became vicious only later under Nehru's influence.

Rajju Bhaiyya had virtually become a prachaarak as he gave all his free time after his teaching duties to the Sangh. Thus, for twenty-five years he was a teacher as well as a prachaarak, a rare combination. His first assignment when he was formally designated as prachaarak was to look after the Prayag division. He sought permission from his father if he could stay at home. His father said, 'I have no problem, as long as you don't organize any RSS meetings as it is a government bungalow. You can invite friends.' Both stuck to their principles (Sharda 2018, 97). In fact, Rajju Bhaiyya believed that this disciplined frugal way of life was a gift from his father to him.

He would take classes in typical prachaarak dress of dhoti-kurta and carry a cloth bag on return from his RSS related tours. He would prepare for his lectures at night even while travelling (Sharda 2018, 54). He was such an excellent teacher that even students who were not from his department would come to listen to his lecture (Sharda 2018, 55). Mr V.P. Singh was his student and paying his homage to his teacher, he once said that his professor could make even boring topics very interesting (Sharda 2018, 51). He refused promotions as that would reduce his time for RSS work. He was not just helpful to his students but also to his colleagues as head of department. There are a host of stories about his individual attention to his students and teacher colleagues, and how he helped them in every possible way to study and work better and progress in their respective careers (Sharda 2018, 55).

Even years after he left teaching, his interest in science and his subject had not waned. While he was in the US in 1982, Shridhar Damle arranged a programme for his interaction with senior scientists of the prestigious Fermi Lab, famous for nuclear research. He tried to put it off by saying he was not 'up-to-date.' But, when he had discussions with the scientists, the latter were amazed with his knowledge in the field (Sharda 2018, 48).

He was moulded by first-generation prachaaraks like Bapurao Moghe (his chief mentor), Bhaurao Deoras, Nanaji Deshmukh and Madhavrao Deshmukh, among others (Sharda 2018, 70–81). Though they were not very senior to him in age—the entire RSS rank and file was very young at that time—they were more experienced than him in terms of Sangh work. He was much loved for his affectionate nature and calm personality. The biography cited here has major parts from his own audio recording about his life and times.

People outside the RSS who left a mark on him were Purushottamdas Tandon, Lal Bahadur Shastri and Sant Prabhudatt Brahmachari. Later, he had warm relations with Acharya Kripalani, Dr Lohia and many other politicians too.

One quality of his, of being selflessly friendly with everyone he met, resulted in mutual respect with many, including senior social workers and politicians. He treated his staff with love and respect. He had a deep regard for Tandonji whose son was his classmate. Even at his young age, Tandonji (also known as Rajarshi) had a lot of affection and respect for Rajju Bhaiyya. He would discuss many issues with him while he was a teacher at Allahabad University. He was active in the Cow Protection movement too (Sharda 2018, 134). Leaders of the Congress were so simple and selfless at that time that Tandonji didn't want help even from his own sons after retirement. He would repair his jackets and kurtas himself when they tore (Sharda 2018, 138).

Deendayal Upadhyay was his senior colleague. Rajju Bhaiyya recounted a story about him. He had arrived for a big programme in Rajju Bhaiyya's area. Rajju Bhaiyya noted that his kurta needed some repair so he requested him to change. Deendayalji only had one more kurta, and it was dirty as he had been travelling. Prachaaraks generally carried only two sets of clothes. Finally, Deendayalji said, 'People are coming to hear me, not to see me (Sharda 2018, 80). This simplicity has been the hallmark of the RSS and its prachaaraks. Though he came from a very well-to-do family, he followed a life of simplicity. Infact, in his old age, if someone gifted him a shawl or any other outfit, he would say, 'Why waste money on me, I don't even have so many days to live.' This shows the simplicity and thrifty nature of all prachaaraks, even though, with time, the RSS had much better resources than before.

Rajju Bhaiyya was a senior worker of the RSS by the time the first ban on the RSS was imposed in 1948. He led the satyagraha against the RSS ban in his division. His behaviour was exemplary. He would take care of his juniors. Such was the mutual affection that when the jail authorities wished to shift him to B grade, which was a higher grade, from C grade, and separate him from his swayamsevaks, they created a human chain around him at night so he could not be taken away. Finally, the authorities relented. He preferred to stay with his karyakartas in grade C (Sharda 2018, 85). Even criminals in the jail respected him because of his affectionate nature and calm demeanour (Sharda, 92).

His compassion for his juniors saw him stay up three nights in a row when one of his young protégé was recovering from a deadly disease. By this time his mind was made up that he would dedicate his life for the betterment of society. He notes,

> After being released in 1949 from jail I had decided that I would not marry. I told my mother clearly that due to the type of life I was leading, I may keep getting into and out of jail. Any lady who married me would suffer due to this. Therefore, I would not marry. (Sharda 2018, 34)

He developed good relations with Lal Bahadur Shastri during this period of ban. His father was going by train to meet him from Lucknow to Prayag while he was in jail. Shastriji was in the same train. Upon being asked about the purpose of his travel, his father told Shastriji that he was going to Prayag to meet his Rajju. Shastriji told him to ask his son to stay away from such an organization. But his father said he didn't know about the organization but knew his son. If he was involved in that organization, the organization couldn't be bad. Shastriji asked the father to ask Rajju to write a letter explaining about the work of the RSS. Rajju Bhaiyya wrote a long letter, based on which Shastriji sent the release orders for five or six people immediately (Sharda 2018, 88). Later, that letter was published in *Panchjanya*. He had a very good relationship with Shastriji till the end of his life.

Once, Rajju Bhaiyya invited Shastriji to attend an RSS meeting to understand how they worked and what they discussed. This was actually contrary to what Congress leaders alleged and Shastriji had presumed. Rajju Bhaiyya told Shastriji that he could attend any meeting of any level; he was welcome to see what they discussed. To this, Shastriji confessed,

> You can move around with me anywhere, your people have full faith in you. Nobody will doubt you. Nobody will say you have become a Congressman. But, if I go to your meeting, I will be stamped with an accusation—Lal Bahadur Shastri has become an RSS man who believed in RSS viewpoint.

Surprised, Rajju Bhaiyya asked, 'Is even an old worker like you not given this much credibility? And you are the home minister. It is your duty to find out the true nature of everything happening under you.' But Shastriji responded negatively (Sharda 2018, 136). This showed the stark difference between the organizational culture of Congress and that of the Sangh. While people within Congress could never have complete faith in each other, relations within the Sangh were built on trust and brotherly bonding.

When Shastriji became the prime minister, the only non-political leader to be invited to an all-party meeting to discuss the war with Pakistan in 1965 was Guruji (Sharda 2018, 137). When Shastriji planned to go to Tashkent, Guruji was alarmed. He sent a message through Atal Bihari Vajpayee that he must not go, but by that time he had already left. Regarding his mysterious death, Rajju Bhaiyya believed it was a Russian conspiracy. But due to compulsions of maintaining good relations with them, the Indian leadership kept quiet (Sharda 2018, 137).

Bhaurao Deoras with Nanaji Deshmukh and Rajju Bhaiyya

were one of the earliest to branch out into allied fields from pure RSS work and start Saraswati Shishu Mandirs in 1950s. Hanuman Prasad Poddar, the founder of Geeta Press of Gorakhpur, also gave his support to this endeavour (Sharda 2018, 77). It is now a 25,000-strong school network.

Political Intelligence of Rajju Bhaiyya

Rajju Bhaiyya's biography gives us some idea about the politics of the time. As an observer, he noted,

> Nehruji by this time had come to control Congress completely. Gandhiji had asked for the dissolution of Congress so that new parties could come up [with] different views and ideologies. [The] Congress at that time had diverse leadership like Hindu Mahasabha, Socialist and Communists. [The] Hindu Mahasabha stream was led by Dr Munje, Madan Mohan Malaviya and Rajendra Prasad. Jaiprakash Narayan and Ram Manohar Lohia presented the best of Socialist thinking while Krishna Menon [and] S.A. Dange [represented] the Communist end of the rainbow. [The] Congress was just a co-ordinating platform. Sardar Patel had founded a labour union under [Indian National Trade Union Congress] INTUC. He too was side-lined. (Sharda 2018, 102–03)

Nehruji, inspired by Russian communism, wished to implement cooperative farming in 1952. To counter his suggestion, Chaudhary Charan Singh did a deep study of its ill-effects. But, as soon as he began to present his point of view, Nehruji interrupted him, 'Does anybody else have to add anything?' No one dared to stand up. So, voting was done and the resolution passed, stopping Chaudhary in his tracks, as if his views had no value (Sharda 2018, 104).

Rajju Bhaiyya too was witness to the 1952 Jan Sangh debacle and its effect on the Jan Sangh and RSS workers. When he was prant (state) prachaarak, the Jan Sangh had been formed and nearly all the swayamsevaks took active part in its first elections. However, despite big preparations and hard work, only four MPs were elected while about twenty to thirty became Members of Legislative Assembly (MLAs). It was a huge setback. This resulted in deep disquiet and frustration among the swayamsevaks. It was a young team and Guruji had let the youth experiment. The organization slowly came out of this shock with a lot of hard work and began growing and succeeding again (Sharda 2018, 105).

Rajju Bhaiyya's political understanding was very sharp even at a young age. When Rajarshi Tandon asked him whether he should accept the post of governor being offered to him by Nehru (probably to assuage his hurt feelings after he was eased out of the post of President of the party, so he didn't leave the Congress), Rajju Bhaiyya told him, 'I am too young but since you have given me respect and asked me this question—they are offering you sweet rasgullah of governorship to keep your mouth shut. They would not allow you to express your opinion or voice your opinion against [the] Congress. Rajarshi agreed with him and refused the post (Sharda 2018, 139).

Dr S.P. Mukherjee, the founder of Bharatiya Jan Sangh, also had affection for him and respected his political acumen. During that time, four to five MPs and MLAs in Rajasthan wished to quit the Congress and join Jan Sangh. He said with a smile, 'Let us ask our young professor the answer—what would he do in such circumstances?' Rajju Bhaiyya told him,

> I do not know much about these things, but these people are coming to Jan Sangh as a reaction to something. And when that action is over, they can go back to the parent party. A party can't be built by such reactive people. In the beginning, one should only take people who are conscious of principles and will not leave the organization on any pretext. (Sharda 2018, 143)

Mukherjee laughed and said, 'Rest assured, this is what I am going to do.'

The personal equations that Rajju Bhaiyya had with various social and political leaders were put to good use from time to time. He went with Prabhudatta Brahmachari to Chief Minister Govind

Ballabh Pant to request for a ban on cow slaughter. Pant had lot of affection for Rajju Bhaiyya as he was a bright son of the first Indian chief engineer in UP. When the talk of the Cow Protection Bill came up, Pant told him, 'You don't know, Rajju, how complex is the issue of getting a bill passed.' When Rajju Bhaiyya refused to budge, he said, 'You are half my age, when you reach my age, you will understand how to bring about unanimity.' Rajju Bhaiyya responded, 'Pantji, I am living my life at twice the speed of yours.' Pant laughed aloud and said, 'OK, Rajju, you win. We will bring the law.' Soon, the UP government passed the Cow Protection Bill (Sharda 2018, 107).

The year 1968 proved to be an important year for re-alignment in Indian politics when three seats fell vacant and the Opposition decided to fight it together on the suggestion of Ram Manohar Lohia. The three opposition candidates were Acharya Kripalani, Ram Manohar Lohia and Deendayal Upadhyay. Rajju Bhaiyya worked for Lohiaji. Kripalaniji and Lohiaji won while Upadhyayji lost because he refused to play caste politics. These successes in by-elections improved the relations between ideologically divergent parties and led to the formation of Samyukt Vidhayak Dal ministries in 1969.

Rajju Bhaiyya recalled how he bonded with Ram Manohar Lohia earlier too in 1962 when he stood against Pandit Nehru, and Prabhudatt Brahmachari had asked Rajju Bhaiyya to help him in that election. Swayamsevaks campaigned for him selflessly without any expectations across all villages. Lohiaji was, in fact, surprised at the liberal and forward-looking views of Rajju Bhaiyya and the RSS. This friendship survived many decades till Lohiaji tragically died because of poor medical support. Lohiaji was a hardcore nationalist and socialist. He had deep faith in dharma and Indian heritage. He started Ramayan Mela in Chitrakoot. He used to say that the character of Ram was equally important for all sections of society in India. He also had abiding love for all things swadeshi (Sharda 2018, 149-150). Lohiaji had lost in 1962 too but he won in the 1968 by-elections.

His relations with Kripalaniji were so good that he went to give a lecture under the auspices of the Deendayal Upadhyay Lecture Series of which Rajju Bhaiyya was president much later in life. Kripalaniji also had a wonderful equation with Nanaji Deshmukh till his last breath. He would complain to Nanaji if he didn't come to meet him often (Sharda 2018, 147).

Rajju Bhaiyya had a deep regard and love for Kripalaniji, who was then the general secretary of All India Congress Committee (AICC) and stayed in Swarajya Ashram in Prayag, the place gifted by Motilal Nehru to the Congress. This affection and relationship from the 1960s lived on in the hearts of both until Kripalaniji's death. His only argument with Rajju Bhaiyya and the RSS was this—why use the word Hindu and not Bharatiya (Sharda 2018, 145). He objected to the word 'Hindu' and asked why the RSS couldn't change it to Bharatiya. Rajju Bhaiyya's argument would be this:

> For us, both are same for our society. What was the speciality of Bharat that was not speciality of a Hindu? You will say, talk about truth, non-violence and other good qualities. Respecting all belief systems, *sahishnuta* [spirit of coexistence], sacrifice and simple life—all these are qualities of Bharatiyata. But all these are contributions of Hindus. Both are same. What is the one good quality that Islam or Christianity has taught us? This is the reason we are abused and criticized. Tomorrow, a new word could be coined for you too. You have created a big Socialist party therefore you could be called a party that fights, that quarrels, and [people] will start opposing you. You will be called some other party's agent. We believe that we should put forth our views clearly. We treat our goal of nurturing our country's culture as [the] prime objective, and culturally, Bharat is Hindu Rashtra.

Kripalaniji finally said, 'What you say is right, and in [the] future this will be the main point of struggle.' This discussion ended there (Sharda 2018, 145–46). In the current political environment, we find the views of Rajju Bhaiyya and Acharya Kripalani still relevant. This ability to converse with people of opposing views without any rancour, with affection has been the hallmark of RSS leaders.

As a Senior Prachaarak

Rajju Bhaiyya would mould a karyakarta very lovingly and with care. He would inspire them to do better and rise high. He once told a prachaarak, 'Do not keep talking about yourself. We should try to find out that person's area of work, his talents, etc., [by engaging in] affectionate conversation. Such information can be useful (Sharda 2018, 118). His nurturing of young Sangh karyakartas was legendary. A swayamsevak once wrote a patriotic poem about the motherland and recited it to Rajju Bhaiyya when he visited his area. He liked it and asked this karyakarta to complete it and send it to him. The swayamsevak was too petrified to send it. He could not imagine that a senior leader would remember this conversation. But next time when they met again after many months, Rajju Bhaiyya asked him about his poem. The young karyakarta took a piece of paper from his pocket and recited it diffidently. Rajju Bhaiyya liked it and suggested a few changes. Then he took out a piece of paper from his pocket, tore it and threw it in the wastepaper basket. He explained to the karyakarta that he had kept his version ready in case the swayamsevak had not done so, but it was not required any more (Sharda 2018, 201–02).

His compassionate, humane nature is illustrated by an incident not known to many. While going to Bhagalpur on Vikramshila Express, his colleague Swami Chinmayananda saw that the berth occupied by Rajju Bhaiyya at night was occupied by someone else while he was sitting quietly at the corner of the berth. When he tried asking him, he signalled him to be quiet. Later, he told him that when he had gone to the washroom early in the morning, he saw a boy who was almost ten years old hanging on to the handle of the door in the cold. So he got him in and put him to sleep on his berth. He didn't want to disturb his sleep. He sent a karyakarta for some milk at a station and fed it to the boy. At Patna, he asked karyakartas to find out about the child and ensure that he reached home safely (Sharda 2018, 197).

He had a knack for explaining difficult ideas in a simple manner. Once he explained how to make a shakha more strong and impactful. He used a simple formula for this. He called it the 5-S Formula.

- S1: *Sankhya* (Good attendance in large numbers that can make the shakha experience a lot of fun)
- S2: *Sanch* (Structured teams that can conduct programmes in a shakha)
- S3: *Samskara* (Progammes that impart values)
- S4: *Sampark* (Regular contact with swayamsevaks and people in the locality)
- S5: *Sneh* (Warm relations and programmes that enhance brotherly bonds)

He never raised his voice and was very gentle and was careful if by any oversight he had hurt a person. If he felt he was severe, he would write a letter seeking apology for his angry words. Even if he was sick, he would attend a programme so that it would not suffer because of his absence (Sharda 21018, 205-206).

He was very interested in sports. While reading about lawn tennis player Illie Nastasia, he once explained to a swayamsevak how the spin on the tennis ball worked mathematically. He would teach laws of physics using games as examples (Sharda 2018, 67). No one knew of his mastery in horse-riding. He once showed his flair for it during the RSS ban of 1975–77 when the team was going for a meeting. He had got an unruly horse to ride by mistake and he tamed it confidently. He went on to to tell his colleagues, 'If I cannot discipline a horse, how would I discipline the society?' (Sharda 2018, 89)

He was a stickler for protocols in public life. He took care to follow the right protocol when he met RSS swayamsevaks who were in government posts. In one case, he directed a chancellor of a university not to come to meet him at the station as it would be against the dignity of the post. In another instance when a minister came for a programme, he called him up on the stage, telling him that a minister cannot sit below a Sangh official as he is a minister. Dignity of the minister must be maintained, though he was much junior to him. He would allow his ex-students to touch his feet as a guru but would not allow swayamsevaks to touch his feet (Sharda 2018, 191-192).

He was totally egoless and good-humoured. A young student of standard X once stood in front of Rajju Bhaiyya and asked him to introduce himself (*parichay*, as it is called in the RSS), when he visited their shakha as Sarkaryavaah. Rajju Bhaiyya simply introduced himself, 'My name is Rajendra Singh and I am a Sarkaryavaah of Sangh' (Sharda 2018, 122).

This feeling of all swayamsevaks being equal and being able to talk to the top leaders gave swayamsevaks moral strength and a sense of oneness within the organization. He loved nature. He travelled to scenic places once a year on his own expense and a major chunk of his salary and savings would go as guru dakshina (Sharda 2018, 123).

He had an abiding love for music. He used to played the violin but gave it up when he became busy with Sangh work (Sharda 2018, 67). Rajju Bhaiyya wrote many songs and poems for the RSS and also set them to music. One of his poems is still sung in RSS shakhas and programmes.

> *'Nirmanon ke paawan yug mein,*
> *Hum charitra nirmaan na bhoolein.'*

Meaning,

> In these times of national reconstruction,
> We should not forget about building character.

Another popular song that is still sung is:

'Dason dishaon mein jaayen,
Dal baadal sa chha jaayen,
Umad ghumad kar har dharti ko,
Nandanvan sa sarasaayen.'

Let us spread in all directions, like clouds.
Let us green this earth with our energy.

I had the privilege of listening to this song in Mumbai, soon after he had written and set tune to it.

He would encourage everyone and help others fulfil their dreams. When some team members of *Panchjanya* objected to Tarun Vijay publishing his book on Kailash Mansarovar under the auspices of *Panchjanya*, Rajju Bhaiyya scolded them and told them, 'He is our boy. He is doing good work—why object to it. This is not correct' (Sharda 2018, 204). At another time, when an editor wished to resign from a weekly due to some differences with his colleagues, he gently chided him saying, 'Don't pay any attention to such criticism. Focus on your work; don't get upset by petty issues. Never criticize someone in writing. Because, that person may be useful in the organization in some other capacity' (Sharda 2018, 212).

He was very careful about money and funds. When the RSS was in dire straits economically in the early days, he told some swayamsevaks in a meeting, that though you don't spend much, please try to save money wherever possible. Such was his impact that one prachaarak started eating only once a day. He lived like this till the end (Sharda 2018, 120). Rajju Bhaiyya himself would eat at railway or bus stations to avoid inconveniencing swayamsevaks and also save money (Sharda 2018, 126). If someone booked him upper class tickets, he would cancel and buy third class tickets with his own money. In Kerala, after a successful public programme, he chided swayamsevaks in his own sweet style telling them that putting on the lights before time could have been avoided. Fancy decorations could have been avoided. It could have saved money (Sharda 2018, 127).

A young vistaarak who was deputed to assist Rajju Bhaiyya during a workshop, out of curiosity, peeked into his diary. He was shocked to find that the expenses of his Sarsanghchaalak were as low as that of that of a vistaarak. It was somewhere in 1990, when he spent only ₹300 a month on himself (including conveyance and related expenses) (Sharda 2018, 129). Till he was active, he would try to use his personal funds and Provident Fund that he had saved during his term as professor. When a fund was being raised for Uttarkashi earthquake he silently sent a cheque as a blessing, noting 'this cheque is from the savings during my teaching job' (Sharda 2018, 197).

He was a director from 1966 to 1970 of Rashtra Dharma Prakashan. He had very warm relations with workers there just like he had with the directors and managers (Sharda 2018, 121). He wouldn't mind travelling on the back seat of a scooter to save time and money (Sharda 2018, 130). Whenever he travelled, he would shop for simple, useful items and gift them to his RSS workers (Sharda 2018, 120). He hardly shopped for himself, it was always for his juniors and workers in the RSS office where he would be.

His sense of detachment and complete dedication to the nation is illustrated in another incident. Rajju Bhaiyya's father had gifted him his Prayag house. He had confided to a prachaarak that he was doing this since his other brothers could manage a house for themselves, but since this son of his had dedicated his life for society, he had decided to gift it to him. This bungalow in Prayag was vacant after his father expired and his mother went to stay with his other brother. When a senior worker suggested that he could give this bungalow for Saraswati Shishu Mandir, he agreed immediately and gave it out on a nominal lease. He kept just one room for his own use once in a while. The nominal rent he charged the trust was used to maintain the building (Sharda 2018, 123).

He was impressed with Balasaheb Deoras quoting Sanskrit shlokas. He wished to improve his grammar and improve his recitation. For this, he would keep a Sanskrit *Chandamama* in his prachaarak jhola. When he felt it was useful for improving his language skills, he paid for an yearly subscription for the magazine (Sharda 2018, 209).

For a three-year period, he used to go to Kerala each year for a month for Ayurvedic treatment. In that period, H.V. Sheshadri, who was Sarkaryavaah at that time, was also there in Thrissur. Many other local swayamsevaks and karyakartas too were there and many seniors would visit him during the time. He arranged a *Sanskrit Sambhashan Varg* (Sanskrit-speaking classes) for ten days, for two hours each day run by another RSS affiliate 'Sanskrit Bharati.' A teacher would come every day. It was a inspiring sight that two of the top-most RSS leaders, both in their sixties, were still in student mode learning Sanskrit (Sharda 2018, 210). He always encouraged the Sanskrit Bharati and its workers.

Rajju Bhaiyya lived the life of a simple common man. Even at an advanced age, he went for his treatment to AIIMS. Though his team knew the doctor, they could not get an appointment. One of his relatives was a director in the institute, but he went there as an ordinary patient and waited in queue for two hours. When asked about this, he simply said, 'I should also experience the difficulties that an ordinary citizen faces to get treatment' (Sharda 2018, 252).

Emergency Struggle

He was a key underground leader during Emergency in 1975–77 and was entrusted with the task of keeping in touch with government officers, teachers and opinion leaders apart from taking care of the underground struggle for the North region (Sharda 2018, 154). The Emergency was the litmus test for the organizational network of the RSS and the ability of its workers to keep it running in the worst of external conditions.

His excellent equations with bureaucrats and politicians, many of whom were his one time students, were useful. He was assigned the job of meeting bureaucrats and other people in public life to keep track of what was happening in the government. He witnessed the exchange of important information during Emergency and other times. He later told how Indira Gandhi was upset that only ten or twelve people from the list of 2,000–3,000 prominent RSS persons given by her were arrested. Police officers had told her that RSS leaders stayed with different families as their relatives. They didn't know most of them by face. At that time, Rajju Bhaiyya thanked RSS founder Dr Hedgewar who had insisted that prachaaraks should work anonymously without expecting any recognition (Sharda 2018, 163). This approach unwittingly worked to the RSS's advantage in a difficult situation. He used to say that the RSS is a family organization and that is why it and its workers and leaders survived the Emergency.

Rajju Bhaiyya was a bold person who moved freely in any situation including in the courts where police used to be present in heavy numbers. He would travel with a fake identity as Gaurav, dressed in Western clothes. He would carry some foreign currency and coins to regale people with knowledge and humour. This way, he avoided inquisitive questions too (Sharda 2018, 166). Once Rajju Bhaiyya went right into the High Court chambers wearing a lawyer's gown to meet an RSS lawyer! He then went back after discussing various issues and asking about the well-being of RSS swayamsevaks. He would attend court hearings too this way (Sharda 2018, 171).

Based on his experience during Emergency struggle, he opined that there were two distinct types of people whom he met during the time. One, who were bold and courageous who wished to do something. Others were scared and worried and did not wish to do anything. For example, he recalled that when he tried to meet his ex-student V.P. Singh, he refused to meet Rajju Bhaiyya fearing the police watch over him (Sharda 2018, 166).

He pointed out how regular meetings and exchange of ideas in the RSS could result in some good ideas. One of the ideas was to fight the election of the Bar Council in Allahabad that the Sangh nominee won easily against a Communist candidate who got less than fifty votes compared to the six hundred votes of the RSS candidate. This boosted confidence of the workers. When Advocate Virendra Pratap Chaudhary was arrested, a signature campaign was organized to put pressure on government. It was expected that a hundred lawyers would sign the petition but nearly six hundred signatures were collected in which Shanti Bhushan too played an active role (Sharda 2018, 170).

He attended Acharyakul Sabha called by Vinoba Bhave to persuade him to pass a resolution to relax censorship on newspapers and remove the ban on non-political educational and social service organizations as beneficiaries were affected. This could ease the situation and reduce tensions. The sabha made this recommendation and this news was published (Sharda 2018, 172).

Rajju Bhaiyya shared Sarsanghchaalak Balasaheb's views that the struggle against Emergency was a 'war of nerves. One who has stamina would win.' He was prophetic (Sharda 2018, 164).

When he met Dr T.N. Singh, who was not yet arrested during this period, he showed despondency, asking if the situation would change. Would dictatorship end? Rajju Bhaiyya told him calmly, 'You are not aware what is happening in the world outside. I move around. I feel that Indiraji will have to give a call for elections and I am sure that she will face crushing defeat.' Singh was surprised and said, 'You are the first person who is so confident' (Sharda 2018, 173). Later developments proved Rajju Bhaiyya's political assessment correct.

Even during these difficult times, Rajju Bhaiyya tried hard to see that teachers of Saraswati Shishu Mandir and workers of Vanvasi Kalyan Ashram didn't suffer as schools were shut by the government. They were not getting salaries. He talked of a Muslim inspector of schools who visited a few schools as per government directives who wished to take over these schools. The inspector requested the government not to disturb these schools as they were offering good education, the likes of which even his district didn't have. He felt there are good people everywhere and if they have courage they could do well (Sharda 2018, 176). This was the kind of goodwill the RSS had even among non-Hindus due to its selfless service.

Prominent Opposition leader of that time Chaudhary Charan Singh was released sooner than other leaders and Indira Gandhi was trying to woo him to divide the Opposition. Rajju Bhaiyya realized it and requested some journalists to be in touch with Chaudharyji, appreciate his good work and patriotism and remind him how the Nehru family had been persecuting him. This idea worked. So, he went for the combined Opposition meeting called by Jaiprakash Narayan in Bombay, even though he had refused earlier to attend it (Sharda 2018, 177). Rajju Bhaiyya, thus, saw to it that Indira Gandhi couldn't break the Opposition unity, especially in the north, and succeeded in keeping various parties and factions together for the formation of the Janata Party.

There was talk of a Constitutional amendment that would secure Indira Gandhi's future control when there was pressure from the world over to conduct elections. It was decided that a meeting be held inside a hall and there should be lectures and resolutions to oppose the amendment. The response was outstanding. Many leaders came for the seminar. Many legal luminaries including Soli Sorabji, Daftary and political leaders such as Charan Singh and Acharya Kripalani attended the programme. M.C. Chagla couldn't attend but sent an encouraging letter. Fiery lectures were made. A hall with a capacity of three hundred persons overflowed with people, way beyond the expectations of the organizers. People were pleasantly surprised. Similar programmes were held in other places too. The Allahabad programme was organized in Shanti Bhushan's house. Elections were finally declared due to global pressure and positive reports from intelligence agencies (Sharda 2018, 179–80).

In those gloomy times, Rajju Bhaiyya went to meet Prof. Kothari. He asked Rajju Bhaiyya about his opinion on how many people from the Congress would win. Rajju Bhaiyya said he didn't have data of other states as he was concentrating on UP and Bihar. He was confident that the Congress would not win a single seat. Kothari was stunned. He chided him that he was a man of science and should keep some margin of error as it seemed impossible. But Rajju Bhaiyya was correct. In the entire northern belt, the Congress won just two seats each from Madhya Pradesh, Bihar,

UP, Haryana and Rajasthan (Sharda 2018, 181).

The important lesson he shared with his swayamsevaks was that since the spirit of the nation was morally strong, people of India would not bear with a leader who oppressed them for long. He also noted that it was a good idea to keep meeting people, talking to them and explaining the details to them. People could be readied for a struggle by ensuring these small steps and TV propaganda doesn't work then. He added that the atmosphere changes slowly and other corresponding changes then take place (Sharda 2018, 181). In any scenario, people-to-people contact and relations are much more important than mere talk and propaganda.

These small anecdotes tell us that the RSS can work at any level in the society—from the common citizen's level to the government, from opinion leaders to political leaders. It has capabilities at all levels. This period showed how the RSS is ready to get into a political arena when required for the good of the nation but withdraws when the situation improves. This happened in the period leading to Emergency, during and after Emergency. The Sangh by its sheer reach in every segment of social life had to take a position, no matter what crisis or situation in the country.

His good work during the Emergency did not go unnoticed among the top leadership of the RSS. He was appointed Sahsarkaryavaah (joint general secretary) when the Sangh began its activities again after its ban was lifted. Within a few months, he was elected as Sarkaryavaah in 1978. It is noticeable that the then Sarkaryavaah H.V. Seshadri had demitted office due to ill health, but agreed to be his deputy when Rajju Bhaiyya was proposed as Sarkaryavaah. This shows total dedication of the RSS workers at any stage of life and absence of any ego.

Rajju Bhaiyya as the Top Office-Bearer

Rajju Bhaiyya's scientific temper, keenness about numbers and eye for detail was seen in his reporting style as the Sarkaryavaah. He was the first Sarkaryavaah who asked for written reports from the states and presented statistical details of the Sangh's work.

This initiative became a regular practice in national reporting at all levels.

Behind his calm affectionate persona was a disciplinarian who was as strict with himself as he was with others, though in an affectionate way. He visited Kerala when he was Sarkaryavaah. At that time there was a lot of struggle between Communists and RSS swayamsevaks. Many swayamsevaks were sent to jail. Some were even given life imprisonment. Rajju Bhaiyya went to meet them in jail with the permission of the jailer. Rajju Bhaiyya met them and conversed with them for a considerable time, giving them solace and confidence. He reminded them of the discipline, respect for authority, feeling of brotherhood and other sanskaars learnt in shakha and how they should nurture them even in jail. He stressed that it was important to keep talking to each other and discuss and recite Sangh prarthana and bhajans when they had free time.

During this time there was terrorist violence in Punjab and the Sangh had established a fund 'Punjab Peedit Sahayta Samiti' for these victims of violence. Those swayamsevaks donated whatever they had earned in jail to this fund. They even gifted Rajju Bhaiyya a piece of craft they had made. The jailer was surprised. There were no fiery lectures, nor talk of revenge, and nor any assurance. Those were times of Communist domination and even the jailer used to get threats. He said that it was the first time he saw a leader so calm and clear in his mind and one who advised his followers to follow jail rules and respect the jailer. He saw Rajju Bhaiyya off with respect (Sharda 2018, 189).

Rajju Bhaiyya was the Sarkaryavaah during the Ram Mandir movement and played a crucial role as the interface between the movement and the government. It was a period when there was heady gain in the strength of the RSS and its affiliates like the VHP. Ram Mandir turned into a huge mass movement. However, it was important not to let the movement get out of hand or spiral out of control. There was every chance of the organization losing its moorings when BJP came to power in 1998 on the back of the Ram

Janmabhoomi movement. Rajju Bhaiyya with his calm demeanour kept things under control in those years.

He had full faith in a karyakarta and gave him the responsibility and full support of handing the situation. Vinay Katiyar disclosed that during the Ram Janmabhoomi movement, he was criticized by some members of the team for his decisions. He was upset so he talked with Rajju Bhaiyya about it. Rajju Bhaiyya told him not to worry. 'I am with you, if there is any problem, just say without reservation that I have done this on the directions of Rajju Bhaiyya' (Sharda 2018, 195). Rajju Bhaiyya was coordinating the agitation with other organizations on behalf of the Sangh.

This period saw the BJP finally becoming the party of governance in 1998. Due to his good relations with other political parties and senior BJP leadership, Rajju Bhaiyya could steer the complex relationship between the RSS, its affiliates and the government.

In the 1990s, when conservation of environment and protecting ecology was not much of a talking point, he worried about it. He discouraged misuse of energy or natural resources in any form. In an HSS programme in the Netherlands, when somebody handed him a paper napkin as was the custom there, he took out his handkerchief, explaining how a paper napkin was against the environment as it led to the cutting of trees and wastage of water in addition to the energy consumed to manufacture it (Sharda 2018, 128).

He gave great importance to purity of character like all other leaders of the Sangh. A prachaarak had gone to BJP and came to meet him seeking his advice. He explained the qualities required by a prachaarak in politics to him,

> A prachaarak's nature should be all encompassing, touching everyone, taking everybody along and he should be popular and gentle as the Triveni waters. Just as Triveni doesn't stop anyone from bathing in it, and removes all sins, the nature of a prachaarak should be like this. Follow the same nature even

> in Jan Sangh. (Sharda 2018, 130)

His pride for Indian languages and uncompromising nature is evident from another incident. A doctor had presented his MD thesis in Hindi. It was not accepted though it was a government institution. When he heard about it he became very uneasy. He knocked at every possible door to get it accepted. He even met the then president, Giani Zail Singh. He asked the doctor to prepare a petition to go to courts if required. This took him to the famed legal luminary Laxmimal Singhvi. Finally the rules were amended, an index of Hindi definitions of English terms was prepared and his research thesis accepted (Sharda 2018, 193).

Speaking about importance of language in imparting the right education, he said,

> Our national talent which is spread over lakhs of villages of our country has to be given an opportunity to develop. Due to the use of English language in imparting education, it has become difficult to educate our people in rural areas today. Unless science reaches our village students, their scientific talent and thoughts cannot be developed. If science is taught to a village student in a language which he does not know, what will be its benefit to him? Today fifty percent of the capacity of our village students is lost in learning English alone. If the medium of teaching is mother tongue of the students, or atleast in the language of their communication, we can develop the talents of our children. But unfortunately, we have not understood this fact.[13]

His innate nature was to have great faith in goodness of all human beings. Dr Mohan Bhagwat was a prachaarak in Vidarbha when Rajju Bhaiyya was the Sarsanghchaalak. He told Mohanji,

> All people are basically good. We should deal with them with the belief that they are good. Someone's conduct may change

[13]Taken from Rajju Bhaiyya's Vijayadashami address in Nagpur in 1994.

> momentarily due to anger, envy or due to something else at that time. Basically, people are good in whom we can put faith, and we should work on this premise. (Sharda 2018, 195)

Prof. Rajendra Singh aka Rajju Bhaiyya had a soothing and calming presence and an aura of a rishi. I had many chances to see this for myself. His affectionate nature won him countless friends across the globe. In a world without internet or mobile phones, he could keep in touch with his ex-students and friends.

He was always optimistic and positive, when he was told about his diabetes. He said, 'Let me enjoy the sickness. I have got a lifelong friend now' (Sharda 2018, 214). He would always carry a medicine box with him due to various ailments but never complained.

One of the critical subjects that rose in the RSS was the issue of globalization and liberalization of the Indian economy from 1991. The initial critique was presented by veteran labour leader Dattopant Thengdi. It evolved into a policy of swadeshi by the time Rajju Bhaiyya took over as the Sarsanghchaalak of the RSS. Dattopant Thengdi floated Swadeshi Jagaran Manch. Being a proud Indian science teacher with a scientific mind, Rajju Bhaiyya supported swadeshi thoughts.

On the subject of Swadeshi, he said,

> Our country cannot progress either on the basis of foreign capital or depending on the foreign technology. We have to be very cautious about those, who wish to sell such dreams to us. All the areas in which we have marched forward in achievements like space technology, missile technology software, etc., are accomplished by our own capabilities. No one helped us in our efforts in these directions, but enough hurdles were thrown at us. Our patriotic scientists accepted this challenge in the national spirit and today they stand head and shoulders above others with the success our scientists accomplished. Big industrial houses do not need capital. Funds will have to be invested in research. We have immense

> capital of talent. We can use our own talent which is flowing out to foreign countries. Even today, the world is astonished by their manifold achievements. Due to lack of modern facilities for research and respect for talents our bright youths are going out of our country. Now the time has come for us to stop this outflow of talents and put them unto the wheels of national progress in the fields of science and Technology.
>
> [...] A few of our industrialists can come together to invest their capital and start new industries for the production of certain items. For this, we have to develop the idea of cooperation in our society. We see that as of now, cooperative societies laws are made so cumbersome that they put less time in business and more in quarrels. This means our governments are not in favour of cooperative enterprise. The world over, wherever multinational companies have succeeded in entrenching themselves, they have poked their nose in the economy and policies of those countries.[14]

There were mass campaigns for boycotting MNC products. There were seminars for building up public opinion against globalization without liberalization for the local companies. Papers were presented explaining the issues with the Dunkel draft—new rules of Intellectual Property Rights and GATT that favoured developed nations at the cost of emerging economies. Some good karyakartas were deputed for this specific work of Swadeshi Jagaran Manch. Major fairs were organized to promote swadeshi products. There were also protests against power projects that were awarded to giant MNCs.

The good thing that happened is that the concept of Swadeshi took root in the Indian psyche and many new companies rose and grew on this idea. It is also true that the indigenous companies that changed their working processes and improved their quality to suit the new liberal economy's environment grew, while those

---

[14]Rajju Bhaiyya's Vijayadashami address in Nagpur in 1994.

that stuck to archaic license raj culture and systems lost out and shut down. This campaign also revived the philosophy of 'integral humanism' in BJP's lexicon, and took a place of pride in its later manifestoes.

His urge to stay away from the limelight was ingrained in him just as all other RSS workers. When someone wished to publish a short booklet on his life to celebrate his seventy-five years of life, he refused flatly (Sharda 2018, 215). So much was his exhortation about simplicity in life and conduct, that he gave a lecture on 'working for the Sangh with simplicity' in ABPS, while the Ram Mandir movement was at its peak (Sharda 2018, 215).

Rajju bhaiyya was committed to rural development. He stressed on rural development in sewa projects by giving a simple guideline that all villages should be *Kshudha mukt, Bhay mukt, Shikshan yukt* (free from hunger, free from fear and imbibed with education). This message carries with it all aspects of social and economic issues of rural India. It was during his time that rural development became one of the focus areas of RSS sewa projects.

He laid a lot of stress on nurturing Bharatiyata. He said, 'You may use different dresses for your work. But when you attend public or social programmes, at least wear [an] Indian dress. Our dress is an important part of our culture, [the] more we wear it, [the more we] will we nurture it.' To stay rooted to ones roots, he suggested that we must visit our native village at least once in a year. (Sharda 2018, 218) He himself followed this habit throughout his life.

He was a conservationist of resources and against any kind of wasteful expenditure. His suggestion to reduce conspicuous consumption in marriages was simple. 'Whatever expenses you incur, can you donate ten per cent of it for a good social cause?' (Sharda 2018, 218) It was a practical suggestion that would make any person think about these kind of expenses.

He was the first senior RSS leader to visit foreign lands. He visited Kenya as Sarkaryavaah in 1979, Maynmar in 1981, the US, the UK and Canada in 1982. His second visit to Kenya was in 1989. After being appointed Sarsanghchaalak, he visited the UK again and mainland Europe in 1994, and in 1997 went to Mauritius, South Africa and Kenya. His last visit in 1998 was to Japan and Hong Kong (Sharda 2018, 224).

In response to a question on BBC Radio on whether the RSS should be considered a militant organization, he replied, 'We are neither militant nor submissive. We are not even aggressive; we are assertive.' Everywhere he went, he stressed upon the role of Hindu sanskriti and traditions to nurture world peace. He stressed that Indians overseas may support 'sewa' work in India but can also do 'sewa' locally (Sharda 2018, 231, 233).

A swayamsevak from England, who was a very senior scientist, visited Rajju Bhaiyya after he had handed over the baton to Sudarshanji and retired to Pune in a Sangh facility. He discussed with Rajju Bhaiyya the problem of India progressing in modern science but Indians losing touch with Sanskrit and traditional science. The Indian education system seemed to be running in two separate streams without a connect between science and philosophy. He asked whether it is possible to see the two merging together. Rajju Bhaiyya told him, 'You are expecting another Vivekananda. Yes, he will come. But it is also possible that he may come from the Hindus living in the West' (Sharda 2018, 247). His was an open liberal mind.

Though he was a hard-nosed scientist, he realized the limits of science in personal growth and this view reflected his thinking about life. A science professor had come to meet him to discuss new advances in gene therapy that could be used to cure many serious ailments. Listening to the professor, Rajju Bhaiyya recited a couplet (Sharda 2018, 255):

Paal le ik rog naadaan zindagi ke vaste,
Sirf sehat ke sahaare zindgi katati nahin.

Meaning,

Have some hobby or interest O ignorant,
One cannot live a good life just with good health.

He had deep interest in the science of ancient Bharat and had studied this subject with scientific mind. He did not go by myths, but quoted scientific texts with proper references. Since he was a scientist, his lectures would be full of facts and figures on this subject. He referred to the wonderful research of Gandhian Dharampal whose book *Science and Technology in 18th and 19th Century India* was published around 1964. He searched for a copy and got it. He wished it to be disseminated widely.

He left behind instructions that he should be cremated wherever he died, as the entire motherland was his home. This was a lesson to all Indians about the sense of belonging to the nation and not just his or her birthplace.

Rajju Bhaiyya: The Leader

Rajju Bhaiyya rose from the ranks of the RSS having passed through many organizational processes and rose on his outstanding merit, as has been the case in the RSS always. There is no concept of a godfather. There are too many checks and balances, the biggest being consensus-based decision-making process on any issue.

In the elevation of Prof. Rajendra Singh from a full-time karyakarta to a prachaarak and then to various positions till he reached the post of Sarkaryavaah and Sarsanghchaalak, we see the systemic filtering processes of the RSS at play. We also see that caste, region or closeness to Nagpur had no bearing in the progression path of the karyakartas. Those who can't survive the rigour of this multi-layered filtering system get side-lined by the process, and not by an individual or a group of individuals. These checks and balances are not understood by outsiders. A lack of understanding about the working style of the RSS leads to talk about regionalism, caste, or closeness to a particular RSS leader for one's rise in the organization.

A very senior prachaarak once told me, 'Rajju Bhaiyya was conscious of not having come from "Gangotri" of the Sangh that is

Nagpur.' He was also a late entrant like Guruji. His position at the top broke the myth that the RSS was controlled by Nagpur-based Maharashtrian Brahmins. In fact, his successor, K.S. Sudarshan too was not from Nagpur, nor was he a Maharashtrian.

Rajju Bhaiyya came from a well-to-do privileged family. But he never took advantage of those privileges either within the family or outside. This is what endeared him to people. He lived a very disciplined life on his own salary as a professor even when he was a prachaarak till he retired after completing twenty-five years as a teacher. After he retired, he used his own pension and retirement funds for himself and for helping others. His scrupulous adhering to financial frugality is legendary.

He had very acute understanding of politics and due to his friendly nature, had warm relations with friends across all party lines. This helped him and the RSS at various times in getting its views across to people. This knack for keeping friendships and relations alive, helped the pro-democracy movement against Emergency in a big way. But like all RSS leaders, he had a detached view of politics. Whether it was 1952 or the 1967–69 period or the 1975–77 period, or the Ram Mandir agitation, once an activity or episode was over, he would simply cast aside his political side and return to normal Sangh work.

In 1977, the success of the underground movement and of the Opposition in ousting a dictatorship raised the expectation of swayamevaks too. When some people were discussing political power and RSS work, he quoted a doha (Sharda 2018, 190):

Jin madhukar ambuj ras chaakhyo, kyon kareel phal khaawe,
Paramhans ko chhaadi mahaatam aur nadi mein nahaave

Meaning,

[...] Those who have tasted the juice of mango, why would they eat bitter fruit.

One who has the wisdom of a paramhansa [swan that can separate milk and water] would not bathe in a river.

He had penned a very famous Sangh poem (Sharda 2018, 190):

> *Path ka antim lakshya nahin hai,*
> *simhaasan chadhate jaanaa.*
>
> Meaning,
>
> The ultimate goal of this path is not to capture the chair of power.

It is widely believed that his dedication to RSS work may have resulted in India losing a top scientist. When asked about it, he would humbly discount this talk. However, a senior prachaarak once disclosed that when he asked Rajju Bhaiyya about it, he had told him that his name was indeed recommended by C.V. Raman to Homi Bhabha when he founded the Bhabha Atomic Research Centre. He was approached again for atomic research but he politely refused saying his priorities in life were different, and neither money nor fame could change them. (Sharda 2018, 47)

Being a man of science, he had a scientific temper. When the rumours of Ganesh drinking milk spread like wildfire, he explained that it was no miracle but a simple matter of surface tension. He went on to say, 'God can't be so cruel that he will drink so much milk where millions of children thirst for a few drops' (Sharda 2018, 68). While speaking in Kenya about science and religion, he said, 'For unveiling the truth, the path of science is the practical way.'[15]

It was during his term as Sarsanghchaalak that BJP came to power at the Centre—the first purely non-Congress political party to achieve this feat. In this, his work in expanding the work of the Sangh in the north, especially in UP and Bihar as well as his understanding of politics played a big role. It was a culmination of years of dedicated organizational work on the ground.

He was the first top leader of the RSS to go overseas and address Hindus and meet the Western media there. He could change the discourse about the RSS and Indians in their own adopted lands.

---

[15]Taken from his lecture in Kenya University on 13 January 1997.

His view that possibly a new Vivekananda might even come from overseas showed his innate liberal thinking and open mind. In an interview to a radio station in the UK, he was asked why the RSS was aggressive. He said, 'RSS is not aggressive, it is assertive about Hindu identity.' That was his ability—to express a big idea in a nutshell.

He is credited with the intense expansion of Sangh work in northern India. His scholarly scientific enunciation of Hindutva gave a direction to RSS karyakartas about how an intellectual approach could be used to present a case for the Sangh philosophy to people-at-large in a simple way.

His insistence on figures and written reports as Sarkaryavaah helped the RSS to have better data and better analysis. It also brought order to the meetings when people made presentations.

Though he was Sarsanghchaalak of the RSS for a comparatively shorter period, he left his indelible mark on the RSS and the society. He created bridges with different parties, organizations and people with his brilliant, warm and calm personality. He created an environment that made leaders at various levels realize that the RSS was approachable and open. He had the satisfaction of seeing Hindutva becoming the central pole of socio-political discourse in Bharat.

K.S. Sudarshan: An Intellectual with Enormous Cross-sectional Reach (2000–2009)

Sudarshanji was born in Raipur in the then Madhya Pradesh (MP) (now in Chhattisgarh) in June 1931. His forefathers came from Shenkottai taluka of Tirunelveli district and moved to Karnataka. His father had joined the forest department and was posted in MP. He studied in different parts of MP. He was the eldest of three brothers in the family (Tarun Bharat 2012, 65). He became a swayamsevak in Damoh at the age of nine and excelled in physical as well as intellectual activities. He stood fourth in board exams of matriculation.

He received his Bachelor of Engineering in Telecommunications (Honours) from Jabalpur Engineering College (formerly Government Engineering college) in Jabalpur with a gold medal (Anand 2019, 210).

His family's movement across south to central India saw him excel in Tamil, Kannada, Marathi and Hindi. His mother tongue was Tulu (Anand 2019, 209–10). These movements and his personal interest in languages made him a polyglot. When he was deputed to look after the Northeast, he also learnt Assamese, Bengali and Odia.

He never worried about 'What will people say?' He did what he felt was right. He would go to his engineering college in a kurta and pyjama or dhoti. Since one couldn't wear lose clothes in an engineering workshop, he wore his RSS shorts with a shirt. At the farewell programme of his college, while other students sang filmi songs, he sang the RSS song, '*Jaag utha hai aaj desh ka wah soya abhiman*'. After the programme, a professor quipped, 'He is an example of simple living, high thinking' (Tarun Bharat 2012, 69).

Life as a Prachaarak

Eknath Ranade was the inspiration behind Sudarshanji's decision to become a prachaarak by the time he finished his engineering (Anand 2019, 210). He became a prachaarak in 1954, with his first posting in the Raigarh district of MP (now in Chhattisgarh). He rose rapidly through the ranks due to his extraordinary physical and intellectual prowess. After lifting of the RSS ban post-Emergency, he was posted in a sensitive Northeast region as a kshetra (regional) prachaarak. He took over as the all-India head of physical training, and then later head of intellectual training—the only Sangh leader to grace both posts. In 1990, he was appointed Sahsarkaryavaah of the organization.

After he had become a prachaarak and had gone home to meet the family, he came home bare foot one day and said with regret that somebody had taken away his slippers in the temple but as a prachaarak he did not have the heart to spend money on a new pair. His mother gave him ₹10 (a big amount in the 1950s) to buy a new pair. He went out, bought a chappal made of rubber tyre for Re 1 and returned the rest to his mother, saying that if he lost this pair, he wouldn't feel so bad (Tarun Bharat 2012, 70).

During his tour as a prachaarak, once he reached a village very late. Deciding not to bother the host family, he slept on a platform of the village temple. Some Congress workers saw him the next morning and told him, 'See, the RSS doesn't value such a well-educated talented person. Come to the Congress, we shall get you to meet Nehruji and you can reach sky high.' He told them, 'If I had personal ambitions, I would have accepted the post of Assistant Director of All India Radio in Delhi. Sangh work for me is my lifelong mission and I will do it till my death.' (Tarun Bharat 2012, 71)

I am reminded of Rajju Bhaiyya's example, who would sleep on a hawker's trolley if a train reached too early, because he didn't want to wake up a swayamsevak staying in the RSS office.

He looked stern, and actually he couldn't suffer nonsense. But, he had a child-like nature. He could play with children, draw cartoons, tell them stories or teach them yoga playfully. If he got angry or irritated for any reason, he never carried it with him. He would forget the matter once the matter was over. Though he did not show it, he had a very soft heart. Dr Bhagwat was witness to a poignant scene of him crying silently looking outside a window before he was to visit the home of a prachaarak who had recently passed away (Tarun Bharat 2012, 8).

When a Sangh-inspired daily *Swadesh* began publication from Indore, he was prant prachaarak. They were working on an old printing machine. It broke down one night. There was no mechanic to repair it. He spent the entire night and finally repaired it (Tarun Bharat 2012, 70). When he visited Indore, he would try to find time to visit the *Swadesh* newspaper office. When he visited their new office, he took a round of the entire building. Then he asked them about electricity consumption and whether they had tried using solar power. His concern for the environment had led him to study the subject well. He asked them to check it out thoroughly and see if they could adopt it (*Swadesh Smaranjali* 2012, 5).

He had studied biochemic medicines well and carried them in his bag. If any person needed some immediate medical attention he would provide it and it was often quite effective. He advised other karyakartas to study it as well. As there were only twelve of them, so it was not difficult to study and understand them. In case of a serious problem, he would advise the patients to be taken to a hospital. But there are stories abound of his medicines working even in serious cases when there was no help around (*Swadesh Smaranjali* 2012, 15).

Even as the Sarsanghchaalak, he preferred to sit on the ground during a meeting like everybody in a meeting. He was very meticulous and would note down all the activities in the meeting in his diary. When he stood up to speak, one could immediately feel the power of his personality and his intellect.

I had attended many of his meetings.

He was a purist and perfectionist in every sense. He would not like to mix languages while speaking. He would correct mistakes in any newspaper or article and inform the person (*Swadesh Smaranjali* 2012, 19). His knowledge of Hindi and Sanskrit would surprise even great scholars. When he went to Delhi, he would mark mistakes in *Panchjanya* weekly with corrections in the margins and return the issues to editor Tarun Vijay. He inspired the *Panchjanya* team to start a column on good language. The column gave Hindi substitutes for English words or incorrect words that had become common (Tarun Bharat 2012, 51).

His brother Ramesh recalls his firm conviction in whatever he did. Once he was visiting the US with Sudarshanji to watch the *arangetram* performance of his niece. In the disembarkation card, he filled 'Bharat' under country name. His brother requested him to write India or at least write India along with Bharat, since Americans would not be aware of the word 'Bharat.' He refused, saying that if they don't know, they should be told. As expected, there was ruckus at immigration, with Sudarshanji insisting that India's Constitution has given the name of his country as 'Bharat.' After a lot of debate, the irritated customs officer had his luggage checked all over again. It took him an additional 45–60 minutes to come out but he refused to compromise on his convictions (Tarun Bharat 2012, 70).

He also did not shy away from a confrontation if the Sangh was attacked or presented wrongly. In his first speech in Kolkata, after he became Sarsanghchaalak, he challenged the then chief minister of West Bengal, Jyoti Basu, saying, 'You have maligned the RSS by accusing it of Mahatma Gandhi's assassination. Either you retract your statement or we will initiate action against you.' Basu, when posed with this question, in a press conference, immediately back-tracked saying, 'I have never given such a statement. Anyone who has published it has misquoted me' (Anand 2019, 223).

He would never leave a task incomplete. He would not look at a watch nor allow others till the task was over, like finalization of a resolution during ABPS or any other task. No matter for him was casual. He paid the same attention to a small or big job. Generally, the Sarsanghchaalak doesn't get into details of resolutions and it is left to the delegates and later the committee to finalize the resolutions as his word can influence the opinions and the resolutions, but according to Ranga Hariji he was an exception who took deep interest in these affairs. Many purists would consider this habit beyond the call of his duty. But, that is how he worked. No details were small enough for him to pay attention.

The Multifaceted Genius

His sharp eye in physical drills was legendary. Even as an RSS Sarsanghchaalak when he visited any shakha or a camp, he could detect mistakes from a distance and would then teach the person till he got it right. The same was true for RSS prayers, songs and Sanskrit shloka recitation. Dr Mohan Bhagwat recalled that the day Sudarshanji passed away, he had corrected a swayamsevak's pronunciation of a shloka in the morning shakha and made him repeat it five times before he was allowed to go (Tarun Bharat 2012, 10). When he was arrested under Maintenance of Internal Security Act (MISA), he took the physical training books to jail and would practice his moves thousands of times to achieve perfection. He studied martial arts with a martial arts specialist in jail during the Emergency. Then after studying it further, he finally designed '*Niyuddha*'—the martial art based on ancient Kalaripayattu from Kerala that became part of physical training in the RSS syllabus. He had also developed a new manual for the folk dance form lezim (called *yogchaap* in RSS parlance) when he headed the physical training department (Anand 2019, 205).

It is worth noticing that his kneecap was destroyed totally in a scooter accident earlier when he was the prant prachaarak. A new cap was not fitted. But with sheer willpower and physiotherapy he could recover ninety-five per cent of the strength of his knee and went on to train people in physical fitness (*Swadesh Sudarshan Smriti* 2014, 162).

Even at an advanced age, he kept himself fit and kept his skill of martial arts sharp. He would sportingly ask others to grip him or attack him with cane or lathi and show them how he could come out of the grip or counter the attack (*Swadesh Sudarshan Smriti* 2014, 15).

His depth of knowledge on various topics was legendary. Nobody knew how he was able to find time in his busy schedule. He would request for a book from friends or visit libraries if he found that a book had certain references he wasn't aware of. Dr Mohan Bhagwat gave an example of Sudarshanji's study of Assam and problems in the Northeast when he reached there and observed the seriousness of the situation. He would spend long hours in libraries, meet people and make notes. Sometimes, he would pick up books or go to libraries for a new topic or on hearing of some new subject.

Dr Mohan Bhagwat was witness to his hard lifestyle. Their physical training classes for the teachers in Utkal (Odisha) training camp would begin at 3 a.m. and last till 4.45 a.m. Then the physical training of students would end at 7.30 a.m. Thus, he would be teaching physical drills for four hours. He would be busy the whole day till night. He would be on the ground after his bath, personal exercises and puja before others came to the ground, which means he would be getting up much earlier.

He could work without sleep for days and if required could recover by sleeping for long hours once in a while (Tarun Bharat 2012, 7). After his first heart attack, he told Mohanji with a heavy heart that he would not be able to do physical drills anymore. But he still carried on with some efforts. He did not go for surgery but depended on an *urad dal* paste to be applied on the chest and drinking gourd juice. After he recovered, he shared his experience with others (Tarun Bharat 2012, 10).

As all-India *Bouddhik* pramukh, he tweaked the *Bharat Bhakti Stotram* (till then called *pratah smaran,* to be recited in the morning), so it could be recited at any time of the day. He added many more names and restructured it. I have mentioned more details in the chapter on Balasaheb Deoras. The practice of '*subhashit*' or some good sayings from ancient scriptures in Sanskrit and *Amritvachan*—inspiring quotes from great Indian leaders—were introduced by him as a part of training camps and shakhas. We can understand his prowess and why he had the unique distinction of heading both the physical education and intellectual training of RSS at national level. He introduced a shloka called *Ekatmata Mantra,* which explains the underlying unity of Hindu thought about the Supreme Being. It reminds us that there is one Supreme Being called differently by different sects and sampradayas from the Vaidika period to the present. This shloka is the RSS view on unifying philosophy of Hindu culture that manifests itself in different forms. We can, thus, see his stamp both in physical and intellectual training that evolved in the Sangh. Bringing the famed Kalaripayattu to mass level of RSS shakhas was his signature contribution.

Once, he and Bajranglalji went to meet Acharya Mahapragya. He asked Sudarshanji why the Sangh insisted so much on the word 'Hindu' and that the Sangh should think of some other word that is more acceptable. Sudarshanji then spoke fluently for about ten minutes explaining the root, emotions, etymology and history of the word 'Hindu.' Acharyaji was astonished. He said, 'I had heard about your scholarly knowledge but today I have experienced it myself. You are a walking encyclopaedia!' (*Swadesh Sudarshan Smriti* 2014, 38) Despite such intellectual depth, he would always prepare his speech, whether it was for a gathering of fifty or five thousand. He was very particular about facts and figures. He kept revising his speech till the last moment. He stressed on intellectual rigour and would not shy away from getting into discussion with anybody on such matters.

It was Dr Hedgewar's view that was followed by all Sarsanghchaalaks—that nobody is the Sangh's enemy and the Sangh does not work only on the basis of current issues; it's a long-term journey to re-establish ancient traditions of Hindu civilizations in the modern context. Sudarshanji was always open to any discussion with any friend or adversary. He was always flexible to accommodate them. A Leftist author of the book *Khaki Shorts and Saffron Flag* once came to meet him at the RSS office in Delhi without any prior appointment. He was Sahsarkaryavaah at that time. Without bothering about protocol, Sudarshanji invited him in with respect and responded to all his questions.

He was always positive and magnanimous. He said, 'My work is to bring in and connect individuals and I should do my work. Whoever comes in our contact, we should make an effort to connect that person with us, it doesn't matter who the individual is' (Anand 2019, 214).

He was a person who did not believe in the war of perception but in war of ideas. He told Rakesh Sinha once, 'In this world, only facts and logic get an idea accepted. The people who are on weak wicket do politics of perception. Galileo's factual discovery destroyed hundreds of years of perception of Christian civilization.' He was clear—emotional initiative, work and writings have limitations. In the Mahabharata of ideologies, it is most important to write sharply with clear facts (Tarun Bharat 2012, 93).

The day he announced his retirement and handed over the baton to Dr Mohan Bhagwat, he simply walked down the stage and sat on the ground with the delegates. Raghu Thakur, a veteran socialist thinker, noted, 'In his lifestyle, he was close to Mahatma Gandhi, in his thoughts he was close to Lohiaji and Shri Deendayal Upadhyay, and as far as his organizational style was concerned he, of course, belonged to the RSS. In a nutshell, he belonged to all. He was a true Bharatiya' (Anand 2019, 212).

The Humane Being

During Emergency, he had great relations with political leaders of all political and religious hues in the jail. A socialist leader recalled, 'When a few people in Indore started giving written apologies to get out of jail, many of us found it very humiliating and objectionable. We often used to criticize our friends fiercely who went out this way. But he gave a different argument to defend such people and avoid bitterness.' He said,

> Everyone gives according to his or her capacity. If someone wants to donate ₹100, let him do it. If someone wants to donate ₹50, let him. If someone wants to donate only ₹25 he should be allowed to do that. After all, someone is donating according to his/her capability. Why should we stop one from doing what they are capable of?' (Anand 2019, 213)

His approach was very humane towards others. He did not judge others from his own contribution to the society, but encouraged anyone who could do his or her bit.

In jail during Emergency, he would organize lectures of all leaders in jail about their ideology and views. Civil discussions and debate would follow. Once he gave lectures for three days on the concept of nationhood in jail. Birth and death anniversaries of great personalities would be celebrated in the jail. He would give lectures on various personalities. His deep knowledge about prophet Zarathustra of Persia, Prophet Mohammed of Muslims and Jesus Christ surprised people. This resulted in very good relations with all religious and political leaders who were in jail (*Swadesh Smaranjali* 2012, 35).

His deep compassion for fellow beings, irrespective of their station in life, showed in his day-to-day conduct. Once Sudarshanji came from a tour at 9 p.m. when he saw a marriage invitation from a watchman of a government office. His house was in the government office compound where he stayed in a 15x12 room. One of his sons used to attend shakha daily. So, the invitation was for the entire shakha. No one had imagined Sudarshanji would attend the wedding even after returning at such a late hour. But he immediately told others in the RSS karyalay to get ready to attend the marriage. It was the wedding of a daughter. The baraat of fifteen to twenty people was about to arrive. He saw that the room was in a mess. He immediately began sweeping it and asked others to clean the place urgently. By the time the baraat arrived, everything was ready. Watching the appointed priest not performing the rituals properly, he sat down and chanted shlokas and completed the marriage ceremony himself. He also explained the significance of those rituals to the bride and the bridegroom. He set an example that even less expensive weddings can be done in a good and tidy manner. He advised the family that a daytime wedding could have saved the cost of electricity (Tarun Bharat 2012, 8–9).

Role in National Crises

When Sudarshanji was deputed to the Northeast in 1977, first he learned Bengali and then, Assamese. He could give lectures fluently in both these languages. He also studied Church activities in depth and exposed them. He studied the tribes of the Northeast and suggested ways and means to protect them from the influence of Christian missionaries. Several schools and hostels for students were set up (Anand 2019, 203). While he was active in the Northeast, he worked with local tribes, reviving their indigenous faiths, promoting education and health for them. These sustained efforts by the RSS have seen the rise of movements of indigenous faiths in the Northeast now.

By the time he understood the region, the Assam issue had taken a turn for the worse. During an RSS meeting, the news of the murder of a Bengali-speaking Hindu bank manager by ULFA extremists came in. He dropped all other subjects and began discussing solutions to this serious problem. He was told about seventy language riots that took place in 1960, 1968–69 and 1970. It was decided to discuss the issue thoroughly with scholars and leaders of society and bring out a pamphlet on behalf of the RSS. He met a large number of scholars and society leaders. The meetings went on till 6 p.m. Then he met with some officers for two hours in the evening.

Finally, in addition to many other points, he made the important suggestion of putting in a demand for the creation of a National Register of Citizens (NRC). Such a document had been prepared during the 1951 census. This could be the basis for tracing immigrants who came after 1951. A copy of this NRC had been given to every police station and district collector's office at that time. He was clear that illegal Bangladeshi Muslim immigrants should be sent back, but Hindus who had come are refugees; and they should be dealt with differently. When the statement was published in newspapers the next day, there was a huge uproar. Agitators and extremists began threatening RSS swayamsevaks, but Sudarshanji was firm (Tarun Bharat 2012, 29–30).

According to veteran prachaarak Shrikant Joshi, he focused on this issue from 1980 to 1985 and gave lectures on the topic all over the country and wrote articles to spread awareness. His insistence on NRC-1951 became a defining point of the agitation. When the agitation was losing steam in 1981–82, he suggested that ABPV organize a public programme on 2 October 1983 to put energy back into the agitation. Thousands of students converged in Guwahati and breathed new life into the agitation (Tarun Bharat 2012, 30) He made the Assam problem into a national issue.

Ashok Singhalji wrote that when he became Sahsarkaryavaah, the Khalistan issue had taken a very ugly and fiery turn. With his active support to the Punjab Rashtriya Suraksha Samiti, founded by an ex-RSS prachaarak, a huge Sadbhavana Yatra was taken out. Thousands of citizens participated in the yatra. Sudarshanji studied the *Guru Granth Sahib* thoroughly, internalized many of its teachings and would discuss various issues with Sikh religious leaders and give lectures based on his deep understanding. He was the inspiration behind Rashtriya Sikh Sangat. He would say, 'Every Sanatani is a Sikh because of his/her faith in Gurubani, and every Sikh is a Sanatani, this is what our history tells us' (Tarun Bharat 2012, 21).

An Objective Intellectual

Sudarshanji's obsession with truth resulted in his busting the myth that Gurudev Rabindranath Tagore had written the national anthem for the British monarch George V. He even told veteran K.R. Malkani, the editor of *Organiser*, that it was wrong news and appraised him of the facts. He then suggested to the editor that there were a lot of misconceptions about this issue in north India and that the *Panchjanya* weekly should write an article about it. The article was written under the title, 'Jana Gana Mana ka Sach' (Anand 2019, 224).

His views on women and their place in society were enlightened and clearly demarcated the Hindu view versus the Western view of femininity. He asserted that only in Bharat do we see women as a mother. Not only this, we also worship God in various female forms (Anand 2019, 23). He told the Rashtra Sevika Samiti Sanchaalika (Chairperson), Pramilatai Medhe:

> There are three views about how to treat women: (i) She is worthy of worship; (ii) man and woman are complementary so think about women's issues from this point of view; and (iii) man and woman are competitive. With this in mind, each will try to show one's superiority and struggle to prove it. If we go by the third alternative then [...] society's affection and sense of unity is destroyed. Therefore, it is not right. If we limit ourselves to treating women as worthy of worship, then a woman does not get an opportunity to put in her efforts and share in social good. Therefore, second option of mutual cooperation became the central thought of Hindu society. This is the concept behind image of Ardhnarishwar. (Tarun Bharat 2012, 24)

Like all the top leadership of the RSS, he was keen to break the social barriers and assimilate Dalits in the mainstream. He would say that we need to instil confidence in them that they can move upwards. This is the foremost requirement (Anand 2019, 227). While speaking on the release of the book *Samarasta* in August 2006, he shared the pains that brethren from SC/ST had to go through. He had read all the books of Dr Ambedkar and also the biography of the Chancellor of Aurangabad University. He went on to say, 'It has been the misfortune of our society that we could not understand Dharma properly. It is sad that Hindu society, its supreme philosophy and its practical aspects got separated.' He explained how over time Hindu society had seen many highs and lows (Tarun Bharat 2012, 132).

He would say,

> There is a deep conflict that manifests itself in lack of coordination between western philosophy that thinks of struggle as the medium of progress, and Indian philosophy that has different values and systems. Because slavery had calcified our systems and institutions, they stopped evolving and became orthodox. So, we got attracted to western worldview. They came from two extremes that saw two kinds of people rise. First, those negating our own systems, traditions and knowledge systems, blindly following western model and second, people ready to face challenges of the new modern world with new systems and knowledge system. The first said, all the old is untouchable, useless, worth throwing away. Talking of the old itself is anti-progress, orthodoxy. So we must borrow everything from the west. The second finds the old structures worth dropping but believes that root inspirations and basic understanding need to be nurtured. (Swaroop 2017, 11–12)

He believed that our own traditions and cultures show us the path to find answers to our problems and solutions to equitable growth. But he was a follower of modern science and technology too. He often quoted a Sanskrit shloka that means, 'It is not necessary that what is old is definitely good. A poem cannot be dropped just because it is new. An intelligent person picks up things after validating them, a fool simply follows others' (Swaroop 2017, 13).

Sudarshanji was a firm believer in Swadeshi. The new post-Independence Swadeshi agitation had started in 1991 in the wake of liberalization led by veteran RSS prachaarak and founder of Bharatiya Mazdoor Sangh, Dattopant Thengdi. His view was that opening the gates to MNCs without adequate time given to Swadeshi manufacturers to get ready to face the competition would kill the Indian industry. He demanded a level playing field so Indian companies can face competition from the big MNCs. The laws for MSME were archaic and reservations of many items from small-scale industries were being removed without worrying about the repercussion on the industry segment that provided maximum employment and was the growth engine of Bharat. The taxation, industrial controls and labour laws too were weighed against the MSME.

He took a strong initiative to write the history of India from a national perspective, and held discussions with scholars like P. Parmeswaran, K.I. Vasu, Dr Sujit Dhar, K.R. Malkani and Devendra Swaroop. He added more people like Dr Bajranglal Gupt to the team to take his idea forward. The final outcome of these discussions led to the formation of *Pragya Pravaah*. Each state had small bodies registered locally that would hold intellectual workshops and seminars (Tarun Bharat 2012, 120). He also got prominent scientists involved in this activity (Anand 2019, 203).

Akhil Bharatiya Itihas Sankalan Samiti Yojana had been formed many years earlier in 1979–80 under the leadership of renowned archaeologist Dr Hari Wakankar, a Padmashri awardee, who had discovered, among hundreds of archaeological sites, Bhimbetka Caves, the oldest rock caves in India. He had begun researching on Saraswati river that had dried up. He worked on satellite imagery and other archaeological proofs. However, the governing class at that time had no interest in these findings that could potentially change the entire theory of Aryan invasion. When the National Democratic Alliance (NDA) government led by BJP came to power in 1998, this research received the required boost from Pragya Pravaah under guidance from Sudarshanji. In fact, Dr M.M. Joshi was accused of saffronization because of this (Anand 2019, 204).

He was a passionate advocate of rural development. Subjects close to his heart were organic farming, non-conventional resources of energy, water management and cow protection. After he handed over the baton to Dr Mohan Bhagwat, he spent most of his time to study, promote discussions on these topics and experiment on these subjects. (Anand 2019, 201 and 204) Swadeshi and ancient and modern science were two topics that figured often in his talks.

He was very happy with the work done by Deendayal Research Institute (DRI) floated by Nanaji Deshmukh who also created a sustainable model in Gonda, UP. He encouraged it in every possible way and wished it to become the centre for research on such an economic development model on a larger scale (Tarun Bharat 2012, 80–82).

Sudarshanji was opposed to genetically modified (GM) seeds that were promoted by MNCs and warned about them. He was a firm believer in the cow-based rural self-sufficiency model. He was in constant touch with scientists to find out alternatives to diesel and petrol. He discussed the issue of making petrol from plastic waste and found someone would do it successfully (Anand 2019, 204).

He was deeply committed to water conservation, environment and non-conventional energy. All the RSS offices where he visited, it became an unwritten rule not to give a full glass of water to guests as mostly they would take a couple of sips and leave the rest. This led to a huge amount of water wastage if taken in totality (*Swadesh Smaranjali* 2012, 6). When he met C.P. John in Kerala and heard him speak on water conservation, he went to his house the next day and discussed the issue with him for over an hour. He explained how farmers in Kolhapur in Maharashtra had begun using drip irrigation that saved ninety per cent water and got him in touch with the organizers. As an engineer, he had provided the design of rainwater harvesting tanks in Gujarat that proved very successful. He shared it with John (Tarun Bharat 2012, 53). He would encourage young scientists to go for research.

His engineering and technological mind too was always ticking. Surya Prakash Kapoor noted that after the supercyclone in Odisha in 1999, he suggested a project to stop earthquakes. There are seven geothermal regions with 340 hot water springs that can produce 10,000 MW power with binary cycle plants. This would reduce surface steam temperature and pressure, reducing the chances of an earthquake. He presented this idea to Dinanath Mishra who was member of the Planning Commission at that time. However, this project was scuttled by vested interests. He then wrote to many chief ministers about this idea. Chief Minister Narendra Modi at that time signed an MOU with Tata Power for a 5 MW plant. Gujarat alone would have 1,000 MW geothermal power plants. Many states followed this suggestion (*Swadesh Sudarshan Smriti* 2014, 101).

Such was his obsession with environment protection that once while in Kerala, he returned from a walk and asked K.C. Kannan to call the chief minister's office. He talked to CM Ommen Chandi and told him that he had seen huge quantities of plastic scattered all over—why didn't he convert waste plastic to diesel? He explained to him the entire process for its conversion (Tarun Bharat 2012, 46). For him, national interest was above politics.

Inter-Faith Outreach

Exchange with other faiths used to take place earlier too, but he gave it a big push. He considered Muslims and Christians to be a part of the Hindu Rashtra. He was in close touch with their religious leaders. He didn't agree to the idea of calling Muslims and Christians as minorities. He termed this as a fallacy and always held this belief that they were children from Hindu forefathers (Anand 2019, 205) He would say,

> Minorities are those who move from one country to another and then settle there. That way only Jews and Parsis should be treated as minorities. But, even they don't consider themselves as minorities and have amalgamated in the national mainstream. But, 99.9% of Christians and Muslims in India haven't come from outside. They always belonged to this land and changed their religion only a few generations ago. So, just by changing the religion how can we call them minorities? (Anand 2019, 227)

Indresh Kumar, the patron of Muslim Rashtriya Manch (MRM), which was formed with inspiration from Sudarshanji, says that the workers of MRM believe that Sudarshanji's all-encompassing definition of Hindutva led Muslims to believe that Islam is not only safe but respected too. He instilled the belief in Muslims that they are neither minority nor foreigners, but Indian Muslims are Bharatiya Hindus. Sudarshanji believed that we can be believers of different ways of worship, but all of us are the children of the one Supreme Being (Ishwar or Khuda). Our forefathers are common. We all belong to one nation (desh or watan). We are all sons of Bharat Mata. Therefore, our culture is the best humanist culture, and one that we call Hindu sanskriti. We are proud of it because we think for the betterment of living beings of this world, and treat all as brother and sister (Tarun Bharat 2012, 38).

Highly influenced by Sudarshanji's scholarly discourse, Ajmer Sharif's Hazrat Maulana Jamil Ilyasi said in a programme,

> I am from the family of the King of Naharsingh, Bharatpur. My grandfather had converted to Islam. We are Muslims by religion. We worship one 'malik' but our sanskriti or tehzeeb is Hindu. As a true Muslim, I am proud of my Hindutva. Every true Muslim must think on these lines. We should not live in Bharat as two communities of Hindu and Muslims. We are one community due to our nationality. Our mazhab, language, clans are different, but we are one. (Tarun Bharat 2012, 38)

The seed of MRM was sown when Indresh Kumar was prachaarak in Jammu and Kashmir and Himachal Pradesh. He recounts,

> J&K was afire due to terrorism. There was hardly a week when one didn't hear the painful news of people dying while trying to leave the valley. He used to visit Kashmir Valley during those times too. Sudarshanji asked me, 'Are the hearts and minds of all the Muslims in Kashmir Valley filled with opposition to India and violence?' I told him, 'No, it's not true. I have been going to Muslim-dominated areas, visiting their homes and sitting with them. I believe that a much bigger number of people wish for peace and brotherhood. But all of them think they are helpless. The

> government does not provide them protection; in fact, it seems that the government and the media are standing with the separatists. There are Muslims in the media too who are against nurturing the extremists.

In 1997, Sudarshanji, as Sahsarkaryavaah visited Kashmir Valley for two days. He had meetings with many Muslims. This created a firm belief about the possibility of nurturing the seeds of national or Indian views. He also kept meeting Islamic scholars all over India. It was during this time that an idea of forming a *tehrik* or a movement of Muslims began taking shape.

This movement finally became an organization on 24 December 2002 in Chanakyapuri in Bapudham in the presence of a large number of Hindu and Muslim delegates, leaders from both communities and BJP leaders too. Sudarshanji said in his speech, 'The meaning of Islam is *salaamati* [security] and *aman* [peace]. But today the face of Islam is presented as that of a terrorist and a militant and an outsider. Is it not our responsibility to throw away the mask of terrorism and extremism and show its face of peace and brotherhood?' Maulana Wahiduddin too supported this view.

After a feast, some Muslims decided to take up this important but very difficult task. The movement carried different names like My Hindusthan and Rashtriya Muslim Andolan. After five or six years, the name finally decided by Muslim brethren was Muslim Rashtriya Manch: Sudarshanji was present in the programme when this name was finalized (Tarun Bharat 2012, 39).

Since Indreshji used to be in touch with various mosques, dargahs and programmes to spark a fire of nationalism, he was given the responsibility to support and help this organization. The first national conference was organized on 30–31 August 2003 in Delhi where 250 delegates came from fourteen states. The conference passed two resolutions. The first condemning terrorism in the name of Jihad and the second supporting cow protection. They ultimately got 1.35 million signatures from Muslims for banning cow slaughter (Tarun Bharat 2012, 39).

In April 2004, the first All-India Conference of Muslim women was held in Delhi. Three hundred women from thirteen states participated in this conference. Sudarshanji was present on both days. He heard their views and problems. The crux of what he said during the conference was this: The foundation of any civilized society or family is formed on the basis of daughters, sisters and mothers. That society progresses where women are educated, safe and trained in value systems. Therefore, all members of society should educate and inculcate culture in their daughters.

On the 150th Anniversary of the 1857 War of Independence, Sudarshanji explained to the MRM workers how history and the lives of freedom fighters were being removed from history books, and this is unfortunate for the nation. The workers of the Manch decided to celebrate 2007–08 as 'Salaam 1857' and conducted over hundred programmes all over India, beginning with the first huge programme in Delhi where Sudarshanji was present. Inspired by the success of this programme, members of MRM decided to offer prayers to the martyrs at their graves on the *Shabe-raat* (Tarun Bharat 2012, 41).

MRM organized a yatra from Red Fort to Hazratbal on 7 August 2009. A total of 172 members reached Lakhanpur border on 10 August 2009, where they were stopped. Finally, twenty courageous members went up to Srinagar. Similarly, MRM took active interest under the guidance of Sudarshanji and a meeting with 200 Muslims scholars and Maulanas was held in 2009 in Delhi to discuss the Ram Mandir issue. After long discussions in a good atmosphere, everyone agreed that Imam-e-Hind should get his right and the Ram Temple should be built. For this, discussions at all levels should be done. It was decided to meet again after the decision of the court. But before this could happen, Sudarshanji passed away (Tarun Bharat 2012, 41–42).

He motivated Muslim brethren to fight against terrorism. They took out a 'Tiranga Yatra' with a call for 'Mumbai chalo'. Thousands of Muslims gathered in front of Taj Hotel and called for death to terrorists. Many such programmes took place during these years. Such was his relation with the leaders of Muslim community that when Maulana Jameel Ilyasi died, he went personally as an elder brother to dig 'kabr' in the mosque campus and laid a warm sheet on the kabr, saying, 'O brother, this sheet will give you warmth.'

Sudarshanji had done detailed studies of Islamic and Arabic history. He would quote *aayats* and *Hadis* while explaining some issues to Muslims. He would quote Prophet Muhammad to inspire them to study. He quoted the Prophet as saying, 'I receive cool winds from Hindustan', then how can it be Dar-ul-Harb? Hindustan is the true Dar-ul-Aman. Our dear 'watan' is the most sacred land where followers of all the religions of the world stay together (Tarun Bharat 2012, 42).

When Sudarshanji was in Kerala, there were 'Christian–RSS discussions' in many places. Retired SC judge Justice K.T. Thomas was a moderator in one of the programmes. He developed a very good friendship with Sudarshanji (Tarun Bharat 2012, 47).

In year 2001 during a mass contact programme, M.G. Vaidya, RSS spokesperson at that time, was asked by Jon Joseph, a member of the Minority Commission for a meeting with Christian leaders with RSS leadership. Vaidya readily agreed. He made repeated efforts—finally some members of Roman Catholic Church were ready to meet RSS leaders but they put two conditions. One, there should be no Protestant in the meeting and two, they will meet only the Sarsanghchaalak. After some coordination, the date and time was fixed. But on the last day they sent a message that they would not meet in the RSS office or any third place but only in a church. Vaidya was very upset and told them that they could consider the meeting off. He talked to Sudarshanji and told him about the condition. Sudarshanji said, 'OK, we will meet in the Church.' He did not make it a prestige issue, nor did he take it as an ego issue or believed in formalities. Finally the meeting took place and they had discussions for nearly one hour. The next meeting with the Protestant Church took place in Nagpur where twenty-nine delegates representing 27 sects came and met him. They too had nearly one-and-a-half-hour open-hearted discussions. They had food at the RSS headquarters (*Swadesh Sudarshan Smriti* 2014, 28).

Later while addressing an RSS instructors' training camp in Kottayam in 2018, Justice Thomas said that after the Constitution, democracy and the armed forces, the RSS is the factor that has made people in India safe, and that the idea of secularism should not be kept away from religion.

Thomas said he feels the Sangh imparts discipline to its volunteers for protection of the country. He said:

> Snakes have venom as a weapon to defend [themselves against] attacks on them. Similarly, the might of man is not meant to attack anyone. I appreciate the RSS for teaching and believing that physical strength is meant to guard [oneself] against attacks. I understand that the physical training of the RSS is to defend the country and the society at the time of attacks.

He continued,

> If asked why people are safe in India, I would say that there is a Constitution in the country, there is democracy, there are the armed forces, and fourthly the RSS is there. What prompts me to say is that the RSS had worked against the Emergency. The RSS's strong and well-organized work against the Emergency had reached then Prime Minister Indira Gandhi. She understood that it could not go on for long [...] If an organization has to be given credit for freeing the country from the Emergency, I would give that to the RSS.

On the concept of secularism, the former apex court judge said that the idea should not be kept away from religion, and that the Constitution has not defined secularism.

> The minorities use secularism for their protection, but the concept of secularism is much more than that. It means that

> dignity of every individual should be protected. The dignity of a person should be seen above partisan approach, influences and activities.[16]

There are many such examples of people who began seeing the RSS beyond the image created by negative propaganda of the Left-secular groups. One can see the far-reaching impact of Sudarshanji's outreach and inter-faith dialogue.

During his years as Sarsanghchaalak, he took keen interest in Tibet affairs and in 2006, when the birth centenary of Guruji was being celebrated, he decided that it would be incomplete without meeting the Dalai Lama. He met him and was quite vocal about Tibet's cause. He later invited the prime minister of Tibet's Government-in-Exile as the chief guest in his annual address as Sarsanghchaalak on Vijayadashami in Nagpur. He played a pivotal role in setting up of an organization, Bharat-Tibet Sahyog Manch (Anand 2019, 216). He wrote an introduction to the book *Guruji and Tibet* written by Dr K.C. Agnihotri where he stressed that Tibet's freedom is important for India's security but those in power in our country haven't understood it till today. We have not been able to assess Chinese expansionism. The result is that we can see that after Tibet, even Nepal is now getting swallowed by China. After his demise, the Tibet parliament-in-exile passed a resolution unanimously, saying, 'We have lost a true friend of Tibet' (Anand 2019, 217).

His grasp on international affairs was quite remarkable. When he was travelling to Hong Kong, Boris Yeltsin had begun facing huge opposition. He simply said, 'He won't last long. People have tasted democracy and they will not rest till he is thrown out.' Within a week of this, he was dethroned, recalls Ravi Iyer, at that time co-convenor of HSS working out of Hong Kong.[17]

He gave full support to the International Centre for Cultural

[16]https://indianexpress.com/article/india/after-constitution-army-rss-keeps-indians-safe-supreme-court-ex-judge-5010704/

[17]Based on a recording of 25 April 2019.

Studies (ICCS), Nagpur, and allied organizations to support the revival and strengthening of indigenous faiths in the world. This idea was initiated by one of the former senior prachaaraks of Hindu Swayamsevak Sangh, Dr Yashwant Pathak. The first International Conference of Elders of Traditional Cultures and Faiths held in 2003 in Keshav Srishti, in Thane near Mumbai, saw his presence. These cultures and traditions were those that had thrived before the advent of Christianity and Islam but were destroyed or nearly destroyed by the advancing Abrahamic forces presented by these two belief systems. I was one of the hosts as the Secretary of Centre of International Studies (Vishwa Adhyayan Kendra, Mumbai) and could see the sheer devotion and love of nearly a total of 200 delegates from forty-five countries representing seventy-five different ancient traditions of the world. They came from a wide arc beginning from New Zealand and ending with Latin America, passing through Africa and Europe.

The delegates believed that only Hindu dharma won't prey on them but help them preserve their ancient traditions and cultures. They compared Hindu culture to a large ship that could help their smaller boats travel safely and feel secure. Now these conferences are held every three years in India. Any international observer will note that there is a revival and renaissance of ancient traditions and cultures or indigenous faiths all over the world. Many in the West are trying to find their roots and going back to them to get spiritual solace. Now, this meet takes place every three years in India.

As a senior Sangh leader he undertook many foreign tours to address local people there and programmes of the Hindu Swayamsevak Sangh. He would specially go during their training camps to provide guidance. He had excellent personal relations with workers of HSS in different countries.

According to Shyam Parande, in 2002 he had an open discussion session with diplomats from Middle East Islamic countries in the RSS office in Delhi. It was arranged by a swayamsevak from UP who had gone to work in the Middle

East. Ambassadors from Syria, Libya, Sudan, Iraq and UAE were present. This was just a month before the US attacked Iraq. He presented Hindu philosophy and Sangh thinking and connected it to the Muslim world. He also presented his view on globalization resulting in natural and economic imbalance due to western leadership. A diplomat quipped, 'How are you able to present such tasty intellectual food regularly to people?' He could build such relations due to his open dialogues (Tarun Bharat 2012, 110).

Visionary View of Bharat

I had personally heard Sudarshanji talk about the rise of Bharat as a strong nation around 2011–12 many years back. A video of his prediction is available on YouTube. I could find one record in the year 2003 on 12 January in a RSS workshop in Ramtek, Maharashtra. He quoted Dr Pranav Pandya who had said in an RSS Vijayadashami programme that the change of times (*yug parivartan*) began with the birth of Ramakrishna Paramhansa in 1836. He added,

> Maharshi Aurobindo had said that a *sandhikaal* (time-lag between change of two eras) is 175 years. This period is called *yugsandhi*. It is like the time between day and night called *sandhyakaal* (dusk) or between night and day that is called *ushahkaal* (dawn). If you add 175 years to 1836, the year 2011 is the year. It is the year when Bharat's destiny will begin shining like Sun. We are the people who will take Bharat to that stage. I do not know whether I will be able to see this period with my own eyes, but all of you are going to see it. We need to be ready with strength to welcome it, and the base for this is Sangh work. (Tarun Bharat 2012, 152)

We find the social and political changes in the Indian society following the path that he had predicted nearly fifteen years back. He had sharp socio-political understanding, but he was not politically inclined. He laid more stress on pure Sangh and its expansion in other social areas. He was focused on science and technology aspects for the benefit of Bharat and humankind in general. He did not like any dilution in ideology and he was blunt in expressing his opinion. Not for him the diplomatic finesse. He and Dattopant Thengdi were strong proponents of Swadeshi while BJP government had decided to open the gates to MNCs in the hope of investments in industry. There is no doubt that there were differences in opinion between the RSS or the BJP around economic policies. Because of his open expression of views, many in the media exploited and tried to create a wedge between BJP and RSS leadership, targeting Sudarshanji in this game.

In his book, *Sangh Rajneeti aur Media*, Devendra Swaroop calls out the news manufacturing about RSS-BJP division. On 29 August 2001 the newspapers carried a news item about the release of the Hindi version of a book on veteran prachaarak Shri Laxmanrao Inamdar, who had a great influence on current PM Narendra Modi. The book was written in Gujarati by Rajabhau Nene and the then general secretary of BJP and Narendra Modi who had just been appointed as Chief Minister of Gujarat.

The book was released at the PM's house. The manufactured stories revolved around the then Sarsanghchaalak Sudarshanji's presence with a bandaged and dislocated shoulder, whose name was not on the invitation card. The card carried the name of Dr Mohan Bhagwat (Sarkaryavaah then). The fact behind this switch was that Bhagwatji's father had expired on 10 August and he couldn't attend. So Sudarshanji, inspite of being injured, came. If there was a news it was his dignified simplicity and humility that he came as a substitute for a colleague who was technically junior as a show of respect to the post of prime minister. A hidden message behind this presence of the Sarsanghchaalak was deduced as an effort at 'rapprochement.'

During his speech, PM Atalji complained to the media that the news of four senior karyakartas of the RSS kidnapped and killed in Tripura across the border had been suppressed and asked the press to publish that day's news of the book release prominently.

He also affirmed his being a swayamsevak. It was a disappointment for the media that had been talking about Atalji distancing himself from the RSS. Another news manufactured from the news desk was about Sudarshanji's covert meetings with Advaniji, M.M. Joshiji etc. to review the working of the NDA government. A journalist of *Indian Express* claimed that Sudarshanji met Atalji for half an hour before the book release though Sudarshanji had trashed this rumour immediately (Swaroop 2016, 198). Thus, Sudarshanji was a victim of what we today call 'fake news' factories. The differences were honest as far as economic policies were concerned but clash between the two organizations as a very serious issue was manufactured.

Uncompromising Ideologue

When he became the RSS Sarsanghchaalak, the affiliates had grown very big by that time. Many of them had a large cadre base of their own. They had their own full timers or prachaaraks. They had their own structures, philosophy and approach to issues that confronted their specific organizations. All this may have led to some dissonance from what one gets to understand from various interactions. But they were not of the nature that newspapers wanted people to believe. If one were to go back to Balasaheb Deoras's chapter, the reader would note that one of the objectives of Balasaheb's idea of celebrating Dr Hedgewar's centenary by involving all the associate organizations was to bring them together, to have better coordination that had suffered as they grew big. And in its decades of existence as a family from the same ideological mooring, this ability to get over such frictions is a tribute to the inbuilt processes and personal relations that the RSS nurtures.

Sudarshanji's objective approach to various issues saw the RSS pass resolutions cautioning the BJP. It asked the government to be careful when dealing with Pakistan when the then president of Pakistan, Pervez Musharraf had a summit meeting with the Indian PM, Shri Atal Bihari Vajpayee. The RSS resolution in 2003 similarly cautioned the government about dealing with China and the Tibet issue and to keep lessons of history in mind. Since Guruji's tenure, this was a rare resolution about foreign policy, that too when a party supported by the RSS was ruling at the Centre. These resolutions showed that the RSS wouldn't change its position on issues of national interest just because the ruling party happened to be close to its philosophy. Cautioning a friendly party was blown up as a serious friction.

An interview of Sudarshanji in *Walk the Talk* had become highly controversial. About his advice asking old leaders to retire and make way for young leaders, M.G. Vaidya says,

> There was nothing wrong in Sudarshanji's statement about handing over the reins to younger leaders. Not just Bharatiya Janata Party but all public organizations and associations should give responsibility on the young shoulders. This is an unbiased suggestion. [The] Sangh has been doing it for long. No prant prachaarak in RSS is generally above fifty years. Even Sudarshanji's health was not so bad and he could have carried on with the responsibility of Sarsanghchaalak. After Guruji's centenary celebrations in 2007, he had begun planning for handing over the responsibility to someone. In 2009, when the Sarkaryavaah is elected, he declared his successor. Isn't there Vanprasth ashram in Hindu philosophy? Then, where is there a need to feel bad about i? I don't think, Sudarshanji said anything wrong. (Tarun Bharat 2012, 33)

Now, even BJP leadership has taken a stand that leaders above seventy-five years should take a break from electoral politics and government responsibilities.

About Sudarshanji's opposition to Macaulay-inspired education system, Vaidya again says,

> It was not his personal opinion. Sarkaryavaah H.V. Seshadriji too had spoken on the same lines. The purpose behind Macaulay education system was not good. Its purpose was

> to de-Hinduise Hindus. Why should medium of education be English and not mother tongue? France, Germany or Russia don't have English for education. He believed that our languages are rich enough to provide necessary education. And he never shied away from speaking his mind. (Tarun Bharat 2012, 33)

Speaking about Sudarshanji's insistence on Swadeshi, M.G. Vaidya states that every nation in the world has insisted on Swadeshi. Congress too insisted on Swadeshi. We put foreign clothes in a bonfire during Lokmanya Tilak's time. Gandhiji insisted on it. Sudarshanji was a great supporter of Swadeshi. He believed that we could produce fuel from alternative sources. But, people didn't pay much attention (Tarun Bharat 2012, 33). He encouraged anyone who came up with some solution, went and visited him. Now, we find these idea being successfully tried in many places.

It would be a good idea to give a brief understanding about Sudarshanji's, essentially the RSS's views, about Indian development model. One thing that strikes a reader is what Sudarshanji said years back is now the dominant thought on economic development models—basically sustainable consumption, not sustainable development. He, essentially, expanded on the philosophy of Integral Humanism presented by Deendayal Upadhyay. One can see that the current BJP government led by Narendra Modi has also been implementing many ideas like Antyoday or reaching the last man in the queue.

Dr Bajranglal Gupta explains his ideas in *Su-darshan* thus:

> His critique of western model of development was that it is was based on Cartesian Newtonian philosophy that looks at mechanical fragmented view of the universe. This view looks at the world only as material arranged in a certain manner as the basis of all existence and treats material world fabricated together like a machine. This view treats individual and the nature as two separate entities. Each entity is separate from each other hence an individual becomes indifferent to the

> happiness or pain of the society. On the other hand the Bharatiya philosophy treats individual, society and the natural world as integrated entities, thus it is sensitive, believes in cooperation and integrated approach. The future economic development has to be based on this concept of an 'Integral Human.' (Tarun Bharat 2012)

Acceptance of the Darwinian principle of 'survival of the fittest' leads to competition and struggle to protect one's own existence and put down others to become economically stronger and prove one superior. As a result, the economically weak slowly lose the strength to exist and get destroyed. He believed in the principle of *Antyoday*.

The West treated nature as its slave and exploited in an unlimited way to enjoy comforts. Because of this view the world is suffering from pollution and degradation of our ecosystem. Therefore, nature must be treated on the principle of coexistence and harmony. He stressed on nature-friendly, pollution-less technologies. He supported technologies that would result in lower consumption. He went on to rediscover traditional techniques of iron melting that consumed less energy.

He believed that *Arth-Kaam*-driven (economic- and pleasure-driven desires) consumerist lifestyle is the root cause of ills that society is facing. He said we have to go back to '*Dharma, Arth, Kaam, Moksha*' paradigm and create models of economic development based on it. Only consumption and enjoyment has led to a life of only non-human, animal-like enjoyment, leading to a consumerist world. This is why our rishis had commended earning and consumption within ethical mores of dharma. He stressed the wisdom of Upanishads that say *Ten tyakten bhunjitha*—use only what is needed and give up excess. The new environment-preservation thoughts, the new approach to economic growth and welfare, all of these talk about sustainable consumption and avoiding reckless exploitation of natural resources, thoughts that Sudarshanji stressed very strongly.

He would say that if we wish to get rid of poverty, inequity and unemployment we will have to create an economy based on swadeshi, self-dependant and decentralized economy. We can't have large, automated and high energy-consuming manufacturing as it is not suitable for Indian conditions. We need to create plans separately for urban and rural economies based on practical requirements. He suggested creating clusters of ten to fifteen villages for better integral development. He supported strengthening of traditional manufacturing and farming techniques and creating an entire supply chain ecosystem to help export such products. He advocated conserving traditional water resources, using indigenous seeds, biological organic farming, saving biodiversity, nurturing indigenous animals, using indigenous desi cow as the basis of rural life with its multi-purpose, multi-product (*panch-gavya*) benefits. In all, create a balance between '*Jal, Jameen, Jungle, Jeev and Jan* (water, land, forests, animals and people) for integral balanced development. He did not believe in state control or capitalist market mechanism, but cooperative, society-centred economic development.

The timelessness of Sudarshanji's and Dattopant Thengdi's views about Swadeshi is proven now in the post-COVID world and it is being re-interpreted afresh by the BJP government as well as other countries in their own way. We also saw that the return to core values of BJP benefitted BJP and it returned to power in 2014 and 2019 with thumping majority while it had lost power in 2004 and failed to come back in 2009 while it was trying to create a new ideological platform. So, ultimately, Sudarshanji's intellectual clarity stood vindicated.

He gave up the post of Sarsanghchaalak in 2009 when he realized that his memory was slowly deteriorating, and handed it over to Dr Mohan Bhagwat after due process of consultation with senior members of the RSS that had begun by 2007. After retirement as Sarsanghchaalak, he stayed in Bhopal, where he worked on organic farming. He would personally take care of a small organic garden on the roof of Sangh karyalay. He would happily be present in any programme sitting in the audience to listen to this topic (Anand 2019, 205). In Bhopal, he would attend all the meetings that he could, as ordinary swayamsevak, without any special seating arrangement as an ex-Sarsanghchaalak and refused a mic too as he didn't wish to impose himself as a former Sarsanghchaalak (Anand 2019, 215). He gave an important message to the swayamsevaks, that ultimately, every leader in the RSS is basically a swayamsevak, everything else is just a responsibility given to him, nothing more.

Such was his yogic mind that he died while doing *pranayam*, in sitting posture (Tarun Bharat 2012, 9).

Sudarshanji: The Leader

Sudarshanji can be seen as more close to Guruji with focus on Sangh work and little interest in politics. He added new dimensions to Sangh work and intellectual depth to many topics close to the RSS's heart. He had the rare distinction of being the head of both physical and intellectual training departments, a recognition of his brilliance.

He fine-tuned many intellectual and physical programmes. He created an entire syllabus for Bharatiya knowledge based martial arts, training himself to perfection for this. Introduction of many small but significant exercises helped in better training of the RSS cadre in shakhas and various camps and workshops. His fine-tuning of intellectual inputs in daily shakha improved the training methodologies of shakhas.

He gave vigour and direction to the Swadeshi movement initiated by Dattopant Thengdi. He gave intellectual direction to a movement that was working more on patriotism and emotions after Thengdi. Extension of Swadeshi into self-sufficient economic model was possible because of his inputs.

His advocacy of organic farming is finding resonance now across the globe. His insistence on sustainable consumption rather than a sustainable development model can be appreciated now when we see that the devastation of nature in human greed has created immense problems. He had said that if every nation wished to have consumption levels of the US, we would need eight Earths to sustain it. He often quoted the Upanishadic wisdom, *'Ten tyakten bhunjitha'* (Give up that which is not required, do not accumulate).

His reassertion of Antyoday and redefining Integral Humanism has also been accepted to a great extent by PM Narendra Modi who has gone in for highly ambitious programmes that benefit the last person in the queue. We can thus say that he was a visionary who was not distracted by the prevalent thinking. He was a 'change-oriented' person.

All the Sarsanghchaalaks had spoken of a larger definition of 'Hindu' and tried to extend the sphere of Hindutva to include large minority groups like Muslims and Christians. But he took the courageous step of promoting inter-faith dialogue with various communities on his own initiative without worrying about ultimate results or probable failure. He was instrumental in the formation of the first national Muslim organization—not an easy task in a community controlled by orthodox clerics.

His support for promotion of international brotherhood between like-minded civilizations was another path-breaking initiative.

His encouragement to India-centric research of history has set in motion a rewriting of well-researched history. His weight behind Itihas Sankalan Samiti led to rediscovery of Saraswati river that has virtually destroyed the narrative of the Aryan invasion theory of and changed the narrative about India's ancient and current history.

His prediction about cataclysmic changes in India's socio-political life and renaissance by 2011–12 based on his deep study seemed like a pipe dream at the time the prediction was made. He spoke about it fifteen years before it actually happened, but we see those changes as also the possible chaos he predicted during this changeover.

There was possibly some dissonance with the first BJP-dominated government. But it also gave a message that the RSS would not compromise on its principles or issues dear to its heart. Support to BJP was not absolute or unconditional but only in the interest of national good, which was in line with what even Balasaheb Deoras had stated.

He was always open to vigorous open dialogue with anybody, not letting any formality or egos come in the way. According to Sarkaryavaah of the RSS Suresh Bhaiyyaji Joshi, a Sarsanghchaalak plays an important role when it comes to structure, scope and direction of the organization and Sudarshanji played an effective role in all these areas for nine years (Anand 2019, 201). If we look at his term in perspective, his uncompromising intellect left a strong imprint on socio-economic policy making. Sudarshanji gave a definite direction to the Sangh with his clear assertive, non-apologetic enunciation of Hindutva and indigenous economic policies.

Dr Mohan Bhagwat: An Open-minded Reformer with a Ready Smile (2009-)

Dr Mohan Bhagwat is a third-generation swayamsevak in the family. Mohanji's grandfather was from Satara and moved to Nagpur. He studied Law from Allahabad University, got a government job but refused it because he was a patriotic member of the Congress party. He decided to set up private practice. He was a member of state Congress committee. Senior Bhagwat began to practise in Baroda and then moved to Chandrapur. He was a friend of Dr Hedgewar who ultimately appointed him as the district Sanghchalak when he founded the RSS. He was given the oath of the RSS personally by Dr Hedgewar.

Mohanji's father Madhukar Bhagwat was born in Baroda and joined the RSS at a young age when they moved to Chandrapur. He went to Fergusson College in Pune and became a prachaarak around 1934. Interestingly, his father was fine with him being a prachaarak. However, Doctorji first asked him to work for the Sangh in Pune before he became a prachaarak. He was referred to as the father of the RSS *ghosh* (band) of Pune as he had played a big role in its formation. He was later deputed to Gujarat as a state prachaarak and created a foundation for the Sangh there. When Madhukarji's lawyer brother lost his wife, Madhukarji was asked to return to the family to share family responsibilities.

Madhukarji returned to Chandrapur and got married. His wife was from Satara. Her father too was a lawyer. Madhukarji remained a prachaarak till 1951. After Mohanji's birth, he returned to Chandrapur to study law and begin his practice. He was

Chandrapur karyavaah during this time. Thus, it can be seen that Mohanji's family had a tradition of lawyers as well as RSS. He had two more sons and a daughter. One of Mohanji's younger brothers is a lawyer too. His mother was socially very active and played an important role during Emergency. She worked for women's empowerment in her area since her youth. Mohanji studied in Chandrapur till standard X and then moved to Nagpur for further studies. He completed his Bachelors in Veterinary Sciences (BVSc) there and ran a shakha in the college too. He was a good singer and an expert player of the flute and drums. He took part in various cultural activities including drama and college orchestra. He then began his Master's programme. However, he left it half way during Emergency and became a prachaarak. After this, his visits to Chandrapur decreased. However, because of his affectionate nature, he visited his family regularly to meet his siblings. Not only this, even while he was on any college tour, he would make it a point to visit his relatives there.

After his responsibilities increased, the visits became rarer, especially after he became Sarkaryavaah in the RSS. But he made it a point to visit home during Ganesh festival. Such was his dedication to his work that when his mother died, the then Sarkaryavaah Sudarshanji told his father that he could send Mohanji back. But, he refused and came only on the tenth day of her death. When his father died, he was in a remote area and came home on the third day but stayed back till the thirteenth day until the completion of religious ceremonies.[18] A prachaarak is a family man only for the outside world, but in reality he is like a mendicant without saffron clothing.

Like all prachaaraks, he has worked in many states and regions of Bharat. He was deputed to the Northeast like most of the RSS prachaaraks from Maharashtra. He was the all-India physical training in-charge. He was also in-charge of prachaaraks'

[18]Based on a telephonic interview with Ravindra Bhagwat, younger brother of Mohanji, on 25 August 2019.

care and coordination. In 2000, he became Sarkaryavaah when Prof. Rajendra Singh retired in favour of Shri K.S. Sudarshan as Sarsanghchaalak and Shri H.V. Sheshadri stepped down as Sarkaryavaah. He was nominated as Sarsanghchaalak of the RSS on 21 March 2009 by Sudarshanji who retired due to ill health.

Mohanji recalled, while paying his tribute to Sudarshanji,

> Sudarshanji had finished his Matric exam with top honours from Jubilee High School in Chandrapur. He probably used to visit our house; I was very young at that time. When Sudarshanji became prant prachaarak, my father told me, 'See, Sudarshan was a merit holder in board exams and now he is prant prachaarak. You should also study well and become a prachaarak. You need to study very well if you want to be a prachaarak.' (Tarun Bharat 2012, 6)

Sudarshanji's brilliance touched and influenced Mohanji. Routine visits from senior RSS workers and prachaaraks to his home had an abiding influence on his personality.

There is thirty-four years of tapasya or hard work as a prachaarak behind this genial personality. He has a ready smile and relaxed presence that is always open to new ideas. He has been overseas to address People of Indian Origin (PIO) at various occasions and visit programmes of the Hindu Swayamsevak Sangh. His last visit was to Chicago to address the World Hindu Conference organized by the Vishwa Hindu Parishad.

An Open-Minded Organizer

Balasaheb Deoras used to say, any experiment is welcome. If it fails, it is no problem. If it succeeds, share it with others so the idea can be spread. Dr Bhagwat believes in the same approach. He adds that there can be no compromise on principles of Hindu Rashtra and Hindutva; beyond this any other new idea and approach is welcome. I have been to many of his meetings and seen his open-minded approach to any new idea. It is common to hear him say, 'Why not? Let us try.'

With him, one doesn't feel overwhelmed that one is sitting with a very big leader. It is easy to talk to him without any hesitation or reserve. Like his predecessors, he discourages people from taking his photograph. After a meeting at my home, a swayamsevak requested for a photograph. He asked him, 'Why do you wish to take my photograph?' The flustered swayamsevak said, 'For my memory.' He said with a smile, 'But, I am still around, no?'

When Dr Bhagwat took over, the coordination between different affiliates of the RSS was at a low ebb, as we noted in the chapter on Sudarshanji. Dr Bhagwat's first job as the head of the large family tied by a common national vision and philosophy, was to inject warmth and confidence in these relations and improve coordination. Results of his exertions have been visible. He has been able to create the right environment and confidence between different organizations. Given the current political and national environment, it is evident that there is much better coordination between associate organizations than there was before. Considering that many of these organizations have conflicting organizational goals, it is no mean feat.

However, as the head of the RSS, his prime focus remains the organization's growth. Like all Sarsanghchaalaks, he too believes that shakha is the life breath of the movement. It is the powerhouse that provides right human resources for various organizations with nationalist approach and helps them grow. In this, he has a highly capable Sarkaryavaah as an associate in Shri Suresh aka Bhaiyyaji Joshi. A soft-spoken and humble leader, Bhaiyyaji Joshi hails from Thane district in Maharashtra. He has been working at the minutest details, fine-tuning the working of RSS shakhas as per changing times. His vision is to reach the last village of Bharat with a shakha there before 2025. It seems that the RSS might achieve this ambitious target given its steady increase in shakhas and rising number of swayamsevaks going to RSS training camps. There is such eagerness among the youth in joining the one-week primary training workshop (*praathamik varg*) that the RSS had to put in some qualifying filters to keep the numbers manageable.

Infrastructure creation and organizing trained manpower for the training is no mean task as the workshops are at district levels. Despite this, the number of participants for these workshops all over India total around 100,000. No organization in the world can boast of accretion of such qualified numbers.

Reaching Out to Untouched Sections of Society

Dr Bhagwat's significant contribution has been to reach out to those segments of society that had previously remained outside the purview of the RSS. This included leaders of various sects and religions as well as industry, commerce and opinion leaders. He has been meeting political leaders too as a goodwill gesture. The idea for these meetings has been to explain the RSS's views on various national and local issues and get their feedback, and also remove their misgivings about the RSS. The response has been uniformly gratifying.

The visit of ex-President Shri Pranab Mukherjee followed by an industrialist like Shiv Nadar to Nagpur illustrates the warm relations he has been able to strike with people from varied ideological backgrounds. He has been able to explain the RSS to various segments of society, which illustrates his communication skills. This is evident from the attendance of top opinion leaders at the annual Vijayadashami festival, that also happens to be the RSS's foundation day, in Nagpur.

One of his earlier decisions as RSS chief was to approve a change in the RSS uniform from half-length to full-length trousers. This was done after receiving feedback from the youth who are attracted to the RSS. Many traditionalists, though, still felt an emotional attachment to the earlier uniform. This small step was an indication to the youth that the RSS was flexible and open to change with the changing times.

Judicious Use of Media

Media-related activity in the RSS was introduced in the 1990s after nearly seventy years of its existence. However, it had not picked up speed or spread the way it should have. It hadn't yet created a space for itself in the media and or gained traction in public perception. Dr Bhagwat's openness to changing dynamics of the society and world with changing modes of communication influenced this activity in a big way.

From the beginning of his term, the RSS has taken up media interaction more aggressively, embracing emerging technologies. Dr Bhagwat adopted a more easy-going approach with media. One can witness a sea change in how the RSS is now looked upon by the media and people in general due to this openness. The RSS has shown readiness to let its swayamsevaks appear on TV shows and put forward their views on socio-political issues. More opinion leaders and intellectuals, not directly involved with the RSS, are being invited to programmes organized by the RSS and its affiliates. As a consequence, its detractors seem to be getting isolated and frustrated with only hardcore Left and faux secularists backing their views.

All the Sarsanghchaalaks have addressed press conferences and public meetings. Prior to this, they had addressed meetings primarily in small groups or in associations outside the organization. Some of their meetings used to be public meetings, but they were generally attended by sympathizers. Never had a Sarsanghchaalak gone public using the media (and social media) to let the world at large hear the RSS point of view on issues concerning Bharat. There has been a quantum shift in public perception about the RSS after the three-day live interaction with select opinion leaders from all segments of society.

Dr Bhagwat's famous three-day meeting called 'Future of Bharat' was held on 17–19 September 2018 in Delhi. It was path-breaking in many ways. It was for the first time that the senior-most RSS functionary had spoken to a global audience about the RSS, its basic principles, its work and its views about India's socioeconomic and political issues. The growing acceptance of the Sangh was also illustrated by the fact that many TV channels broadcast the programme live on all the three days without any marketing or canvassing. It had been organized in a month's time. Millions viewed the programme on TV and social media. TV channels had debates and discussion on his views, which are basically the RSS's views. The debates on electronic media and digital media after the programme did not have the usual caustic twist that was common earlier. Not only did he speak over three days for nearly one-and-a-half-hours, he also took questions and did not shy away from responding to them. There were hundreds of questions. A team of RSS co-ordinators assessed the questions and clubbed them together based on subject and concern so that most of them could be addressed. This entire exercise and the elucidation of the RSS by Mohanji was a big surprise for many. At the end of the day, no participant left the programme unsatisfied with his or her answers as they were forthright and honest responses. This programme was organized in the light of sustained attacks on the RSS by the opposition parties. It showed the readiness of the RSS Sarsanghchaalak to engage with people with diverse opinions. This single event has opened up the RSS to the people at large and revealed its friendly approach and readiness to engage with diverse groups of people.

Restating the RSS Philosophy

Since his views tell us the position of the RSS on issues confronting the nation at this point in time, I will provide a synopsis of his lecture and Q&A session in Delhi. They will tell us in a nutshell, how the RSS has evolved since the times of its founder Dr Hedgewar and yet stayed true to its foundational principles and organizational methodologies as implemented by Dr Hedgewar since 1925 and taken forward by various Sarsanghchaalaks. It is a typical example of change with continuity or dynamic equilibrium. In his three-day speech, he elaborated nearly all the points related to the RSS and also many other aspects of Indian cultural and economic renaissance.

Dr Mohan Bhagwat spoke of four major streams of social awakening that rose after the failure of the First War of

Independence in 1857. One stream believed in armed struggle even though the struggle of 1857 had failed. It remained active in various forms of *gadar* (rebellion) with many groups of revolutionaries remaining active and ended with Subhas Chandra Bose's era in 1945. The second stream that evolved, believed that our people don't have enough political understanding of what is important. Therefore, the need for political awakening was considered essential. This led to a big political movement in the form of the Congress. Leaders from the third stream believed that the society needed to be reformed. There are so many selfish interests, so many differences. They felt that there is lack of character in the people. There are differences in terms of states, languages, castes and sub-castes. There is lack of education and poverty. It would not be possible to fight the British without removing these obstacles. This stream was led by many great social reformers whom we remember even today. The fourth stream strove to take people back to their roots. The founder of Arya Samaj, Swami Dayanand and the disciple of Ramakrishna Paramhansa, Swami Vivekananda gave a message to stand firm in our roots and remove poverty and ignorance, while spreading the message of sewa, or service to the people (*Bhavishya ka Bharat*, Dr Mohan Bhagwat, Page 14, Vimarsh Prakashan, 2018). This book is the printed version of his speech and Q&A session.

Rabindranath Tagore wrote a long essay called 'Swadeshi Samaj' in which he talked about the integral view, and getting rid of incessant fights because we have a tradition of working with diverse views. This change can take place at the social level—not at the political. Dr Bhagwat went on to quote Sir Manvendra Nath Roy from his 'The Radical Humanism.' Sir Roy had founded the Communist Party but later formed his own Radical Humanist Movement. He believed that superficial changes, without changing the society, will not succeed in changing the nation. He had felt the need to reach out to the common people and change their thinking and quality. It seems to be a long route but if this is the only route then it is the shortest route. 'Any shortcut will cut you short,' he said (Bhagwat 2018, 16). He quotes Dr Abdul Kalam Azad and Dr Varghese Kurien to stress this point further.

Dr Hedgewar chose the fourth path when he founded the RSS that is changing people and society, while keeping political issues aside. According to him, the RSS, as an organization, strives to create selfless people of character and discipline, because it wishes to bring in changes to create a society that is more harmonious—a society that does not exploit and is not divisive. Our behaviour tells us that we wish to see another Shivaji but not in our homes. He said, 'Ideals are like stars that we can never reach, but we can plot our charts according to them.'

He explains that the Sangh wishes to create good swayamsevaks in each and every lane of every village, those who have high character and treat the society and nation as their own. One who doesn't look at anybody as an enemy is devoid of any divisive view and earns the love and respect of society. This is the goal of the RSS—to have groups of such dedicated people all over India (Bhagwat 2018, 20).

He goes on to enunciate other core values of the RSS. Social behaviour can change only with a change in people's behaviour. He asserts that for people all over the world this is the only mantra for social renaissance. Without good people, any system will fail. A poor system will corrupt people. So both must be good.

We have huge diversities but our philosophers and rishis have told us that we may describe things differently but they are essentially the same. '*Ekam sat, Vipra bahudha vadanti.*' Meaning, there is one truth, scholars call it differently (Bhagwat 2018, 23). There is no need to fear diversities. This underlying harmony is the second value of the RSS. Then there is the value of *sanyam* (patience). If we wish to live together, we have to give up certain things to accommodate others. We are part of a whole—the society and the nation. A human being cannot live alone, by himself. Every component of society has contributed to our well-being. This *kritagyata* (sense of obligation) is another important value (Bhagwat 2018, 23–24). For him, Hindutva is the collective expression of values that come from unity, harmony, sacrifice, patience and a sense of obligation that provide us with an integral view of life (Bhagwat 2018, 45).

He stresses that there was no lack of planning to serve the people since Independence yet results were not great. We have to be deserving of the fruits of such plans. We have to be a deserving society. Society needs discipline and civic sense. To create a great nation, one doesn't need to die daily for the nation, but one has to live daily for the nation. When there is occasion to die for the nation, those societies have produced thousands of such people ready to give their lives, who have learnt how to live. This is the man-making, making of the people who know how to live for the nation, that the RSS talks about and the methodology is the RSS shakha (Bhagwat 2018, 26–27).

Dr Bhagwat repeatedly said that though he may explain the RSS methodology, but rather than going by what he has said, people should join a shakha to understand it. He explains how simple programmes are used to disseminate the right *sanskaars*, imbibe right values and how these programmes have evolved over time. We have seen glimpses of such programmes as they evolved over time. These are the habits that lead swayamsevaks to their work in fields such as disaster management, which RSS swayamsevaks carry out without any training. The RSS is now trying to create a programme in its training camps for disaster management, but so far it is basically being done through values, discipline and habits created by daily shakhas.

In his lecture, he explained how various organizations that emerged with inspiration from the RSS, now work independently, autonomously and are self-dependent. They are working in their respective fields and have rich experience of that field. Since they are all swayamsevaks, they meet and talk to each other about various issues, but members are free to support or work for any organization.

Not just RSS-affiliated organizations but the RSS is ready to help any positive work. There is no insistence on ideology except that they should not be anti-national. He explains how *samanvay baithak* (coordination meeting) is only conducted to keep their value systems alive by being in the Sangh atmosphere for some time. At these meetings, members discuss and exchange ideas, but there is no insistence on accepting any idea. That is left for the organizations to decide (Bhagwat 2018, 36–37).

He also explained how the 'Rashtra Sevika Samiti' came up and why women were not part of RSS shakhas. Dr Hedgewar had explained to the founder Laxmibai Kelkar that she could work with women and the RSS would help her in every way, but he could not include women in shakhas due to the intensely physical nature of its programmes and the atmosphere prevalent at that time in society. The Sangh helped the Samiti as and when the need arose. They run like parallel tracks. He underlined the fact that apart from shakhas women are part of every organization run by RSS affiliates and are present in large numbers. He stressed that the RSS is not an organization of sanyasis, but of families. Thus, families of swayamsevaks also work with the Sangh (Bhagwat 2018, 37).

He reminds us that men and women complement each other, and for a meaningful life they need to work as equals. Both should take equal responsibility in taking decisions, and women should have a major role in nation-building (Bhagwat 2018, 44). On the question of women's safety, Dr Bhagwat talked about special programmes of *Kishori Vikas* for young teenage girls for training in self-defence and to learn about safety and hygiene issues. He stressed the Indian view that every woman—except one's wife—should be looked upon and treated with respect like a mother, and that ideal sanskars need to be given to men. Men need to learn to respect women (Bhagwat 2018, 77–78).

Dr Bhagwat reiterates the principle followed by Dr Hedgewar; that is staying away from power politics. This remains sacrosanct and no office-bearer of the RSS is allowed to be an office-bearer of any political party, thus keeping a clear distance from electoral politics (Bhagwat 2018, 40). In an answer to a question, he said that politics should be for the good of the people. Power is for the people's well-being. Divisive talks take place only when this fundamental view is missed and politics means to grab power (Bhagwat 2018, 99).

He agrees that the word 'Hindu' doesn't exist in our scriptures and gained currency sometime in the ninth century. However, since the world has labelled us thus, and all issues put to us to resolve are as Hindus, the Sangh has used this word to respond to multiple challenges. For Sangh, Bharatiya (or Indic or Arya) is the same. It has no issues with those who use these words. Arya is not a word for a race; rather, it is the Sanskrit word for 'civilized'—an evolved human being. The distinct issue with Bharatiya viz-a-viz Hindu is that Bharat denotes a geography too. Though this has kept changing with time, it is the oldest name of this land. However, the essence of this philosophy depicted by the word 'Hindu' remains the same, and is not bound by geographic boundaries (Bhagwat 2018, 48).

He also reiterated the difference between religion and dharma, and said that while there is no word like 'religion' in Bharatiya languages, there is no word like 'dharma' in the Western lexicon. Dharma is unique to all Bharatiya languages. Religion is a way of worshipping the Supreme Being with certain rituals and belief in a certain book and prophet or messiah. Dharma is universal—dharma is for all human beings and is not constrained by geography. All spiritual streams—Sanatani, Jain, Bouddh, Sikh and Arya Samaj are born out of the Bharatiya idea of well-being of the world, and not a particular kind of people or followers. Hindu dharma talks of *Vasudhaiv kutumbakam*, that is, people of this earth are one family (Bhagwat 2018, 49).

In the West, nation and state are co-terminus. When state goes, nation goes too. For us, the state may have kept changing but the nation did not. The nation didn't end with state. Nation is ancient. Just like nation, dharma is perennial—*shaaswat*. He quotes Dr Ambedkar, who said in Parliament while piloting the Hindu Code Bill, 'What do you understand of dharma—values or codes? You believe "code" is dharma. Codes change and must change. I am changing the code, not the values.' For us, dharma is a set of values—not way of worship (Bhagwat 2018, 49). Dr Bhagwat recounts that wherever we went in the world, we did not go to war, we didn't win a nation through violence nor did we pillage a society. We shared our knowledge and civilizational values with other nations. That is why even today, those nations who were once Hindus, still respect us and love what we shared with them (Bhagwat 2018, 52).

He quotes Dr Ambedkar to tell us that the Liberty, Equality and Brotherhood enshrined in the Indian Constitution were not taken from the French Revolution but from our own soil, from the thoughts of *Tathaagat Buddha*. The basis of this brotherhood is our dharma, our common forefathers and our common cultural heritage. Many people criticize the RSS for saying that we are all Hindus. Some may feel proud while some may not. Some may not say this due to material considerations or political correctness, but privately they accept this.

Putting to rest any controversy, he asserts that the Sangh accepts and respects the Indian Constitution since its very beginning, as it has been put together on the basis of consensus in the nation. The RSS respects all the symbols and sentiments attached to the Indian Constitution. He stresses that the Sangh works on the basis of a sense of brotherhood enshrined in the Constitution. When the Sangh espouses,

> This is a *Hindu Rashtra*, it does not mean that we don't want Muslims. The day we say we don't want Muslims, it will not be Hindutva. Hindutva talks of this world as a family. The day we say only Vedas are valid and only Vedas will be allowed, the Bouddh viewpoint that doesn't believe in Vedas will not work, it will not be Hindutva then. We talk of this Hindutva because it is the only philosophy that gives basis to this sentiment of brotherhood. This thought is not a reaction to anything. It is a thought of '*Sarvesham avirodhen*'—taking everybody along, without any opposition from anybody. (Bhagwat 2018, 57-58)

One can note that this view, that Muslims and Christians are also sons of this soil and are Hindus for us when they believe it is their motherland and all of us Bharatiyas have common forefathers, has been repeated by Shri Guruji, Balasaheb Deoras and other Sarsanghchaalaks at various times. Balasaheb Deoras said they are welcome to join the RSS. There have been Christian and Muslim swayamsevaks, workers and also prachaaraks. So, what Dr Bhagwat said was reiteration of this very view.

Dr Bhagwat clarifies that the Sangh does not believe that it alone will bring in renaissance of Bharat. It has no such false ego. The nation does not progress because of any one person, an organization or a government. No nation has progressed before the society is unified, raises its quality, rises above its differences and individual interests. He challenges us to find out if any nation in the world has risen without at least a hundred years of such gigantic efforts and come to any conclusions. He gives examples of the UK, the US, France, Cuba, China and Japan in recent history to buttress his argument (Bhagwat 2018, 59).

While responding to questions and answers in this programme, he clarified many words and ideas and addressed misgivings. For example, he says that Hinduism is a wrong word. Any 'ism' closes any further thinking. The word closest to Hindutva is *Hinduness*. He quotes Radhakrishnan, who said, 'Hinduism is a movement, not a position, a process, not a result, a growing tradition, not a fixed revelation' (Bhagwat 2018, 65). Dr Manmohan Vaidya has noted that Hinduism was used probably because Dr Radhakrishnan wrote in English. If he were to write in Hindi, he would have used the word 'Hindutva.' Just as Veer Savarkar used the word Hindutva as he wrote in Marathi. If he were to write in English, he might have used the word 'Hinduism.' That is why he also says that Hinduness is closer to what the RSS wishes to convey.

In response to another question about inter-caste marriages for social harmony, he unequivocally supported this idea to reduce caste conflicts. Sangh has always supported and encouraged inter-caste marriages. He said that, if one were to find out the percentage of inter-caste marriages in Bharat, it would be found highest among the Sangh swayamsevaks (Bhagwat 2018, 67).

He even asserts that to call casteism as *jati vyavastha* or caste system is wrong. Today, it is not a system it is a non-system (*avyavastha*). He reminds us of the words of Balasaheb Deoras about throwing out all ideas promoting social inequality, lock, stock and barrel. He recounts why the RSS has never given any thought to caste and shared his experience that he didn't even know the caste of his fellow Sahsarkaryavaah (Bhagwat 2018, 69). He explains how the Sangh has slowly evolved from being a dominantly Brahmin-led organization to a mass organization encompassing all the sections of the society by empowering everyone. He also talks about the presence of people from all sections who have slowly risen in its ranks and leadership. He reminds us of the RSS sewa work taking place in gypsy communities too (Bhagwat 2018, 70).

On reservations, he is unequivocal that the RSS supports all the constitutional provisions that try to remove social inequality and give equal opportunities to deprived sections of the society. Representatives of the people will decide how long this provision will last according to the constitution. The Sangh supports the constitutional view. He raises the issue of the creamy layer, as well as the issue of more and more people asking for reservation. For this, he suggested that the Constitution has provided various forums for such decisions (Bhagwat 2018, 85). Similarly, regarding the Atrocities Act, he suggested that the law should not be misused and law should be applied fairly (Bhagwat 2018, 85, 87).

He stresses upon the need for reforming education with the inclusion of teaching of value systems of various faiths. He believes that the level of education is not going down; it's the quality of those providing education that has gone down, and therefore the level of the recipients. He gives examples of how people have risen on the basis of their own qualities and inclinations and why education should not be imposed uniformly without giving a chance to a person's individual inclination (Bhagwat 2018, 72). He suggests that there is no need to wait for a new education policy and government schemes. People in educational institutions can work within their powers to improve the level of education in their own institutions.

He stresses upon the importance of Sanskrit, as it is the repository of our knowledge and mother of nearly all Indian languages as well as a few global ones. According to him, the government doesn't pay attention to it because we don't give it importance. For us Indians, all languages should be our own languages. We should learn the local languages of where we stay and also learn our mother tongue. Our basic education should be in our respective mother tongues. We can and should learn foreign languages, but this should be dependent on our requirements and interests (Bhagwat 2018, 76).

Addressing the question of strong reactions to Hindutva and violence against Hindus, he said the anger is not against the philosophy of Hindutva but a distortion of the Hindu worldview in the last 1500-2000 years through distorted rituals, orthodoxy and unjust behaviour of many in the name of dharma. If we conduct ourselves based on time, place and situation and reform our conduct and traditions, then this anger will dissipate, because as a thought, Hindutva is pure and enlightening. He quoted Dr Hedgewar who said that a thought may be great; however, one doesn't become great by speaking about it but by immersing it into our own behaviour (Bhagwat 2018, 79).

He criticized lynching, saying that cow protectors don't lynch people. They work for the betterment of the society and work with positive views. People have to be explained how the cow is useful not just as a productive asset till her last moment but also as a wonderful cure for emotional disorders—something tested by jail inmates and doctors. Nobody knew about medicinal properties of A2 milk of Indian cows but now medical science accepts it (Bhagwat 2018, 81).

He was asked why the Sangh opposes conversions it it believes all religions and faiths are similar. To this he quoted a saint, Gulabrao Maharaj, who was asked the same question, and he had answered, 'If all religions are same then where is the need to convert?' Why should only the Sangh oppose it? The history of conversion world over tells us that all societies should oppose it. He also said that if someone converts out of conviction and understanding of religion, then there can't be any opposition, and gave the example of a famous scholar. However, promoting a religion with money and allurement is wrong. Spirituality is not for sale (Bhagwat 2018, 82).

On population demographics, he articulates the views of the Sangh clearly. He says that looking at a fifty-year projection, population demographics are a serious issue of discussions. He illustrated how China changed its policies as situation arose. (It adopted one child policy for years, then changed it back to larger families.) We also need to understand how much our country can bear and also the composition of population in terms of age. We must also think of mothers who give birth to children, as also the demographic balance. Policies should be applicable to all citizens as the problems will be faced by all citizens. Demographic imbalances arise out of conversions and illegal migrations. All these are challenges to the national sovereignty and must be treated strictly (Bhagwat 2018, 84).

He explained that every individual has certain special qualities but they are also part of the society and society should make place for them as per our traditions and this has been done earlier too. He was expressing his views on Section 377. As per changing circumstances, people with such differences should not be left out of the society and should have the scope to rise as per their wishes and efforts. We will need to find a social approach to tackle it (Bhagwat 2018, 88).

On the supposedly 'controversial' views in *Bunch of Thoughts*, a collection of Guruji's speeches, about Muslims being treated as enemies, he explained that lectures must be viewed within the historical context in which they were given. To understand Guruji's views, people should read his *Shri Guruji: Vision and Mission*, which has select writings from his *Complete Works* published in multiple volumes. His views carry a perennial message and are not contemporary reference points (Bhagwat 2018, 90).

He further added,

> [The] Sangh has problem basically with the tag of 'minority' itself. We never used the word 'minority' ever, before the British or before Independence. We had so many diverse religions and languages. With these terminologies our differences have increased. We need to talk of things that bring us together not fragment us. If there is imaginary fear in the minds of the people, they should visit RSS shakhas. [...] Muslims feel much safer where there are shakhas. Our appeal is to the national sentiment, not to individual faiths. Even minorities respect and take pride in same culture and love for the motherland—and that is Hindutva—so where is the question of fear?

He invited people to visit RSS programmes and hear what its members speak and see their conduct (Bhagwat 2018, 89). He concluded that one must look at the conduct of Sangh swayamsevaks in the field rather than simply going by the words of some.

Regarding Jammu & Kashmir, he reiterated the Sangh's views that Article 370 and 35(A) must go. The view of the RSS on dividing the state into three units was for better governance, better law and order that can result in better development. For bringing in normalcy and bringing back the unhappy youth to the mainstream, he explained that swayamsevaks may not be organizing many shakhas but scores of swayamsevaks inspired by the RSS are running social and educational programmes in Jammu & Kashmir too. There, discussions on national views take place. They also hoist the Indian flag and sing Vande Mataram and the national anthem (Bhagwat 2018, 92).

As this book gets written, we find that Article 370 has been nullified and 35(A) alongwith it, the Jammu & Kashmir Constitution has gone too. It would be good to point out that Article 35(A), hidden in the annexure of the Indian Constitution, was ferreted out and brought before the Indian people by an RSS-inspired think tank. It was a totally unknown law till the year 2005. It was never discussed or spoken about since Nehru's time.

Replying to a question about internal security, Dr Bhagwat pointed out that development and the sense of being one with the society is important. But no compromise can be made on unity and integrity of the nation. Action of the government should be strong and direct. One may talk with various groups but that should be on the grounds that there would be no compromise on the nation's integrity. Elements who speak anti-national language and those who support them must be isolated—such should be the sentiment in the society. Only then will internal security be strong (Bhagwat 2018, 93).

The Sarsanghchaalak also expressed agreement over Uniform Civil Code, but also said that citizens of different faiths and traditions will have to give up some of their views in the interest of changing times. The government should consult people and slowly build a consensus and implement it (Bhagwat 2018, 94).

> During Q&A he said that None-of-the-Above (NOTA) in elections is not a good idea as people who press the button ultimately help the least desirable to win. Democracy is about choosing the best among the available, as it is not possible to get a candidate who is one hundred per cent desirable. Things shouldn't become worse due to NOTA. So, this option should not be used at all. We need to reform the electoral system. People have not talked about changes in the basic electoral process; they have only suggested some reforms here or there. These should be discussed and the required changes must be brought in (Bhagwat 2018, 96).

Dr Bhagwat underlines the importance of rural development. By development, the RSS means that good qualities of village life such as mutual cooperation, treating nature with respect and feeling of brotherhood should be maintained while basic requirements of schools, roads, electricity should be provided. Only through rural development can Bharat progress and swayamsevaks are working towards it. Rural development has been one of the focus areas of sewa since the last few years for the RSS.

He is also an advocate of swadeshi economics because security of our financial systems springs from self-dependence. Swadeshi does not mean shutting the door to the world. He says,

> I will use an item that gives employment to my village, my city and not bring it from outside. Similarly, we shall import only that which cannot be produced here. The world has come closer, no doubt. It is true that the world trade runs on give and take, but it cannot be one sided give-give or take-take. He reminds us that after 2014 the atmosphere has changed and many people are returning after their education abroad and working in India. (Bhagwat 2018, 100)

On the Ram Temple issue, he affirms that as a part of a larger movement, the Sangh wants a grand temple to be built. Shri Ram is one of the most worshipped Gods for a majority of Indians, although He may not be God for all. Muslims call him Imam-e-Hind. There are enough scientific and historical proofs that the temple existed earlier too. Once the temple is built, a major cause of friction between Hindus and Muslims will end. If it happens with the goodwill of the Muslims, fingers that keep pointing to them will more or less stop being raised. We must find a solution that can help in the construction of the temple at the earliest (Bhagwat 2018, 102). Another historic decision has been taken by the courts while this book goes to print, allowing building of the Ram Temple in Ayodhya at the site where it existed.

He dispels the notion that once a directive is received, all thought processes stop in the RSS. He explained that even before a directive is issued, there is a very long process of deliberations. Only when there is consensus, is a decision taken. So there is enough thinking. After a consensus is built, there is only application of the idea and its conversion into an actionable task. Democracy doesn't mean clashes. Consensus is the essence of democracy that the RSS follows.

Answering another question, he explains that the Sarsanghchaalak's post is by nomination and not by elections, and clears the notion of division of power within the RSS by clarifying that the Sarsanghchaalak is just a friend, guide and philosopher. The real executive powers are with the Sarkaryavaah who is elected with due process of the constitution of RSS by elected and ex-officio members. To elaborate the point, he noted light-heartedly that if the Sarkaryavaah decides to end this programme, he would have to end it. Thus, there is a very intelligent division of power in RSS hierarchy (Bhagwat 2018, 105–06).

In conclusion, he exhorted the audience that they were free to take his views or reject them. They could join the RSS or they could do something they liked, but they should not remain inactive. He appeals to all to begin this work at the earliest.

> All of us must contribute to make this nation great and stand on its own self personality. Sangh swayamsevaks will also try to help those who wish to work to the best of their ability. But, let all good people stay in touch. [....] The Sangh doesn't want to record in the history that the nation's renaissance happened because of RSS. We wish to write that there rose a generation in this country that worked hard and made Bharat a 'Vishwa Guru' again. (Bhagwat 2018, 112)

He appealed to all to begin this work of national renaissance at their end at the earliest.

His latest visit to the US to deliver the inaugural keynote address in the second World Hindu Congress organized in the first week of September 2018 was a landmark visit wherein he addressed Hindus from various countries of the world for the first time from outside India. It gave a good perspective of how the RSS looks at the global scenario with Indians present in more than 115 countries and dominating the socio-political and economic spaces of some.

Firstpost carried the gist of his speech. I have used it to provide a summary of his views on the place of Hindus in the global scenario.

Speaking at the second World Hindu Congress that coincides with the 125th anniversary of Swami Vivekananda's speech at the Parliament of World Religions in 1893 in Chicago, in September 2018, Shri Mohan Bhagwat said collaboration and oneness is the most urgent need for Hindu society to progress. Shri Bhagwat used stories from the Mahabharata to explain right-distancing from leadership, obedience, dissent and patience for results and why it's important to get in line once there is a consensus. Bhagwat began and ended his 40-minute speech with quotes from the Bhagavad Gita. 'Luck follows your efforts,' he began. 'What are the values, what goals you have, should never be forgotten,' he added.

He further said, 'In the initial days of our work, when our karyakartas used to talk to the Hindus about organizing them, Hindus used to tell them, *sher kabhi jhund mein nahi chalta* (a lion never walks in a pack). But even if a lion or a Royal Bengal tiger, that is, the king of the jungle is alone, wild dogs can attack and destroy him. Coming together of the Hindus is in itself a difficult thing.' He added, 'If you don't dream, nothing is possible.' That is, dream high as nothing is impossible for Hindus.

We are both ancient and postmodern. What humanity will need twenty years from now, we are thinking today, we all have to come together. People today are in dire need of wisdom,' he said. Bhagwat compared Hindu society's status quo with a precise moment in the Mahabharata when the Pandavas in exile suddenly found their fortunes turning around. 'That is the moment when luck starts performing *pradakshinas* (circumambulations) around you,' Bhagwat said.

He said Hindu society is home to more 'meritorious people' but 'we don't work together.' Reiterating his call for team effort, the RSS chief said the Hindu society will progress and prosper only when it works as a society, and that some organizations or parties working alone will not suffice. Bhagwat stressed on teamwork and collaborative effort throughout his talk. Bhagwat talked about the Hindu principle s*umantrite suvikrante* or think collectively, achieve valiantly.

It is generally acknowledged that the RSS was, earlier, lagging behind on the intellectual frontier. Sudarshanji had given it a good push in this direction. Now it is abuzz with many successful programmes. Earlier the RSS had purposely decided to focus on work on the field and expand in every segment of social life, rather than put in efforts into intellectual semantics. Now it has joined the ideological battle. One can see the foment and the unease in rival left camps as a result of this new challenge to their hegemony.

New Dimensions of RSS Growth

There have been two major developments in the recent months that show that the RSS is entering into another wave of evolution under the guidance of Dr Mohan Bhagwat. A massive survey of Indian women was done by Rashtra Sevika Samiti and Stree Shakti involving nearly 43,000 women from all strata and diverse geography of the society to get their views on their personal lives, family and society. The report was released by Dr Bhagwat and also presented to the government of India. Dr Bhagwat declared that the RSS with its allied organizations would work out new projects for social upliftment and solutions to women's issues based on this survey. He hoped that government too would be able to craft its plans based on this ground report.

Then, a few days later RSS Sarkaryavaah Shri Bhaiyyaji Joshi released another survey report. The RSS did an internal survey of it young swayamsevaks upto an age of thirty-five years. Around 16 lakh or 1.6 million took part. The information given by the volunteers was their age, education, profession and their area of interest. Based on the inputs received from the survey about the interest of a swayamsevak in a particular work, they would be asked to work in his area of interest. These volunteers for social change will be divided into two age groups of eighteen to twenty-five and twenty-six to thirty-five. Some interested seniors would also join in. The subjects shortlisted are rural development under five heads: education, health, farming, social harmony and self-reliance. One thousand villages have been identified as proposed model villages. Of these work has already begun in 300 villages. Other areas of concern are environment that includes water conservation and its availability, reducing use of plastic and conservation of environment. These youth will be trained according to their aptitude and choice given by them in the projects where their skills can be used.

The RSS has been, for some years, stressing the importance of family as the basic building block of our society and a treasury of our sanskaars. The activity is called '*Kutumb Prabodhan*'. Bhaiyyaji Joshi talked about nurturing the family system that is the key component of India's heritage, strength behind its cohesion and secret of its survival as a civilization. We must strengthen this institution of family. There will be special training for young families about nurturing Hindu values at home for self and children. He also observed that the RSS is not talking of joint family as that is not possible in current changed urban scenario. But, we can still stay together, meet together and celebrate together. He disclosed that 100,000 youth will be trained for social reforms. Noticeably, none of the goals of social reforms and development are religion specific, so any member of the society can take advantage of these initiatives and help create momentum.

Significantly, Bhaiyyaji Joshi also clarified that it is not just formal training, but training can be informal and outside the RSS workshops. I am aware that it is happening already in small ways. The RSS has reached this stage over ninety-five years of sustained work in the field that is basically done at individual level—person to person. It is this capital earned with ninety-five years of work that the RSS wishes to invest in a rapid change in social behaviour, nurturing family system, environment, developing villages in a holistic manner, conserving and providing water to more families, providing basic and better education, basic health facilities and help people achieve self-reliance to lead a dignified life.

The organization is eager to utilize the humongous organized power of the people to help society take a quantum leap in different dimensions of national life. I perceive a sense of urgency now, probably to reach certain targets it has set for itself by 2025, the year when it completes 100 years. Over years, the RSS has achieved most of the objectives it has set, though at a steady, slow pace. Because the entire work is voluntary, being done by people performing their daily duties of life too. Now, it is planning to increase the velocity. There are good chances that it will achieve the objectives it has set out to achieve. RSS is but an organization of individuals who wish to do good work for the society and see Bharat as a prosperous proud nation. If it succeeds with determination of its swayamsevaks and well-wishers, it will bring about unprecedented positive change in our society.

Dr Mohan Bhagwat: The Leader

Dr Bhagwat is the incumbent Sarsanghchaalak, so it would not be wise to analyse his impact on the RSS at this stage. However he has completed ten years of his term. It is possible to have some idea about his influence on the RSS and Indian socio-political life in these ten years.

He has been able to create a sense of harmony between different affiliates who are working in different areas of social life, sometimes with different agendas and ideas. Some of the all-India organizations are big and have their own mass base. It's not an easy task.

The RSS is no more a closed organization, not even a mass activist organization; but it has become a mass movement. People from different walks of life, without typical RSS training through its shakhas, are joining its various organizations. They do not understand nor have they imbibed the RSS style of working that earlier workers had, as the growth was not this fast. To absorb them and keep working without any major hiccup is a challenge for the senior workers. It is a speciality of its flexible structure that various Sarsanghchaalaks have been able to create systems that can absorb some shocks or tremors. But, it is equally the skill of the person at the helm of the affairs that facilitates such mutual adjustments within.

His ability to help a smooth transition from the previous older leadership to a younger leadership in the BJP gives us an idea of his skills in man and organization management at a very critical juncture in contemporary history. Keeping the waters calm with organizations like Bharatiya Mazdoor Sangh, VHP and Swadeshi Vichar Manch pushing their different agendas, requires sagacity and great teamwork. Balasaheb Deoras had successfully decentralized decision-making process in the RSS. The process has been further strengthened by the present incumbent.

There has been a sustained attempt to show him as more political than earlier Sarsanghchaalaks. But he is closer to the thinking of Balasaheb Deoras in accepting that if the situation demands, the RSS won't hesitate to work in the political arena. His call to swayamsevaks to work for *'shat pratishat'* or 'cent per cent' voting raised the overall voting percentage in all elections. The 2014 elections saw a major shift in voting patterns and higher involvement of voters that changed the political landscape in a big way. Now, this idea to vote and own some responsibility of electing the right people has become a habit for voters and India has seen sustained rise in voting percentages. This is a positive contribution by the RSS to participative democracy.

Understanding the pulse of the society, Dr Bhagwat has opened up the RSS to the society in a way no other Sarsanghchaalak had done so far. Its people friendly image and eagerness to satisfy people's curiosity and respond to criticism, rather than keeping quiet has worked wonderfully well to create a positive image of the RSS in the minds of common citizens and the intelligentsia. I have also heard many opinion leaders say in wonder, 'We're surprised, we never knew the RSS is such a reasonable and open organization.' This is a notable change in the perception of the RSS. Readiness to engage with the RSS, to get to know it better is palpable across social strata.

Dr Bhagwat's readiness to experiment with new ideas with a positive frame of mind has created a very pleasant atmosphere for young karyakartas and swayamsevaks to experiment with social outreach programmes. His readiness to utilize all media platforms has been helpful to the RSS in disseminating its views to a larger audience.

The RSS has always been keen to get more women involved in the social field and has encouraged participation of women. It has passed resolutions about women's role in building of the society. However, for the first time in 2009, there was a completely women-centric resolution in ABPS advocating women's empowerment.

His stress on reforming the Hindu society is well recorded. His reminder to Hindu society and asking RSS swayamsevaks to begin implementing reforms where there already are shakhas shows a sense of urgency. He has reiterated the theme of 'One well, One temple and One cremation ground.' To some it may look symbolic but it is a massive attempt at social transformation and harmony. It is a tough social reform that requires major change in mindset. Reading about atrocities on SC/ST brethren tells us how rusted our social mores have become. But considering how the RSS has slowly and steadily followed its objectives and fulfilled them sooner or later—this may also be achieved in coming years.

Broadening the definition of Hindutva and reasserting the openness of the RSS to include larger sections of the society who feel they are out of the ambit of the RSS has made it more appealing to the people. The RSS is no more the 'best avoided' option.

Dr Bhagwat has carried forward the RSS tradition of evolving without disconnecting with its fundamental ideas and key principles. There is still more to come. His Sarkaryavaah's and his goal of reaching every village is an ambitious target set for its centenary year in 2025. These, coupled with massive social projects outlined above, are ambitious targets with innovative approaches, to utilize its youth power and organizational skills in training with new toolssets for the RSS. Thus, the coming years promise to be eventful for the RSS and the nation.

Evolution of Organizational Methodologies and Elements of RSS

By now, readers would have noted that the RSS has been an innovative organization right from its birth. This is because of the novel approach adopted by its founder and new methodologies that were introduced by its later leaders towards building a strong organization. For example, the very idea of gathering daily for an hour to pray for the motherland was unique and never done before at the social level.

The reader would have also noted some of the new ideas that were introduced for physical and intellectual training in the RSS. This chapter will provide an overview of all these changes and understand how the training methodology evolved seamlessly over the years. Many activities were added and many jettisoned over nine decades of its organizational life.

Physical Fitness and Prayers

Physical fitness programmes began from *akhadas* from where Doctorji recruited young boys for his mission of nation-building for the freedom of Bharat. Then, finding that it was difficult to provide a nurturing environment of togetherness and team-building, the daily shakha was introduced. This daily shakha had many energetic games—all of them indigenous and traditional 'Bharatiya' games. Indigenous because they promoted physical fitness, built strong team spirit, had moral lessons embedded in them and hardly used any resources, not even a big ground. In addition to these, Doctorji also gave lectures and held long discussions for intellectual stimulation.

His young swayamsevaks now wanted some kind of structured training. For this, Doctorji roped in his friends for physical and military training, such as parades. For public programmes, the need for a uniform was felt, so it was also introduced. He introduced a military-style band to create an impact and thrill in parades and physical drills.

Change in the Sangh prayer is another landmark in keeping with its growth all over India. The current prayer was introduced in 1939 after the Sindi workshop. The ten-day long meeting was done fourteen years after the RSS was founded and when it was realized that it has reached eighteen provinces, and there needs to be a more organized and systematic approach. Lesson—large organizations are continuously evolving entities, don't straitjacket them into pre-defined rules. Before 1939, the prayer used was a mix of Marathi and Hindi shlokas. The first stanza was taken from a prayer that was commonly sung in schools at that time.

Namo matribhoomi jithe janmolo mee,
Namo Aryabhoomi jithe vadhalo mee.
Namo dharmabhoomi jiychyach kami,
Pado deh Majha sadaa tee name mee.

Meaning,

I bow humbly to the motherland where I was born. I bow humbly to land of Aryas (the civilized) where I have grown. I bow humbly to land of dharma for whom, may I give up my body. I always bow to you.

The second stanza was taken from an Arya Samaj prayer with slight modifications.

Hey guro, Shri Ramdoota, sheel hamko deejiye,
Sheeghra saare sadgunonse poorn hindu keejiye.
Leejiye hamko sharan mein Ram panthi ham banein,
Brahmachaaree Dharmrakshak veervratdhaaree banein.

> Meaning,
>
> O' Guru (Hanuman), ambassador of Bhagwan Ram, bless us with character. Bless us with all the positive qualities at the earliest and make us complete Hindu. We seek refuge in thee that we become followers of Ram. May we be celibate brave protectors of dharma.

The last two lines of the prayer were:

> *Bharatmata ki jai!*
> *Rashtraguru Shri Samarth Ramdas Swami Maharaj ki jai!*
>
> Meaning,
>
> May Mother Bharat be victorious. Salute to Shri Samarth Ramdas, the Guru to the nation.

The new Sanskrit prayer was written and set to tune by scholars based on a brief given by the RSS leadership during the Sindi workshop of 1939. Sanskrit was chosen as it is the root for most Indian languages. Thus, it was felt that it would create a sense of oneness and acceptance everywhere across the country. The current prayer is provided in Annexure IV. This prayer was set to tune and sung for the first time in the training camp of 1940 in Nagpur by Yadavrao Joshi.

The RSS orders, its prayer and many of its songs are in Sanskrit. Even the orders being given during physical drills are in Sanskrit. It is the most unifying language. Thus, without any lecture on unity of the nation and unifying role of language, Sanskrit made this sense of unity easy. The shakhas and programmes in different states conduct day-to-day communication and meetings in local language. People organizing RSS shakhas outside India use English or the native language of the country in which they are working. For the five-year camp in India, Hindi and English are the languages of choice. The Sangh is working very smoothly for decades now, without any friction or hitch all over Bharat. People who create friction in the society over language need to learn a lesson from this approach.

When the British started shadowing the RSS and released orders that made it difficult for the RSS to work, many terminologies and programmes were dropped and its uniform was modified. Guruji sent out letters indicating that military designations were not required for the organization, so they were being dropped and some teams were disbanded. He also made the uniform simpler and less military-like.

Inspiring storytelling has also been a part of shakha programmes since years. Somewhere down the line, *Bodh Katha*—stories with morals to help young people understand good values—became a regular standard feature of RSS shakha.

Changes in Physical Training and Training Workshops

The physical training has been an essential part of RSS shakhas and training camps. Military discipline and physical rigour were of the highest level, because the goal was freedom of India. Strict discipline and physical strength were the basic requirements. As the Sangh evolved and times changed many items of training were dropped while new ones were introduced. At one time, apart from *danda* (wooden staff) training, there were other training activities using sword, dagger, spear and cane. All of these were jettisoned and new items like yoga and *niyuddha* (martial art) were introduced. There used to be training in *lezeem*, which was dropped a few years back. There were no RSS resolutions passed to make these changes in its national meetings or ABPS. These were administrative decisions made by the respective teams headed by a central leader in charge of that activity.

When daily evening shakhas for young boys was becoming impractical in a trade-dominated area in Nagpur, Balasaheb Deoras introduced morning and night shakhas. Also, with changing timing of schools and introduction of coaching classes, late evening shakhas and weekly shakhas for young students were found to be more accessible. The need to reach out in remote areas of Bharat led to the concept of monthly get-together. Just a few years back, weekly and monthly shakhas were not recognized for number crunching. From one-hour shakhas, the morning and night shakhas were shortened to half an hour in many places. As times changed, these changes became an accepted norm.

When disaster management became a part of the country's policy, the need for training swayamsevaks interested in it was felt. Live on-field training sessions on environment and social service were introduced. Environment and rural development are now areas of focus for the RSS and are part of its additional training module.

An impression was gaining ground internally and externally that RSS shakhas were dominated by ageing swayamsevaks, and the RSS as an organization was ageing too. To get a better idea of the reach of shakhas in various segments of society, the reporting system of shakhas was changed recently by the current Sarkaryavaah. Earlier reporting mentioned only morning, evening and night shakhas. Of these, only the evening shakhas were meant for youngsters. In the changed scenario, the reporting is now modified to *Proudh* (elders) shakhas, *Vyavasayee* (attendees below forty-five years) shakhas, *Tarun* (youth) shakhas and *Vidyarthi* (school and college-going) shakhas; the reporting is no longer based on the timing of the shakhas. It was found that shakhas were predominantly of *Vyavasyee, Tarun* and *Vidyarthi* categories, that is, between the age groups of sixteen years to forty-five years. Programmes for different age groups were devised accordingly.

There was also a change in its three-term training workshops. One of the most important training sessions, which used to happen once a year in the past was also changed to accommodate a changing lifestyle. The training camps used to be of forty-days' duration. The duration slowly changed to thirty days, then twenty-five days; and now the first year training is only for twenty-one days. A primary training (*Prathamik Shiksha Varg*) of seven days was introduced a few years back. This is the first-level training that teaches the basics of RSS philosophy and methodology of conducting a shakha. This became acutely important as thousands of young people started joining the RSS through the 'Join RSS' option on its website. This one-week-long training also became a filter for the subsequent stages, so that only trainees who were genuinely interested in running shakhas and taking on higher responsibilities would join the next level programmes. The most recent innovation is splitting the first-year training in two parts, keeping in mind difficulties of IT professionals in getting long leaves. They can now do this course in two parts. The condition for certification is that both trainings should be completed in one calendar year. *Proudh Sangh Shiksha Varg,* for swayamsevaks above forty-five years, is another innovation for people who missed these training in their youth due to professional or family compulsions, but now want to contribute to the Sangh.

As work fast expanded, the gestation period of its workers to mature for the next-level responsibility became shorter. Promotion to higher levels came faster without the need for field experience and intellectual training. *Yojak Varg* (Training of Trainers) that is a new idea for training senior karyakartas was introduced five years back. Senior prachaarak Ranga Hariji was asked to address the first camp, so that basic training material could be designed. In the published version of his lecture, he notes, 'I pay my humble respects to the departed elders of Sangh with *sashtang namaskar* and I take forward my work' (Ranga Hari, 2019, 7). His acknowledgement tells us that this is another step in the continued evolution of RSS work.

Songs as a Tool of Intellectual Training and Nurturing EQ

Doctorji used to sing patriotic songs. Balasaheb Deoras turned this irregular practice into a standard protocol by making it a regular feature of shakhas and public programmes. Slowly, songs became a major source for building intellectual and emotional qualities in the RSS cadre. Many critics claim that the RSS has not produced much intellectual content for training its swayamsevaks. This is true to some extent. One of the reasons given by RSS leaders from the past was that the RSS was doing nothing new—it was just retelling and re-presenting the native Bharatiya intellectual capital that was already built over thousands of years of this civilization.

However, such arguments miss an important aspect of intellectual training that is not understood by RSS observers. This is the importance of songs (or *geets* as RSS workers refer to them). In fact, most swayamsevaks too don't easily realize the importance of RSS *geets* in character building and moulding their thoughts, enriching their EQ. It is a subtle subconscious change. The Sangh has been able to build up a swayamsevak, intellectually and emotionally, through songs that stay with him for life. Ranga Hariji says, 'A swayamsevak may not have read *Bunch of Thoughts* by Shri Guruji, but he would have imbibed his teachings and thoughts through songs.'

If you begin counting the number of songs adopted in different states from songs in other languages, the number would easily go into thousands. No organization in the world can boast of such varied and large number of songs with different themes. Most of the songs were in Marathi and Hindi initially. Slowly, original songs were also written in Tamil, Malayalam, Kannada, Telugu, Gujarati, Punjabi, Odia, Bengali, Assamese, Rajasthani and also Sanskrit. The RSS has songs in thirteen different languages. Ranga Hariji adds, 'These songs can be divided into at least six categories: praying to the motherland, singing praise of the motherland, songs about social conditions and the urge to change or reform them, songs about liberating the society from oppression, importance of organizing the society, and aspirational songs.'

If one were to do a research on Sangh *geets*, they would reflect the changing environment in the society and evolution of the RSS in its thought process through changing times during its nearly century-old existence. While songs before Independence were prayers of surrender of self to the cause of the motherland, or inspiring songs of bravery, of sacrifice or praise to the motherland, themes for later songs were on the lines of aspirations for the nation, songs about bringing in change, songs about social harmony, urge for a prosperous, strong and equitable nation, and so on.

Not all songs were written by RSS workers, many were adopted from existing literature by poets. Some songs by Sane Guruji, a Gandhian with socialist mindset and a trenchant critic of the RSS, were adopted in Maharashtra. One of the Marathi song is—'*Balasaagar Bharat hovo, vishwaat shobhuni raho*' (May Bharat attain great strength and shine gloriously in the world).

Thus, songs being sung in RSS shakhas and other programmes are high-quality training material with well-defined ideas. The practice of *Vaiyaktik* or *Ekal* (solo) *geet* started in Pune. Since it was appreciated by people, it was taken up by others. Soon, it became a standard feature in any programme, to be sung generally before a lecture. These songs are not sung in daily shakhas.

The idea of building up the organization through songs is a contribution of the Sangh to organizational theory. Ranga Hariji says, '*Bouddhik* is *shruti* while songs are *smriti*. Not many people would have read RSS literature but the songs carry its views. The message seeped into the heart as geets had to be learnt by heart at that time.'

Inclusion of More Material for Intellectual Training in Shakhas

A collection of shlokas called *Praatah Smaran* (morning remembrance) to commemorate great sages and leaders in different fields of Bharat, had been sung for many years in the morning shakhas and training camps. A need was felt to make it more inclusive and more updated so that it could be sung in any shakha at any time. A new version was created and introduced a few years back. This is called *Bharat Bhakti Stotram*, and it can be recited at all shakhas at any time of the day or night. *Ekaatmata Mantra* was introduced to enhance the feeling of unity of various faiths born out of Bharat. It is a reminder of how the followers of Hindu dharma follow different paths—followers also address the Supreme Being with different names—to reach the same Supreme

Being. The *Ekaatmata Mantra* is reproduced in Annexure V.

Subhaashit (noble thought from a shloka) is also a later addition. Ranga Hariji recounts that when he joined the RSS seventy-five years back, there was no *subhaashit*. It was consciously introduced by Sudarshanji. Earlier karyakartas such as Babasaheb, Bhuskute, Balasaheb used Sanskrit *subhaashits* routinely and frequently. It was Babasaheb Apte who insisted on using Sanskrit in various intellectual programmes. But, Sudarshanji made it compulsory for *Sangh Shiksha Vargs* when he was *Bouddhik* pramukh. Hariji also contributed to *subhaashits* when he took over from Sudarshanji.

To understand the significance of such simple tools, one can compare another Hindutva movement. We can then appreciate the RSS methodology better. Though Veer Savarkar, a leading figure of the Hindu Mahasabha, was a poet par excellence and wrote highly emotional poems as well as highest quality articles and books, his intellectual message of Hindutva did not help build the organization. As a result, the Hindu Mahasabha withered away as a dry intellectual exercise.

An average swayamsevak, like most people, may not be an avid reader and may not go through RSS literature. However, elements such as *bodh katha, subhashits* and *amrit vachan* (quotes from great personalities) seep through his consciousness and enhance his understanding of the philosophy of Hindutva and the RSS. By doing this, the Sangh can involve even illiterate swayamsevaks, farmers, and tribals; reaching out to people on the ground in our vast nation and growing strong in all sections of the society.

Changing Processes and Imperceptible Evolution in the Organization

Till Guruji's time, there was the concept of *ek chalakaanuvartitva*—one leader whose decision was final. Balasaheb Deoras slowly did away with this idea, and the top leadership of the RSS became a team whereby decisions were taken in a collective manner. Right from the time of Dr Hedgewar, the RSS had a decision-making process that was built on consensus, but it was ultimately the decision of the Sarsanghchaalak. Slowly, from Deorasji onwards, decision-making was decentralized and only a formal nod was taken from the top leaders for deciding the direction of any activity.

The working style of the RSS, its methodology and its components, everything has evolved over the decades. These changes go unnoticed for outsiders. For insiders, however, these were only temporary distractions that required a little retraining before things settled down again. When half-pants were jettisoned in favour of full trousers, it created more noise outside than within the organization. Some swayamsevaks were amused, some who were associated with the Sangh for long felt a little lost without that identity and perhaps a little upset too, but soon everything fell into rhythm again.

In the last three decades, the linguistic or limited geographic nature of the top leadership at the Centre has changed unimaginably. As an ingrained culture, the Sangh never talks about the caste or language of its swayamsevaks or leaders. With rise in trained workers and prachaaraks from various regions, now it is possible to interchange senior workers from different regions. Earlier there was no scope for such an exchange. It was a natural process and the RSS doesn't believe in enforced or quota-based appointments. There have been big changes in the composition of state-level and national-level teams with people coming from varied social strata, including members from SC and ST communities. No doubt, this change will result in more changes at the top too. But, this must be a natural process of progression, and not an enforced change meant to impress outsiders.

One can understand why the RSS has continuously grown despite many social and political changes in nintety-five years of its organizational life. The RSS has not shied away from changes as it understands that one who doesn't adopt to change, perishes.

I have talked of the role of the Sarkaryavaah, the elected general secretary of the RSS, as the executive head. The focus of the Sarkaryavaah is the day-to-day working of the RSS, growth of RSS shakhas and allocating duties to different senior karyakartas and prachaaraks. He is responsible for implementing various policies adopted during ABPS and Kendriya Karyakarini Mandal meetings. The complete list of names of Sarkaryavaahs since the inception of the RSS is provided in Annexure IV. Readers must also note that many of them went on to become Sarsanghchaalaks in the future. The three Sarkaryavaahs—Bhaiyyaji Dani, Eknath Ranade, Balasaheb Deoras—belonged to the first shakha started by Dr Hedgewar. Ranadeji was relieved of Sangh responsibilities when he took up the two massive projects of the RSS—Vivekananda Rock Memorial and Vivekananda Kendra.

One Sarkaryavaah, who left a strong imprint, especially in the field of intellectual content creation and sewa, was Shri H.V. Seshadri. He served as Sarkaryavaah from 1987 to 2000. I have put a short note about him in Chapter 4. He wrote many books. His most famous books in English are *RSS: Vision in Action* and *Tragic Story of Partition*, among many others.

As the Sangh expanded and more and more affiliate organizations grew, it was difficult for a Sarkayarvaah to manage the show. After Emergency and the second ban on the RSS was lifted, there was a change in policy and a post of Sahsarkayavaah (joint general secretary) was created. Sahsarkayavaahs are given the responsibility of specific verticals within the organization and the task of coordinating with affiliate organizations, and guiding them whenever needed. Sahsarkayavaahs also regularly meet with the leaders of other teams. The number of Sahsarkayavaahs was four initially, and it has recently been increased to six. They along with other all-India office-bearers are stationed in different parts of Bharat, in different cities, making a two-way feedback mechanism easier. We can thus see how the structure of the organization has been tweaked and modified to ensure better and faster growth.

Since the RSS was born in Nagpur, it was but natural that during its initial years its workers were from Nagpur and then from Maharashtra for many years. This was not about Maharashtrians dominating the RSS; rather, it was a natural progression. Hariji notes that the Ramkrishna Mission too had its initial support system in Bengal and its volunteers also came from Bengal. Even today it carries traces of Bengal. Natives of its place of origin carried forward its message. In the same way, RSS trainers and prachaaraks also came naturally from Nagpur and Maharashtra. The nomination of Prof. Rajendra Singhji as Sarsanghchaalak broke this much highlighted and imagined wall. Not only was Rajju Bhaiyya not from Maharashtra, he was also not a Brahmin. After this, Sudarshanji took over. He had lived in various parts of the country, but was born in Raipur in Madhya Pradesh and traced his ancestors from the south of the Sahyadri ranges.

There are many other senior workers and leaders who did not become Sarkaryavaah or Sarsanghchaalak, but immensely assisted in the growth and evolution of the RSS through their silent contributions. From amongst the first-generation and early second-generation prachaaraks, some of the names that come to mind are those of Appaji Joshi, Babasaheb Apte, Bapurao Moghe, Bhaurao Deoras, Dadarao Parmarth and Moropant Pingley. Moropant Pingley, though well known within RSS circles as a master strategist, is hardly known outside the RSS. He was the man behind the hugely successful Ekaatmata Yatra, that later spawned multiple reformist activities with the help of various sants, heads of sampradayas and *math* heads. His biggest contribution was the strategic planning of the Ram Janmabhoomi movement. He worked out the different phases of the movement that made what was an Ayodhya-specific issue, into a national and finally an international issue. From offering aarti to Bhagwan Ram at a specific time across India, to Ram Shila poojan—people offering bricks for the Ram Temple from nearly all villages across India—to many other steps to keep up the momentum, was a result of his ideas. It is a challenge to keep an agitation active over thirty years, but his ideas saw this happening.

There were some sterling prachaaraks who moved out to create huge organizations—Dattopant Thengdi, Dadasaheb Apte, Ashok Singhal, Deendayal Upadhyay, Nanaji Deshmukh, Atal Bihari Vajpayee, L.K. Advani, Balasaheb Deshapande, Bhaskarrao

Kalambi and Shyam Gupt just to name a few.

As noted previously in the book, when Balasaheb Deoras said that there were six Sarsanghchaalaks outside while he was in jail during the Emergency, he was not too much off the mark. This statement showed the huge talent pool in the RSS and the strength of its decentralized working.

The RSS does not go by constitutionally defined states. To promote intensive growth in addition to extensive growth, political states are further divided into smaller units. Thus, the number of prants (states) in RSS operations as of now is forty-three. For example, Maharashtra has four prants, Uttar Pradesh has three prants, Odisha and Assam have two prants each, and so on. These numbers have increased as the need for deepar reach and improvement in various regions was felt. Because of this, kshetras (regions) which comprise a number of prants in a region have also increased. Earlier it was Uttar, Dakshin, Poorva, Pashchim and Madhya kshetra. Now there are eleven kshetras.

Earlier, the prant prachaarak in a state looked after all the activities of the Sangh. As different verticals became active and required more attention, prachaaraks have been allocated to different verticals too.

There is a major degree of autonomy for the team looking after an activity to decide its actual course of action. Its democratic and federal functioning is based on mutual trust and is a major factor that has helped the sustained growth of the RSS, its affiliated organizations and its work in nearly every arena of social life. Viewing the Sangh as a static, orthodox, monolithic organization is the biggest mistake critics make. Its flexibility and readiness to adapt to changing times is its strength.

Expanding the Scope of Hindutva

From the very inception of the RSS, there have been many questions about who is a Hindu and what is Hindutva. Many scholars maintain that Hindutva as a term predates V.D. Savarkar's exposition of Hindutva in his seminal work *Hindutva: Who is a Hindu?* According to Makarand R. Paranjape, Hindutva, like most modern ideas in India, was born in Bengal in the nineteenth century. A Bengali essay titled 'Essentials of Hindutva' was published in 1892 by Chandranath Basu.[19] In this essay, the author explains that 'Hindu' as a geographical term with common cultural features across Bharat was supposed to have been coined by outsiders. It was, however, accepted as the identity of people living in 'Hindusthan,' which was the land of Hindus, just as Turkmenistan is the land of Turks, Uzbekistan is the land of Uzbeks, and so on. Thus, the undercurrent providing dynamic flow of life to this nation, rightly or wrongly, got its name, Hindu. Whatever be the root of this word, it did get attached to people populating Hindusthan or Bharat.

In a meeting in Pune addressed by Dr Hedgewar, a person arrogantly countered him by asking, 'Who is that fool who says Bharat is a Hindu Rashtra?' Dr Hedgewar, without quoting any book or scholar—calmly but firmly, responded, 'I, Dr Keshav Baliram Hedgewar, say that Bharat is a Hindu Rashtra' (Vaidya 2019). However, whenever Doctorji was asked, 'Who is a Hindu? Define Hinduism or Hindutva, he would avoid a debate on the subject and simply shrug it off. To him, the conventional definition was acceptable.

---

[19]Refer to https://www.dnaindia.com/analysis/column-hindutva-before-savarkar-chandranath-basu-s-contribution-2411145 (last accessed on 4 June 2020).

Lokmanya Tilak was the first political leader and thinker to answer the question, 'Who is a Hindu?' According to him, whoever follows the Vedas is a Hindu, '*Pramanya Buddhirvedeshu Upasyanam Aniyamah.*' However, his analysis excluded Jains and Buddhists who are very much a part of Bharat (Vaidya 2019).

Then in 1923, Swatantryaveer Savarkar came up with a broader definition, stating that all the people living on this land from the Himalayas to the Indian Ocean, who treat this land as their fatherland and holy land are all Hindus (Savarkar 1999).

> *Aasindhusindhuparyanta Yasya Bharatbhumika*
> *Pitrubhu Punyabhushchaiva Sa Vai Hinduriti Smrita*

This definition, however, excluded Bharatiya Christians, Muslims, Parsis and Jews as people who propagated faiths that considered their sacred places of worship or their gods to be outside Bharat—this meant that they were not Hindus. Thus, Savarkar's definition carried a connotation of religion.

According to Savarkar, Hindutva is different from Hinduism. Hindutva is not a word but a history. It is not just a spiritual or religious history of our people, but history complete in itself (Savarkar 1999, 2). Such was his devotion to Bharat that he said, '*Yadihaasti na sarvatra yannehaasti na kutrachit*' (Verily, whatever could be found in the world is found here too. And if anything is not found here it could be found nowhere.). (Savarkar 1999, 71)

According to Savarkar:

> Ye, who by race, by blood, by culture, by nationality possess almost all the essentials of Hindutva and had been forcibly snatched out of our ancestral home by the hand of violence—ye, have only to render wholehearted love to our common Mother and recognize her not only as Father land (*Pitribhu*) but even as a Holy land (*Punyabhu*) and ye would be most welcome to the Hindu fold. (Savarkar 1999, 71–72)

Did he keep the door open for non-Hindus if they reconverted to their old faith, or did not consider the holy land (*punyabhu*) superior to the fatherland (*Pitrubhu*)? One could consider this possibility because he did say in the same book, 'It may be that at some future time the word Hindu may come to indicate a citizen of Hindustan and nothing else...' To provide a geographical dimension to Hindu Rashtra, Savarkar also quotes *Vishnu Purana* that clearly defines Bharat and Bharatiya (India and Indian) (Savarkar 1999, xi).

> *Uttaram yatsmudrasya, himaadreshchaiv dakshinam,*
> *Varsham tad Bhaaratam naam Bhaarati yatr santatih.*

> In essence: the land north of the (Indian) ocean and south of Himalayas is called Bharat and the children of this land are Bharatiya.

This is much in line with how Chanakya in 4 BC and Kalidasa in AD 4 defined Bharatvarsh in their writings.

In 1888, Muslim intellectual and educationist Sir Syed Ahmed Khan had propagated, for the first time, that Hindus and Muslims are 'two nations' who cannot live together (Lan Jiang and Dong Li 2016, 4–5). This view came after the 1857 War of Independence that was fought jointly by Indians irrespective of their religions. Contrary to what Gandhiji wished to achieve, the difference between the two communities was accentuated during the Khilafat Movement. Failure of the Khilafat Movement led to violent bloodshed let loose by Muslims in Mallapuram in Kerala and it spread to India before it died down by 1924. Thus, this agitation proved to be the major breaking point between the two dominant communities.

Before he went to Kala Pani, Savarkar too espoused Hindu–Muslim unity. His book, *1857: The First Indian War of Independence,* presented the entire struggle as a joint struggle by Hindus and Muslims. He presented a picture of unity between the two communities. It was published in 1909. He was deported to Kala Pani in 1911 and was there for nearly eleven years till 1921. It was his experience in Kala Pani with Muslim wardens and their jihadi mentality even in prison that made him think that for

Muslims, religion came before nation. He saw the Moplah violence and a series of riots upon release. This changed his essentially non-religious approach to the struggle for independence and national unity. It brought about change in his view on nationality and extra-territorial loyalty of Muslims. The ideology of Hindutva by Savarkar came from deep intellectual churning in this period and he presented it in the form of the book, *Hindutva* in 1923. Hitler's *Mein Kampf* was published in 1926. Thus, those who link his Hindutva to Nazism do so in ignorance or are vicious liars.

A commonly accepted definition at the time stated that Hindus were citizens of Bharat with roots in the nation and a common culture, irrespective of their *sampradayas* or sects. This is how Swami Vivekananda, the monk behind Bharat's renaissance, spoke of Hindus. For Dr Hedgewar, the first condition for independence was that Hindus, as defined in such commonly held view, be united and awakened for renaissance of Bharat as a nation, because the major cause of the downfall of Bharat was disunity, internal fights on language, caste and region between Hindus. So, their unity was a must. It can be safely said that during his time, the term 'Hindu' in literature, art and songs implied that Muslims, Christians, Jews and Parsis did not fit into the prevalent definition of Hindu.

Interestingly, the Constitution of India too defined Hindu in a negative way—any person who is not a Muslim, Christian, Parsi or Jew is a Hindu, unless he proves that he may not have been dealt with the instance of Hindu customs, rites and rituals. Treating Sikhs and Jains as minority community is a latter-day development. But, it shows that our elders who wrote the Constitution saw every citizen of India as Hindu unless specified otherwise. Perhaps this is how Dr Hedgewar saw it and saw no reason to get into a debate.

Dr Hedgewar's Hindutva and the commonly accepted definition of 'Hindu' carried no hatred for any faith as we have seen in his pronouncements. However, he realized that unless Hindus overcame their differences and inferiority complex, Bharat could not achieve its full potential. Guruji followed the same definition. He always stressed upon the common cultural aspects of Hindus living in the geographical mass called Bharat.

Guruji's first attempt at expanding the fold of Hindus took place in 1957 when he responded to his felicitation on his fifty-first birthday. He appealed to minorities, especially Muslims, for *Ghar Wapsi*, that is, a return to the roots. He reminded them that they had the same forefathers as Hindus. They came from the same heritage that Hindus carried. Thus, they were closer to Hindus than to people from distant lands whose religion they now followed. He noted that these minorities had been converted either under force or allurement of safety and easier life a few generations back, to their new faiths. According to him, the panacea to this problem lay in a return to their ancient fold as they were also culturally Hindus.

However, he modified his stand later in life, when he supported the idea of 'Indianization' or *Bharatiyakaran* floated by Prof. Balraj Madhok for Bharatiya Jan Sangh. This interview, towards the end of his life, quoted earlier in the chapter on Shri Guruji, should be taken as his final view on minorities as it was his last. In his interview to Dr Saifuddin Jeelani, he reiterated that Indianization did not mean conversion to the Hindu fold, but an acceptance by the minority of their common ancestry and cultural roots. They could happily follow their faiths, but they needed to own up to their culture like Muslims of Indonesia or Malaysia do, who say that they have changed their faith but not their culture.

Guruji gave an even broader definition of Hindu, saying that Bharat as the motherland of people with common ancestors and common traditions has provided a unique identity to the people living in Bharat for centuries. This identity is Hindu. In the traditional Bharatiya sense, the people form the 'nation,' not a 'state.' We were one people, irrespective of all the different rulers, or states with different languages. Ranga Hari quotes Guruji as saying, 'I am ready to open even my temple for them.' Balasaheb Deoras, as Sarsanghchaalak, also said that all those born in India are Hindus—Hindu Muslims or Hindu Christians.

Thus, the RSS differed from Savarkar's definition that

considered *punya bhoomi* as one of the defining criteria for being a Hindu to claim equal rights in Bharat, even as both talked of Hindu Rashtra. Another difference with Savarkar was that the RSS considers Hinduism and Hindutva as synonyms, appearing differently because of linguistics. Hinduism is an English term while Hindutva is a Sanskrit and Bharatiya term. Dr Manmohan Vaidya often says that if Savarkar had written in English, he might have used the word 'Hinduism' or if Dr S. Radhakrishnan had written his book on Hinduism in any Bharatiya language he might have used the word 'Hindutva.'

All Sarsanghchaalaks stressed upon the difference between 'dharma' and 'religion,' which was at the root of controversies around the supposed communalism of the RSS. Dharma is the rule of law and ethics irrespective of one's faith. It defines the duties of an individual or an organization vis-à-vis the other members of the family, society and nation. Dharma is not attached to the faith a person belongs to. Though Hindus have coined this term, it is by definition secular, rather religion-neutral. Defined by rishis, dharma is that which holds the society together—*dharayati iti dharma.*

Guruji stressed that incorrect translation of key words of the Hindu civilization had led to much misinterpretation. According to him, they should not be translated and be used as they are. He gave numerous examples such as *rashtra, dharma, varna, samskriti,* and so on. Rajiv Malhotra later expanded the idea and coined the term, 'Sanskrit non-translatables.' He said that by sticking to the original Indic term, we will convey the correct meaning. This will also ensure appreciation of differentiation between our philosophy and Western philosophy. This will better preserve Hindu cultural ideas.

The Supreme Court of India has also defined Hindu as a civilizational concept, 'Hindutva/Hinduism is a way of life of the people in the subcontinent' and is a state of mind—not a religion. The question that arises then is what is this way of life?

Swami Vivekananda in his speech at the Parliament of the

World's Religions in Chicago in 1893 said,

> We believe not only in universal toleration, but we accept all religions as true. I am proud to belong to a nation which has sheltered the persecuted and the refugees of all religions and all nations of the Earth. I am proud to tell you that we have gathered in our bosom the purest remnant of the Israelites, who came to Southern India and took refuge with us in the very year in which their holy temple was shattered to pieces by Roman tyranny. I am proud to belong to the religion which has sheltered and is still fostering the remnant of the grand Zoroastrian nation. I will quote to you, brethren, a few lines from a hymn which I remember to have repeated from my earliest boyhood, which is every day repeated by millions of human beings: 'As the different streams having their sources in different paths which men take through different tendencies, various though they appear, crooked or straight, all lead to Thee.'[20]

This, in a nutshell is the spirit of Hindutva or Hinduism as Vivekananda defined it succinctly.

RSS thinkers noted that all faiths or religions born out of this *dharmic samskriti* or Indic culture shared some common elements. In short, they may be enumerated as follows: (*i*) belief in the theory of karma, (*ii*) belief in rebirth, (*iii*) concept of mukti or nirvana or *shunya*, (*iv*) worshipping and showing respect to nature, and (*v*) sharing of the most important philosophy of pluralism, that is, *Ekam sat, vipra bahudha vadanti*—there is one truth, scholars call it differently. This pluralism and respect for others' viewpoints differentiates Hindu dharma from the Abrahamic religions such as Islam and Christianity. The belief of these religions is that there is only one God and all other gods are false. People who don't believe in their religions are sinful or *kafirs* and must be converted (to

---

[20]Refer to https://www.business-standard.com/article/current-affairs/full-text-of-swami-vivekananda-s-chicago-speech-of-1893-117091101404_1.html.

save them from hell). This exclusivist thinking lay at the root of all the conflicts in the world. There is a stark difference between the inclusive Hindu *darshan* or philosophy and exclusivist Abrahamic ideology.

As Swami Vivekananda explained in his Chicago address:

> If the Parliament of Religions has shown anything to the world, it is this: It has proved to the world that holiness, purity and charity are not the exclusive possessions of any church in the world, and that every system has produced men and women of the most exalted character. In the face of this evidence, if anybody dreams of the exclusive survival of his own religion and the destruction of the others, I pity him from the bottom of my heart, and point out to him that upon the banner of every religion will soon be written in spite of resistance: 'Help and not fight', 'Assimilation and not Destruction', and 'Harmony and Peace and not Dissension'.

Thinkers also tried to put together commonalities that bound Indians, irrespective of their faiths, across India though there were apparent diversities in their behaviour and celebrations. The oft repeated slogan of 'unity in diversity' needed to be crystallized. As the current Sarsanghchaalak Mohan Bhagwat says, 'It is not unity in diversity. Actually there is underlying unity that is expressed in diverse forms, and we celebrate this diversity.'

The RSS has more or less followed this stance on who is Hindu. However, there have been efforts in defining Hindu as a non-religious or cultural term, since we say that dharma is not equal to religion and Hinduism is a way of life.

In a conversation with Ranga Hariji, a veteran RSS thinker, he brings out some interesting common features of the Hindu civilization that have no religious base but are purely cultural. He gives an example of a common practice followed by shopkeepers whereby they put a little extra vegetable (or whatever else is being purchased) while they weigh it for their customers. In many languages, it is called *runga* but there are different words across

India for the same dharmic approach of a shopkeeper. Some of the words that Ranga Hariji learnt from local sources for the word *runga* are *vasaru, osaru, sheen, saviayan, setu, chunga, choga, happa, navadana, mandani,* amongst others. The underlying principle is, if there is a mistake in weighing, it should be on my side and the customer shouldn't pay for it. This is 'dharma' of a trader. There is a concept of the opening deal of the day or a season in a business. It is called *bohoni.* This concept is there in all regions of Bharat. Some other words for this concept are *bhavani, boni, tikappa,* and so on. He gives examples of many indigenous games like *lagori,* where a pile of flat stones is felled by a ball thrown by a player. This game is known by many different names. There is *attya pattya,* in which two sides have to cross each other—the game is known by names such as *uppata, noon, loon, gitte.* Another one is a game played with pebbles or *stappu;* it is a game of square boxes with stones or pebbles to be picked up with a hop and jump. So, we see, all these games with different names are played across Bharat. They have the same unwritten rules, some supposedly played by girls only or some by boys only. They don't identify with any religion but are signs of common cultural threads. All these existed before sports committees came up or marketing of games began. No directives were passed for these games by a sports committee! There were no rule books written! Similarly, most festivals of Bharat are based on the agricultural calendar and are known by names across the nation. Not disrespecting books or money, worshipping the balance in the shop or worshipping the plough in farms before its use is another cultural trait. Such examples show us that culturally India remains one nation though language, local culture and faiths may differ. He calls this unifying quality '*Hinduness*'. Hinduness of Bharata is an idea of dynamic civilization, not constrained by hardbound definitions.

Thus, the scope of the words 'Hindu' and 'Hinduness' has been expanded over time by the RSS. Dr Mohan Bhagwat took it another step forward by saying that every person born in this land is a Hindu because Hindustan is a land inhabited by Hindus. It does not carry a religious connotation though 'Hindu' also represents a faith system that is pluralist because it respects different paths to reach the same Supreme Truth.

The RSS has time and again reiterated that Hindu Rashtra is not a theological construct. It is not a concept of a nation state that is alien to Hindu culture. Rather, it is a nation that is independent of the ruler's faith and survives the ruler, unlike the Western concept of a nation state where the collapse of a ruler resulted in the collapse of the nation state.

According to Ranga Hari, the word '*rashtra*' has been used seventy-two times in the *Rig Veda*. It is also used as a concept of committees (*sabha*) or team (*samiti*). These words have been in currency even during Chanakya's time. No ancient Hindu text defines nation in terms of a religion or a ruler's faith. The idea of secularism as seen from the Hindu prism is much different from the Western concept that was born out of an idea to keep the Church away from the affairs of the state, thus, defined secularism as a separation between the Church and the state. It, thus, implies an irreligious state, though in a democracy like UK and other secular states, the government of the days takes oath on the Bible.

Another dimension is added by VHP's foundational documents that define 'Hindu' on a global level written in Sanskrit.

भारतीयर्षि प्रोक्तान् इहामुत्रार्थ साधाकान् ।
योगीकरोतिसश्रध्द्र सत्सिध्दान्तान्सनातनान् ॥
महात्मभिः दीव्यशीलैः काले काले प्रवर्तितान् ।
सम्प्रदायानाद्रियतेयः सर्वान्पारमार्थिकान् ॥
यत्रकुत्रापिजातः सः वास्तुया कोपि जन्मना ।
सच्छिलोदार चरितः सः हिन्दुरिति स्मृतः ॥

Bhaarateeyarshi proktaan ihamutraarth saadhakaan,
Yogeenkaroti sashraddham sat siddhantaan sanaatanaan
Mahaatmabhih deevyasheelaih kaale kaale pravartitaan
Yatra kutraapi jaatah sah vaastu yaa kopi janmana
Sachhilodaar charitah sah hinduriti smritah

> The sages of Bharat (said to) the followers, cults and those who are related to the high spiritual path, who are here or anywhere, who had spoken (said to them all):
>
> He who accepts and follows the oldest [Sanatana] rules, which are given by great souls at every time with complete faith, wherever he goes or in whatever birth [if] he narrates [all those Sanatana rules] with great affection, he who of noble character is known as Hindu.

This is an excellent definition of 'Hindu' for Hindus globally. This definition excludes geographical constraint. However, keeping in view VHP's objectives, it is more religious than territorial.

For the RSS, working within Bharat and for Bharat, this definition of Hindu doesn't work because it has to be more inclusive, expansive and also have geographical boundaries. The RSS has been striving to expand the definition of Hindu and Hindutva to include more communities within its definition of Hindu and Hindu Rashtra. In this regard, Ranga Hari quotes from the poem 'Outwitted' written by Edwin Markham to explain the Hindu approach better:

> He drew a circle and kept me out,
> Heretic, rebel, a thing to flout.
> But Love and I had the wit to win:
> We drew a circle and took him in!

He suggests that this has been Hindu behaviour all through its history. But for this, we couldn't have assimilated various people like the Shakas and Hunas into our fold. When the Shakas and Hunas came, Hindus had the skill to draw a larger circle and bring them in. This is Hindutva, a self-expanding idea.

A shloka from *Atharva Veda* is much wider in scope in explaining the concept of Hindutva. It says, 'Various types of *bhashah* [linguist] people, various types of *aacharana* [behaviour] people, all of them are together, fed like milk from one udder.' This assimilative approach is not taken or cannot be taken by religious heads because gurus speak as per scriptures within religious bounds. However, the RSS can express such ideas as its Sarsanghchaalak is not a religious head, nor is it a religious organization, thus, not bound by scriptures. That is why, Dr Bhagwat said during his Delhi programme that all the people born in this land and believing this to be the land of their ancestors are Hindus. Dr Hedgewar was right in his formulation when he attempted to solve problems of society as he saw them during his time. Similarly, Dr Mohan Bhagwat is also right in his formulation, because he views problems through the lens of his time. The Sangh has evolved imperceptibly in this period.

Considering all these factors and confusion between the term Hindu 'the religion' and Hindu 'the civilizational cultural entity', can we begin to demarcate religion from dharma and draw differences between religious and cultural definitions.

Hindutva or Hinduness has an expanding, evolving definition. Savarkar, too, was aware that nothing is permanent, including his definition of a Hindu. He noted in *Hindutva*.

> It may be that at some future time the word Hindu may come to indicate a citizen of Hindustan and nothing else; that day can only rise when all cultural and religious bigotry has disbanded its forces pledged to aggressive egoism, and religions cease to be 'isms' and become merely the common fund of eternal principles that lie at the root of all, that are a common foundation on which the Human State majestically and firmly rests.

This is the most open view of Hindutva as a dynamic construct one can think of, and it comes from a scholar, who is labelled as most rigid.

Explaining that Hindu Rashtra is not a theocratic concept, Manmohan Vaidya quotes Perry Anderson from his book *Indian Ideology*:

> There was something unique about the antiquity of the

> subcontinent and its tremendous impress of oneness, making its inhabitants throughout these ages distinctively Indian, with the same national heritage and same set of moral and mental qualities. Indeed a dream of unity has occupied the mind of India since the dawn of civilization.

This unity and uniqueness known to the world as Hindutva (Hinduness) should be felt, realized and manifested in all walks of social life. This is the realization of the Hindu Rashtra. This has nothing to do with a theocratic state. Rather, a theocratic state is alien to Hindutva and Bharat. (Vaidya 2019)

Today, the view of the RSS presented by Dr Mohan Bhagwat may not be accepted by a large number of people, but the Sangh will have to present its viewpoint and keep its doors open to expand and be expansive in its reach. It may not happen now; it may take some more years. After all, even its original idea of a Hindu organization, renaissance of Hindu society and Hindu Rashtra had hardly any takers. Considering the way the RSS generates and develops ideas and structure, this subject is still open to new interpretations.

Taking all these arguments together, can we then define what is genuine native Bharatiya culture or Bharatiya nationalism? The RSS calls it 'Hindutva' or 'Hinduness.' New terminology may be thought of and inserted into social discourse for wider discussions. To keep terminology simple, will it be better to call it cultural nationalism or genuinely native nationalism? Some may even call it cultural, national or economic nationalism. To keep the discourse simple, can we use the term 'Bharat Rashtra' instead of 'Hindu Rashtra'? Only, the time ahead will tell. For the present, the RSS is not changing these words even as it expands the scope of important keywords. We are an ever-evolving civilization and the RSS is an ever-evolving organization.

Epilogue
RSS: The Organic Organization

One can look at the evolution of the RSS from an organizational perspective through the following timeline:

1925–1940: Foundation of the RSS, creation of its processes and structure, and its reach in different parts of India. Basically, this was the seeding of the plant.

1940–1946: Rapid expansion of the RSS across India. High growth, especially in northern and western regions of the country.

1946–1949: The turbulent period of Partition, the RSS worked as a protector of Hindu society, rescue and rehabilitation of Hindu and Sikh refugees, supporting Indian army in throwing off first Pakistani attack on Jammu & Kashmir, the Congress offensive against it, persecution, struggle to lift the ban and clearing of all charges against it and lifting of ban.

1949–1974: Rebuilding of the RSS from near zero all over again, setting up of new organizations by RSS swayamsevaks covering nearly all the dimensions of social life in India. Helped the cow protection movement to come out of its shell and reach wider society. Collected signatures from twelve million citizens. Emergence of RSS-inspired organizations in different countries. From an organization based on shakhas to a massive social organization. The RSS moved into public space by openly supporting the anti-corruption movement and reaching out to non-RSS leaders and organizations.

1974–1985: The RSS takes part in anti-corruption movement and works hard for restoration of democracy after imposition of draconian internal Emergency. Able to overcome political untouchability. From being kept on the fringes, it becomes a mainstream organization. Hindutva becomes a recognized philosophy in political arena. Mass conversion of Hindus leads to a huge counter programme, Ekatmata Yatra reaches 80 million Indian citizens. Biggest ever outreach by the RSS. Move from social organization, to activist mass organization. Hindutva on way to become a movement.

1985 onwards: Ram Mandir agitation sustained over period of thirty years, evolution of Hindutva and RSS Hindutva and the RSS into mass movements. From a local legal case, it became national issue of cultural pride. Participation of people from all nooks and corners of Bharat in this agitation, run in multiple phases with innovative programmes making it the biggest movement of all times. More national organizations come up. Transforms from its earlier avatar of cadre based organization to mass activist organization to a mass movement. All the efforts by combined Left-Secular forces fail to stop or marginalize Hindutva from becoming the central pole of social and political discourse.

At a philosophical level, Darwin's theory can be considered true for social organizations. The basic premise of his theory is that if you don't adapt to the changing environment, you will become extinct. This principle is illustrated in Bharatiya tradition as Dashaavataar, with the Supreme Being shown to be progressing from non-vertebrates, various life forms to human being. This evolution is an adaptation of nature.

There have been four major ideological streams, or to put it in Indian ethos—*vichar pravaah* in India in the last 100 years presented by four groups: Congress, Socialist, Communist and the RSS. Of these, only the RSS has survived and thrived while others have lost or are losing steam. The reason is, the RSS constantly adapted to its changing environment, while the others did not.

The RSS may look like a staid, non-dynamic organization if a lazy, intellectual aerial view is to be taken. This is the mistake most critics make. However, if you look at the organizational evolution of the RSS and its ever-expanding organic nature, you will find that there has been continuous fine tuning and modifications. Many inflexible, rigid organizations are being run by autocratic, oligarchic or feudal leadership (in the sense of total submission of loyal followers to the leader) with a closed system, with a few elite at the top dictating the movement. They have gone down when confronted with existential crises. The RSS, however, sailed through. In fact, it adapted itself to emerging scenarios and moved on to expand its base and grow. In modern terminology, we can say that the Sangh has a management system with feedback mechanism that works both ways—from cadres to top leadership and from top leadership to the cadres. The mechanism of its continuous 'baithaks' or meetings that stumps many is the router of this feedback. This allows the RSS to adapt and flow with the new knowledge systems.

Dr K.B. Hedgewar initiated a historic change in Hindu society's perspective. This is his lasting contribution to the social framework of the oldest living civilization. Hindu society has been an individualistic spiritual society focused on moksha or nirvana for the self. Hindus have no concept of collective liberation as expounded by Abrahamic religions. They have no history of collective action except during military action. While they do come together on occasions like the Kumbh Mela, it is a crowd of individual seekers for self-realization, rather than a collective gathering for a social purpose.

Dr Hedgewar attempted an unbelievable and previously unthinkable change in the Hindu mindset to bring about a unity of purpose and action at the societal level. A social unity that focused on worldly, materialistic pursuits—whether it was for attaining freedom or creating a prosperous, disciplined and courageous society that took pride in its past achievements but also looked to the future with optimism—not with pessimism of a slave society that had gone into a shell. It was a difficult task, given that the British had succeeded in convincing Hindus that theirs was a moribund backward society with an unjust social (caste) system that killed widows and married off children—an unscientific society that had nothing to be proud of and a society that was never a nation.

Dr Hedgewar went on to create a modern organization with a modern structure, chose a Western uniform, musical band, and so on. He did not link his work to *maths,* temples or any religious sect-based organization. This is where he deviated from Swami Vivekananda's approach who created Ramkrishna Mission, Sri Aurobindo who built a spiritual centre in Pondicherry, or Swami Chinmayananda who created Chinmaya Mission. To this list, one can add organizations such as the Brahmo Samaj and other similar religious reformist institutions. Even some top leaders in later times, like Tilak, used religious symbolism and Hindu traditions to transform an individualistic society into a united society to create an enlightened collective conscience. When we look back, we realize such institutions lost their energy over a period of time and the directions set by their founders. Dr Hedgewar's creation, on the other hand, without any outward religious symbolism or spiritual goals, changed this approach and succeeded in the long run. We may call it the first well-structured non-religious Hindu organization that was interested in worldly pursuits, albeit with Dharmic underpinning.

When Guruji succeeded Dr Hedgewar, he faced the most turbulent times in the history of the RSS. Just as he had begun expanding the RSS at breakneck speed to achieve Dr Hedgewar's goal of three per cent of the population of rural Bharat and one per cent of urban Bharat in RSS uniform, the 1942 Quit India Movement commenced and diverted its energy and its swayamsevaks. From 1946 to 1947, RSS volunteers were completely involved in protecting their Hindu and Sikh brothers against rampant violence and their rehabilitation during the years following Partition as well as saving Jammu & Kashmir from Pakistani marauders. This happened at a heavy cost to life and property of these swayamsevaks. His heart bled with them and for them. Guruji led the organization from the front. The organization also faced oppression, violence, losses to its swayamsevaks and later a ban for one-and-a-half-years on the false pretexts of Gandhiji's assassination in 1948–49. It was the organizational set-up built by Dr Hedgewar that saw the RSS through these turbulent times.

After the ban was over, the period 1949–50 saw many divergent views about the utility of the work of the RSS. There were doubts about its working methodology and even the very idea of using the word 'Hindu.' The self-doubts in the minds of some senior workers were so agitating that Guruji had said, 'If nothing works out, I will begin from the beginning.' It was in these trying times that Guruji created a superstructure built on the foundational principles of Dr Hedgewar, which was able to support a complex organization in the years that followed. He re-energized the cadre and rebuilt the organization. His fine-tuning of the superstructure has seen diverse, powerful social groups aligning with the Hindu dharmic view of life.

No other organization could have survived such persecution and government pressures as the RSS did in 1948. However, Guruji's silent yet innovative approach took it forward and ensured that it reached every corner of Bharat.

His term saw its expansion into new areas of national life. The organization took dynamic changes in its stride. During his time, India saw the emergence of new social organizations such as Akhil Bharatiya Vidyarthi Parishad (ABVP), Vanavasi Kalyan Ashram (VKA), Bharatiya Mazdoor Sangh (BMS), Vishwa Hindu Parishad (VHP). But, the RSS was not held back by any dogma or compartmentalized thinking. Not many have noticed that though Shri Guruji had a spiritual aura, and observers believe that he injected *'adhyatmikata'* in the RSS, most of the organizations that came up during his time were non-religious in nature. Only VHP works for religious cause and religious reforms, all other organizations have been working for tangible worldly objectives that would lead India to high prosperity, or *'param vaibhav'* as RSS prayer says.

Balasaheb Deoras took the organization to the next level. It is under him that the organization reached the next orbit of national life as envisioned by its founder. He set the RSS on to a path of social outreach as the next stage of evolution or 'unfolding' as Dattopant Thengdi called it. The RSS had taken a clear position on social evils that bedevilled Hindu society and worked without propaganda to reform Hindu society on caste discrimination. Balasaheb was very open in enunciating the RSS's views on these issues that affected Hindu society. He energized the RSS cadre to get into sewa (social service) projects in a big and organized manner and encouraged interaction with other social movements. He floated the idea that each shakha must be part of its locality and pick up one social service project in its own locality, thus expanding its social outreach. His aggressive espousal of Sewa (service), Samarasta (social harmony) and Sangharsh (struggle) infused a new consciousness into the organization. He was able to break the image of the RSS as an upper-caste organization.

He was an outgoing social organizer with a political mind. He had seen the suffering of swayamsevaks during the ban when no political party came out in support of the RSS. When Dr Shyama Prasad Mukherjee reached out to Guruji to support him in the launching of the Bharatiya Jan Sangh, the precursor of the BJP, Balasaheb was a leading light of the group of young team of Guruji. It was Guruji who had requested Balasaheb to support Mukherjee. Subsequently, Guruji deputed some of the best brains of the RSS to Jan Sangh.

The decision to give open and direct support to the anti-corruption movement was a bold move by Balasaheb. First it was the Gujarat Navnirman Andolan and later, Shri Jaiprakash Narayan's movement. It was under his leadership that the RSS fought against the Emergency, and it played a key role in the restoration of democracy. His strategy of not demanding for the ban on the RSS to be lifted, and instead focusing on fighting dictatorship was an intelligent move. However, the RSS had to pay a heavy price in terms of its swayamsevaks losing their jobs and businesses and their families put to great difficulties. This phase may be seen as another turning point in the evolution of the RSS, as its popularity and appeal increased and idea of the political untouchability against the RSS practically died.

He was able to guide the RSS to the next orbit by harnessing the seething dissatisfaction in the society that had built up on the issues of corruption, Emergency, mass conversions, atrocities on Kashmiri Hindus and weak-kneed response to the Shah Bano issue. These factors saw the emergence of Ram Janmabhoomi agitation and it became the rallying point for the masses. It may be argued with benefit of hindsight that if governments of the day had taken firm action in Jammu and Kashmir and had stood by the courts in the Shah Bano case, they would have got people's support and the nation would have moved in a different direction with confidence.

The creation of a media cell for the RSS was a critical departure from the conventional RSS line of thinking. Being an organization that is circumspect about publicity and media, it took some years before this activity became mainstream. He was the first Sarsanghchaalak who gave it an organizational push.

Prof. Rajendra Singh (better known as Rajju Bhaiyya) along with Nanaji Deshmukh and Bhaurao Deoras added a new dimension to the work of the RSS in the 1950s when they entered the education field. He was on the field again when new political alignments were taking place. He was there when the first non-Congress alliance took shape in 1968-69. These developments paved the way for the emergence of more stable opposition alliances. Dr Lohia and Deendayal Upadhyay were the political architects of the changing politics. He played a key role in 1977 when Janata Party was being formed for the forthcoming elections. As a true swayamsevak, he would detach himself easily and go back to his original passion, Sangh work. Rajju Bhaiyya's role in the democratic struggle against the Emergency along with other top RSS leaders can be considered an important factor in this fight and its success. This struggle bolstered the image of the RSS and changed the way political parties looked at it. Despite the best efforts of Socialist groups, they could not sully the image of the RSS, nor slow down its work.

The RSS launched a massive movement to fight mass conversion that had begun from Tamil Nadu in 1982. Ekatmata Yatra was the biggest mass contact programme in India that was novel in every way. The veteran first-generation prachaarak, the think tank of the central team, Moropant Pingley along with Rajju Bhaiyya as Sarkaryavaah, saw to its massive success.

I have noted elsewhere that Balasaheb Deoras had decentralized the decision-making process. When Socialist leaders wondered how the RSS underground struggle was going on smoothly when its chief was in the jail, he had told them, 'Sarsanghchaalak may be in jail but there are six Sarsanghchaalaks outside.' He was underlining the importance and success of the collective leadership of the RSS.

The Ram Mandir (or Ayodhya Movement) was a huge change in the socio-political life of India. It was the time when the RSS became a mass movement in every sense. To keep swayamsevaks and volunteers balanced during this period of euphoria was not an easy task, Rajju Bhaiyya was able to wean away swayamsevaks from becoming too street smart and bring them back to regular Sangh work. His exhortation, *'path ka antim lakshya nahin hai, singhasan chadhate jaanaa'* (The ultimate destination of our path is not to gain power), was to cool down the euphoria and bring the swayamsevaks back to regular Sangh work of social awakening. During his time, the RSS-inspired work for overseas Hindus, viz. Hindu Swayamsevak Sangh, also got a new impetus with his trips. He was the first Sarsanghchaalak to travel overseas and the result was highly encouraging for the activists there. It was during his leadership of the RSS that India got its first swayamsevak-led (Atal Bihari Vajpayee) government at the Centre.

Sudarshanji will be remembered not only for creating new training material for physical as well as intellectual training for the RSS, but also for his intellectual push towards a 'swadeshi,' rural-based self-sustainable economy that cared for conservation and ecology. The most remarkable development during his time was improved relations with minority communities with his sustained dialogue with Muslim, Christian scholars and various religions and sampradayas. One of the outcomes was the formation of the Muslim Rashtriya Manch.

With his sustained intellectual exertions and fieldwork, the RSS was able change anti-outsiders sentiments to anti-infiltrators sentiments to a large extent in the Assam Agitation. Sudarshanji's idea of a National Citizen's Register was finally endorsed by the Supreme Court. His espousal of citizenship rights to non-Muslim refugees (who had to migrate because of persecution by majority community) from neighbouring countries led to an amendment to the Citizenship Act, and this has been accepted by the present Narendra Modi government. His energetic support to Itihas Sankalan Samiti led to the demolition of the Aryan invasion theory and change in the entire narrative of ancient Indian history.

Dr Mohan Bhagwat has carried on the work of evolution of the organization with changing atmosphere and social requirements. Today, the RSS is looked upon as a modern organization, open to society at large. One could, actually, say that his ascent to the top post from 2009 has ignited the next stage of evolution of RSS work, especially after 2013.

Though the media cell in the RSS began after seventy years of the RSS's existence in the 1990s, Dr Mohan Bhagwat has encouraged it to take a more proactive approach. Under him, the RSS is seen as more open to the media and its tools of communication. His understanding of the importance of the media as a dissemination tool to reach out to people and present its viewpoint as witnessed in his three-day address in 2018 has seen a groundswell of positivity in favour of the RSS.

His open-hearted interaction with cross-sections of the society, with thought leaders has resulted in changing the mindset of the influential people. His takeover as Sarsanghchaalak has seen appreciable expansion in the RSS shakha network as well as huge improvements in coordination and harmony between different affiliated organizations.

He has been advocating far-reaching reforms in Hindu society with his promotion of the idea of 'One well, One temple and One crematorium' in villages. It is not a rhetorical call. If we see the casteism still prevalent in Hindu society, we can understand how difficult but critical this project is for social harmony.

Dr Bhagwat's new idea, with his Sarkaryavaah Bhaiyyaji Joshi, of taking decisions based on large data and not the earlier approach of anecdotal experience and discussions in the meetings has far reaching potential. The mass survey of women and much bigger survey of young swayamsevaks to chalk out new development programmes, new approach to skill enhancement and training of workers based on the projects they will take up, and moving into social areas that had not yet been taken up by the RSS adds new dimension to the evolution of the RSS.

At various times, the RSS has been able to fine-tune its approach and tweak its organizational setup with the help of technology. Its structure is sturdy, yet flexible; its leaders are firmly rooted in the basic philosophy of the RSS but at the same time open to changes. The systems have evolved into an open architecture that can absorb people from different streams of the society and reconcile differences within different organization within this framework. This success comes from nurturing talents, close warm relations and patient collective decision-making.

The RSS as an organization is more system-driven than personality-driven. This system filters out people who cannot perform at a higher level and also recognizes those with potential and facilitates their rise within the organization. The major success of the RSS has been that it has remained a personality-neutral and circumstance-neutral organization. When the first Sarsanghchaalak, Dr Hedgewar, passed away, people speculated if the RSS would survive. When the second Sarsanghchaalak, Shri Guruji, expired, there was huge speculation in the media—who will lead it after Guruji and whether the RSS would slow down. This speculation was based on observers' experiences with other organizations. The critics of the RSS were hopeful that the RSS will wither away with change in leadership. But, nothing of the sort happened. It showed the maturity of the ordinary swayamsevak who was not swayed by all this speculation. After Balasaheb Deoras, the question of succession and gossip about the RSS's growth has stopped. This is the measure of the success of the RSS as an organization.

The RSS is, possibly, a wonderful case study for management students and gurus to understand an organization that is unique, with an open architecture and one that has grown organically and seamlessly after the lows of 1949. It has a strong network or a self-renewing nervous system that keeps it on a healthy growth path.

In the ten years prior to completion of its 100 years of existence (from 2015 to 2025), the RSS has shown a resolve for a quantum leap. One can't be sure of what the future holds, but looking at the past record of the RSS, we can be reasonably sure that the RSS will be able to contribute richly to India's renaissance on her way to re-establishing herself as the Vishwa Guru.

Annexure I

Glossary of RSS Terminology

Sarsanghchaalak (सरसंघचालक): Mentor or guide of the Sangh, head of the organization
Sarkaryavaah (सरकार्यवाह): General Secretary, topmost elected office-bearer
Sahsarkaryavaah (सहसरकार्यवाह): Joint General Secretary
Sanghchalak (संघचालक): Guide and guardian of local activities and local volunteers
Prachaarak (प्रचारक): A person who dedicates a major part of his life to the Sangh expecting nothing in return
Vistaarak (विस्तारक): A full-time worker who dedicates a brief period to the Sangh
Shakha (शाखा): Daily assembly or gathering for imparting (Sangh) samskaaras
Upashakha (उपशाखा): Various shakhas in the same area
Mukhya Shikshak (मुख्य शिक्षक): The one who is responsible for conducting regular shakha activities
Karyavaah (कार्यवाह): Secretary of the shakha, main leader of a shakha
Gatnaayak (गटनायक): Team leader of a small area which falls under the purview of shakha
Karyakarta-Karyakram (कार्यकर्त्ता-कार्यक्रम): Worker-programme
Baithak (बैठक): Meeting for discussing, deliberating and decision-making
Pravaas (प्रवास): Visiting and staying in other places as a part of Sangh work
Sampata (सम्पत): Command given for arranging swayamsevaks in a specific manner before the commencement of a programme

Danda (दण्ड): Lathi
Veekira (वीकिर): Command given at the end of a shakha programme
Bouddhik (बौद्दिक): Intellectual exercise programme, or intellectual discourse
Samataa (समता): Physical training programme for self-discipline
Chandan (चंदन): Joyful gathering for having snacks
Sahabhojan (सहभोजन): Gathering for having homely meal
Saanghik (सांघिक): Congregation of swayamsevaks belonging to more than one shakha
Ekatrikaran (एकत्रीकरण): Gathering of various shakhas, gathering of main workers
Sangh Shiksha Varg (संघ शिक्षा वर्ग): Training programme scheduled over three years for teaching Sangh programme
Shivir (शिविर): Camp
Rakshak (रक्षक): Security in-charge of Shivirs
Prabandhak (प्रबंधक): In-charge for looking after the programmes conducted by the Sangh
Saarvajanik Samaarop (सार्वजनिक समारोप): The public programme at the end of Shivir and Varg
Deekshant Samarop (दीक्षांत समारोप): Special Convocation for trainees at the end of a Varg
Vividh Kshetra Sangathan (विविध क्षेत्र संगठन): Other organizations inspired by the ideals of the Sangh

Annexure II

List of Sarkaryavaahs since the Inception of RSS

Sarkaryavaah is the executive head of RSS, elected by the Akhil Bharatiya Pratinidhi Sabha (ABPS) that has both elected and ex-officio members. The role of the Sarkaryavaah is very important in running, strengthening and shaping up the organization in its day-to-day operations. He plays an important role in policy-making and its execution. Given below is the list of Sarkaryavaahs since the foundation of the RSS.

1.	Balaji Huddar	1929–1931
2.	D.R. Limaye	1931–1934
3.	H.V. Kulkarni	1934–1937
4.	G.S. Padhye	1937–1939
5.	M.S. Golwalkar	1939–1940
6.	Bhaiyya Saheb	1940–1945
7.	Bhaiyyaji Dani	1945–1956
8.	Eknath Ranade	1956–1962
9.	Bhaiyyaji Dani	1962–1965
10.	Balasaheb Deoras	1965–1973
11.	Madhavrao Muley	1973–1977
12.	Rajju Bhaiyya	1977–1987
13.	H.V. Seshadri	1987–2000
14.	Dr Mohan Bhagwat	2000–2009
15.	Bhaiyyaji Joshi	2009–

Annexure III

Graphic of RSS Organizational Structure

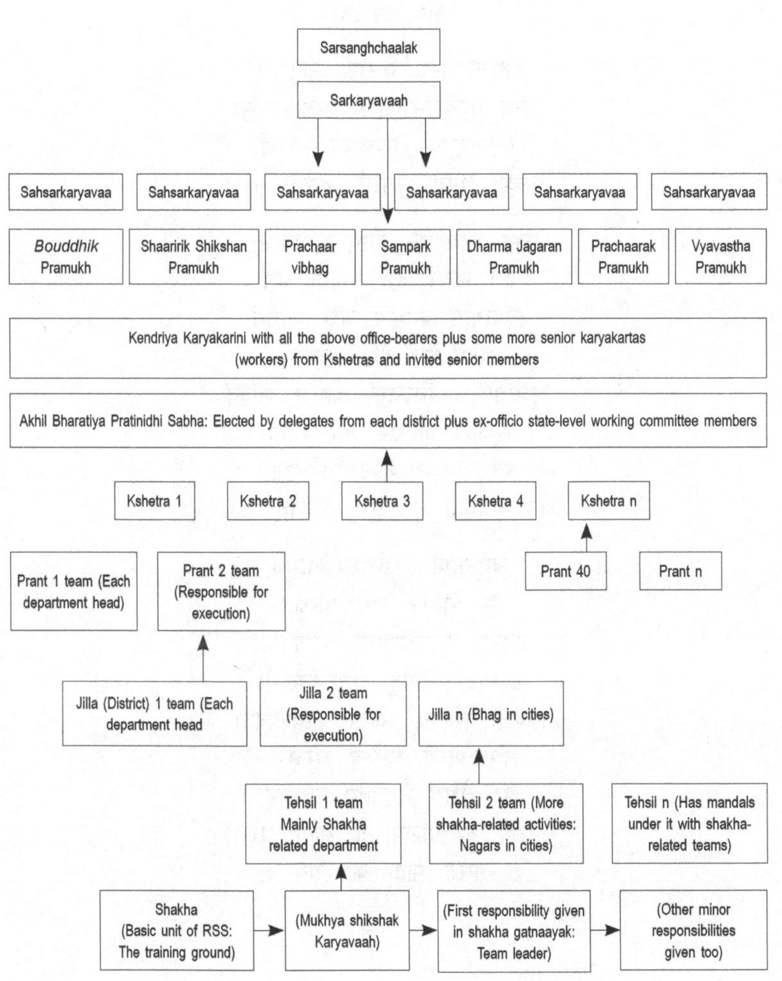

Annexure IV

RSS Daily Prayer and Its Meaning

संघ प्रार्थना

नमस्ते सदा वत्सले मातृभूमे
त्वया हिन्दुभूमे सुखं वर्धितोऽहम्।
महामङ्गले पुण्यभूमे त्वदर्थे
पतत्वेष कायो नमस्ते नमस्ते ।।1।।

प्रभो शक्तिमन् हिन्दुराष्ट्राङ्गभूता
इमे सादरं त्वां नमामो वयं
त्वदीयाय कार्याय बद्दा कटीयं
शुभामाशिषं देहि तत्पूर्तये।
अजय्या च विश्वस्य देहीश शक्तिं
सुशीलं जगद्येन नम्रं भवेत्
श्रुतं चैव यत्कण्टकाकीर्णमार्ग
स्वयं स्वीकृतं नः सुगं कारयेत् ।।2।।

समुत्कर्षनिः श्रेयसस्यैकमुग्रं
परं साधन्र नाम वीरव्रत
तदन्तः स्फुरत्वक्षया ध्येयनिष्ठा
हृदन्तः प्रजागर्तु तीव्राऽनिशम्।
विजेत्री च नः संहता कार्यशक्तिर
विधायास्य धर्मस्य संरक्षणं
परं वैभवं नैतुमेतत् स्वराष्ट्रं
समर्था भवत्वाशिषा ते भृशम् ।।3।।
।। भारत माता की जय ।।

English translation:

I forever bow to thee, O loving motherland!
O, motherland of us Hindus, thou hast brought me up in happiness.
May my life, O great and blessed Holy land, be laid down to thy cause.
I bow to thee, again and again.

We, the children of this Hindu nation, bow to thee in reverence, O almighty God.
We have girded up our loins to carry on Thy work.
Give us Thy holy blessing for the fulfillment of this purpose.
O Almighty, grant us such might that no power on earth can ever challenge,
Such purity of character as would command the respect of the world,
And such knowledge that would make easy the thorny path
That we have voluntarily chosen.

My we be inspired with the spirit of stern heroism,
which is the sole and ultimate means of attaining the highest spiritual bliss,
with greatest temporal prosperity.
May intense and everlasting devotion to our ideal ever inspire our hearts.
May our victorious organized power of action, by Thy grace,
fully protect our Dharma and
lead this nation to the highest pinnacle of prosperity and glory.

Salutations to Bharat Mata.

Annexure V

Ekatmata Mantra Recited in RSS Shakhas

एकात्कता मंत्र

यं वैदिका मन्त्रदृशः पुराणा इन्द्रं यमं मातरिश्वनमाहुः ।
वेदान्तिनोऽनिर्वचनीयमेकं यं ब्रह्मशब्देन विनिर्दिशन्ति ।।1।।
शैवा यमीशं शिव इत्यवोचन्
यं वैष्णवा विष्णुरितिस्तुवन्ति ।
बुद्धस्तथाऽर्हन्निति बौद्धजैनाः
सत्-श्री-अकालेति च सिक्खसन्तः ।।2।।
शास्तेति केचित् प्रकृतिःकुमारः
स्वामीति मातेति पितेति भक्ताया।
यं प्रार्थयन्ते जगदीशितारं
स एक एव प्रभुरद्वितीयः ।।3।।

Ekatmata Mantra

Yam vaidikaa mantradrishah puraanaa, Indram Yamam Maatrishaanmahuh I
Vedaantinonirvachaneeyamekam Yam Brahmashabden vinirdishanti II1II
Shaiva yamisham Shiv ityavochan yam Vaishnaa Vishnuriti stuvanti I
Buddhastathaa Arhinniti Bouddha Jainaah Satshri Akaaleti Sikkh santah II2II
Shaasteti kechit katichit Kumarah Swameeti Maateti Piteti bhaktyaa I
Yam praarthayante Jagadeeshtaaram sa ek eva Prabhurdwiteeya II3II

That whom the ancient visionary Vaidik rishis called Indra, Yama, Maatrishvaa and that indescribable One whom the followers of Vedanta indicated as 'Brahma,'

Whom Shaivas praise as Shiv and Vaishnavas as Vishnu, Bouddh and Jains call Buddha and Arhant respectively, and Sikhs call Satshri Akaal,

The Lord of the Universe whom some call Shaastaa, some Kumarswami and some as Swami, Mother or Father, and pray with devotion—that God is One and the Incomparable.

Acknowledgements

It took nearly three months of meetings and discussions at Rupa Publications before we zeroed on this topic. I thank them for coming up with this challenging topic that covers ninety-five years of an organization that has its presence in varying degrees all over the nation and present in all the dimensions of national life.

I express my heartfelt gratitude to Shri Ranga Hariji, a veteran prachaarak and the foremost thinker of the RSS, who gave rare insights about the RSS and its philosophy. His insights are refreshing and often surprising. I say surprising, because he is eighty-seven years old, yet very unorthodox—a modern thinker with unsurpassed breadth of study of ancient and modern knowledge. He has been indulgent and supportive to a novice like me since I began writing. His inputs have enriched this book immensely.

I must also thank my friend Dilip Karambelkar, a delightful intellectual who has a different take and analysis on issues that confront society. He has been a prachaarak, with an unorthodox and uncommon perspective about the RSS and national issues as a journalist. It was great to have long discussions that helped me analyse many issues better in this book.

There is no book on the current Sarsanghchaalak, Dr Mohan Bhagwat. I thank his younger brother Shri Rajendra Bhagwat for sharing some of their family history and anecdotes about Mohanji to help me understand his family atmosphere that moulded his personality.

I bow humbly to the senior swayamsevaks of the first and second generation of RSS who worked tirelessly, selflessly without any expectations of any fruits, to create a solid foundation for RSS in a highly challenging and negative atmosphere like true *karmayogis*. Each of those thousands have left an imprint on the evolution of RSS.

It is customary to thank one's wife and children for being cooperative. And, I must confess that but for my wife Shyama's support to one, who is more immersed in social activism and writing about RSS rather than earning money, I could not have done what I am doing today. My loving hug to my children who have been very supportive of an unconventional father who hasn't provided much comfort in their lives apart from giving them the full freedom to pursue their dreams.

Above all, I thank the Supreme Being for always being with me.

Bibliography

Anand, Arun. *The Saffron Surge* (Delhi: Prabhat Prakashan, 2019).

Bhagwat, Mohan. *Bhavishya Ka Bharat: Rashtriya Swayamsevak Sangh ka Drishtikon* (Delhi: Vimarsh Prakashan, 2018).

Das, Durga. *Sardar Patel's Correspondence, 1945-50. Volume VI: Patel Nehru Differences—Assassination of Gandhi* (Navjivan Publishing House, 1973).

Deoras, Balasasheb. *Punjab Problem and Its Solution* (Delhi: Suruchi Prakashan, 1984).

Deoras, Balasaheb. *Samajik Samata va Hindu Sanghathan* (Nagpur: Shree Bharati Prakashan, 2014).

Dr Hedgewar Smriti Special Edition, *Yugdharma*, Nagpur, 5 April 1962.

Gandhi, M.K. *The Collected Works of Mahatma Gandhi*, Vol. 96 (Gandhi Ashram, Sevagram, Wardha).

Hari, Ranga. *M.S Golwalkar: His Vision and Mission* (Kochi: Kurukshetra Prakasan, 2008).

Hari, Ranga. *The Incomparable Guru Golwalkar* (Delhi: Prabhat Prakashan, 2018).

Hebalkar, Sharad. *Shri Balasaheb Deoras* (Pune: Bharatiya Vichar Sadhana, 2000).

'Hindu-Muslim Tension: Its Cause and Cure', *Young India*, 29 May 1924.

Karandikar, V.R. *Teen Sarsanghchaalak* (Pune: Snehal Prakashan, 1999).

Lan Jiang and Dong Li, 'The Evolution of Sir Syed Ahmed Khan's Political Identity', *Cross Cultural Communication*, July 2016.

Pachpore, Virag Shrikrishna. *Deoras Parv* (Pune: Snehal Prakashan, 2011).

Palkar, N.H. *Dr Hedgewar* (Pune: Bharatiya Vichar Sadhana, 2000).

Ranade, Eknath. *Story of the Vivekananda Rock Memorial* (Chennai: Vivekananda Kendra Prakashan Trust, 2013).

Rashtra Sevika Samiti, *Karmayogini Mausiji* (Mathura: Sevika Prakashan, 1996).

Savarkar, V.D. *Hindutva* (Mumbai: Swatantrayveer Savarkar Rashtriya Smarak, 1999).

Sharda Shastri, J.C. *Memoirs of a Global Hindu* (Vishwa Adhyayan Kendra, 2008).

Sharda, Ratan. *Prof. Rajendra Singh Ki Jeevan Yatra*. (Suruchi Prakashan, 2018).

Sharda, Ratan. *Sangh and Swaraj* (Delhi: Prabhat Prakashan, 2019).

Sharda, Ratan. *RSS360* (Delhi: Bloomsbury India, 2018).

Seshadri, H.V. RSS Vision in Action (Bengaluru: Sahitya Sindhu Prakashana, 2000).

Sinha, Rakesh. *Dr Keshav Baliram Hedgewar* (Publication Division, Ministry of Information and Broadcasting, 2004).

Shri Guruji Samagra Darshan (Delhi: Suruchi Prakashan, 2005).

Swadesh Smaranjali, Swadesh Group, Indore, 2012.

Swadesh Sudarshan Smriti, Swadesh Group, Bhopal, 2014.

Swaroop, Devendra. *Sangh Rajneeti Aur Media* (Delhi: Prabhat Prakashan, 2006).

Swaroop, Devendra. *Sangh Beej Se Vriksha* (Delhi: Prabhat Prakashan, 2009).

Tapasvee, M.G. *Rashtraya Namah* (Delhi: Prabhat Prakashan, 2001).

Tarun Bharat Publications, *Su-darshan* (Nagpur, 2012).

Thengdi, Dattopant. *Dr Ambedkar Aur Samajik Kranti Ki Yatra* (Lucknow: Lokhit Prakashan, 2015).

Vaidya, M.M. *Panchjanya*, 11 March 2018.

Vaidya, M.M. 'Modern Untouchability Thrives Among "Liberals" in India,' *The Sunday Guardian*, 18 August 2019.

Wadhwani and Motwani. *9 Years of RSS in Sindh: 1939–1947* (Mumbai: Bharatiya Sindhu Sabha, 2006).

Index